Deceiving Elvera

Peg Herring

DECEIVING ELVERA

© Peg Herring, 2020

Printed in the USA

Copy Editor: R. Hodges

Deceiving Elvera is a work of fiction. The names, characters, and incidents are entirely the work of the author's imagination. Any resemblance to actual persons, living or dead, or events, is entirely coincidental.

ISBN: 9781393678892

Gwendolyn Books: USA

Acknowledgments

For some time, I've wanted to write a novel that's less about whodunit and more about relationships. It's scary to step outside what I've been doing for years, so I'd like to thank the people who encouraged me to do that, especially Kelsey, Samantha, Sherron, P.J., Luci, and Lynn.

I'd also like to thank George for information on Mackinac Island in the 1960s and Kelsey for help with scenes set in Thailand. Any mistakes readers might encounter are mine as I tailored events, characters, and geography to fit my story.

Chapter One

With the blare of horns up top and the chug of engines deep in its bowels, the cruise ship *Happy Wanderer* left Singapore's Marina Bay Cruise Centre, gliding in the fierce morning sunlight past other vessels like a dignified matron at a crowded wedding. As the city's unique collection of buildings faded from view, voices rose at a meeting in the employee lounge.

"Now in Cabin Three," Marilyn said. "I've assigned Glynis—"

"I had her once already," Glynis interrupted. Her accent was Australian, her manner assertive. "It's someone else's turn."

"Not me," a Lao woman begged. "I cried every day the time I got her."

"Two weeks with Miss E? No, thanks," a man in the back grumbled, and several crewmembers near him nodded agreement.

"Who are they so afraid of?" one of the new hires asked.

"We have a frequent guest who's plain ornery." A round-faced man from Oklahoma spoke softly, so Marilyn couldn't hear. "Miss E goes through stewards like a puppy tears up chew toys."

"She's an old, dried-up prune that lives on Wild Goose cruise ships full time." The speaker, a burly man in a white cook's coat, tilted his head left then right, causing a cracking noise. "They say it's been years since Elvera Tharp slept on land."

"This woman is difficult to please?"

The man made a rude noise. "*Impossible* is a better word."

Apparently sensing the mood in the room, Marilyn dropped for the moment the question of who would serve Cabin Three. "Alrighty then. Quick like a bunny, let's go through some other things. As most of you know, we'll be visiting several ports in Thailand, make one stop in Vietnam, and end up back in Singapore in fourteen days. I'm posting a revised schedule with last-minute changes and some reminders about our conduct code and recording procedures." She waved a clutch of papers. "Please read it."

After clarifying several other points, Marilyn returned to the topic that had caused the earlier flap. "I would like a volunteer for duty in Cabin Three." The smile she flashed looked fake, even to those who didn't yet know her well. "Ms. Tharp prefers that one person prepares and delivers her meals and does her daily cleaning. That employee also runs errands for her as needed." In a hopeful tone she added, "He or she is excused from some other duties in order to be available as required."

"But no one who's been her steward cares to repeat the honor," the guy in the cook's coat warned.

"True," a woman agreed. "I felt like I was gonna throw up every time I went there."

That opened a new flood of comments. "She called me once in the middle of the night," a man with a Scandinavian accent reported. "Her slider was stuck, and it had to be fixed right away. It was three a.m. by the time I got it open, and she kept yelling at me to hurry." He waved his hands on either side of his face in imitation of a flighty woman. "She wanted to watch the sunrise, and it had to be that morning."

"The food is never to her liking," a Malaysian woman said. "Always there is something wrong."

"She's a right knocker." That was Glynis, the Australian who'd started the complaints. "Chucked a wobbly once 'cause I left her scissors in the wrong spot." She ran a hand through her wiry hair. "Thought she was gonna stab me with the bloody things."

Example after example followed, in differing accents and with varying levels of English competence. The *Happy Wanderer's* crew were a diverse lot, about half from Southeast Asia and the rest a world-wide mix. All employees were required to speak English, since most Wild Goose Cruise Line passengers were American, Canadian, or British.

An earnest-looking young African man said, "At breakfast my first day, she said if I did not trim my hair by noon, she would do it for me."

"She didn't like my tattoos, so I had to cover 'em, no matter how hot it got." It was the man in the cook's jacket again, and as he spoke, he showed off an inked figure of a mermaid on his forearm.

Over the babble, a voice came clearly. "I'll serve Ms. Tharp."

The room went quiet as everyone turned to see who'd spoken. Whispers through the crowd provided a name, Michael Kanda. Standing alone at the back of the group, the middle-aged new hire had said nothing to that point. At his offer, expressions among his crewmates revealed everything from disbelief to gleeful anticipation. Someone laughed, a prolonged giggle that lingered like a musical riff in the air.

To everyone's disappointment, Marilyn rejected the offer. "You're new to sailing and to Wild Goose Cruises, Kanda, so you're bound to get something wrong. I don't want to get hit with the fallout." Her East Coast accent distorted the *r*'s and flattened the vowels, *Yow-ah. Fawl owt.* Some in the crowd frowned as they struggled to decipher her meaning.

A woman groaned, and someone objected, "He volunteered, for Pete's sake."

"Let him try," the tattooed man urged. "Mikey looks like a ladies' man to me. He might charm the old bat right out of her granny-panties."

Marilyn shot him a glare. "If I need input from you, Darrin, I'll ask."

Glynis spoke in her friend's ear. "Got a bit of a Dwayne Johnson look, our new bloke. Wouldn't mind knocking boots with him."

Briefly confused at the unfamiliar idiom, the other woman elbowed her friend. "Oh, knocking boots. But see the crucifix he's wearing? I bet he's the prim and proper type."

"Doesn't mean he won't want a good time." Glynis raised a brow. "We'll see how it goes."

Ignoring the wave of whispers, Kanda made a case for himself with calm assurance. "While I'm new to cruising, I've been in domestic service since I was fifteen. I can handle a demanding old woman."

A rustle of anticipation followed his assertion. Some nodded in approval of Kanda's spirit. Others seemed pleased at the prospect of being off the hook. Those who knew Miss E best smiled at the new man's innocence. "Lamb to the slaughter," someone observed softly.

After chewing at her too-bright lipstick for a few seconds, Marilyn made her decision. "We'll let lunch be a test." Speaking to the tiny Lao woman, she ordered, "Ha'o, go along with him and pour a little oil if the waters get troubled." Though her eyes revealed reluctance, Ha'o nodded acquiescence.

"Thank you." Kanda made an almost formal bow to his supervisor. "I'll work to justify your faith in me."

Marilyn shook a plump finger in his direction. "One complaint from that—" She rephrased, and again those who knew the guest under discussion smiled knowingly. "Ms. Tharp is a frequent, valued passenger. We don't want her upset, ever."

"I understand, and I'm very good with difficult people."

At his slightly pompous tone, Glynis' friend raised a brow knowingly and mouthed, "Prissy."

"Great." Marilyn began packing up her notes. "Alrighty then. Let's get to work."

Under Ha'o's watchful eye, Michael prepared his first meal for Elvera Tharp in a tight corner of the fluorescent-lit galley. "She hates mustard," his guide informed him as he loaded the tray. "Even when the menu calls for it, don't take any to her cabin."

"She'll throw it at you." A woman nearby who was filling baskets with warm, fragrant rolls touched her shirtfront in apparent memory. "Take extra salt packets. The old biddy definitely isn't watching her blood pressure."

Ha'o gave her coworker an admonishing look. "Miss E isn't that old. And she doesn't mean to be difficult."

The other was unwilling to concede either point. "She acts old, like some shrunken cartoon character. And she does mean to be mean."

Catching Michael's eye, Ha'o frowned to indicate the comments were overly judgmental. Still, her reluctance to serve Elvera Tharp lent credence to their coworker's argument.

When the tray was ready, an appealing roast beef sandwich on crusty bread with *au jus* on the side, a tub of coleslaw, a crisp dill pickle, a can of Coke set next to a drinking glass polished to a shine ("Never let her see a smudge."), and a slice of German chocolate cake with pecan-caramel frosting, he asked, "Anything I should change?"

"You forgot the flower." It was one of two men of similar build and coloring, either Bao or Duong. Michael didn't allow himself to glance at the name badge and reveal he hadn't yet learned which was which.

"She gets a flower with every meal," Ha'o explained. "For breakfast and lunch anything will do, but it's always a red rose with dinner."

His dark eyes met Ha'o's, his brows crunched. "Why does this woman get such special treatment?"

"Orders from the top." Ha'o seemed to feel that was enough

explanation. "I'll go to the back and get some vases. Use crystal for lunch and breakfast. At evening she likes the silver ones." She left, heading toward drawers along the back wall where such things were stored.

"It might sound like Ha'o is fond of the old witch," Bao (or Duong) warned when she was out of hearing, "but really, she's glad it's you assigned to Cabin Three and not her."

Michael examined the tray critically. "Is Miss E as bad as all that?"

The man's eyes twinkled. "Do you know any grandmotherly old ladies who call you Sweetheart and feed you cookies?"

"I've met a few, yes."

"Well, Miss E is the exact opposite: the grandma you can never, ever please. And the cookies are all for her, so don't expect a single crumb, as in a tip, when we get back to Singapore. She moves on to another ship in the line and harasses the next steward in her path."

"I worked on the *Laughing Sailor* for a while," a diminutive man with a shaved head said, "This guy came on board asking about her once, and we were pretty sure he was a cop. I think the police are keeping an eye on Miss E for some reason."

"A cop?" Bao/Duong said incredulously. "Are you kidding?"

The small man made a grimace. "Well, he asked a bunch of questions about Miss E, and he *acted* like a cop."

His co-worker was obviously dubious. "How does a cop act, Lu?"

"I don't know. Tough, you know? Like we'd better cooperate, or we'd be in trouble."

"What did he find out?"

"Nothing, as far as I could tell. I mean, she's a grumpy old lady, but that isn't against the law anywhere I know of."

"That wasn't a cop." The other man said dismissively. "More likely a conman wanting to relieve the old lady of a big chunk of her money. Rich people got to watch out for guys like that all the time."

Ha'o returned at that point with a vase and a bright pink, soft-scented flower. She fussed with it for a few seconds, making sure it sat at precisely the right angle, and then said to Michael, "We'd better get down there. The worst thing you could do is be late your first time."

They took the fastest route, an interior elevator. Ha'o seemed nervous, fingering her waistband and shuffling her feet. "She doesn't like me," she admitted. "I did everything I could think of to make Miss E happy but never got the tiniest sign I'd done anything right." After a moment she added, "I get really clumsy around her. It's hard for me to think when I feel like someone's mad at me."

The elevator opened with a muted rumble, revealing a softly lit corridor lined with doors staggered along both sides. It might have been a hotel anywhere in the world. There was no visible hint they were heading almost directly north across the Gulf of Thailand, and only a gentle feeling of movement it was easy to forget when the waters were calm. Monsoon season was only weeks away, but with luck they'd complete their circuit with fair skies and placid seas.

Outside the door to Cabin Three, Michael examined the tray one last time to be sure everything was perfect. He smoothed his uniform shirt, straightened his tie, and checked his hair in the reflection of the stainless-steel plate cover. Ha'o smoothed her dark hair and checked her uniform for lint. Then she tapped three times on the door, just loudly enough to be heard by ears seven decades old.

"Yes?" The single word conveyed impatience.

Ha'o nodded to signal that Michael should answer. "Lunch, ma'am."

"Come in."

Squaring his shoulders, he slid his passkey into the slot. Despite his eagerness to see the room's infamous occupant, Michael watched the tray carefully as he entered. Duong (or Bao) had warned that whatever remained of a sloshed drink might be dumped on the floor for him to clean up. Ha'o caught the door so it closed softly behind them.

Once he was sure the tray was level, Michael took his first look at the notorious Elvera Tharp. Though she was seated, he could tell she was tall, and thin to the point of boniness. Her thick, iron-gray hair was pulled back and fastened at the base of her neck with a bit of navy-blue ribbon. Her oval face had a deep, permanent frown line etched between the brows. A faded scar showed white from eyebrow to chin, pulling the left side of her mouth slightly out of shape. Though it might have detracted from her looks, the scar instead called to mind a statue from ancient times, flawed but in no way diminished.

Michael's new charge examined him openly and without regard for courtesy, and he thought he now knew what a gladiator released into an arena with a lion must have felt like. Meeting her gaze only long enough to nod in greeting, he took in the room he'd be responsible for cleaning.

Miss E sat in the center, on an upholstered chair flanked by two small tables. Atop the one on her right was everything a person who didn't move around much might want within reach: tissues, a pitcher of water with a half-filled glass beside it, a book of crossword puzzles, a hand-held video game of the type he hadn't seen for years, a hairbrush, a nail file, a TV remote, and a tablet computer. The other table was buried under an array of tools he deduced were for jewelry-making: tiny pliers, a divided basket with different types of beads, rolls of wire and string, and small plastic bags containing fasteners of several types. Off to one side but within reach stood a wheeled walker with a storage compartment beneath the seat. The place smelled medicinal, like minty liniment.

Miss E's first words were directed at his companion. "He's new."

He took the lead in a firm tone. "Yes, ma'am. My name is Michael."

Tharp's nose wrinkled. "Michael, you said?"

"Yes, ma'am." He set the tray on the dining table.

"Not a name I've ever been fond of."

What reply was acceptable to that? Silence seemed the safest option, so Michael merely looked at her, his demeanor blank and unthreatening.

Ha'o stepped in with a falsely jolly tone. "It's good to have you aboard again, Miss E. It's been a year since your last time, right?"

A steel-gray eyebrow rose. "I imagine the kitchen help is leaping with joy."

Ha'o's tone went saccharine. "Miss E, we love having you with us."

Tharp looked at Michael. "Do you share Little Mary Sunshine's exultation at my presence, Handsome?"

"That will depend on how well we get on together."

Ha'o couldn't leave it alone. "He doesn't mean you won't get along, Miss E. He means—"

A quick movement of the woman's arm sent the TV remote sailing in Ha'o's direction. She squeaked once and ducked. The device hit the wall and clattered to the floor, its batteries spilling out and rolling until they banged against the cabin wall. "Let him speak for himself, Shorty."

Though the action shocked him momentarily, Michael decided the missile hadn't really been aimed at Ha'o. Tharp's goal had been fear, not injury. While Ha'o apologized as if she'd done something wrong, he retrieved the remote, reassembled it, set it back in place, and returned to Ha'o's side, careful to show neither fear nor anger.

For a bully, Miss E was surprisingly forgiving. "You meant well, I suppose, but this new man and I need to come to an arrangement without you interfering. You may go."

Ha'o hesitated, caught between the task she'd been assigned and their guest's demand. Meeting her gaze, Michael inclined his head toward the door. Ha'o left the cabin, her shoulders slumped. Michael waited to see if Tharp had more to say. When she didn't, he turned to business. "Your lunch, Ms.—It's Elvera, with the second *e* long, right?"

Her nose rose a half-inch. "You may call me Miss E. *If* I decide you can stay."

Maintaining a pleasant expression, he nodded. "Miss E."

"I'm going to call you Mike. Michael sounds snooty." After a pause she added, "I like Mickey, but your dusky skin and almond eyes are too Asian to fit with an Irish nickname."

It appeared she couldn't keep from being offensive, or perhaps she didn't care to try. Michael stuck to his reason for being there. "Would you like your meal served where you are, Miss E?"

"No. There." Dragging the walker toward her, she rose and limped toward the small dinette table. Her body leaned oddly to the right, the hip on that side so damaged that she had to swing the leg forward with each step. Tharp's dependence on assistive devices was the commonly accepted reason for her taking meals in her stateroom. Though the crew made every accommodation for walkers, wheelchairs, and the like, she chose not to take advantage of the ship's accessibility.

"Five restaurants we got," one of the dishwashers had commented to Michael. "Some with views of the water that would knock your socks off, and others that let you forget you're at sea. Some are formal enough to please the upper-upper crust, with a quartet playing classical music; others are casual, with golden-oldies piped in. With all we offer you can get any kind of meal, from burgers to octopus steak, and people from all over the world to talk to. Miss E eats alone. Every meal. Every day."

Glynis had summed it up in a few words. "She don't like anybody."

Michael unloaded the tray, making an attractive setting with the various dishes and accoutrements and setting them down carefully to avoid excess noise. Popping the top on the soda can, he poured her drink into a glass, careful to fill it to about three-quarters, as Ha'o had instructed. Last, he set the vase at table center. Sliding the tray under his arm, he stepped back. "Is everything satisfactory?"

Her chin jutted, pulling the skin around the scar tight. "Do you generally leave guests standing like cattle at a feeding trough?"

Hurriedly Michael set the tray on the mini-fridge and pulled the chair out for her. She sat, smoothing her blue-and-green kaftan theatrically. Moving the walker back a little, he swept the scarlet napkin—The ship's colors were silver and scarlet, its logo a red goose with silver wings—from beside the plate and laid it on her lap. She made no acknowledgment of the service.

Stepping back, Michael again put the tray under his arm, clasping his hands before him. "Is there anything else, Miss E?"

She glanced at him disdainfully. "For one thing, don't stand with your hands over your privates. Your precious jewels are safe with me."

"Sorry." He dropped his hands to his sides, but they felt weird hanging there. He tried putting them behind his back, but he really did feel vulnerable that way, and it was hard to keep the empty tray in place. In the end he folded them at his waist, like a kid about to solo in the Christmas choir.

Picking up her fork, Tharp tasted the coleslaw and frowned. "It's not as sweet as I like it."

"I brought sugar packets." He pointed. "There."

"I'm not blind." Taking up the sugar, she dusted the top of the slaw, stirred it with her fork, and tasted again. "Better." She examined the sandwich, removing the bun and sniffing at the meat. "Tell them I'm satisfied." She raised a finger. "Not pleased, Mike. Satisfied."

Michael wondered if that meant he was dismissed, but, having been warned to make no assumptions where Miss E was concerned, he remained in place. Was the next move up to him? If so, what should it be? Wish her *bon appetit*? Make conversation? Sing a Broadway tune?

"I like a good roast beef sandwich, don't you?" Her eyes were dark as old brownstone. "I hope you aren't one of those vegan types." Unsure how eating habits related to his ability to wait on her, Michael shook his head. "Good. I can't stand people who see food as a test of character."

"Hmm."

After another bite she swallowed and observed, "Your English is quite good."

"I spent several years in the U.S."

She looked up at him. "Doing what?"

"Personal service." He bowed. "They don't call us butlers anymore, but that best describes what I did."

"But you were born in Thailand?"

"Yes, ma'am."

She switched to Thai. "Did your parents encourage learning?"

"My father is responsible for my education," he replied in the same language. It was a slanted truth. Attending school had provided Michael temporary respite from the man's casual mistreatment.

"And where was this?"

"A tiny village north of Bangkok that no one's ever heard of." An image came to mind: a cluster of slant-roofed huts set into the deep-green cleavage between two hills, plagued most of the time by pressing heat and unrelenting damp: sometimes one, sometimes the other, and sometimes both at once. A school and a church built by an ambitious American couple who eventually tired of the work and went home, ceding control to the village elders. In the fifteen years he'd spent there, the place had never felt like home.

She jabbed a crooked finger at him. "I'll bet you've eaten beetle chili and deep-fried frog skins a few times. Yum-yum, crunch-crunch, yes?"

It felt like criticism: his homeland was primitive, its food disgusting. *You volunteered for this.* "Yes, ma'am. I have."

"I lived in Thailand once upon a time." She took another bite. "They say insects provide protein, but I'll take beef over bugs any day."

Picturing Marilyn looking over his shoulder, Michael shifted his feet slightly and made another noncommittal noise.

"Tell me about your parents."

Americans were notoriously nosy, but he'd learned to deal with their intrusive questions. Making the sign of the cross he said, "Good people, ma'am, but they're dead now."

"I see." She took a bite of the pickle. "How did you get a spot on the *Happy Wanderer*?"

"After my last employer died, may he rest in peace, I saw an advertisement for serving staff on Wild Goose Cruises. It sounded like fun, seeing the world on a big boat."

"Ship," she corrected. "If you're going to work at sea, you should learn the correct terminology."

"Sorry. I'll remember next time."

Dipping the sandwich, she took a bite, chewed, and swallowed. "You've no doubt heard things about me."

He had, all morning long. "Miss E is well-known on the line," one smart aleck in the kitchen had quipped, "the same way Jack the Ripper is well-known in England." Her fussiness made her a frequent topic of conversation among Wild Goose staffers. If he pretended otherwise, she'd know he was lying.

"I have heard positive things." *People are positive you're horrible to work for and positive they want nothing to do with you.*

Setting aside her crust she asked, "How old are you?"

"Thirty-six." He added a tried and true method of pleasing women. "About twenty years your junior, yes?"

The telltale brow shifted. "Mike, you're a good-looking man, and charming as well, which I imagine has helped you get what you want in life. However, I see beyond such things as looks and charm." With a watchful air she added, "Besides, your looks have already begun to fade."

Michael forced himself not to glance in the mirror on the far wall to discern the faults she'd noticed. She was baiting him, and he would not rise to it. Keeping his gaze on Miss E, he made a sound that indicated polite acceptance of her opinion but no real interest in it.

"Be honest with me. No flattery. No foolishness." She took up the pickle. "Now, what do they say about me?"

He took a deep breath and let it out before answering. "You live full-time on Wild Goose ships, taking whichever cruise strikes your fancy at a given time. I suppose that means you enjoy travel."

Pushing her empty plate aside, she set the cake in its place and sniffed it appreciatively. "I have private quarters, cleaned regularly by someone other than me. My meals are provided without effort on my part, mostly on time. I see the world when I want to and close the blinds when I don't."

"You don't have a home anywhere?"

She shrugged lightly. "Nothing to tie me down." Cutting a large bite of cake, she asked, "How did you come to be my steward?"

Another test. "They sent the new man into the lion's den, or lioness, in this case, to see how he'd manage."

She chuckled, and a sprinkle of cake crumbs flew onto the table. "Now you're being honest. One sweet young thing insisted it was a great honor to wait on me." She took a sip from her glass before asking, "What happens if I reject you?"

"I think you'll get Ha'o back. Possibly Glynis, though she objected quite strenuously."

A frown creased her brow. "Ha'o is entirely too chipper, one of those who believes if you're just *nice* to everyone they'll be *nice* back. And that Glynis! Has she hit on you yet?"

"Um, no."

"She will. In my day they called women like her man-eaters." She wiped a dot of moisture from the table with her napkin. "She wanted to give me pointers on how to 'update my look.' As if I give a rat's ass about my look or some thirty-something's opinion of it."

"Of course not."

His attempt at conciliation earned him a glare. "No matter who they send, sooner or later my stewards can't resist sticking their noses into my business. Do you think you can refrain from doing that?"

"I will do my best, ma'am."

"All right then." Pausing dramatically, as if she were about to award a prize, Miss E said, "You may tell Marilyn I want you to bring my dinner this evening." Raising a finger, she added, "Remember to be honest. The rest you'll learn as we go."

"Thank you, Miss E. I have every intention of serving you well."

Outside the cabin, Michael slumped briefly against the bulkhead and closed his eyes. Wiping his mouth with the back of a hand, he tasted salt. *The first time is the worst. Once she trusts you, things will get easier.*

"How'd it go?" Marilyn asked when he entered the galley.

"I managed to escape without wearing the coleslaw. Is that good?"

"Ha'o tells me Miss E was in her usual nasty state. If you've changed your mind, I can still assign the duty to someone more experienced."

"No. I want to do this."

Marilyn made a dismissive gesture. "Then that's how we'll go."

When she moved away, Ha'o approached carrying a tub of

sweet-smelling lemongrass. "I'll take Miss E if you want. You're new here, and I think she was getting used to me by the end. Maybe if I try again, and if I'm really careful..." She trailed off, unable to assert with any assurance that she'd be more successful in a second attempt.

"I'm taking it as a challenge." Michael frowned. "Any idea why she's so…angry?"

"She has a lot of pain, I think. And maybe not such a happy life. She doesn't seem to have any friends or family, no visitors, no mail."

"Too bad. I wonder what happened to everyone."

"She doesn't say much about her past. I know she grew up in Chicago, this big city kind of in the middle of the U.S." After a pause she remembered something more. "And she spent her summers on some island where they don't allow cars. It sounds like she really liked it there."

Chapter Two

Chicago, Illinois-May, 1965

"They don't have any cars up there, none." Mother spoke as if it were the neatest thing ever. "Only horses and bicycles for transport."

"Horses?" Elvera gave her a look. "I can imagine what the place smells like."

Father had inherited a house on Mackinac Island, a few miles off the tip of the Michigan mitten. The island, once important to the fur trade, was now a popular vacation spot. Clever city fathers had frozen the place in time, which drew tourists charmed by its Victorian architecture and ambiance. Father had showed her a photo taken from the air: trees, water, a small cluster of buildings, and more trees. He also had a picture of the house. Taken from the road, with purple-tipped lilac bushes obscuring the view, the photo lacked detail, but the house was at least as big as their home in Highland Park. Still, it was on an *island*. According to E's friends at school, people went to Mackinac for a day, maybe two, rode around in a horse-drawn carriage, bought fudge, and then left. No one stayed for the whole summer, but that's what Father had decided the Tharp family would do.

E had excellent reasons for objecting. One, this island wasn't in the Mediterranean or the Caribbean, where the cool people went. Two, it was hundreds of miles to the north, in Lake Huron, which meant the water would never really get warm enough for swimming. Three, it was primitive, with none of the stores available on Chicago's famous Loop. Four, Franklin Tharp's family trips were notoriously boring. He drove at precisely fifty miles per hour, his voice droning all the way about the Battle of This or the First Man to Do That. He'd brag to everyone in the city about their "historic" summer home, but Elvera recognized that spending their summer vacation in a remote spot was simply another way for her parents to pinch pennies.

And who gave a care about history anyway?

Worst of all, Elvera wouldn't have her brother along to relieve the boredom. Drake had been sent to some awful boarding school where they made him march in columns and say, "Yes, sir, thank you, sir," when they let him eat, sleep, or breathe. Father had encouraged him to "do well" in his new adventure. "With the training you get at Spooler Academy, you'll already be on your way up the ladder if you're called to the military. You won't get tossed into the ranks with Negroes and hicks from Dogpatch." Drake had repeated Father's words in an excellent imitation of the overly loud voice he used when giving his children advice. "'Service in the military stands a man well later in life, when he prepares to run for public office.'"

Drake hadn't even tried to explain to Father that he had no interest in a political career. He didn't talk to Mother about it either, since she'd never disagree with a Franklin Tharp edict. If allowed to do as he chose, Drake would have finished high school in Chicago and then joined the Peace Corps. While E was sorry to see Drake leave home, she agreed with Father on one point. Serving in the Peace Corps was no way to get ahead in life.

Her brother's absence meant E would travel alone in the back seat, without his whispered, humorous observations or his help changing the subject when Father started lecturing on the Death of Polite Society and the Perils of Immodest Young Women. Though a little too tied to honor and duty to suit E, Drake was funny, sweet, and not yet petrified, the way her parents were. Being with them for the summer, with no Drake and no friends her own age, was going to be horrible.

Elvera tried explaining to Father that modern child psychologists recommended teens be given input on important family decisions. That argument had been futile. Her father's endless litany of tired phrases cut off any intelligent discussion she tried to have with him. She had to go to church because, "The family that prays together stays together." She should be careful with boys because she had "a gift meant only for her husband." (That one she didn't fully understand, though stuff she heard at school gave her an idea.) Father kept repeating that going to Michigan might "expand her opportunities." When she asked how, he said, "George Romney, the governor of Michigan, has a house not far from ours. His son Mitt is only a little older than you."

Mother seemed shocked at that. "Aren't they Mormons, Franklin?"

Father shrugged the problem away. "George could be our next President, or one of his sons someday."

On the extremely unlikely chance that she'd meet some boy, make him fall for her, and marry into the Republican elite, Elvera would be exiled from her friends for three whole months. Father would work in the city and drive up on weekends, "When I can get away," which would seldom happen. Work was always "busy" and Father's promises evaporated like morning fog in the bright light of reality. E would be left with her mother for weeks on end, constantly reminded that she wasn't quite thin enough, pleasant enough, or clever enough (not *intelligent*—smart girls scared men away) to capture a "good" husband. According to Mother, Elvera would never "fit in" and "do well," because of her "outspokenness" and "disrespectful attitude." Sometimes it got so bad she put her hands over her ears and screamed, "Shut up!" When that happened, Mother complained to Father, and she got long, stern lectures about obedience to the Fifth Commandment.

There were times when she wanted to scream at him to shut up too, but no one told Father that. Telling anyone to shut up was unforgivably rude, and E wasn't allowed to point out that her parents said the same things over and over and over, even if she was extremely polite about it. Father was the boss of the family, like Jesus was the head of the church, and Mother was his "helpmeet," a term E didn't really get. Still, her Bible, her priest, and her parents were certain they had it right. No matter how stupid his ideas were (meaning Father, not Jesus), they all had to go along.

"It's cooler up there," he said when she asked for the twelfth time why she couldn't stay in Illinois. "You'll get to really explore nature."

But her friend Camilla had been to Mackinac Island, and she said it was stupid unless you were dying to know every single thing there is to know about Indians. When E had pronounced it *MAK in ak,* parroting Father's pronunciation, Camilla corrected her. "It's *MAK in aw,* both the island and the town. People up there laugh if you don't say it right." She claimed you could only get a decent radio station late at night because of the ionosphere. And, though there were lots of tourist shops that sold fudge and souvenirs, there wasn't a movie theater for miles. That meant Elvera would be the only person in her circle who'd miss *A Hard Day's Night* when it came out in July. A thousand-to-one chance to charm the governor's son was not even close to being worth that.

The drive north was long, and Elvera dozed in the back seat of the 1960 American Motors Ambassador Father had snapped up "for a song" when an elderly neighbor died. She sat with her feet up, since the floor was stacked with clothes and linens that smelled of lavender from sprigs her mother had tucked into the folds. Without Drake she had the whole seat to herself, but it felt weird to be back there alone. She had no one to read funny signs to, like the "Short Funeral Home" and "Bull Available for Stud." Drake would have snickered at her impression of the waitress with the gap-toothed grin who asked, "What'll it be, Pop?" like Father was ninety-two years old. But Drake was off studying military history and, if his letters were to be believed, starving to death because the food at the Spooler Academy for Young Men was ninety percent inedible.

After the first hour, the scenery was all the same: fields, woods, and towns not big enough to have a Woolworth's, much less something interesting. Elvera wished she were small enough to climb into the back window, like she had as a kid, and nap with the watery June sunlight warming her back. She was too long for that now, with arms and legs that didn't always work together smoothly. Mother made pointed comments about the danger to the nice things in the house when one's daughter was more like a Great Dane puppy than a decorous young lady.

When they stopped in a tiny town called Gaylord (another time she missed Drake's knowing smile), a young attendant hurried outside to wait on them. "Fill her up," Father ordered, "and you may check the oil."

"Yes, sir." The guy opened the tank with the key Father handed to him. Once he got it back, Father went inside to find the rest room. The attendant put the nozzle in and then went to work cleaning the windshield. He was kind of cute, though he had a bad case of acne. Elvera noticed him peering at her, and when their eyes met, he smiled. Unsure what her response should be, she looked away.

"All set?" Father had come up behind the kid, who glanced at the pump. While he'd been eyeing Elvera, the dials had stopped spinning and the bell had sounded.

"Yes, sir." Taking the nozzle out, he set it back in its place with a clunk. "That'll be two-twenty."

"Oil's okay?"

The kid gulped. "I'm sorry. I forgot to check."

"You forgot." Father's voice turned frosty. "What are you here for, young man?"

"Sir?"

"Isn't your job to provide service to this station's customers?"

"Um, yes, sir."

"And did I not ask you to check the oil in my car?"

"Yes, and I'll do that right now, sir."

"But you had to be reminded to do your job."

"Um, I—"

Father put up a hand. "I don't need to hear excuses, son. Even a gas jockey can contribute to the world, but only if he knows his job and stays focused. Do you understand that?"

"Yes, sir."

The kid's acne seemed to have caught fire. He glanced at E, who turned her gaze to the traffic on the street. Hurrying to the front of the car, he opened the hood. Father followed and stood with his fists resting on his hips, his suit jacket pushed back so his suspenders showed. Though E could only see through the slit between the hood and the car, she could tell the guy's hands fumbled nervously as he removed the oil cap, tested the level, and replaced it. Mother didn't seem to have noticed the exchange. Either that or she pretended not to.

Handing two dollar bills and two dimes to the attendant, Father got into the car. "Ready for the last leg of our journey, girls?"

Mom said she was. Elvera said nothing. The attendant had turned his back to them as he cranked the dials back to zero with jerky movements, his spine lightning-rod straight.

When they reached Mackinaw City, Father turned in at a ferry dock where a sign said, "Fastest Boats to Mackinac Island." Getting out, he spoke to a man in a uniform shirt at a small wooden kiosk. Money changed hands, and the man followed Father to the car, where he started unloading boxes and suitcases and stacking them onto a cart another man pushed forward for the purpose.

Suddenly E realized that for the next three months, she would be without motorized transport. She remained in the car, which seemed like the last vestige of civilization as she knew it.

"Come on, Elvera," Father said impatiently. "The ferry leaves soon."

"I'm going to hate Mackinac," she muttered to her mother as

she obeyed the command. "Camilla says it's all grass and fudge shops."

Mom put on her patient expression. "You'll be fine once we get there, Ellie."

"E," she corrected. "I hate it when you call me Ellie."

Pursing her lips, Mother avoided either nickname. "Elvera. You can help me plant a flower garden."

"I hate flowers."

"Saying you hate things is rude, dear."

"All right then. I *despise* flowers."

At a loss, Mother fell silent.

E had to admit the view was spectacular. The Straits of Mackinac lay on three sides: to her right, Lake Huron and the island almost eight miles away (according to Father). On the left was Lake Michigan, more familiar to her from its southern end, where lay home and the city she was already missing. Splitting them was the Mackinac Bridge, completed less than ten years earlier. Once a ferry had been required to get from the Lower Peninsula to the Upper. Nowadays ferries went only to the island, making the trip several times each day while passengers left their cars behind in Mackinaw City.

When their belongings were loaded on the cart, the first man pulled while the second pushed it toward the open ramp of the ferry. Elvera followed her parents across a metal plank-way and onto the enclosed passenger deck. The lake sparkled in the sunlight, but the breeze that swept off it was cool. E shivered. Chicago had been warm for weeks now, but this far north they hadn't heard it was summer.

"Do you want to ride up top?" Father asked, but she pointedly took a seat on a bench along the side. "Suit yourself. We're going to enjoy the view." Mother gave the bench a look of longing, but taking a scarf out of her coat pocket, she covered her lacquered hair and followed her husband up a narrow metal stairway to the top deck.

Elvera watched out the window as tanned crewmen hurried here and there, undoing ropes and wrapping them in neat coils. A strident horn tooted, causing her to jump, and a low vibration under her feet signaled engines shifting into gear. The boat went backward for a while, moving away from the dock like an overburdened turtle. Everything stopped for a moment, and then the sound changed to a higher pitch. A forward surge made E grab hold of the seat. They were off.

The noise was irritating, and the smell of diesel was nauseating. As the boat picked up speed, the cabin temperature dropped. Water splashed along the side, spattering the windows with teardrop shapes that flattened and ran backward along the glass. Looking at the gray expanse ahead, Elvera wondered what would happen if the boat sank. It was some relief to see a wooden box nearby that said, "Life Preservers Inside," but the fact that the boat owners acknowledged the possibility of sinking wasn't encouraging. She shivered at the thought of the chilly, choppy waters of the straits enveloping her.

"I have an extra sweater." Elvera turned to see a girl about her age standing before her. Her long hair was dark brown, like E's, but curlier and gathered into uninspired pigtails fastened with rubber bands. She was as thin as E and perhaps an inch taller. Her clothes were awful: a cheap cotton skirt and a button-up blouse in a floral print under a corduroy jacket. She held out a blue, cable-knit sweater, obviously home-made and apparently taken from a canvas bag slung over her shoulder.

"My mom's always cold," the girl said. "She makes me carry around a coat *and* a sweater."

Torn between the chill in the air and her distaste for the garment, Elvera chose warmth. There wasn't anyone she knew within hundreds of miles, so it didn't matter if she looked like a dork. Taking the sweater, which felt heavy and scratchy, she pulled it on over her long-sleeved blouse, a favorite since it had a fashionable mandarin collar. "Thanks."

"My name's Cathy."

Busy with buttons she replied, "Elvera."

"That's a pretty name, and I bet nobody else at your school has it. There are three Cathys in my class alone."

E rolled her eyes. "It's from Mozart's Piano Concerto Number 21. It's called *Elvira Madigan*, but my dopey mother misspelled it."

"Dopey mother" apparently called for a change of subject. "Are you staying on the island?" Cathy gestured toward the window, where the sun's rays seemed focused on the dot of land in the dark waters ahead.

"Yes. You?"

"My mom manages one of Billy Mason's shops. This will be my third summer up there."

"A shop?"

"Yes. Stuff for the tourists—souvenirs, rain hats, all that. Where are you staying?"

"We have a house."

Her brows rose. "You own a place on Mackinac?"

"Someone in my family built it a long time ago, but lately no one goes there much." Elvera shrugged. "Indians? An old fort? Hooray."

Cathy smiled at mention of the fort, and E guessed she'd been there and liked it. "Where is your house?"

"On the hill, behind the…Great Hotel."

"*Grand* Hotel." Cathy shrugged to show the correction was well meant. "That's it, that big, long, white building." She pointed to a spot some distance above and back from the shore, and E squinted to focus her gaze. The place looked like an oversized plantation house, with a Colonial-style porch running its whole length. An array of American flags flapped in the breeze at intervals, and a wide, green lawn in front matched the green roof above.

"From what Father said, our place is beyond the hotel and higher up, in the wooded area at the center of the island."

"It's nice up there," Cathy said. "The trees smell good, and you can't hear the noise from all the tourists. You'll like it, I think."

Elvera examined the girl speculatively. She'd know the area well, even places not meant for tourists. "You should come and visit once we get settled in."

Cathy's face lit. "Really?"

"Yes." Elvera looked again at the Grand Hotel, which grew larger as the boat grumbled its way through the water. "My parents will be glad to see I've met someone my age."

That was a fib. Mother, who constantly nagged E about choosing the "right" kind of friends, would take one look at Cathy and get that pursed lips look that said she wasn't happy. Father would remind her about the Romney boy, who was sure to show up at some point. But Elvera kind of liked Cathy, whose smile was slightly crooked and who'd obviously jumped to the conclusion that the Tharps were wealthy. It would be nice to have a friend she didn't feel she had to compete with every single minute of the day, the way it was back home in Chicago.

Elvera was surprised to learn that Cathy was on the ferry by herself. "Mom came over earlier to open the shop. I stayed in Mackinaw City to finish eighth grade."

"You got yourself to school every day?" Mother and the housekeeper regularly joined forces to get Elvera up and dressed in the morning, and she usually let them know she wasn't happy about it.

"Oh, no. There are lots of people at my house, even with Mom gone," she said with a grin. "Five females and a baby boy. It's kind of like living at the circus."

She didn't mention a dad, but Mother's voice sounded in E's head. *Ladies don't ask questions that might make others uncomfortable.*

A blast of the horn warned that the ferry would soon dock. Elvera removed the sweater and returned it to Cathy, who folded it neatly before returning it to her bag. Setting one foot and then the other on the bench seat, she pulled up dingy cotton socks that had sagged around her ankles. "Maybe I'll see you again soon." Though her voice didn't rise at the end, it was a question.

"Yeah." Her mother's nagging resurfaced, and E corrected herself. "Yes. Give us a couple of days to settle in and then come up. It's called Braddock House, but Father says we'll probably change the name."

Cathy chuckled. "Good luck with that. You can make it 'Elvera's Mansion' or the 'Mickey Mouse Castle,' but the locals will still call it what they've always called it."

They parted then, Cathy skipping lightly off the boat and turning once to wave before disappearing into the milling crowd at the dock. People pointed at buildings and carriages and consulted directional signs. Elvera waited for her parents to descend the stairs and then joined them as they stepped onto Mackinac Island, Michigan, a Great Lake and a world away from Chicago, Illinois.

It was noisy, as docks tend to be. For a while the passengers huddled in a comforting herd, trying to decide what to do first in this new place. Horse-drawn carriages and drays of several kinds lined the street above them, some battered and others fancy, like the one in *Cinderella.* "Carriage tours of the island," one man called, while another bawled, "Haul your luggage to the Grand Hotel."

Elvera surveyed her new community. Up a steep hill straight ahead was Fort Mackinac, which she already knew about from Father's endless description. They'd be visiting soon, and she was apparently supposed to be excited that she'd get to see a cannon fired by men in costumes of whatever era it was when they fired cannons. Like loud noises and stinky black powder were a big, hairy deal.

Above the docks was the main street, and to the left was the town's business section, a few blocks of shops housed in two-and three-story buildings. Their cheerful fronts were mostly white, trimmed in Victorian colors, decorated with gingerbread, and protected on the ground-level by colorful awnings.

Hearing a shout, E turned to see a black-enameled coach pull up on the street with the words "Grand Hotel" on the side. A laughing couple hurried up to it, and a few words were exchanged with the driver, who wore a long red uniform coat. Gallantly, he offered a hand to the girl and helped her board. Her companion handed over their suitcases and then followed, settling in as the driver stowed the cases and took his seat up front. He urged his gray-white horse forward, and its hooves clopped sharply on the roadway, the sound dimming and finally fading away. *How nice,* E thought, *to sit on a velvet seat and look down like royalty at those on foot.*

Any dream of riding in a carriage was soon shattered. Choosing a man of about thirty with a single horse and a battered wagon, Father spoke briefly with him and returned to his wife and daughter, obviously pleased. "That fellow will take our belongings up to the house. We'll walk, so we get to see the island."

As usual, he'd chosen the cheapest method of doing things. Mother said nothing, though she looked down at her three-inch heels and then enviously at Elvera's Keds.

They strolled through the congested business section, where a sense of liveliness permeated everything. Hundreds of people shopped, sold, walked, rode, and talked, creating a blur of movement and a babble of noise. "It's hard to imagine all this energy lasts only three months of the year," Mother said wonderingly, and Father grunted agreement.

Elvera was silent, taking in the differences between Mackinac

Island and any other place she'd ever been. It smelled like horse manure, as she'd predicted, but for some reason she felt optimistic about the summer. While it wasn't the Riviera, the mood of the island was bright, and she'd already met someone interesting. The experience might be tolerable.

When they'd passed the shopping district, Father consulted a map he'd brought along and turned onto a street leading sharply uphill. The incline was steep enough that Mother, who constantly fought her weight, was soon gasping for air and trying not to limp. By the time they rounded a bend and saw the house fifty yards ahead, Elvera felt sorry for her. They all stopped, Mother to catch her breath and Father and E to get a first impression.

Trees separated Braddock House from its neighbors, making it appear to stand alone. It had a turret on one end that brought to Elvera's mind oil lanterns and lost sailor lovers. A long porch trimmed with gingerbread held pieces of outdoor furniture. E imagined her mother in a crisp apron, serving iced tea to guests who sat on wicker chairs and admired the view of the lake below. "Pretty," Mother said, and for once E didn't disagree.

As they got nearer, however, the favorable impression faded, like the flavor in the Bazooka gum E was not supposed to be chewing. Up close the place was run-down, filthy, and in dire need of repairs. The porch roof had a large hole directly over the door, and leaves and other debris had piled up, almost hiding the steps. The wooden deck wobbled under E's slight weight, and she imagined one or both parents falling through. Would that be funny or tragic? She never found out, because Father spotted the danger, guiding his wife around the weak spots as he dug an oversized key from his trousers pocket. Inserting it in the lock, he wriggled it a few times until the mechanism responded with a scrape, and then stood back like a doorman, inviting them to precede him inside.

The place smelled disgusting, a combination of dust, damp, and mouse droppings. The furniture was centuries old—well, not quite, but maybe from the nineteen thirties. The only toilet, which E needed desperately, had a nasty ring of red at the water line. It worked, but when she flushed it made a noise like the guts of the house were being sucked into the ground.

Mother walked through the downstairs rooms on tiptoe like she expected the ceiling to collapse on her head. Father took on the fake-cheerful voice he used when they weren't supposed to complain. "I've hired a couple to do the heavy work," he informed them. "The husband will make the necessary repairs to the structure, and the wife will do the cleaning and such."

"Oh, good," Mother replied, but Elvera had never heard her sound less pleased. Accustomed as she was to invisible economies in Chicago, Mother obviously didn't know where to start with a neglected, century-old house on an island in the middle of nowhere.

"I'll be around until Sunday noon," Father said, as if that would be plenty of time to fix everything. "After that I'll have to get back to the city before the business falls apart."

It seemed things were always close to falling apart these days. Once a simple banker, Franklin Tharp had started a new firm that expanded an individual's credit through use of a card he carried with him. "It's much like the popular Diners Club card," E had heard him say a hundred times, "except a man can use in all areas of life, not only in restaurants. He'll use a credit card when he shops in a clothing store or buys gasoline." People often frowned at that, but Father would soldier on. "Credit revolves, so a fellow doesn't have to pay the full bill at the end of every month. It's being done in California already, and I mean to help financial institutions in Illinois provide the same service to their customers."

The business hadn't grown as father had hoped, because, according to Mother, people weren't yet educated as to the possibilities buying on credit opened to them. To help spread the word, she'd entertained a seemingly endless line of bankers at dinners and parties almost every weekend through the first half of 1965. Seeing her so attentive to the men, so sweet to their wives, E claimed that being in the room was like eating a dozen Bit O' Honey bars all at once. Mother had replied stiffly that because of her braces, E wasn't supposed to have one candy bar, much less twelve.

The worst part for E was being forced to meet their guests and smile politely when they praised her for the paper napkins she and Mother had folded into flower-like nut cups and set beside each plate. She hated being told by Mr. Charles or Mr. Barkin (She could never keep them straight) who always laid a heavy hand on her shoulder and said how tall she'd gotten since last time. "I'm supposed to get taller," she wanted to say. "That's why it's called growing up." Of course, that was rude, so she fake-smiled, escaping as soon as possible to her room, where she told her poster of Bobby Darin how much she hated every single thing in her life. "I promised Father I'd be really nice to the bank people if I could stay home this summer," she'd told Bobby one night after one of her parents' cocktail parties. Bobby didn't answer, knowing that proposal had been doomed from the start.

The first night on the island was awful. Elvera was terrified by every noise. They hadn't yet found her bed sheets, so she had to sleep wrapped in a blanket. She got the urge to pee in the night (too many orange sodas on the road) and had a terrible time finding the bathroom in the unfamiliar place. By morning, her optimism from the day before had evaporated. She was grumpy, and the disrespect she was prone to came out in every response she made to her mother's forced cheerfulness.

After the family had breakfasted on bananas and Tang, Laura and Darby Wolf showed up at the back door. Darby, a man of about forty with greasy hair and dirty fingernails, did the talking. Within minutes he was thumping through the shed, looking for scrap lumber to use for mending the porch steps. After that he got a ladder and, with Father's inept assistance, fixed the hole in the porch roof. "Much of what needs to be done is cosmetic," Father said at lunch. Ignoring the house's mustiness, dated appliances, and faded furniture, he praised its classic lines and Victorian architecture.

"Once it's cleaned and aired out, we'll be quite comfortable."

Who's we? E wanted to say. *You'll go back to Chicago and leave us in this musty old tomb.*

Mother said, "It will be nice, won't it, Ellie?" Since Father was looking at his plate, E rolled her eyes to let her mother know she was displeased with both the situation and the hated nickname. Mother looked down at her sandwich and said, "Laura seems competent. She made this lunch out of practically nothing."

Laura didn't appear to be that much older than Elvera, though her solemn demeanor suggested maturity. She'd bought a few food items in Father's name at the island's only grocery store. "You'll want to get most of your supplies from the mainland," she advised, "because everything's expensive here. Make a list, and I'll bring it when we come on Mondays."

Mother frowned. "I didn't realize it would be difficult to get ordinary things like groceries."

"Island life's an adjustment." Laura's tone indicated no judgment of that fact. It simply was.

Elvera's life to that point had been noise and light, and it took a while for her to get used to the silence and complete darkness that surrounded the house at night. By ten o'clock the woods around them were inky black and seemed threatening. Despite being assured there were no bears or cougars on the island, her imagination conjured them waiting just out of sight. Even in the daytime it was quiet, since their house wasn't on the way to anywhere. For days, the only people E saw were her parents; Laura, who was nice but not chatty; and Darby, who didn't talk much at all. It was like being in the isolation booth on some quiz show.

Mother was less anxious once the main rooms of the house were opened, aired, and cleaned. She teased that Elvera should never be bored, since there always seemed to be another room full of mouse droppings and spider webs to dispose of. Father ignored any negatives, even when their single toilet overflowed and for the whole day everyone had to use an actual outhouse that sat in the back yard like some prop from *The Beverly Hillbillies*. "It's a good thing our ancestors left it there," he said with a chuckle. "We could have been in big trouble." Elvera wanted to slug him. As far as she was concerned, being forced to use an outhouse *was* big trouble.

Worst of all, her parents were adamant that Elvera could not go anywhere by herself. After the promised trip to the fort, which was every bit as boring as anticipated, she was ordered to stay on the property. The town offered excitement, even if it was only watching people from all over the nation, even the world, walk by, and the woods called out for exploration, offering piney smells and shadowy places where one could disappear for a while. If she even hinted she'd like to investigate the area, dire warnings came in two different voices. She might get lost or run into some unsavory character bent on doing things she didn't completely understand. When she argued there had to be at least as many unsavory characters in Chicago as there were on Mackinac Island, E got her mother's last-ditch response to complaint: "If you can't find yourself something useful to do around here, I'll find you something."

By the time the girl from the ferry boat showed up, Elvera was desperate for diversion—and for a friend.

Chapter Three

"I sent a man down to do some adapting in Miss E's bathroom," Marilyn told Michael as he and Ha'o set up the dinner buffet. "She's gotten less mobile since her last trip with us, but she refused to trade her favorite cabin for a handicap-accessible one." She put a hand on Michael's arm, and he forced himself not to pull away. "When you take her dinner down, suggest a shower chair. She's touchy about her limitations, but we can't have her falling in the bath."

"I noticed she moves a lot slower now," a nearby woman remarked. "You think she'll need a wheelchair soon?"

"Not my place to speculate." Michael's tone made it clear he wasn't willing to gossip about his charge.

"You can't buy health," the woman opined in a righteous tone. "Someday we'll find her dead in there, curled around a pile of hundred-dollar bills." When Michael looked confused, she quirked a brow. "We figure Miss E's got money hidden in her cabin. That's why she'll only have one steward—so she'll know who to blame if it comes up missing."

Darrin stood at the grill, flipping chicken breasts with deft flicks of his wrist. "We'll have to watch our pretty new boy, yeah?" he said over the hiss of frying meat. "If Mikey buys tons of bling when we get to Koh Samui, we'll know what his game is."

"I'll bet Michael isn't a snoop, like some I could mention."

Ha'o's words seemed to sting, and Darrin said in an injured tone, "The nasty old bat deserved it. She said right to my face that having a lot of tats means I'm desperate for attention." His shoulders twisted as if to deflect the criticism. "They're art, and everybody with a brain knows it." He sniffed defensively. "I didn't appreciate being insulted by old Scarface, so I paid her back a little."

"By invading her privacy," Ha'o said. "That was mature of you."

"Shouldn't have told anyone," Darrin muttered. "Bunch of pansy-asses around here."

Once he'd turned away Michael asked, "What did he do?"

Ha'o spoke softly. "Everybody really is curious about how Miss E pays for stuff. She must be well-off to live full-time on cruise ships, but no one has ever seen anything to do with finances: no credit cards, checks, money orders, nothing. She doesn't get mail. She doesn't have a phone, as far as I know."

"She banks online. That's pretty common these days."

"That's what we thought." Ha'o pushed her glasses back in place with a wrist. "But when Darrin got mad at her, he searched everything in her room, even her tablet. She has a PayPal account for selling the jewelry she makes, but it had only a few hundred dollars. There was no bank app or anything else to do with money."

"How does she pay for these trips then?"

"It has to be cash. That's why everyone wonders where it's kept."

"In a safe, one would suppose."

"Nobody's seen a safe in there." Ha'o touched her lips as if chiding herself for gossiping. "It's not our business, but we wonder, you know?"

"Would I really get blamed if she were robbed?"

"Well, nobody else goes in there." Ha'o grinned. "If you plan to steal her money, today would be perfect. You can blame it on the plumber."

Michael's smile was brief. "Does Miss E ever leave her cabin?"

"Almost every time we stop, and it's always something to see." Ha'o giggled. "She's ready the minute the boat docks and sometimes doesn't get back until after the last whistle. Drives the deck officers crazy."

"They let her get away with that?"

"What Miss E wants, she gets." Setting a cover over the remaining half of a carrot cake, Ha'o offered a theory. "I think maybe Miss E mixes real gems in with her beads and then sells an emerald or ruby when she needs cash. None of us would know the difference, right?"

Michael took a single rose from the cooler and set it in a silver vase. "You were right before. It's none of our business."

"True." Ha'o grinned as Michael picked up the tray. "But it's fun to imagine a handful of diamonds hidden among the rhinestones, right?"

On his way into Cabin Three, Michael met a young man wearing a tool belt and a frustrated expression. "She's in a foul mood," he warned. "I had orders to install a hand-held showerhead, but that woman said I made more noise than was necessary. It gave her a headache."

"But you got it done?"

"Yeah." He jabbed a thumb over his shoulder. "Claims she's made do with a bucket and a rag, so she doesn't need me to make her life easier." The plumber went on his way with a grin, able to take a lighter view now that he was done with Miss E for a while.

Michael knocked. "Dinner, ma'am."

Hearing her give permission, he entered. Miss E sat with glue gun in hand, attaching a bit of beach glass to a slab of copper. The unique smell of heated adhesive made his nose twitch as he set his tray on the dining table. Checking the strength of the seal with her fingers, Miss E put her work aside and rose. "You may set the table while I clean the gunk off my hands." She held up smudged fingers.

"Some of the substances I work with are poisonous, not a healthy accompaniment to a meal." Using her walker, she moved to the bathroom, and Michael heard the splash of water in the sink.

The chair Miss E favored was set directly under the ceiling fixture, allowing the best possible light for her work. Recalling Ha'o's theory, Michael stepped quietly forward and peered at the tray of beads. In the colorful array he saw mostly glass beads mixed with wood, bone, stone, and cloisonné. Nothing uncommon or valuable.

Freed from Miss E's watchful glare, he studied the cabin with interest. It was bigger than some staterooms he'd seen, about two hundred square feet, with a small dining area to the right of the entry door. Beyond the table and two chairs, a mini fridge topped with a microwave sat in the corner. On the longer wall, a futon-type couch filled the remaining space to the bathroom wall. Opposite the bath was the bed, and between was a sliding-glass door that led to a balcony where the sea turned gold, amber, and red as the sun's rays slanted across it.

Beside the bed was a dresser topped with personal items, a hairbrush, a tube of skin cream, and a long-handled shoehorn. The bath/bedroom area could be closed from view with a canvas curtain that now stood open. The remaining wall, on his left, was dedicated to storage, parts of it open and others fitted with doors. Aside from the cluttered area around Miss E's chair, the cabin was neat but impersonal, in the way of rented spaces. He saw no safe or lockbox, and no obvious spot where one might be hidden.

Moving back to the table, Michael began setting out the meal, being careful to put items down precisely and with as little noise as possible. Recalling Marilyn's order that he interest her in a shower chair, he started with what he thought was an innocuous question. "How are you feeling today, Miss E?"

The sound of running water stopped abruptly. "Don't do that." She appeared in the doorway, hands white with soapsuds, face pinched with anger. "I don't tolerate inane questions from the help."

"I—"

She held up soapy fingers as she made three points. One: "We're practically strangers, so it's unlikely you truly care how I'm feeling." A second: "My condition at any given moment is none of your business." A third: "You saw me five hours ago. Since I'm still upright, it's safe to assume my health is unchanged since then."

Michael felt his face warm. "People ask after each other's health to be polite, Miss E."

Her chin rose sharply. "Well, I don't like it. To answer truthfully, I'd have to list everything that currently hurts, aches, or malfunctions. Otherwise, I'm required to lie and say all's well when it isn't."

Michael had spent the afternoon wondering how to deal with his charge's prickliness, how to get her to talk to him and possibly even like him. He'd noted her reaction to Ha'o's servile jolliness, and she'd responded badly to his initial attempt at charm. He guessed the stewards before him had done everything possible to avoid making Miss E angry.

Had anyone tried the opposite approach?

"Should I say, 'Here's your dinner, ma'am, and I don't give a fuck how you are?'"

Her face froze. For a moment Michael was sure he'd done the wrong thing. He pictured himself being ordered from the room. Miss E would no doubt demand he be fired, maybe even put off the ship at the next port.

When she spoke, her voice was calm. "It's better than some meaningless pleasantry neither of us cares about."

He tried to hide his relief. "You did ask me to be honest."

Her mouth twitched briefly with what he thought was humor, the scarred side moving less than the other. The smile, if that's what it had been, disappeared, and she pointed a finger at him. "Don't assume you've figured me out on your first day. You aren't that clever."

"I will assume nothing where you are concerned, Miss E." Despite the warning, he felt they'd crossed a barrier, and that pleased him. Returning to his duties he said, "I understand your impatience with useless niceties. The other day I called the phone company's helpline. I spoke to three different people, and I was thanked so often by each of them that I almost forgot what I contacted them for in the first place."

"Then we agree," she said formally. "You won't ask questions you don't need an answer to, and I won't congratulate you for doing your job." She disappeared again, and Michael caught a whiff of lavender soap as he suppressed a grin. As if she'd thanked him for anything.

A moment later she stepped back into the doorway. "Of course, the solution you chose is improper. You'll need to find something between obscenity and obsequiousness."

"Is a simple good morning or good afternoon tame enough for you?"

"It beats a pop quiz about the condition of my bowels." She leaned a shoulder against the doorway. "Do you know what old age is, Mike? It's the daily discovery that your body has more ways to betray you than you ever imagined. Solve one problem; another arises."

"And talking about it does no good."

She shrugged. "Some enjoy sharing the details of their personal deterioration. I try not to, so it's easier to be around those who don't expect me to make up cheerful lies." She disappeared again. The splash of water stopped, and he heard a jar lid being removed.

"My inquiry did have a purpose." He raised his voice to be sure she heard. "My bosses think you should use a chair in the shower, but everyone's afraid to ask you about it. Will you let them bring one in?"

After a pause she said, "I'll consider it."

Slowly, so as not to make an audible sigh, Michael let the air out of his lungs. He'd accomplished his mission, and he thought he'd made progress toward getting Miss E to accept him. Dealing with her was like tiptoeing through a minefield. Still, it wasn't as if this were the first difficult relationship he'd taken on.

Rick came to mind. Though not prickly like Miss E, the man had been a challenge, refusing to accept responsibility for anything, ever. "A guy does what he has to, Michael," he'd say after a long day and a few glasses of Dewars. "You deal with people the way they force you to."

"Are you thinking of your ex-wife?" Michael had asked, but the answer had been a sniff, another slug of Scotch, and repetition. "A guy does what he has to do."

Michael shouldn't have been surprised, he reflected, when Rich turned on him. Miss E might do the same, he reminded himself. Nurturing the delusion that we're forced to do the things we choose to do is a way of life for most people.

When she came to the table, Michael pulled out a chair and handed Miss E the scarlet napkin. She examined her meal but apparently found nothing to criticize. The setting was balanced. The chicken fettucine looked appealing. The flatware sparkled.

"Don't lurk like a mugger in an alley, Mike. Stand over there."

He stepped to the opposite side of the table. "That's better." Shaking an exorbitant amount of salt onto her entree she said, "You wear a crucifix."

He resisted the urge to touch it. "I had a Christian upbringing."

"Catholic?"

"Um, no, ma'am. Evangelical."

"Is that so." She set her elbows on the table, letting her fork dangle for a moment. "If you had to put your beliefs into a single sentence, what would it be?"

After a moment he said, "God helps those who help themselves."

"That's neither Biblical nor Christ-like."

He shifted his feet. "Since God made me as I am, I prefer to put my faith in myself."

She didn't argue the point. "Will you want Sunday mornings off to go to church?"

"That's not necessary, though if you'd like to attend services, I'd be happy to go along to help out."

She made a negative gesture. "I lost interest in outward observances long ago."

"Were you raised in the church?"

"My family was Catholic." It was said as if it didn't matter, and her next words clarified her position. "Every faith has books, deities, and traditions, yet each tells its adherents to reject the books, deities, and traditions of the others." She tilted her head to the side. "It seems unlikely to me that a creator would share secrets with only some of the beings he or she created." Putting a finger in her dessert pudding, she tasted it.

"Then you don't consider yourself a religious person?"

"There has to be a balance between the faith we're taught and the truth we feel inside, and too much of either is disastrous. We constantly walk a line between arrogant belief in our own righteousness and meek acceptance of the righteousness of others." She raised a brow. "Does that offend your dogma, Mike?"

"Not at all. It helps me to understand you better."

Her eyes turned a shade darker. "And why should I care how well the guy who cleans my bathroom understands my level of piety?"

Michael judged it too early to test her tolerance a second time. Laying a hand on his chest, he said, "Once I know your feelings on a subject, I won't have to guess what I might say that will offend you."

For some seconds Miss E looked up at him, her eyes like walls that blocked entry to her thoughts. Finally, she turned to rolling noodles onto her fork. "How did you imagine you could get away with saying *fuck* to an old biddy like me?"

He made a theatrical bow, like a magician who'd performed a clever trick. "You appear to have seen something of the world, so I guessed you've heard improper words before this."

"A few." With a chunk of chicken on her fork and a faint smile on her face, Miss E looked past him, as if a memory had captured her. "But when I was a girl, sex, and especially that word for it, was a huge taboo."

Chapter Four

Mackinac Island-June, 1965

Meeting Elvera Tharp was the coolest thing that had ever happened to Cathy. Though it almost killed her, she made herself wait until Monday before acting on the invitation to visit. When she judged the Tharps had had time to get the house opened up and their clothes unpacked, she put on her favorite outfit, yellow shorts and a navy cotton blouse, pulled a brush through her tangly hair, told Mom she'd be back for supper, and followed directions one of the cart drivers provided to Braddock House.

Having no phone, Cathy couldn't call ahead to see if Elvera was home and willing to have company. She imagined some family outing, E's dapper father and pretty mother sitting on a blanket on the hillside at the fort, a picnic spread between them while E watched the traffic on the bridge through binoculars. Or all three of them on horseback, cantering around the island with crisp clip-clops, Mr. and Mrs. Tharp side by side while Elvera led the way, her hands sure and relaxed on the reins. Cathy had no equestrian experience except a few stolen rides on a neighbor's ponies, but she guessed E took lessons regularly, probably with an English saddle and a cool riding outfit like girls wore on *Spin and Marty*.

As she left the stretch of shops that lined the shore, the hubbub of tourists laughing, arguing, and calling out, "Look at this!" quieted behind her. Trees took over, though it was hard to tell how they sustained themselves on the rocky ground. As she walked, Cathy sang "Teddy Bear," by her all-time favorite, Elvis Presley, softly to herself. Elvera had mentioned loving music too, so she looked forward to comparing favorite songs and artists.

Braddock House was beautifully made, with graceful lines and lots of gingerbread. It needed work, but she recalled Elvera saying it hadn't been lived in for years, so that was understandable. A guy in overalls stood halfway up a ladder, nailing a piece of trim back into place. He glanced at her once and then returned to work. Cathy stood at the gate, hoping one of the Tharps would notice they had company. When that didn't happen, she gathered her courage, approached the door, and knocked.

Mrs. Tharp answered, wearing a housedress that was slightly tight, low heels, and an apron. Though in her mid-thirties, she seemed older, possibly due to some extra pounds she carried around her waist. When Cathy asked if Elvera was home, she seemed unsure how to respond. Her repetition in a cool, high tone, "Elvera?" suggested she'd never heard that name before. Cathy was sure she was about to be sent on her way, politely but firmly.

What did you expect? she asked herself. The Charbonneaus weren't the kind of people who came calling at homes like this one. Even lifting the brass handle that hammered against the fancy plaque beneath it had made Cathy feel unworthy. She couldn't picture herself relaxing on one of the freshly scrubbed and precisely placed wicker chairs on the veranda. Her mouth wouldn't form the words, "Elvera invited me." In fact, she was tempted to turn and run.

Luckily, Elvera came clomping down the stairs at that moment. She wore leather shoes, had covered her hair with a bandana, and held a cobweb-coated broom in hand. "That's Cathy, Mom. We met on the ferry, and I asked her over."

"Oh." Mrs. Tharp's smile was as thin as an onion slice. "Do you live on the island, Cathy?"

"Summers I do. My mom manages Billy's Trading Post."

"I see." Elvera's mother looked like she'd eaten something sour. Cathy wished she'd had the nerve to lie and say she was staying at a hotel, but no one who saw her cheap clothes and home-cut hair would believe that anyway.

"I offered to show Elvera the island." Mrs. Tharp took hold of the screen door with both hands, as if Cathy might wrench it open, rush past, and drag her daughter away. Flashing what she hoped was a trustworthy smile Cathy said, "I'll have her back by suppertime."

"I don't know, dear. Elvera's father doesn't like her going off on her own."

"But I won't be on my own, Mother. I'll be with Cathy."

Mrs. Tharp's smile was as weak as the Kool-Aid served at church picnics. "I'm sure Cathy knows her way around, but that's not—"

"She's going to show me where to find Indian arrowheads." Sliding under her mother's arm, Elvera pushed the door open and joined Cathy on the porch. "Father will think that's cool."

They left the yard, wading through weedy grass that tickled their elbows, crossing the road, and taking a trail that left the bright sunlight behind and sprinkled them instead with speckles of light here and there. "You lied to your mom," Cathy said after a while. "I never said anything about arrowheads."

E's eyes twinkled. "Don't be a goofball. Everyone lies to their parents."

"I don't." When her new friend looked surprised Cathy explained, "Father Yates says lying is as big a sin as stealing, because lies steal someone's trust."

E tilted her head comically, making her chin point almost due west, batted her eyes, and made a "Duh-h-h" sound.

Realizing how dumb she must seem, Cathy cleared her throat and tried again. "I don't always do what Father says. He's pretty old..."

"My mother is a pain in the ass about me going anywhere on my own. Sometimes I lie to shut her up."

"But she said your dad didn't want you to—"

"And he's not even here." She sounded angry about that.

"Mother worries too much. A fib is good, because it makes her less nervous." Dismissing that, E asked, "What are you going to show me first?"

They'd reached a fork in the road. "Would you rather see the island from up high or a spooky cave?"

"Definitely the cave."

"Devil's Kitchen it is."

As they started again E said, "Tell me which direction we're going. I need to get oriented."

"West. We'll turn south in a bit." Cathy pointed. "Once we clear the trees, you'll be able to see the Mackinac Bridge."

"I'm glad you showed up." E sounded breathless as she hurried to keep up with Cathy's long strides. "Exploring will be lots more fun without my parents along. And Father can't be mad, since I have a guide."

It was Cathy's first inkling the rich city girl's life wasn't perfect. "You're not allowed to go places by yourself?"

"If I even *mention* leaving the yard, I get this huge lecture about dirty old men. To hear them tell it, there's always at least one crouching in the bushes at the property line, chuckling like some sort of demon while he waits for a chance at me." She paused. "Doesn't anyone ask where you're going when you take off?"

"I always tell Mom where I'll be, but she isn't much of a worrier."

As they walked the shady path, the girls exchanged vignettes of their lives. Cathy described the public school she attended in Mackinaw City, with kindergarten through twelfth grade housed in one noisy, crowded building that smelled like hot wool all winter due to dozens of mittens left on the radiators to dry. E told stories from St. Mary's Catholic High School, where nuns inflicted punishment with impunity, convinced of their own righteousness. "I had a friend who teased her hair to make it puffy," she reported.

"Sister Clare washed it out in the bathroom sink and made her sit in class dripping wet afterward. And don't *ever* come to school wearing makeup!" She rolled her eyes. "I think nuns like being mean, don't you?"

"The only time I ever meet any is during our two weeks of catechism every summer."

"They're horrible. I think they get training in how to embarrass you so bad you'll never recover."

Cathy frowned. "I don't remember the ones we had being that way."

"You, Miss Cathy Charbonneau, are a goofball." E made a queen-like gesture, as if bestowing a title on her new friend. "But I'm pretty sure I like you that way."

Cathy felt her face warm at the compliment. Pointing, she said, "The cave is up ahead." In her hurry, E tripped over a tree root but caught herself gracefully. She probably took ballet lessons too, Cathy decided.

The cave, just off a road that circled the island's exterior, was in some ways a disappointment to visitors, being small and not deep enough to bring Tom Sawyer to mind. "Doesn't it look like a face?" Cathy asked.

"Spooky." Elvera approached and stuck her head inside. Her voice echoed a little as she asked, "How did it get black like that?"

Cathy shrugged. "They say evil spirits lived in there, cannibals who ate anyone who got too close. That's why it's called the Devil's Kitchen."

"You're kidding."

"I think it was really waves crashing on the limestone." She grinned. "But it's still cool."

"I agree." Elvera ran a hand along the edge and then wiped the dirt on her pants. "I'll bet Father doesn't even know it exists. I can't wait to tell him." Cathy was beginning to understand that although E resented her father in some ways, she also wanted desperately to please him. Never having known a dad, Cathy didn't get it, but that's how it seemed.

"I'll bet boys and girls come here to do the dirty deed." Elvera made a comically shocked face. "They probably made up the stories to keep other people away."

"The dirty deed?"

"You know." Leaning close she whispered, "The f-word."

She'd seen it a few times, even heard a boy at school say it out loud once, but Cathy didn't get what it was. She knew how animals made babies, but she was sure people didn't do it that way. Did they?

"Yeah, they do," E said when she asked. There followed a discussion filled with euphemisms and half-truths, but even at that, Cathy learned more than her mother had ever told her, or ever would, about sexual intercourse. Cathy welcomed the information, since she'd been uncomfortable revealing her ignorance to her friends in Mackinaw City. It seemed okay to question E, who was naturally more sophisticated, since she came from a big city and was rich.

After that first day, Cathy went to Elvera's whenever she could get away. There were times when Mrs. Tharp saw her coming and stepped onto the porch, her full skirt protected from dirt by an apron that matched some color in the print, to tell her Elvera was too busy to have company. Those days were disappointing and a little embarrassing, since Cathy suspected Mrs. Tharp was fibbing. She didn't like E spending time with an island rat, but E insisted Cathy shouldn't worry about it. "She can like it or lump it," she'd say.

The fact that E liked spending time with her made facing Mrs. Tharp's disapproval worth it. One day after she turned Cathy away, saying "Ellie" was "out with friends," Cathy heard a rapping on glass above her. Turning, she saw E at the window of the turret that rose above the second floor. Elvera had mentioned that she often went up there to get away from her mother, who didn't like climbing the narrow spiral staircase that led to it. After gesturing for Cathy to go to the back of the house, she disappeared.

"Why didn't you come in?" she said when they met at the kitchen door.

Unwilling to make trouble Cathy said, "I, um, thought you might be busy."

"She said I was gone, didn't she?" E was angry. "She doesn't want me to have any fun, ever."

From behind E came the sound of metal on wood. A woman with a long black braid hanging down the middle of her back was cutting ham into thin slices with a knife. "Laura," E told her, "from now on Cathy's going to come to this door. I want you to let her in." When Laura nodded gravely E wisecracked, "Just watch so she doesn't steal the good silver."

Though she didn't look like she smiled often, Laura got the joke. "I'll keep an eye on her at all times."

Mrs. Tharp eventually discovered the new arrangement, but she apparently wasn't assertive enough to send Cathy away once she was inside the house. Though Father Yates said it was a horrible sin to judge others, Cathy thought Mrs. Tharp was like one of her neighbor's chickens. She pecked at Elvera all the time, finding fault with this and that. If E tired of it and shooed her mother away, she went, making humming, hen-like noises that signaled futile discontent.

When Mr. Tharp wasn't there, Mrs. Tharp's authority melted away. E rolled her eyes a lot, got snippy, and was even mean to her mom, calling her a cow once, right to her face. Cathy couldn't imagine what would happen to her if she talked to her mom like that. Not that she ever would.

Mrs. Tharp always ended up threatening to tell E's father what she'd said or done, but E laughed that off. "She forgets most of it," she told Cathy, "and Father doesn't want to hear her troubles anyway."

Laura Wolf wasn't much of a talker, but over time she and Cathy developed a comfortable relationship. If Elvera wasn't at home, Laura would invite Cathy inside to wait for her. Settled on a stool in the corner, she often got a taste of whatever the housekeeper was making for the family's next meal, or better yet, for dessert. Over time Cathy learned that Laura and Darby had two children, a two-year-old and an eight-month-old. Her weekly day off was Sunday, so on Saturday night Laura took the late ferry to St. Ignace, the town at the north end of the Mackinac Bridge, to see them. On Monday mornings she took the earliest boat back to the island, after spending as much time with her girls as possible.

"I'll bet you miss them."

Laura shrugged. "It's only four months. The money's good, and my sister-in-law watches my kids with her own, so I know they're okay."

Cathy observed no signs of affection between Darby and Laura. He spoke to her in grunts, and she answered in soft tones that indicated caution, even fear. When he passed behind her in the kitchen, Laura's shoulders tensed. When he wasn't around, she spoke more freely and sometimes laughed aloud.

"How did you and your husband meet?" Cathy asked one day as she waited. Mr. Tharp had driven up for the weekend and taken E on what she termed a "forced learning experience" at a local museum.

It took a while for Laura to answer. "I grew up at the Indian orphanage in Harbor Springs," she finally said. "I was about to age out when Darby came along." When Cathy frowned at the term she explained, "When you turn eighteen, they can't keep you there anymore. I didn't have any place to go, but one day when I was outside watching the little kids at recess, Darby came up and said he needed a housekeeper. I could live in, and I wouldn't have to pay rent." Her dark eyes turned darker. "I was too dumb to get the idea, but I soon found out."

Cathy had been balancing her chair on its back legs, but she leaned forward, causing the front legs to crash against the floor. "He wanted a…a girlfriend?"

A huff of air signaled disagreement with Cathy's word choice, but Laura replied, "Yes. A girlfriend."

"That's not right. You should—" She stopped, unsure what one might do in such a situation.

Laura twisted her shoulders. "At least he married me when I got pregnant. Some don't."

"You know other girls who go with—" She almost said *old men* but switched to "—guys they don't love?"

Laura's smile said how naïve that sounded. "Darby's okay most of the time. And I have my babies."

Struck by the idea that a woman she knew and liked had been forced, by circumstances if not exactly by Darby, to marry a man twenty years her senior and in no way her match, Cathy found she'd lost her desire for an afternoon of paging through fan magazines. Looking at the clock she said, "I'm supposed to help with unloading at the store. Tell E I'll come back tomorrow, will you please?" Nodding, Laura went back to her work.

That night Cathy told her mother, outrage coloring her account. "They let him take Laura out of that orphanage. Nobody said a word."

Margaret sipped at her rum and Coke. "Who was supposed to stop her, Cath? If she wanted to go with him, they couldn't very well say no."

"But she's twenty and already has two kids by a guy who treats her like she's stupid. She isn't, Mom. Laura knows lots of stuff."

"Not every girl gets Prince Charming, Honey. Laura didn't have many prospects, but now she has a home and a family. What more can someone like her ask for?"

Cathy gave up the argument, though it went on in her head. Women were supposed to be getting liberated. They were supposed to have choices in life. Her mother didn't get it, probably because she was from the old "wives submit to your husbands" generation. That was what the Bible said, but Cathy didn't think it meant you had to accept a mate who was old and grumpy and didn't bathe very often.

Though she wondered what Elvera would think of the situation, Cathy knew instinctively that Laura wouldn't want her to tell. People who lived in northern Michigan did what was required to survive. The Tharps' money allowed them choices that people like Laura and Cathy never got. Nobody would ever force Elvera Tharp to marry some man she didn't want.

Elvera found Cathy Charbonneau almost too much to believe. She'd never been south of Gaylord, which sat on the 45th parallel and represented in Elvera's mind the last dividing line between civilization and wilderness. Cathy never asked Elvera to visit the quarters she and her mother had at the back of Billy's Trading Post, but from their conversations Elvera learned that the apartment smelled because there was a horse stable nearby. The only bathroom in the building was upstairs, smelled like mothballs, and was shared with Billy's other summer workers. Cathy's mom made toast in the morning by roasting bread on a long fork over their two-burner stove, like hot dogs at a campfire. Cath considered soda (She called it *pop*) a huge treat, and she'd never had a McDonalds burger, in fact, had never even heard of them, though everyone in Chicago was aware of the new "fast food" craze.

The Charbonneaus didn't have much money; that was clear. Cathy's dad had walked out when she was a baby, leaving the state of Michigan entirely. He refused to pay child support, so from

October to May, Margaret Charbonneau cleaned houses and worked as a substitute bus driver. She made good money during summers on the island, which got them through the long winters. Still, judging from Cathy's casual comments, the family struggled to survive.

"My gram's arthritis got really bad last year," Cathy told E. "We moved her in with us, but then my cousin Delia, who's got three little kids, had to give up her place. Her husband got two years in jail for stealing stuff from hunting camps." She said it almost casually, as if prison had been a foregone conclusion for the man. "Our house isn't big, and now it's bursting at the seams." She grinned. "It's kind of a relief to be here, where I can turn around without stepping on a toddler."

When Cathy visited on rainy days, showing up at the back door with her shiny plastic hounds-tooth raincoat dripping moisture, Elvera went downstairs to escort her to her room, knowing her friend was uncomfortable with Mother's tight-lipped smiles and judgmental once-overs. Once they were in E's room, Cathy became herself again, diving into E's record collection, reading her magazines, and eyeing the neatly arranged clothing in her closet. Once when E went downstairs to get sodas, she returned to find Cathy fingering the crisply ironed blouses. "Everything smells nice," she said shyly. "Like Tide."

Observation revealed that Cathy owned two pairs of pants, two skirts, four shirts, and two awful, hand-knit sweaters. She was proud of a pair of Jamaica shorts she'd recently been given, and though they looked cute on her, they were a shade of yellow Elvera wouldn't have been caught dead in. She had one dress for church on Sundays, a plaid shift with a big bow at the center of a Peter Pan collar. Though she had more clothes back in Mackinaw, Elvera doubted they were of any better quality than the ones she'd seen. They wore the same size in everything except shoes, but there wasn't a single item in Cathy's wardrobe E envied. Cathy, on the other hand, loved trying on Elvera's dresses. She started wearing her hair loose and parted down the middle, as E did (because Michelle

Phillips did). She also began smiling with her mouth almost closed, so a slightly crooked eyetooth didn't show. Still, when she forgot her new-found dignity, Cathy grinned like the Cheshire Cat.

Billy, Mrs. Charbonneau's boss, remarked once that the girls looked like sisters "—except for your friend there is kind of pale." Hearing that, E resolved to be at least as brown as Cathy by the end of the summer. There was an article on how to tan rapidly in her *Teen* magazine, and she bought mercurochrome and baby oil and mixed them together in a spray bottle. She tried to get at least an hour of sun every afternoon, dozing on the grassy back lawn in her two-piece. She had to keep moving her towel as the shadows crept over her, but Mother had a conniption if she went out front. "What if some man sees you half-naked, Ellie?" That launched the familiar lecture about how men had no control of their "urges," reacting "sexually" to sights, smiles, and even scents. Women had to look, seem, and smell modest, so men's "juices" didn't start flowing.

Though Elvera was never invited to the Charbonneaus' apartment, she sometimes hung around the store while Cathy helped her mom, restocking the tables on the sidewalk, cranking out the awnings when the sun got hot, and straightening T-shirts left in a heap by careless shoppers. When Billy came along to check that things were "shipshape," he often slapped Cathy's mom on the rear. E's mother would have called the cops if a man did that to her, but Margaret only giggled.

Billy was like no one Elvera had ever met before. He actually paid attention to the girls' plans, offering tips on where they should explore next and teasing them about their skinned knees when they came back. "At least you're getting to know the real island," he told E. "Most fudgies (the Islanders' term for tourists) don't get past the smell of horse shit." That was unusual too. The men Elvera knew would never say *shit* to a young girl on purpose. If it happened to slip out, they always said, "Sorry," or "Excuse my French." Billy said it without hesitation or embarrassment. He also shellacked horse turds and sold them in his shops as "the only true souvenir of

Mackinac Island." Laughing at his own cleverness he'd say, "Everybody up here sells stuff that's shitty. I sell the real thing, and people love it."

The girls agreed that Billy was weird as they agreed on most things. Their differences were minor, like favorite singing groups. Elvera was interested in the British Invasion bands, while Cathy preferred "real American" music, like Buddy Holly, Chuck Berry, and Elvis. It wasn't a big problem, since E liked everything, even what Mother called "low-class" genres like country western. "I don't love it," Cathy explained, "but it's pretty much all we get on the radio this far north."

Elvera had brought her portable record player and a few dozen records, but the arm on the turntable was jostled somewhere on the trip, and the singers sounded like they were underwater. Cathy showed E how to tape a penny to the needle to weigh it down, and they played the 45s over and over, until they both knew every word. When Father was around, they lowered the volume and sang along softly, lest he start a lecture about "that noise."

Cathy paged through the newest *Look* magazine while Elvera sprawled on her canopied bed, sifting through her records. "I wish I had straight hair like yours," Cathy said. "Even when I iron mine, it curls back up in no time."

E shrugged. "You want straight hair. I want to sing like Mama Cass."

"You be Cass. I'll be Petula Clark."

"Or Dusty Springfield." E waggled a finger between herself and her friend. "To be honest, I don't think either of us has a chance at a singing career. I sound like a crow, and you mess up the words something awful. I mean, 'Date Ripper' instead of 'Day Tripper'? That was hilarious."

"No *Ed Sullivan Show* for us," Cathy agreed amicably. "We'll have to go into the record books as the world's biggest fans of rock and roll."

Chapter Five

Cruise-Day Two, 5:00 a.m.

Soft music played as Michael passed through the lamp-lit dining room. A few early risers were already seated at tables along the windows, sipping coffee and waiting for breakfast to appear. One man seemed to be watching as he passed, and Michael felt his neck tense. When he looked again, the guy was reading something on his phone. *Stop being paranoid.*

Since it was Mother's Day in the U.S., the program director had ordered a variety of treats for the ladies, making it sound like all moms deserve halos and wings. Darrin, who held a bowl in the crook of his arm as he mixed batter for crepes, took a less optimistic view. "We get to work twice as hard, making 'tributes' to the moms on board. And where are all those loving moms? Since it's a sailing day, the old biddies will spend it in the casino, gambling away their kiddies' inheritance."

Ha'o entered the kitchen carrying a large envelope. "I'm collecting for Marilyn's birthday," she announced. "I'd like to get her a spa day, because she works really hard to make things run smoothly around here."

"Great." Taking out his wallet, Michael extracted a five, folded it in half, and slid it into the envelope. "Before you go on, can you show me how she wants the tables set up for the brunch?"

Though it had been explained in detail earlier, Ha'o was the patient type. "Sure." Setting the envelope and her keys on an empty shelf, she led the way to the dining room.

"Wait," Michael said. "Let me get a pencil and paper, so you can draw me a diagram."

Again Ha'o agreed amicably, and he returned to the kitchen, coming back with a piece of scrap paper and a stubby pencil. After shaking her head at the imperfect tools, Ha'o drew a picture of the usual setup, narrating as she worked. "You need room here for people to pass through without dropping food on the ones already seated." She handed him the drawing and tossed the pencil into a nearby trash can, where it rattled briefly on the metal bottom.

"Thanks," he told her. "I have trouble getting a picture in my head with verbal instructions alone."

When they returned to the kitchen, Glynis was topping fruit cups with whipped cream and crushed nuts. She gave Michael a look of obvious invitation, but he ignored it, hurrying to his cubby at the back of the room. Before long she appeared at his elbow. "Some of us are meeting up tonight. Fancy a drink or ten?"

"No, thanks. I need to be sharp should Miss E call."

"Yeah, right. She's a demanding old bitch."

Michael sniffed. "She knows what she wants, that's all."

Glynis grinned. "I know what I want too. Shall I demand it?"

He treated it as a joke. "You don't have the pull Miss E has."

She stepped closer, and he caught the scent of heavy perfume. "She ain't looking for a pet to spend money on, you know."

Recoiling in disgust he said, "I don't care that Miss E has money. I think she needs—I don't know. A friend, maybe."

"Yeah, right. Every good-looking guy your age wants an elderly woman for his friend." She tilted her head at the grill area. "Darrin tried snuggling up to her a couple years back and got nowhere. All Miss E is interested in is griping about the service here and making her bracelets."

"I wondered about that. Who buys her stuff?"

"People on the internet, I reckon. She puts pictures up on some site and people order them." She tapped his arm playfully. "I'm telling you, she's got her beads. She don't want no gigolo."

"I'm not after money. I only want to be a competent steward."

"Yeah, right." Glynis gave a haughty sniff. "Tell you what. You come 'round and see me when you're ready for a woman with warm blood in her veins."

He pretended not to hear, and she waggled her fingers seductively as she walked away.

As one of Michael's co-workers helped him set the tables in a long line for the buffet. he asked, "What does Miss E call you?" With a grin he added, "Usually I was *idiot*, with a few *imbeciles* tossed in for variety."

"He'll be begging for daycare duty by the end of the week," said a man who passed, hefting one end of a table. "Twenty bratty kids at a time is still less stressful than working for Miss E."

Pride made Michael reply, though he shouldn't have. "I think we'll get along all right. She told me a little about herself."

"The two of you *talked*?" the first man asked. "She didn't just gripe about what you did wrong?"

Though Michael shrugged to indicate he couldn't explain it, he felt a flush of pride at their surprise. Apparently, he was already more successful with Miss E than any of them had been.

A woman who was spreading tablecloths interjected, "Wait till she's hung over. She's ten times worse."

Michael trailed her into the kitchen, where the smell of bananas blended with frying crepes. "Miss E drinks?"

"Guests in the adjoining cabins hear her staggering around her room late at night," she replied after looking to see if Marilyn was within earshot. "She has blackouts too. Can't remember where she put things."

"Come on, Marie," Darrin called from the grill. "Michael's

fantasy is becoming Miss E's boy-toy, but her being a drunk offends his religious feelings."

"Ignore Darrin," Marie murmured. "He's a jerk."

"It's okay," Michael replied. "I've run into his type before."

"Did I drop money somewhere in here?" Ha'o stood in the doorway, her face pinched with concern.

Everyone glanced around their immediate area, but no one saw the missing cash.

Peering into her collection envelope she said, "I know I had more than this in here." She took out a bill. "I have the five Michael gave me. I remember because it was folded, but the rest is gone."

"Where were you before coming here?" Michael asked.

"On deck, collecting from the pool crew." She grimaced. "If the money fell out up there, it's probably in the gulf by now."

"I'm sorry, Ha'o," Michael said as she rattled the envelope, apparently hoping the money was caught in a corner.

"Not your fault." She stowed the envelope under her arm. "I should have tucked the flap in tight."

Since Miss E had no children, the day's first visit presented a problem for Michael. Should he mention it was Mother's Day or ignore the holiday entirely?

When he knocked at her door and was given permission to enter, Michael got the impression she'd been waiting for more than breakfast. He almost asked if she was hungry but caught himself in time. *No inane questions.* "Good morning, Miss E."

"What have you brought me today?"

Lifting the cover, he set a dish on the table. "Crepes with whipped cream and cherries."

"Well, well. Is it my birthday?"

So much for pretending it was an ordinary breakfast. "It's a special treat for Mother's Day."

She eyed the generous portion topped with a drizzle of chocolate. "I'm nobody's mother, but if they're handing out treats to those who might have been, I'll take one." Sitting down, she cut a section from the center, where the whipped cream was piled highest, and ate it, making a little purr of enjoyment.

As she cut another bite Michael said, "The spa is offering one free service to all the ladies on board. I could arrange for a massage therapist or a nail technician to come here if you'd rather not leave the cabin."

"No way. I hate being touched." She shivered dramatically and then added, "When I can't take care of myself, I will simply lie down and die."

That accounted for her bare, square-cut fingernails and blunt haircut. Apparently, Michael had stood still for too long, because Miss E fluttered a hand at him. "You may tidy the room while I eat."

Picking up items of clothing and daily living, he put them in places he hoped were acceptable. Twice he showed her things he didn't see a spot for, and between bites she indicated where she wanted them stored.

Remembering the comments about her drinking, Michael looked for liquor as he cleaned. There was nothing in view, but when he opened a cupboard near the sleeping area, he found a dozen bottles on a shelf that had racks to keep them upright and separate, so that even in rough seas they'd remain intact and wouldn't clink together.

"Why are you banging around in there?" Miss E demanded.

"I'm trying to learn where things are kept."

He picked up a pair of running shoes and she barked, "Leave those right where they are."

He glanced at her slippered feet. "Going out for a jog with friends later?" When she looked up sharply, he added, "Well, you aren't exactly known for running—or for mingling with others, for that matter."

"My running days are long gone." Pushing her plate aside, she took up the fruit cup. "And as for mingling, at my age, one comes to understand that society is redundant."

"What do you mean?"

"No matter where a person goes on this earth, she meets the same people over and over. The outsides change, but not the insides." She chopped at her fruit as if it had offended her. "They fall into two types: competitive sorts who see life as a game they need to win, and cotton-heads who see it as a gift they should appreciate every moment of every day." She delivered the last few words in a breathy lilt, and Michael could almost hear Ha'o saying them exactly that way.

"If life isn't a game or a gift, what is it?"

Miss E spooned out a bit of pineapple and ate it. Then she started on the cherries, digging them out one by one. Having decided she wasn't going to answer, Michael went back to dusting. Finally, she said, "Mostly, life is a challenge. Each morning you have to ask yourself, 'Will I contribute something to the planet today or simply deplete its store of breathable air?'"

He chuckled. "Are you saying the earth is full of oxygen thieves?"

"I am."

"Are you afraid you might be one of them?" It had to be difficult for Miss E to justify her own existence, since she contributed nothing to the world except negativity and cheap jewelry.

"Me?" Her gaze drifted to the sea outside the cabin. "No. Not yet."

"What are your current achievements if I may ask?"

She turned cold. "You may not. I don't explain myself to the domestic help."

"Sorry." Michael tossed a paper towel into the lemon-scented trash bag he'd brought along. "I was attempting to make conversation that wasn't about your health or the weather."

She snorted what might have been a laugh. "Well, in lieu of making conversation, you can make the bed. And don't tuck the sheets in too tightly at the foot. I need to be able to move my legs."

A few minutes later, as he backed out of the cabin with the tray and the bag of trash, Michael felt a jolt. Someone coming down the corridor had collided with him, and dishes hit the floor with varying sounds—none of them pleasant. Some broke; others rolled away. Before he knew it, a hand grabbed his collar, and he was slammed into the bulkhead.

"Watch where you're going, Mikey." Darrin's expression hinted that the accident pleased him more than it bothered him. "You might be pretty, New Boy, but you're clumsy as shit."

"What's this?" Miss E opened the cabin door, her face pinched with irritation. Darrin backed away.

"I'm sorry, Miss E," Michael said. "We bumped into each other, and it made quite a commotion."

"It certainly did."

"I'll get this cleaned up right away." Bending, he began picking up bits and pieces and tossing them onto the tray. Darrin stood over him, making no move to help.

"All right then," Miss E said. "Be quieter about it."

Michael was in the records office when he heard a noise and turned to find a clerk frowning at him from the doorway. "What are you doing?"

Literally caught with his hand in a filing cabinet, Michael saw no way to deny his snooping. Bumping the drawer closed with his hip, he said, "I wanted to know more about Elvera Tharp. She seems lonely, and I wondered if she has people who care about her."

"Not that I know of." Realizing she shouldn't have admitted even that much, the clerk cleared her throat. "Feeling sorry for a passenger doesn't mean you get to peek at her file."

Michael backed away. "I understand."

He'd already seen the financial record, which was a surprise. Every line item: meals, lodging, transport, all of it, ended with zeroes. No down payment, no amount owed, and no charges added since the ship left Singapore. Miss E had paid nothing, and she owed Wild Goose Cruises nothing.

"I should report you for this."

Glancing at the clerk's desk, Michael saw photos of her with friends: on a field after a game of softball; at a movie theater, loaded with snacks; and on a sunny beach, dressed to go snorkeling. "Everyone talks about how grumpy Miss E is," Michael said. "I thought maybe if we could get her involved in some activities on the ship, she'd make friends. That's really important, I think."

The clerk's manner softened. "Like they say, people need people." A second later she stepped behind her desk and, as if putting on the mantle of authority, sat down in the chair, which made a *whoosh* sound. "If you want to go on working for Wild Goose Cruises, Mr. Kanda, you need to stay out of my records."

"I will," Michael said earnestly. "This job is very important to me."

Michael's task for lunch prep was with a woman named Callie, and they tore lettuce into bite-sized pieces and tossed it into a large crystal bowl while pots and pans slid and clanged behind them. The inevitable question came up. "How are you getting on with Miss E?"

Michael gave his usual answer. "I think things are going well." Reaching for another head of lettuce, he asked, "Why is Miss E so irritable?"

"I was working on the *Traveling Lady* when I was assigned Miss E duty," she replied, pushing her glasses back into place with her shoulder. "She drove me crazy, so I googled her, thinking if I got some background, it might help me get along with her."

"That was a good idea."

"It didn't really change anything." Sighing, she smacked the base of a head of lettuce on the table, breaking the heart loose so it pulled easily from the center. "I did learn that she ran her own company back in the day. It was successful for a while, but then she lost everything in some big-time meltdown."

"Not everything was lost," he countered, "or she wouldn't be able to afford to live like this."

"True. She probably stashed money away in a secret bank account offshore or whatever." Letting Michael finish the lettuce, Callie took up a jar of olives, tapped the bottom sharply against her hand, twisted the lid off, and drained it. "Isn't that what rich people do?"

"It's certainly possible."

Callie dumped the olives onto a tray and tossed the empty jar in the trash. "If she does have money, she sure doesn't spend it on clothes, and that's odd. The article I found said Elvera Tharp had her own fashion line. I don't recall the name, but—"

"Mizz."

"What did you say?"

"I said she's miserable." Michael shook his head sadly. "She turns people off with her nasty comments and tantrums."

Ha'o, who was working nearby, joined the conversation. "One time I said I believe that when life gives you lemons, you should make lemonade. I got this big lecture about not telling people how they should feel." Ha'o tucked a strand of hair behind her ear. "I was trying to help."

The baker's assistant set a tray of cupcakes down near Michael. Mixed scents reached his nose, chocolate, lemon, and vanilla. "I hear you're a hit with Cabin Three," the man said. "Does that mean we'll have fewer broken dishes this time?"

Another man snickered behind them. "Miss E likes you, Kanda? Let me offer my sincere condolences."

Michael smiled earnestly. "Really, she's not that bad."

"Keep that attitude, Sunshine, and we'll let you be her steward every time she sails with us."

Chapter Six

Mackinac Island-June, 1966

The second summer of her friendship with Elvera Tharp, Cathy got a part-time job babysitting for a couple in her building. She took their one-year-old to her apartment for a few hours each morning so the mom, who had the day shift, could leave, while the dad, who worked nights, slept until eleven or twelve. It was great to have a little spending money, so she'd be able to buy her own school clothes in the fall and maybe get something she really liked instead of the cheapest skirts and blouses offered in the Penney's catalog. Best of all, the job didn't interfere with her time with Elvera, who seldom got out of bed before ten.

Cathy was less nervous at Braddock House that summer, since Mrs. Tharp had grudgingly accepted her presence. Laura was again there to cook and clean. Darby had taken work somewhere else, since Mr. Tharp had no plans to further improve the house. Cathy thought it was cool, but E griped about the groaning noises the old plumbing made and lights operated by pull-chains that hung from ceiling fixtures at the center of each room. "I have to fling my arms around like a go-go dancer to turn on the light in my room," she complained.

Though it was dated, the sense of order and elegance throughout the place impressed Cathy. No home she'd seen before had a room designed and furnished for each specific purpose of living. Braddock House had a formal dining room with an ornate oak table, eight matching chairs, a buffet, and a sideboard. The kitchen was a separate room, and though the appliances there were old, Laura kept them spotless and they mostly worked. A pantry at one side was stocked with items she'd only read about in books: spices beyond salt and pepper and baking ingredients that seemed exotic, like marzipan and candy sprinkles. Cathy always sniffed when she passed, picking out tantalizing aromas she never smelled at home. Glances into the chest-type freezer stocked with meats and vegetables made her wonder what it was like to decide each day what to have for dinner rather than accepting whatever was available.

Upstairs were the family bedrooms and several reserved for guests, though there never were any. Each was a different color, so Mrs. Tharp said things like, "Let's put that in the green room," and "I think it's in the blue room." It sounded like what Cathy had heard of the White House in Washington, D.C., and she dreamed of being asked to stay over. It happened two weeks into the summer, after a battle of wills between Elvera and her mother that Cathy would never hear about. Cathy slept in Elvera's room, in a slim twin bed exactly like her friend's. Each had a snow-white coverlet with ruffles and slim, white posters topped with a matching canopy. The room smelled faintly of Wind Song, a delicate, distinctive scent Cathy had often squirted on her wrist from tester bottles at the drug store. The curtains were pink and white, but Elvera said next year she intended to go pink and purple. "So much cooler."

When they undressed for bed, Cathy couldn't help but stare at Elvera's underpants. Hers were white cotton, which after only a few washings took on a grayish tinge from Michigan's hard water. Elvera's were silky-looking and pale green, with a little heart on one hip that said *Tuesday*. "Your underwear has the day on it?"

Elvera rolled her eyes. "Mother thinks it's cute. I think it's like I need a reminder to change my skivvies."

"Skivvies?"

"That's what Drake calls underwear. Some military thing." She pulled her nightgown over her head, hiding the garment under discussion, but the idea of having such pretty underwear stayed on Cathy's mind. There was so much of life she'd never dreamed of.

On nice days they traveled the trails that crisscrossed the island, usually up and away from the crowds below. The island had two faces: a small, busy tourist area and great empty spaces most visitors never saw. Cathy showed it all to E: where the horses slept, where the permanent residents lived, and even where the dump was. Despite her stated disdain for her father's history lessons, she stood almost reverently on the high spots while the sun on the water made their eyes squint and Cathy spoke of the island's past. Canoes filled with pelts approaching the straits, propelled by voyageurs with strong shoulders. Indians with their solemn approach to dealing with the pale-skinned strangers in their land. Soldiers with their woolen (sweaty smelling) uniforms and their complicated musketry. Mackinac was a place of meetings, where cultures mixed, but it was also where Man met Nature and the two vied long-term to see who would prevail.

Since neither was much of a letter writer, the girls caught each other up on what had happened since last September. Cathy's gram had died, and the cousin moved in with a friend, leaving their house quiet and empty. "We're like two marbles in a shoebox, Mom says."

E found a gnarled branch, peeled the bumpy bark away, and used it like a staff to help her up the inclines. "How are your brothers doing?"

"They're okay," Cathy replied. "Curtis got married and Caleb's wife had another baby."

"You talk about the twins like you don't know them very well," E observed.

"They're a lot older, and to them I'm just the kid who lives with Mom. We're not close like you and Drake."

"We *were* close until they sent him to that stupid academy." E's brother was clearly her hero, though she sometimes made fun of his devotion to what he considered right. Her conversation was peppered with "Drake says…" and "My brother and I used to…" E sometimes read parts of Drake's letters aloud, and though he made light of his trials, the academy sounded horrible to Cathy. She felt sorry for him, but would she and E have become friends if he hadn't been sent to military school? Drake's absence meant she had E all to herself.

"Don't your brothers ever want to come to the island to visit you and your mom?"

"Summer's their busy time. Lots of wood to cut." Another explanation for the distance in the family went unexpressed. Margaret Charbonneau's sons were embarrassed by their mother's increasing dependence on alcohol. It was hypocritical, since they usually cracked a beer immediately upon arriving home from the woods and spent much of their free time in bars. In their world view, drinking, even to excess, was okay for men, but not for women.

Mornings, Margaret functioned well, though she always had a smoke going. After lunch she started sipping on what she called "my Coke," a description that was about half right. By evening she usually began feeling sorry for herself, asking no one in particular what had made Cathy's dad "up and disappear" when their "oops" child was two months old. "Why?" she'd ask aloud. "What was I supposed to do about it?" Cathy remained silent, aware that nothing she said could plug the hole her father's abandonment had made in her mother's life.

She didn't try to explain her family's dysfunction to E, whose mother was a regular Emily Post and whose brother sounded as different from Curtis and Caleb as a guy could get.

"We always hang around this dump," E said one day when they were listening to records in her room. She picked up the stylus, and Gene Pitney abruptly stopped singing about the eyes of love. "When do I get to have lunch at your place?"

Though Cathy made every excuse she could think of, Elvera insisted she didn't care how small or how grungy the apartment was. Cathy finally chose the upcoming Monday, since that was the day Mr. Mason and a teenaged girl from Petoskey watched the store while Mom took the ferry to the mainland and did the ordering for Billy's three businesses. E wanted to see their place, but Cathy could at least spare her Margaret's nosiness. At work she was busy, but in a relaxed setting Mom would ask embarrassing questions like, "How much do you pay your housekeeper?" and "How do you get your hair so shiny?"

Mrs. Tharp would never pry like that, but then, Elvera's mother had been raised to be a lady. Cathy loved her mom, but Margaret's behavior and Mrs. Tharp's correct comportment were two vastly different things.

After spending the morning cleaning, Cathy stood back and tried to imagine what Elvera would think. They had only two rooms, an all-purpose area and a bedroom so tiny they had to close the door to get to the closet. The main room had a horsehair couch, which they kept covered with a blanket because it was too scratchy to sit on otherwise, and a rickety table whose oilcloth cover had been scrubbed so many times the flowers were wearing off. They had no television or record player. The kitchen was a corner with a noisy, round-shouldered refrigerator, a skinny gas stove, and a sink so stained by hard water it appeared brown instead of white. The place smelled of mold and cigarette smoke. The musty air might be blamed on it being a part-time residence, but Elvera's house sat empty all winter too, and it smelled like Glade.

By 11:45, Cathy had done what she could. Setting a vase of flowers on the table (stolen lilacs, and the vase was an empty peanut butter jar wrapped in tin foil), she stood back to rate her success. The sun was cooperating, so the room was brighter than usual. She'd opened the only window that wasn't painted shut, letting in a soft breeze that helped dispel the dank smell. Her mom's liquor bottles were wrapped in washcloths and hidden under the sofa cushions, where they served to disguise the sag in the middle. She'd scrubbed the sink with Comet until it was, if not exactly white, at least a dignified gray. It was the best she could do.

"Hey, little girl."

Cathy turned to see Mr. Mason standing in the doorway. He pretty much filled it, being both tall and wide. In the past he'd been the guy who wandered into the store from time to time smelling of Listerine, told lame stories, and spoke to Mom in a low voice, saying things that made her giggle. Lately, he seemed creepier somehow. When he looked at Cathy, his eyes didn't reach her face but lingered on her chest and legs. When she walked away, she felt his gaze on her butt. Without admitting to herself why she did it, Cathy had begun wearing jeans more often than the short shorts she used to love.

A few days before, when he'd found her on her knees, pulling sweatshirts out of a box, Mason had smiled like he'd caught her doing something bad. "Hey, little girl," he'd said. "You're getting to be quite a beauty." The smile she managed was as fake as the rubber knives they sold in the shop, but he didn't appear to notice. Taking a white navy cap from a stack, he set it on her head. "Looks good on you. Keep it."

When he was gone, she'd put the hat back.

Now he stood grinning at her, blocking the exit. The muscles in Cathy's back writhed, an instinctive response to danger.

"Mom isn't here."

"Nope." The grin got bigger.

Her hands were suddenly slippery with sweat, and she wiped them on her pants. There was no good reason for him to be there, but if she was rude to the boss, her mom might get fired. What should she do?

"What—um—what do you need?"

"I came to see my little girl. Make sure you're okay."

She wanted to say she wasn't Mr. Mason's anything, but her throat had gone dry. Biting her lip, she stepped back until her rear met the sink. Gripping the rim with both hands, she forced her voice to work, though it sounded squeaky. "I'm fine."

"Good. That's good." Mason took a step into the room. "Is there anything you'd like? Some soda pop, maybe? Ice cream?"

Did she dare order him to leave? *He owns the place, dummy. You can't order somebody off his own property.* "No." Her voice sounded shaky. "I mean, no, thank you."

Mason's smile faltered but didn't disappear. "I'd like to be your friend, Catherine." *Who called her that?* "I could make life easier for you, and for your mom too. All it would take is for you to be nice to me."

"I—It—" What could she say? Was "No" enough? Would he go away if she said it? The glint in his eyes said he wouldn't. He'd planned this. How long had he waited to get her alone?

"I brought you something." Mason put his hands out, fists together, in the classic choose-a-hand gesture. She stared, unsure what to do, as he stepped toward her. "Take your pick."

When she hesitated, he pushed his fists forward, almost touching her belly. "Which one?"

Miserably she pointed at his right hand. "Nope," he said, opening it to show that it was empty. "One more try. That's all you get."

Her stomach roiled at his closeness. This felt bad. *She* felt bad. How could she make him go away? Girls at school told of creepy stepfathers and lecherous neighbors who touched them when they didn't like it. If the girls told, the men said they'd been joking. Sometimes they said the girl flirted, seeking attention. "He said I was a tease," one girl confided, her eyes reddening with shame and anger. "Everyone believed him."

Mason opened his left hand to reveal a silver Crucifix on a chain. "I brought this for you. Isn't it pretty?"

She took a deep breath. "It's nice."

"It's yours." He leaned in, and she smelled beer on his breath. "Turn around, and I'll put it on you."

Cathy didn't want to turn her back, but maybe Mason would go away if she let him put the necklace on. He might be satisfied with that, and once she got away, he'd never catch her alone again, ever.

Mason put out a finger and traced the neckline of her blouse, starting at the collar and descending to the point where button met buttonhole. "Are you going to turn around so I can put your new necklace on or not?"

She'd have done anything to get him to remove that finger from between her breasts. Turning away, she gripped the sink in front and set her teeth. Mason's breath stirred the hairs on her neck, and she saw his hands descend on either side of her. She felt the cross settle at the hollow of her throat. Slowly, Mason pulled her hair out from under it. "There. I gave you something," he said in her ear. "Now you—"

"Hey, Cath. Are you ready to go?"

Equally startled, they turned toward the window, Mason with a jerk of surprise, and Cathy with a sob of relief. Elvera leaned in, her expression pleasant, as if she'd seen nothing improper. Mason stepped back, rubbing his hands on his slacks. "I better get back to the shop," he muttered.

When he was gone, Elvera hefted herself onto the window frame and climbed in. Cathy clung to the sink, feeling as if she might faint. When her legs steadied, she clawed at the necklace, fumbling to release the clasp. Tossing it on the table, she sank into a chair and sucked huge gulps of air into her lungs to keep from crying.

"What was that all about?"

"He—he—Oh, E, I was so scared." The anxiety she'd felt about her friend seeing her apartment was forgotten as Cathy considered what Mason would do next. "Now he's going to—"

"He won't do anything," E interrupted. Pacing a few steps

toward the door, she turned back. "He'll act like nothing happened."

"You think so?"

Elvera pointed a finger at Cathy's nose. "You need to tell the police what that pervert tried to pull."

"I can't." Cathy took hold of her friend's forearms. "Promise you won't say anything about this."

"Cathy—"

"He'll say I asked him to come here." She was again close to tears, and her voice wavered. "Mom needs this job, E. He can fire her, and there won't be anything we can do about it."

After a moment, E sighed. "At least tell your mom, so she knows not to leave you alone with him."

"I guess I should."

E's manner turned brisk. "Let's go down to Murdick's and get some fudge."

"I can't. I don't get paid until Friday."

"Never fear, Goofball. I found a buck in Mother's apron pocket that's dying to be spent."

Mom looked up briefly from her Word Find puzzle. "Catherine Diane, the man was trying to be nice."

"He touched my—he touched me, and it was weird."

Her mother's profile tensed. "It's not right to say things that could hurt a man's reputation, Cathy. Mr. Mason looks at you and sees the daughter he never had."

"But Mom—"

"I suppose you've heard stories from your friends, but I'm here to tell you, Mr. Mason is not some lecher who chases little girls. He's a respectable businessman."

Cathy turned away, angry with her mom and with the world too. Kids had no voice, no power. They were supposed to do as they were told and keep their complaints to themselves.

Concerned for Cathy's safety, Elvera went home and told her mother what had happened. The reaction she got was as cold as the waters of the straits. "What did she do to make him think she was...available?"

"She didn't do anything, Mother. She was in her apartment, minding her own business."

"She must have done something. Girls who behave well don't attract that sort of attention from men."

"D-do—" She tried a couple of times before words came out. "Do you really believe that?"

Mother fidgeted in her chair, letting her *Ladies Home Journal* close in her lap. "Elvera, I know Cathy is your friend, but she's...different from us. People like her—the people she's been raised around—don't have the same values we do. I'm afraid she'll end up disappointing you."

E's face warmed as anger surged through her. "*Cathy* is the nicest person I've ever met. *Cathy* isn't stuck on looking richer than she is or smarter than she is or more important than she is. She's a *real* friend, and I'm sick of your dumb comments about someone you don't even know."

As she stormed out of the room her mother called, "Ellie, you may not speak to me that way." That was followed by, "I will talk with your father about this next weekend."

Billy Mason's three stores on Mackinac Island allowed him to work four months a year and hunt and fish the remaining eight. The souvenir shop Margaret Charbonneau managed was the most lucrative, because few tourists left the island without some sort of remembrance: a horse-shaped knick-knack, a sailor hat, or a cheap cotton t-shirt. Mason's other businesses were a block away and side-by-side: a fudge/ice cream shop and a bar. Between the two was a skinny storage area where he'd replaced the old cork-lined cold room with a walk-in freezer and matching cooler. While the bar was the least financially successful of his businesses, it was where Mason spent the most time, BS-ing with men who shepherded their families to the island, gave their wives ten dollars to do whatever the kids wanted, and retreated to the dark, smoky tavern for a cold brew and a few minutes of peace.

Wednesday was delivery day, and at 8:00 a.m., Mason met the ferry with a horse and cart. On a large block of ice he'd set at the center of the flat bed, he stacked tubs of ice cream from the belly of the boat. Around it he placed kegs of beer and boxes of liquor. At the bar, he drove down the alley and backed the horse up until the cart's tailboard faced the side door. Carrying the booze inside, he stacked it near the door to be transferred to the cooler later. It was more important to get the ice cream into the freezer before it softened. Blocking the door open with a brick kept for that purpose, Mason worked to finish his task before the temperature inside the freezer warmed to the level of the air outside.

As he stacked the last tub on its shelf, a squeak sounded. Turning, Mason saw the freezer door closing and rushed toward it. He was too late. The latch clicked into place, making the door impossible to open from the inside. To make matters worse, the light went off. He was trapped in pitch dark, with the thermostat set at zero.

Remembering the lighter in his pocket, Mason fished it out, flicked the wheel, and examined the door. Though the tiny flame didn't reveal a way to get out, he noticed a piece of notebook paper stuck in the crack. Pulling it out, he held the lighter close and read the block printing: *I took a photograph of you harassing Cathy. Treat the Charbonneaus good or I will give it to the police. Then everyone will know you're a pervert.*

With a snarl, Mason lit the paper and let it burn to ash. Setting his shoulder against the door he pushed with all his strength, but it was firmly latched. In a fit of anger, he punched the smooth metal, succeeding only in hurting his knuckles. By the time someone found him, he'd be chilled through and miserable.

The little bitch from the hill had planned her trick carefully. He couldn't tell anyone what she'd done, or she'd explain why she'd done it. Though she was probably lying about having a photo, she'd seen him with the Charbonneau kid. Mason couldn't afford to call Elvera Tharp a liar and take the chance her father would get riled up about it.

Sitting down next to the door, he fastened his two top shirt buttons and rolled down his sleeves. He'd claim the brick fell over, trapping him inside the freezer. He'd make it a joke on himself, one of those weird mishaps a person can't predict. His wife would laugh and say he should be more careful, and he'd admit she was one hundred percent correct.

As he sat on the cold floor, the refrigeration unit kicked in, working to lower the room to precisely the right temperature for ice cream.

Chapter Seven

Cruise-Day 2 12:15 p.m.

"There's ice cream for dessert," Michael said as Miss E finished a lobster bisque into which she'd crumbled three packets of crackers.

"That sounds good." He was surprised at the rush of pleasure he felt, but it didn't last long. "I hope you brought strawberry."

"Sorry. Only vanilla or chocolate."

Her mouth twisted. "Ice cream is ice cream, I suppose."

Michael opened the cooler he'd prepared. "I did bring plenty of extras." He set two containers with two scoops of ice cream each on the table, adding small tubs of toppings: hot fudge, caramel, nuts, and whipped cream. "Eat all you want. I promise I won't tell your doctor."

"I stopped dealing with doctors some time ago." After dipping a finger into the hot fudge and tasting it, she spoke again, this time in a syrupy, condescending tone. "'Elvera, how many days a month would you say that you feel blue—you know, really down in the dumps?' or 'Ms. Tharp, I need you to draw a clock that says eight thirty-five. Can you do that for me?'" In her own voice she finished, "Medical people are even more intrusive than cabin stewards."

He ignored the insult. "Well, if no one's going to check your cholesterol levels, you can have a real party." Reaching up, he pressed the button that turned on the wall-mounted radio. The Beatles' "When I'm Sixty-Four" was playing, the clarinet making its reedy, happy sound between verses. "There. Mood music."

Miss E glared at him like an angry tortoise. "Turn—that—off!"

Quickly he did as she ordered. "I thought—"

"Well, stop thinking." Taking up both containers of ice cream, she dumped them into her bowl and added every topping he'd brought. "You are here to see I'm fed on time and picked up after. Despite whatever scenario you cook up in your imagination, you won't turn me all warm and cuddly with fancy desserts and oldies in the background."

As ice cream and toppings overflowed the bowl and dripped onto the tablecloth, Michael forced himself not to step forward and clean up her sticky mess. Instead he said stiffly, "If I leaned toward the belief that I might do something that pleased you, Miss E, I admit I was mistaken."

She concentrated on scraping the last bit of caramel from the tub, and when she had it, she licked it off the spoon. "You're not the great schmoozer you imagine yourself to be, Mike. If you want to keep this job, don't analyze me, and for damn sure don't patronize me."

All this over a Beatles' song?

Ha'o would have retreated in tears. Others might have slunk away, cowed. Michael again chose the opposite path. "If I understand correctly, you choose to be miserable. I'm supposed to accept that, even if I kind of like you despite your lousy attitude."

That surprised her, but she didn't give in. "*I* decide how my life goes." She jabbed a thumb at her chest. "Me."

Hearing a note of desperation in her voice, Michael said, "You're afraid your independence is in jeopardy."

"Not as long as I have anything to say about it." She ate a few bites. When she spoke again, her tone was calmer, but bitterness had crept in. "The golden years aren't so golden, Mike. Everybody thinks they know what's *good* for you: the government, the medical community, and of course, over-confident cabin stewards." She rapped the spoon on the tabletop. "Everyone wants to tell me what I should do, how I should live." After a second, she added, "*Where* I should live."

"So you tell them all to go to hell."

"I do." A glint of pride lit her eyes before she sobered again. "But it's a constant battle, keeping the do-gooders at arm's length."

"You shouldn't shut everyone out, Miss E. It's been proven that human interaction prolongs a person's life."

That brought a disgusted grunt. "In the first place, you have no idea how much human interaction I get. In the second place, who said I want to hang around forever?"

"Well, you can't just give up and die. It's not like you're ninety."

She sniffed disdainfully. "Seventy and healthy isn't bad. Seventy and disabled is something else." While Michael tried to think of something encouraging to say, she went on. "Old age is mostly the result of luck: where you're born, how you're treated, what resources you have. A man who reaches a hundred in Miami, Florida, might have died at fourteen if he'd been born in a secluded Ethiopian village." She gave a huff of disdain as she added, "Despite that, people take credit for their longevity as if it's something to boast about." Now her voice turned to a parody of an old man's. "'I'm ninety-three years old!'" She added in a mutter, "As if it takes skill to outlive everyone you ever cared about."

"What's wrong with celebrating one's age, even if it is mostly luck?"

"Nothing, I suppose, but I'd rather be seventy and useful than ninety and lucky." She dropped her spoon into the empty bowl, making a tinkling sound.

"Doesn't it depend on what you mean by 'useful'?" Michael asked. "Maybe that ninety-year-old makes the people around him happy. Maybe he keeps an era alive by telling stories only he can recall."

"Huh!" She interrupted his optimistic description. "Maybe he lies in a bed all day, drooling and being turned every twenty minutes so he won't get bedsores." Setting her empty dishes on the tray, she finished, "I find it sad that our society does whatever it takes to keep the candle of life burning, no matter how horrible the prospect is."

"I think it's because death scares us." He raised his hands and wriggled his fingers. "The Great Unknown."

"But at some point, it's life we should fear." Her voice turned angry. "Go to any nursing home and walk down the hallways. Ask yourself if any poor bastard stuck there isn't praying the Grim Reaper will sweep down the hall and take him out before another breakfast of rubbery eggs with Boost on the side." She bit her lip before asking, "Can hell be any worse than being told when you eat, sleep, bathe, and play Bingo?"

Michael began to understand the choices Miss E had made. By taking cruise after cruise, she had removed herself from anyone who knew her well. No one had any say over her, no relatives, no doctors, no caregivers. Her demanding manner assured that the staff had as little to do with her as possible. How long could she hide her physical deterioration? Without Drake Cruise Lines, would she end up in one of the nursing homes she so despised?

"It's a question life asks each of us," Michael observed. "How long is life worth living?"

"And the answer must come from the individual." She smoothed a wrinkle from the tablecloth. "Being old is like going to the dentist's office with a god-awful toothache. You dread what's coming, but you can't simply turn around and leave."

The ship reached the port of Koh Samui, Thailand's second-largest island, the next morning. Once known for its many coconut trees, the place had become a tourist's paradise, with miles of beautiful beaches and many things to see and do. Listening in on the activities director's talk, Michael learned that the island offered easy transport via a ring road connecting the beaches. Visitors could ride on buses, take taxis and motorbikes, or rent their own scooters in order to see the sights they chose, among them an elephant trek, temples with huge statues, a zoo and aquarium, and Na Muang Falls. There were large hotels in Chaweng, the main population center, with bars, night clubs, and opportunities to sample the sex trade. In short, Koh Samui was the perfect introduction to Thailand's best and ugliest sides.

Ten minutes before eight a.m., when passengers were allowed ashore, Michael stole away from his work to observe the phenomenon he'd been told was Miss E on an outing. As jet-skis buzzed around the harbor and fishing boats wobbled in their wake, she waited with poorly concealed impatience to leave the ship. She wore a flowing, ankle-length, multi-colored kaftan, a gigantic sun hat tied on with a green silk scarf, and oversized sunglasses. The purse she carried was as large as a toaster oven. Instead of her walker she carried a gnarled cane, which she used like a weapon to work her way to the front of the line. There she was forced to stop while the staff set up the going-ashore check-out desk and laid the gangway. While they worked, Miss E glared at the only person still in front of her, a fiftyish German with two cameras hung around his neck. At first, he ignored the obvious message in her gaze, though his shuffling feet betrayed discomfort. When she'd smacked his ankles twice with the cane and apologized without a modicum of sincerity, he stepped aside with a gallant gesture. "Ladies first."

"That's what *I* was taught." As the gate rumbled open, she swept past him like Atalanta on roller skates.

As Miss E crossed the gangplank, a voice called, "Make way, please." Two crewmen passed her, propelling a gurney with a figure strapped to it. When one attendant moved farther forward to pull the cart over the gap, Michael saw that the patient was Darrin, his surly crewmate. "What happened to him?" he asked one of the deck crew.

"Ate something he shouldn't have," she replied. "They say he'll be okay, but he won't be back this trip."

When he returned to the dining room, Michael found his supervisor, Marilyn, waiting with a man whose demeanor practically shouted that he was a cop. Marilyn's eyelids fluttered coquettishly as she introduced him. "Michael, this handsome gentleman is Inspector Lee of the Royal Thai Police. He'd like to speak with you."

Though dressed in civilian clothes, Lee had the air of command common to Thai Royal Police, who are trained similarly to military units. Michael felt anxious, as even an innocent man might be when an authoritative figure seeks him out.

"I have come about an important matter, Mr. Kanda," Lee said in Thai.

Michael made a *wai*. "Of course, Inspector."

When they were seated in a quiet corner of the dining room Lee touched his moustache with a knuckle, a smoothing gesture on either side. "I am looking into the activities of a passenger in your charge, Elvera Tharp."

"She prefers to be called Miss E," Michael volunteered. "What has she done wrong?"

"That is not something I can share with you." Lee's manner warned against further questions. "I believe this is your first voyage."

"Yes."

"This is good, since it means I can be certain you are not part of her...circle."

"I don't understand."

"It is not necessary that you do." Lee smoothed his mustache again. "I only require that you watch for unusual behavior."

"Like what?"

"A visitor perhaps, or a more than casual conversation with someone on board."

"Miss E doesn't interact with others."

Lee waved that away. "Observe, Mr. Kanda, and report to me. It is a matter of your country's security."

"You're saying an American tourist threatens our nation?"

"Tell no one what we have discussed." Lee laid a business card on the table with a crisp snap. "Call me when you have something to report."

He rose, leaving Michael with a dozen unanswered questions. The most pressing one was whether someone had set the new man on board up for a practical joke.

Late in the day, Michael went back out to the deck, though it meant neglecting his duties a second time. He wanted to see if Miss E would return late, as Ha'o said she often did.

Though it was a full ten minutes until the final reminder horn would sound, she approached along the waterfront, head down as if deep in thought. She answered the crewman who greeted her with a distracted air, and before embarking, stopped to survey the area. As her cane thumped on the metal walkway, she glanced up to where Michael stood, but he saw no sign that she recognized him. Overall, the impression was of a different Miss E. Less sure of herself, possibly even worried.

When next he went to her room he asked, "Did you enjoy your time ashore, Miss E?"

She was beading and didn't look up. "It was worthwhile."

"Did you visit Wat Plai Laem? It's quite beautiful."

Her gaze slid from her work to his face. "Why the interest in my coming and going?"

Michael sniffed. "I forgot that you disapprove of light conversation."

Her eyes narrowed to slits. "Try to keep your mind where it needs to be, Mike. Better for both of us."

"Shall I take the table onto the balcony and set your meal up there? You could enjoy the view of the island while you eat."

Glancing out the sliding door, she nodded. "Cities are like women who wear too much makeup. They appear best from a distance."

Chapter Eight

Mackinac Island-June, 1967

When they met on the island for a third summer, Cathy noticed right away that E was different. She'd dyed her hair red, for one thing, and she wore enough makeup for three girls. Cathy had experimented, but she was never able to apply eyeliner evenly or smooth liquid foundation so there wasn't a glaring line at her collar. Most days she dusted on face powder to dull the shiny spots and added green eyeshadow to highlight her brown eyes. And mascara. She didn't have the lashes Goldie Hawn did, but with Maybelline, she came close.

Honestly, Elvera looked like something out of *Plague of the Zombies*, with skin so pale she seemed sick and brows plucked to the thinnest of lines. Her lipstick was white, and eyeliner formed black rings that reminded Cathy of a raccoon her brother had once kept as a pet. Wind Song had been replaced by Tabu, so much it was almost overpowering.

The upside was that Mrs. Tharp was thrilled to have Cathy around. She went out of her way to welcome E's "little friend," and it was almost embarrassing when she offered cookies and soda or dinner with the family. When they were alone in the kitchen, Laura chuckled at Cathy's confusion. "She's hoping your company will turn Elvera back to how she was before she discovered boys and such."

Away from her parents, Elvera became more like herself again, though Cathy still felt as if E spoke from behind a mask. Up in the turret, away from her mother, she said, "We need to get some grass."

Cathy frowned. "Grass?"

"Cannabis." That didn't help. "Pot. Geez, Cath, don't you turn on up here? It's not like there's anything else to do."

"Oh, marijuana." Cathy had learned about it in school. She didn't know anyone who used it; at least she didn't think so. In her world, smoking that stuff wasn't something good people did.

E waved away her concerns. "It's rad, Cath. You're all uptight, feeling like your head is going to explode. Then you smoke a joint, and the world gets mellow."

"Like Donovan? Mellow yellow?"

"That's something else altogether." E said with a smirk. Cathy felt like a kid at a cocktail party, left out but unsure what she was left out of.

The whole summer was odd. Sometimes E was her old self, and they climbed up and over their favorite places on the island. They rented bikes, soaking up the sun as they left the tiny shopping area and followed the road that ringed the island. Along one side was the rocky, steep hillside, tree-covered and cool. On the other Lake Huron joined Lake Michigan, with the Mackinac Bridge spanning the straits. Like ants in parallel lines, cars crawled across it, while the clear water sparkled below. In a meeting place as old as man, Cathy dealt with a different and unnerving Elvera.

The new E spoke of sneaking out at night to find "where the action is." Cathy was glad her full-time job for the summer, selling ice cream and fudge at one of the island's many candy shops, kept her busy. She was also thankful for the cramped apartment, which made it impossible for her to get out without her mom knowing.

That excuse no longer worked when Margaret left for a weekend with Mr. Mason. The trip was supposedly to attend a buyer's show in Detroit, but Cathy suspected there was more to it than that. Mason's wife hadn't come to the island with him this year, which led to speculation among the help that their marriage had fallen apart. Margaret looked out the window when she told Cathy about the trip, and she'd packed a lacy beige nightgown instead of the old T-shirt she usually wore to bed.

It couldn't be what it looked like. Mom was pretty old, so she probably didn't do sex anymore, and Mr. Mason was gross, though he'd left Cathy alone since that one time. When she told E about the trip, Cathy said right up front that her mom would never sleep with Billy Mason. Elvera didn't reply directly, but an elevated brow hinted at disagreement.

"I asked Mrs. Bolton across the hall to look in on you," Mom told Cathy when she hugged her goodbye. Though it was presented as a help, Cathy saw it as a warning to behave herself.

E was thrilled to hear it. "We can finally have some fun."

"I don't want to sneak out," Cathy said, but that wasn't quite true. She did wonder about the fun other kids her age seemed to be having. No one asked her to beer parties back home, and she knew they called her prissy behind her back. Was it wrong to stick to the rules? Was she supposed to ignore the conscience that kicked in when she gossiped or rolled the waistband of her skirt so the hem ended a few inches above her knees? She'd been voted onto the National Honor Society by her teachers, and the church had named her Youth Leader. Her mom bragged to the neighbors about how dependable her daughter was. Should she throw all that away for a chance to drink beer (which she didn't even like) while a bunch of immature kids got wasted?

Apparently, she had to, because E wouldn't take no for an answer. Feeling like a creep, Cathy smiled at Mrs. Bolton and said she'd see her in the morning. She turned out the lights in her own apartment and watched the strip of light under the door across the hall until it too went out. After half an hour to give the old lady a chance to get to sleep, she stuffed pillows under the blankets on her bed and crawled out the window into the cool night.

E waited on the road with a flashlight she didn't need, since the moon was full and the sky clear. "Ready?"

Though tempted to turn around and go home, Cathy said,

"Yes."

"Great. Some people are meeting at Arch Rock. One guy scored some hash." It was like E had started speaking a foreign language. With a sigh, Cathy followed her into the trees and up the sharp incline.

Arch Rock is unusual in that it is made of limestone, a soft rock that doesn't usually lend itself to formations. On Mackinac Island, nature carved out a limestone arch that is fifty feet at its widest point and one hundred fifty feet above the lake. The girls could have reached it by riding their bikes eastward on the ring road then climbing a stairway to the rock, but that increased the chances they'd be seen. Instead they went on foot, following a narrow but well-traveled trail through the interior.

The party was well under way when they arrived. Seven guys and two girls ranging in age from seventeen to twenty sat around a small campfire. Cathy smelled the pot they were smoking before she saw the joint being passed from one to the next. The guy who'd taken the last hit seemed to find it hilarious, and he stomped one foot as he held the smoke inside, finally releasing it with a huff.

"Save some for us," E ordered, and everyone turned to look at the newcomers.

Gazing back at them through the drifting smoke, Cathy wasn't impressed. Some she recognized: guys who worked at the stables or carted luggage from the docks to the hotels. Island Rats knew each other after a summer or two, but Cathy was considered a lost cause as far as having fun went. One guy, Jim, had chased her for a while the summer before but in the end gone in search of faster company.

One of the girls was called Easy Annie, at least when she wasn't around. The other was a tourist, judging from her clothing. She sucked on the joint with an expertise that said it wasn't her first.

Jim moved to make room for them. "Good evening, ladies. Have a seat on Mother Earth."

"I've seen you around," he told E as she sat next to him then slid closer to make space for Cathy.

She smiled, showing straight teeth recently freed from braces. "I've been around."

Cathy rolled her eyes, but E and Jim had already entered a world of their own. For a while Cathy made desultory conversation with Annie, who worked as a maid at the Grand Hotel. She had strong opinions to air. Her boss was an ass. The tourists were a pain, every single one of them. And her roommates were all backstabbing bitches. Nodding occasionally to be polite, Cathy tried to figure out an exit strategy.

While she wasn't an experienced partier, she knew that such events, whether a stoner bash or a hayride at church, followed a common pattern. People would pair off, and relationships would progress or not, depending on the personalities involved. She'd been targeted a few times, but guys always gave up when she failed to respond to their primitive attempts at seduction. When a boy in Mackinaw City informed her she had a reputation as a prude, Cathy had replied she'd rather be prudish now than sorry later.

Girls told stories of how things got out of hand, how they asked a boy to stop but he was either unwilling or unable to do so. Those girls often spent days or weeks in dread, waiting for their next period. One had left town, supposedly to visit an aunt in California. Smiles and knowing nods hinted at the real purpose of her absence: an unwanted baby given up for adoption and never mentioned again.

Remembering all that, Cathy surveyed the group around the fire. Two of the boys were sleepy-eyed and unaware. No danger there. A thin, sensitive type stared off into the distance as if wishing for something. Walter, a guy she knew slightly, had turned his body toward Easy Annie, making a barrier with his legs that signaled she was his for the evening. The last guy eyed Cathy in a sideways fashion. Reaching across the others, he held out the joint. "Here. Try this."

Pulling her feet up, Cathy hugged her knees. "No thanks."

He smiled. "I guarantee you'll like it."

"No."

E stirred from her conversation with Jim. "Oh, for God's sake, Cath, take a hit and pass it on to me. If you're going to be a baby, I'll come by myself next time."

Stung by her tone, Cathy froze. Everyone except the dazed guy looked at her expectantly.

Taking the joint, she put it to her lips and took a puff, as she'd seen her mother do a zillion times. The acrid fumes that entered her lungs made her cough and choke, which the others found hilarious. "Keep at it," Jim advised. "It gets better."

It didn't. Three times joints came around, and each time, she tried. She didn't like the taste, didn't like the smell, and didn't like the sly way the others watched her.

To make matters worse, nothing happened. She felt no euphoria, no floaty sense, no easing of her "uptight" manner. Either she was doing it wrong or the stuff had no effect on her.

Or maybe she hadn't noticed the effects. After what seemed like only a couple of minutes, she realized Jim and E were missing from the circle. Shrugging off the heavy arm of Danny, who'd moved next to her in an attempt to forge a relationship, Cathy looked around. E's flashlight lay on the ground next to where she'd been sitting.

"C'mere," Danny said lazily. "I wanna talk to you."

"I have to find my friend."

He muttered something, but she ignored him, took up the flashlight, and followed a skinny trail. A few yards down she stopped and listened. Nothing. Going back to the fire, she skirted the edge of the clearing until the light revealed a second trail. She followed it up to a flat spot and stopped again to listen. For a while there was no sound, but then she heard Jim's low voice. "Relax and enjoy it, baby."

"I said no." E's voice was firm, but there was a note of fear beneath the command.

"Look, I'm doing you a favor," he said confidently. "I smoke Marlboros, so you won't get pregnant. And once you get past being a virgin, you're going to really groove on sex."

"No!" The word was cut off suddenly, and Cathy plunged forward. In a small clearing in the pines, moonlight revealed two figures. E was on the ground, struggling, as Jim pinned her down with his body and tried to pull off her jeans. Cathy saw E's pale stomach and one exposed breast as she tried to push him away. Without conscious decision, Cathy stepped forward and cracked Jim on the head with the flashlight.

With a roar of pain, he rolled to one side. "What the hell?"

"Leave her alone."

Rising to his feet, he took a step toward Cathy. "You bitch! I oughta toss you off the cliff."

A second later he yelped and stumbled to the side, grabbing his shoulder. Behind him, E had regained her feet. She held a fist-sized rock in one hand, having already pegged the other one at him. "Keep your grubby paws off my friend."

Jim assessed the odds. Two angry women, one with a metal club and one with a makeshift missile. Rubbing his head, he backed away. "I should have figured it out. You two are lesbians."

"Right, jerk," E responded. "Any girl who doesn't go for your obvious charms would have to be queer." Raising her weapon again, she ordered, "Get lost."

Muttering to himself, Jim slunk away, and Cathy hurried to E. "Are you okay?"

Her smile was shaky. "Maybe I'm not ready for the big leagues." Reaching under her shirt, she pulled her brassiere back into place and hooked it. "I thought I wanted to do it, but when it came down to yes or no, I chickened out."

"If you'd really been ready, you wouldn't have wanted to stop." Cathy had learned that from an older girl who rode the school bus with her each day. Debbie had confided she was dropping out of school to marry her boyfriend. "We have to," she'd whispered. "You can't believe how it is, Cath. I couldn't think of anything else but…doing it."

E was brushing sandy soil off her clothes. "Do you know what came into my head? *You're going to let this slime-ball be your first?*" She chuckled, her bravado restored. "It didn't seem right."

Cathy slid an arm around her friend's shoulder. "You don't want to give yourself to some guy that's looking for another notch for his belt, E. You need to save it for someone special."

Though still shaken, E seemed amused by the advice. "Well, old Jim sure isn't special. I bet he hasn't got five dollars to his name."

Tragedy struck the next week. Cathy's mother came to the back of the store, leaving the merchandise unwatched to deliver the news. "Mrs. Tharp died last night. They think it was her heart."

"Oh no." Cathy set aside the sponge she'd been using to clean the sink. "What should I do?"

"I don't think there'll be much you can do. They'll probably head home to Chicago."

Who was with E? What was she feeling? Though she didn't want to intrude on the family's grief, Cathy desperately wanted to see her friend before she left. Changing her shirt, she ran a brush through her hair. Laura Wolf would know what was going on.

When she knocked at the back door, it wasn't Laura who answered. It was a boy, or rather, a young man, with eyes like Elvera's and hair a few shades lighter. Drake. He held a cleaning cloth in one hand, and the smell of bleach hung around him like a cloud.

Cathy always found it difficult to face the recently bereaved. If you said you were sorry, would they burst into tears? If you didn't say anything, would they think you were rude?

"I'm Cathy. I came to tell Elvera I'm sorry. About her—about your mother."

She sounded like a complete idiot, but he didn't seem to notice. "That's very kind of you. I'm Drake, as you already guessed."

"Hi." *Dumb. You're supposed to say, 'Pleased to meet you.'*

After a moment he asked, "Would you like to come in?"

"I don't want to bother anyone. I..."

"You're no bother, but E is gone. Back to Chicago."

"Oh."

Drake smiled ruefully. "I got the call last night, and, hoping to catch her before she left, I came here. I missed her by just a few minutes, Laura Wolf said." His brows arched. "She's riding in the hearse with the, um, body. Very economical." The dry tone might have signaled irritation that Mr. Tharp had not come to collect his daughter. Instead he'd left her, shocked and grieving, to make the long trip home with a stranger and a corpse. Drake had apparently predicted his father's action but hadn't arrived in time to prevent it.

E talked about Drake a lot, so Cathy knew he was now attending college at Villanova. "Father insists he could" —Elvera had mimicked his voice— "'do great things in politics,' but Drake argues that people should use their talents to help the world, not just to make money." Their father wasn't pleased with that, but he and Drake had reached a compromise. Drake would complete a degree in business with a minor in political science. "By the time Drake graduates, Father hopes he'll grow out of his 'do-gooder' phase," E had confided, "but Drake told me he plans to find a job that fits his humanitarian goals, not Father's political ones."

Now, standing in the kitchen that still smelled faintly of Mrs. Tharp's tuna salad, Cathy didn't know whether to stay or go. Drake seemed much as Elvera had described him, attractive in a non-flashy way, fit, and down-to-earth. What she didn't know was how to act around a man she felt she knew but who was in fact a stranger. She didn't want to seem impatient to leave him alone with his grief, but she didn't want to be a pest either.

"I was about to have lunch," Drake said. "And there's enough tuna salad in the refrigerator for ten people. Would you like to join me?"

Pulling her courage together she said, "That would be nice."

The awkwardness of new acquaintance wore off as they prepared the meal. Though he was the host, Drake didn't know where anything was. After he'd opened three wrong cupboard doors looking for glasses he suggested, "Why don't I sit while you get what we need?" As he spoke, he pulled out a chair at the table where she and Laura often sat to talk.

Cathy set out dishes, copying what she'd seen Laura do. "Anything else?" she asked when she finished.

"How about the gold-plated candlesticks?"

For a moment she was flustered, but the glint in his eyes said it was a joke. "I always use silver when dining at home," she replied. "Gold is so ostentatious."

He seemed pleased with her response. "Then let's dispense with them. All I need now is a luncheon companion." Rising, Drake pulled out a chair for her. Feeling her cheeks warm, Cathy sat down. As they made sandwiches he said, "Since I'm here, Father decided I should close up the house before I head home."

"They won't come back to the island this year?"

"No." Drake passed her the bread. "Then an hour after I got here, the housekeeper got a call that her older child was taken by ambulance to Sault Ste. Marie. To..."

"War Memorial Hospital?"

"That's it. Possible appendicitis. I told her I'd do the packing."

Though sorry for Laura, Cathy's mind was stuck on the fact that she'd lost her best friend without so much as a goodbye. "I suppose things will be different now that your mom is gone."

"She wasn't my mom," Drake said. "E never told you that?"

"No." In all the times she'd mentioned Drake, E had never once called him her half-brother.

"My mom left Dad and me when I was a toddler." He shrugged. "I haven't seen her since."

The memory of her own father's abandonment increased Cathy's sincerity as she said, "I'm sorry."

"Thank you." He speared a pickle from a jar and set it beside his sandwich. "I wasn't exactly dear to the heart of the second Mrs. Tharp. Hence my banishment to boarding school."

She almost said she was sorry again but changed to, "That must have been hard."

"It wasn't that bad." He flexed an arm muscle. "Look at me now: rough and tough and hard to bluff."

"Well, then it was worth all those horrible meals you used to write her about."

His expression sobered. "E threw a hissy fit when they sent me away, but it didn't change anything." After a moment he added, "Sometimes it feels like she's the only family I've got."

"She's pretty great," Cathy agreed.

"That's why I came here." He took the last bite of his sandwich and swallowed. "I wanted to get to her before she starts blaming herself for...stuff."

"You mean like fighting with her mom all the time?"

He nodded. "Deep down, E loved Doris. They just—It's a different time for women now, and E didn't deal well with her mother's old-fashioned views."

Cathy had never heard Mrs. Tharp's first name, but she knew what it was like to love your mom and still see her faults. "I bet E wishes you were there with her."

A palm turned upward indicated there was nothing to be done about it. He glanced around. "I will be, as soon as I get this place cleaned out."

"I could help." When he looked at her questioningly, she went on, "I know what E will want in Chicago and what she won't mind leaving for next year." She stopped. "If you think they'll come back."

Drake smiled. "It'll be a battle of wills with Dad, but she won't want to miss your last summer together."

Cathy felt pleased to hear that E had spoken to her brother about her, and apparently in positive terms.

After lunch, Cathy went down the hill to make arrangements. "Is the brother cute?" At Cathy's look of exasperation, her mother said, "I'm just asking. The housekeeper is there to chaperone, right?"

"Right." It was a lie, but Cathy recalled her mom refusing to believe that Mr. Mason had tried to grope her. Did she really think Elvera's brother was likely to ravish her among cardboard boxes filled with his dead stepmother's things? After an hour with Drake, she trusted him ten times more than she'd ever trust Billy Mason. "I'm going to ask Mrs. Commins to rearrange the schedule so I get the next two days off work."

Tuesday and Wednesday flew by as Cathy and Drake packed the family's belongings into suitcases and boxes, covered the furniture with sheets, and went through the cupboards to see what should be thrown out and what would last until next summer. Laura sent word via the cart drivers that her daughter was recovering after an appendectomy, and Drake arranged for her to get the remainder of her summer salary, despite his father's counterarguments.

As they worked, Cathy found herself telling Drake things for which she later chastised herself. Did he really care that she preferred Gerry and the Pacemakers to the Stones? He didn't seem bored with her conversation though, and he even shared his own preferences. He liked the movies *Cool Hand Luke* and *The Graduate*, which Cathy decided meant he was a nonconformist, like Luke and Benjamin. He expressed a desire to see *You Only Live Twice,* which brought to mind a comparison to James Bond. The two were much alike, she decided: handsome, sophisticated, and capable of doing anything they put their minds to.

Drake wasn't interested in being a 007 type. "I'm going into government service," he told her as they covered the upholstered furniture with sheets. "I plan to work overseas, setting up programs that share U.S. know-how with third-world countries." He smiled ruefully. "Father says I'm nuts, and I think Elvera agrees."

"Helping people isn't nuts," Cathy said. "And you'll be doing it on a big scale, not like baking a pie for a church dinner or donating a dollar to the Salvation Army at Christmas."

"Any action taken to help others is worthwhile," Drake argued. "You never know how many ripples go out from a single act of kindness."

"I suppose not," she allowed, though she was thinking that Drake, with his talents, background, and resolve, was far more capable of affecting real change in the world than a girl from rural Michigan.

Cathy helped Drake contact men who came with a horse-drawn trailer to haul the luggage to the boat docks. When she explained the situation to the freight manager, who lived in Mackinaw City and had known her all his life, he assured them that everything would go on the first boat Thursday morning. Drake arranged for a truck to meet him there and transport everything, including Drake himself, to Chicago.

When they left the dock, Cathy stopped and put out a hand. "I'll say goodbye here."

Drake's forehead furrowed. "Oh. I suppose we're done." He took her hand and said formally, "Thank you, Cathy. I'd never have managed without you."

She shrugged. "I wanted to do something for E."

"So that's all I am to you, a stand-in for my sister?"

"I didn't mean it like that—" But he was smiling. Another joke.

"Let me take you to dinner in return for your help."

"Drake, you don't have to."

"Cathy, we packed up or threw out every edible item in Braddock House. I have to eat at a restaurant, and I'd really like it if I didn't have to dine alone."

"Oh." His eyes twinkled, and Cathy said, "If I can do it as a favor to you, then of course."

They went to Little Bob's, a popular spot, and found a table for two in a corner. Cathy felt uncomfortable, being in a restaurant with a boy—well, a man, really. Eating out wasn't a normal occurrence in her family, and dining with a guy, sort of like a date, made it doubly weird. They'd had lunches together in private, but now she felt as if people were judging Drake by the company he'd chosen. What if he was horrified by her table manners? What if she got a gob of ketchup on her chin and didn't know it? What if he didn't have enough money to cover two meals? She ordered exactly what he did, ate her fries without ketchup, and chewed as daintily as she could, sitting straight in her chair and sipping at her root beer.

The conversation concerned practical things, what time he'd arrive in Mackinaw City, how long the trip home would be, and so on. "Are you staying in Chicago for a while?"

"The funeral's on Friday," Drake said. "I'll leave right afterward."

"You won't stick around a while? They say funerals are really for the living, to let them reconnect with friends and family."

He tilted his head to one side, reminding her of Elvera. "What 'they' say isn't always as wise as it sounds."

"What's bad about people getting together?"

When he answered, Drake's words held a tone of apology. "My girlfriend and her mother were close friends with my stepmother. They're both...emotional types, so the funeral is likely to be...difficult." He grinned ruefully. "My classes are an excellent excuse to avoid some of the drama that's likely to go on."

The word *girlfriend* struck Cathy like a blow, but a second later she was telling herself not to be stupid. *He was nice because you're E's friend and because you helped with the house.* Drake hadn't in any way indicated he was attracted to her. *But it felt like we fit together, as if I waited all my life for him to step into it.*

And tomorrow morning he'd step right back out.

Waking early, Cathy put on a jacket and went out to watch the first ferry of the day prepare to depart. Standing under a tree near the fort entrance, she watched Drake come toward the docks on a wagon, sitting next to the driver, his collar turned up due to the brisk wind. While his cargo rolled down the gangplank, he paid the driver and sent him off with a wave. Soon the passengers were signaled forward. Before boarding, Drake turned and looked toward town. She might have called out a goodbye, pretending she happened to see him there, but no. Better if something that might have happened but didn't ended there and then.

With Drake gone, Cathy's mind returned to Elvera. How was she doing? What was she feeling? She got the bartender at Billy's to let her call Chicago by promising to bake him a raspberry pie the first time she got close to a decent oven. He made her wait until evening, when the rates were lower, and promise she wouldn't stay on the line too long.

"Directory assistance. What city please?"

She went through the process and finally heard E's voice. "Tharp residence."

"E? It's me, Cathy."

"Oh, Cath." It broke her heart to hear tears in Elvera's voice. "It's all such a mess. I wish you were here."

"Did Drake make it home?"

"A few minutes ago. He and Daddy are shut up in the study."

"He hated not being with you the last few days."

"I hated it too. I needed him…or you." Cathy heard a sob. "I was so mean to her. What if I—"

"You did not give your mom a heart attack, Elvera."

"But I said—"

Again Cathy interrupted. "She knew you were just letting off steam." Lowering her voice, she added, "I didn't know your mom very well, but I know she loved you more than anything. All the griping she did at you was because she wanted you to have the best life possible. And all the stuff you said back to her? She didn't mind. She knew you have a lot of…spunk."

Suddenly Elvera was laughing. "Oh, Cath, I really needed to hear from you. Knowing I'm Miss Spunk will help me deal with all this."

Was E making fun of Cathy's positive spin on life? It didn't matter if it made her feel better. Losing your mom had to be the worst thing ever, but E had Cathy and her father and Drake. She'd get through it.

Chapter Nine

Cruise-Day Four 5:55 a.m.

The morning after their visit to Koh Samui, Michael prepared a tray of pancakes, bacon, fresh fruit, and coffee.

"I breakfast early," Miss E had informed him earlier, "so I can begin my day." *What does she have to begin?* he wondered. *Another bracelet? Another crossword puzzle?*

Trying to be agreeable, he'd commented, "They say breakfast is the most important meal of the day."

That had earned him a lecture.

"Just when I start to think you have a brain, you open your yap about what *they* say," Miss E groused. "The nebulous *they* should be told that breakfast is not only *not* the most important meal of the day, it's not even required for good health." She'd shoved her walker toward the wall, where the resulting crash was muted by the rubber bumpers. "If you're going to go around handing out advice, at least keep up on the science."

She'd gone on about the necessity of thinking for yourself and the advantages of forming opinions based on logic and research, but Michael stopped listening. Forming an agreeable expression, he'd simply waited for her to be done.

Responding to the pertinent part of that exchange, he arrived with Miss E's breakfast a few minutes before six a.m. Balancing the tray on one arm, he knocked and heard her call out something unintelligible. Assuming it was permission to enter, he used his pass key to unlock the door. There was a scrambling sound, and Miss E raised her voice. "I said *wait*!" She said something else in a hushed but urgent tone, but it didn't seem directed at him. Michael backed away, allowing the door to close. After a few seconds she called, "You may come in now."

When he entered, she was standing at the center of the room, looking frazzled. "Is everything all right, Miss E?"

"Why wouldn't it be?" She moved to the table, bracing herself on one piece of furniture after another. "What do we have this morning?"

As Michael answered, she seemed to be listening to something behind her. He heard nothing but felt anxiety crackling through the cabin like an electrical charge.

"You can go," she said when he'd arranged the meal and set the flower vase at the center. When he looked surprised, she added, "I don't need my room straightened today."

He considered objecting. If she was drunk or stoned on her pills, she might complain later that he hadn't done his job. Taking subtle stock, he decided that though her face was flushed, Miss E was coherent. "Shall I come for the tray in half an hour?"

"Fine." She made a shooing gesture to hurry him out the door.

When he returned, every dish on the tray was wiped clean. "That trip ashore yesterday must have given you an appetite."

He felt a now-familiar chill descending. "Is it your place to notice what I eat or how much?"

"I was joking, Miss E."

"If your idea of a joke is commenting on a woman's eating habits, it's no wonder you're single."

"How do you know I'm single?" The question was out before he could stop himself.

Her confidence and superior attitude had returned. "A middle-aged man who works as a seagoing butler? I'd bet any amount that you've got no wife on shore, no kiddies waiting for Daddy." She gave him a knowing smile. "You're a loner, Mike, and my guess is you always will be."

"I should get back to the kitchen." As he left, Michael hoped the flush of anger he felt creeping up his neck wasn't visible from the back.

Because of that odd encounter, Michael began to suspect someone other than the registered occupant was, or had been, in Cabin Three. Straightening the cushions on the futon the next day, he found a long, black hair that hadn't been there before. He said nothing to Miss E, who was so mellow she only complained once about the noise he made. Asking about the hair was sure to prompt a screed about nosy servants.

Michael put his charge's behavior together with the policeman who'd demanded he report anything unusual. There was more to Miss E than he'd suspected, but that didn't mean he intended to do as Lee ordered. It was possible she'd become acquainted with another passenger while on Koh Samui. Miss E could have invited her—the length of the hair suggested a female—to visit.

While it was a positive step for Miss E to have found someone to talk to, Michael felt unaccountably irritated at the idea. Why hide the fact she'd had company? Had she snickered to her new friend about her cabin steward, a middle-aged, mixed-race man with nothing but his job to cling to? *No wife, no kiddies, no happy home.*

Chapter Ten

Mackinac Island-June, 1968

"I'm getting married in the fall," Cathy told E when they met for their final summer on Mackinac Island. Mr. Tharp had agreed to let her go north on two conditions: first that she take along a chaperone, and second that she ready the house for sale in the fall. She'd invited her mother's older sister, "Drifty Aunt Renee," as her companion. Renee, an animal-lover, was for the most part unconcerned with Elvera's activities. She cared mostly about the "poor horsies" that had to pull those "dreadful" carts around the island and the "pitiful doggies" on the crowded streets whose owners didn't make sure they had water and a quiet place to rest. Renee spent the summer confronting visitors and locals alike over their treatment of animals, which Elvera found embarrassing but also funny.

When Cathy made her announcement, E felt her brows pinch together. "I suppose the next time we meet you'll have two kids and a job waiting tables at Stuckey's."

Cathy gave her a reproachful look. "E, I don't want what you want from life. Even if I thought about college, I can't afford it."

"What if Daddy gave you a loan?" At some point over the last ten months, *Father* had become *Daddy*.

"I wouldn't take his money." Cathy's lips tightened. "And I want to marry Gary."

Elvera knew that look. "Have you slept with him yet?"

Her face turned bright red. "We didn't mean to. It just happened."

"Now he's going to make an honest woman of you. Nice guy."

Cathy's expression turned angry, and sudden fear of losing her made Elvera reach out and pull her close, though she wasn't usually one for hugs. "It's a surprise, that's all. I'm thrilled for you, and I hope I get to meet Gary Wonderful before he takes you away from me."

"Oh, yes." Cathy was obviously relieved. "He's coming up next weekend to meet you. I know you'll like him, E. He's great."

And he was. Nice-looking in a woodsy, cheap-haircut way, Gary was funny and sweet. Cathy had said more than once that he wasn't afraid of hard work, and his scarred, sliced-up hands served as evidence. Still, he seemed endearingly eager to make Cathy happy. He was also a staunch Catholic, which was important to the Charbonneaus.

A few months later, Elvera flew to Lansing on a Thursday afternoon, rented a car, and drove two hundred twenty-eight miles to stand beside her friend in a stone church that was damp and chilly, despite it being only the third of October. After the ceremony, she went with the bridal party to the reception, held in an overheated township hall with wooden floors that squeaked at every step and dying flies spinning in the windowsills. E found it horrible, but she'd never seen Cathy look happier.

She did her best to be amiable to a host of people with whom she had nothing in common. She made only one joke about Cathy's new last name, Przybylski, and that was in a private moment. Before leaving for her honeymoon night at the Perry Hotel in Petoskey, Cathy pulled E into the cloakroom and hugged her fiercely. "I'm going to miss you so much."

"I'll write," E said into her neck. That was when she made the joke, and to be honest, it was to keep herself from crying. "How should I start my letters? 'Dear Mrs. P'? Or 'To the Polish wife'?"

"Call me Cath," the bride suggested. "Like always."

Around the time she turned sixteen, Elvera's father had started telling stories at the dinner table about a young man he'd hired who was some sort of business genius. Her mother had chimed in too, commenting that Richard Terzis was "very handsome" and "so well-mannered." Father would harrumph gruffly, as he did when dropping information his children should take note of, and say something like, "Richard will make some young woman a good husband. Boy knows how to get things done."

At first Elvera paid little attention. Though indeed good-looking, Richard Terzis was almost a decade older than she, and his background was common, to say the least. The elder Terzis worked in "city services," which in his case meant garbage collection, and though he'd started on the bottom rung of that ladder, he'd risen to the top, controlling most of the city's present routes. Rumor said he was mob connected, which was the likeliest explanation for his abrupt rise from poverty to wealth. Mr. Terzis smiled too much and cracked his knuckles every few seconds. Mrs. Terzis wore far too much rouge and had never fully mastered English.

Still, the Terzis had money, while the Tharps struggled more and more to appear to. Tharp Credit Services had difficulty remaining viable against larger competitors like MasterCard. Over time, Elvera realized her parents had a merger in mind: their Old Chicago respectability in exchange for Richard's business expertise…and an influx of cash from his wealthy father.

Once Franklin took Richard under his wing, he was around a lot, rounding out dinner party numbers and making a fourth for tennis or golf. He was a convenient escort for Elvera, since her father believed the guy walked on water. If she wanted to go somewhere Franklin wouldn't approve, all she had to do was get Richard to come along, and it was okay. He walked the line between chaperone and date without objection, at times saving her from her own recklessness but never letting on to her father she'd been anything but proper.

That did not mean she intended to marry the man.

Franklin had pushed Drake into a marriage Elvera suspected

was horrible, though her brother never complained. Drake's wife Patricia was beyond neurotic, and she resented every person her husband cared about. After graduating college and marrying her, Drake had accepted a position with the State Department. While Patti liked the prestige of his work, the job required that Drake travel, mostly to Southeast Asia. Though he'd never even hinted at it, E heard from their friends that Patricia often accused Drake of sleeping with other women during his long absences. E had chuckled when she heard it, though it made her sad too. Drake was as unlikely a philanderer as she could imagine, and Patti was a crazy bitch.

When he was home, Drake did his best to make his wife happy, spending every minute with her and attending glittering social events in Washington D.C. that she loved and E knew he hated. Drake seldom visited Chicago, seldom even called, and over time Elvera concluded it was self-defense on his part. Doing whatever Patricia wanted made life with her as peaceful as he could manage.

Seeing Drake struggle to be cheerful about his marriage, E vowed not to follow her brother's path. She wouldn't be bartered for, and she hated that her father treated Richard like a son. He and Franklin spent whole evenings in the study, talking endlessly about the future of credit. Though Richard seemed completely dedicated to Tharp Credit Services, that didn't mean E would blindly marry where her father pointed.

E wasn't even sure she wanted to marry at all. During her high school period of defiance, she'd gone out with boys who quoted Chairman Mao, boys who didn't cut their hair, and boys who refused to come to the door and meet her parents before roaring away in their souped-up cars. If Father grounded her, she slipped out her bedroom window and slid back in at dawn. But even in her wildest moments, she knew better than to take those dangerous boys seriously. While they went on about free love, they kept track of their conquests like trappers counting pelts, and rebellious or not, E valued herself too much to settle for that type.

Then her mother had died, and Elvera was no longer sure what kind of woman she wanted to be.

Drake might have talked her through it, but he returned to Pennsylvania right after the funeral. Cathy was in faraway Michigan. Her father had no talent for conversation; he only knew how to lecture. By default, Richard became E's confidant, listening to her complaints about her father's aloofness and letting her berate herself for the way she'd treated her mother. He offered no advice, only a willing ear. He did much the same for Franklin, listening to stories about "my Doris" over and over as if he'd never heard them before.

Elvera had her first sexual relationship early in her freshman year of college, with a boy who turned out to be more guilt-ridden than she over their "mistake." He kept apologizing for "ruining" her, as if she'd had no say in the matter. After that disaster, E sought encounters where both sides understood that sex was the end goal, not love, not marriage, not life-long commitment. The biggest barrier to enjoying sex was the fear of getting pregnant, but wiser girls advised her to go to the school clinic and complain of irregular periods. She left with a pamphlet on sexually transmitted diseases and a prescription for the Pill.

While she attended college, Richard Terzis worked his way to Vice-president in Charge of Executive Operations at Tharp Credit Services. When E came home on breaks, he made himself available to her. If she wanted to attend a concert, a ball game, or even an opera, he bought the tickets, arranged transport, and even took along some of her friends if that's what she wanted. Richard never came on to her, and E wondered for a while if he was gay. In the end, however, she concluded he was one of those bland, people-pleasing types with no strong desires of his own.

At dinner her first night home after her freshman year, E gave Richard a covert once-over. Still good-looking, and a bit mysterious. As Mrs. Leon cleared away dessert, he turned to Elvera. "I just bought a Mach 1 in bright blue with a fastback. Would you like to go for a ride?"

A Mustang? A suggestion? A sign Richard might have blood in his veins? "That sounds like fun."

Once they were on Lake Shore Drive, he asked, "No trip to Mackinac Island this summer?"

She'd considered going, but now that Cathy was a married woman, the island wouldn't be the same. "No. Dad put the house up for sale, though he hasn't had a single nibble yet."

He was silent for some seconds, and she sensed his next words were important. "Your father has made some bad decisions in the last few years, Elvera. He's under a good deal of financial pressure."

Things she'd noticed but hadn't analyzed came to mind. Her father's walk had slowed considerably, as if the weight of the world dragged his steps. He'd snapped at her for buying a new coat without asking first. And she'd seen him frowning over the tuition bill for her respected but expensive school in Maryland.

Women attending college to earn an "MRS degree" was a well-known joke, and Elvera had no real love of learning. She'd enrolled because that's what girls of her circle did after high school if they weren't ready to marry. There'd been a college fund when she was younger. Was it gone? Though the Tharps had never had as much money as they'd pretended, the situation had apparently become desperate. Why hadn't Daddy told her?

Because he was a proud man. Because he'd never admit he couldn't provide for her.

E knew why Richard had brought it up. He was letting E know it was time to grow up and accept the facts of life. If they married, the elder Terzis would provide the cash needed to keep Tharp Credit Services afloat. That was the deal. Drake, the diplomat, was the family's public star. E would be the sacrifice that kept the business going.

Glancing sideways as they drove down Lake Shore, E evaluated Richard as a potential life partner. She had no real affection for him. When they were apart, she felt no loss, nor was there joy in her heart when she saw him again. She wasn't attracted to him sexually. The few kisses they'd shared had been emotionless, even chaste. Not what she expected in a husband.

But what do *I want?* She'd felt sexual attraction with some men and an intellectual response with others. But love? E had no experience with it, which she didn't see as a bad thing. Cathy loved Gary, and that meant she'd spend the rest of her life in a tiny town in the boonies, living paycheck to paycheck. If that was love, maybe a business merger was a better bargain.

Still, the prospect of life with Richard left her feeling flat. There had to be a man somewhere with both prospects and the ability to make her pulse flutter. "Your car is great, Richard," she said into the silence, "but I think we should turn back now."

His response was odd. "You won't turn into a pumpkin when the clock strikes twelve, Elvera."

Had Richard contradicted her? And made a joke? Shocked to silence, she waited to see what came next.

Driving to a park less popular than some, he pulled the car into a corner where it wasn't visible from the road. Polite as always, he came around to help her out. They walked along the lake shore, chatting pleasantly about events since they'd last seen each other. The lilacs were past their prime, but their scent lingered even as the blooms shriveled. The evening was mild, the water's gentle slapping at the rocks hypnotic.

When they came to a spot where trees shielded them from view, Richard half-seduced, half-raped Elvera.

He began by kissing her with more ardor than she'd thought him capable of. Then his hands were all over her. He pushed her onto the damp ground, and from there things got mixed up. Had she objected or not? Had he really torn off her underpants? Had she felt pain at the force of his entry? And when it was over, had she cried when he told her he wanted to be with her for the rest of their lives?

The next thing she knew they were setting the date for a wedding.

E made the decisions: colors, bridesmaids, the music for the service, and the menu for dinner afterward. It ballooned into a huge social event her father couldn't afford, but he made no objection, pleased that his favorite employee and his only daughter had come to the point he'd wanted them to for years. Elvera was gratified by her father's happiness. After all the lectures and disappointed expressions, she'd become the daughter Franklin wanted. She also couldn't help but feel a little sly whenever she and Richard slipped away to have sex. Daddy didn't know everything about his second-in-command and his little girl.

Sex with Richard was puzzling. He seemed distant much of the time, but then he'd take her with sudden, urgent ardor in the strangest places: in the (very small) back seat of his car, on the beach under a blanket, and once on the back porch while Franklin napped in a chair just around the corner. Richard walked a line between seduction and force that was emotionally exciting, though often physically unsatisfying.

The newspapers had a field day with the story of an Old Chicago family allying with a reputed mobster, though they were careful to include "reputed" each time they mentioned Carlo Terzis. Richard seldom mentioned his parents, but he commented once that Franklin was more of a father to him than his own had ever been. That admission was the only time E felt she'd seen a real person behind Richard's bland exterior, and it pleased her. That simple confession convinced her it wasn't necessarily a mistake to marry Richard Terzis.

Cathy came to the wedding, of course, but they didn't have much of a chance to talk. Several times during the weekend she stepped in as a buffer between Elvera and some disaster, soothing her nerves, explaining her wishes, guarding her train, and reminding her to thank the priest and smile, smile, smile. Though completely out of her depth, Cathy managed to tread water and hold Elvera up as well, so neither drowned in the sea of chaos around them.

Once the ceremony was over and the confetti swept away, Richard and Elvera moved into an upstairs suite in her childhood home. "There's plenty of room," Franklin had insisted. "Getting a place of your own is a needless expense." Richard agreed, so Elvera began married life in much the same way she'd lived when single: same house, same routine, and same faces at the breakfast table, plus one.

Richard's role at Tharp Credit Services expanded. When he ended contracts with some of the smaller banks, Franklin protested that he'd been doing business with them since World War II. "They can't help us move forward," Richard argued. "We have to trim the fat, or we'll fail." Richard approached larger banks, offering incentives for switching to Tharp Services and guaranteeing higher profits within a year. Aware of upcoming trends in a way Franklin had never been, Richard encouraged consumers to rely ever more heavily on credit. "What if they can't handle it?" E heard Franklin ask more than once, but Richard insisted increased use of credit was good for the company, even if it wasn't the best thing for the individual cardholder.

After the wedding, Richard changed. Though in public he appeared to be a loving and attentive husband, in private he never touched Elvera, not for sex, not in affection, not even in passing. She began to feel like a piece of art, a vase or a painting bought for the sole purpose of impressing others. When she came home one day to find that he'd moved his things to a different room, she became angry. "Richard, what is this?"

His answer came with the mocking sneer of a boy raised in a cramped apartment that smelled of mold and schooled in the alleys of Chicago's south side. "To be honest, Elvera, I've never enjoyed screwing the same woman over and over. I'm finding my own entertainment these days, and I suggest you do the same." After a moment he added, "But for God's sake stay on those little white pills of yours. I don't intend to spend my life raising some other man's bastard."

Chapter Eleven

Cruise-Day 5, 12:43 p.m.

Michael stopped when he saw the note pinned to the corkboard. *M Kanda. Call Lee ASAP*. "Impatient bastard," he muttered.

Ha'o, who was lifting half-empty soup pots out of the warmers, looked over her shoulder at his tone. "What?"

"Nothing. I have to make a phone call, but I can help you clear lunch away first."

"How's Miss E today?"

He smiled, recalling Elvera's opinion of such questions. "In a lot of pain, I think."

Ha'o nodded. "I'm sure you've seen the assortment of pill bottles in her bathroom."

"She said she doesn't deal with doctors anymore."

"No. I think she buys herself drugs when we stop at ports where prescriptions aren't required."

"Do you know how she was injured?"

Forehead creased, Ha'o called up a memory. "One day when I went in there, she was really out of it. She called me Nim or Nin, maybe, and she said something about falling down a mountain."

"Had she been drinking? I heard she has a bit too much sometimes."

Ha'o frowned. "I didn't smell alcohol, but I think she took more pills than she should have."

He paused, thoughtful. "It makes you worry about her hurting herself, either by accident or…you know."

"If that's what she wants to do, I don't know how we could stop her."

When Michael finally called the inspector, Lee was irritated to hear he had nothing to report. "I understand she went ashore in Koh Samui. Did anyone return with her?"

The question told Michael that Lee had more than one source of information. He had decided not to mention his suspicion there was someone in the room with Miss E. In the first place, the inspector's demanding manner irritated him, and in addition, Michael's curiosity outweighed the arguments Lee had offered about integrity and national pride. "She was alone."

Lee was persistent. "Did she bring anything back with her?"

"Nothing I saw, but I couldn't very well go through her pockets."

Did Lee suspect Miss E of smuggling? The loose kaftan she'd worn might have concealed gems, drugs, or... He didn't know what. Still, he'd seen no sign of anything new in her cabin. Michael decided he needed to find an opportunity to investigate on his own.

They anchored in Prachuap the next day, where passengers were given a full eight hours to explore. When Miss E went ashore, Michael was able to make a thorough search of her cabin. He found no one there, no sign there had been, and nothing he hadn't seen before. No packets of *ya ba* or opium, no illegal elephant tusks, no more long black hairs.

He lingered, wishing the room could tell him stories of Elvera Tharp. Standing beside her chair, he turned slowly in a circle, looking at everything, rehearsing what he knew. She took pain pills, sometimes too many, and drank, sometimes too much. She made and sold jewelry, not a particularly lucrative occupation. She didn't much care what she wore. She stayed to herself on the ship but went ashore at almost every opportunity, despite the pain she experienced daily. Miss E was intimidating, but he suspected some of her nastiness was intentional. Michael thought she was starting to like him a little. That was good.

Though he had work to do elsewhere, he remained in the cabin, trying to get a sense of its occupant. He stirred the bowl of beads beside the chair, feeling their smoothness. He fingered the clothing in her closet, cheap kaftans in various colors, simple cotton shirts, nylon pajama pants, and a single pair of sturdy jeans. Moving onto the balcony, he gripped the railing and stood for a few seconds, looking out at the harbor. When his fingers felt a rough spot, he leaned over to inspect the metal. In two places about eighteen inches apart, the paint had been scraped away by friction. Several things might have caused that, and the wear could have happened at any time. But it felt like Miss E's doing. What had she been up to out here?

Back inside, Michael searched the room again and found nothing. It didn't matter. He now knew how the visitor had come to Miss E's cabin.

Michael did not use alcohol often, but at times, when emotion threatened to overcome reason, he found that a shot could slow his raging brain and restore calm. The discovery he'd made was exciting, but he couldn't let himself ruin everything by revealing his mood to his coworkers. He'd seen a bottle of top-end vodka in Miss E's cabinet. It would make a good nerve-settler before he returned to work.

Choosing a glass, he poured himself a healthy jolt. As he put the bottle away, Michael noticed a photo album set against the back of the cabinet, where the bottles hid it from view. Taking it out, he carried it, along with his glass, over to the futon and sat down to have a look. The cover was old and cheap, bright-blue plastic with white letters that said, *My Memories.* In it were images of a ferry, a bridge, a large, white building with American flags along its extensive porch, and two girls, both brunette. Some photos were black and white; others were the blurry images and muddy colors of early instant photos. The girls stood together in several of the pictures, one looking shyly at the camera while the other faced it with confidence. They might have been sisters, except Michael knew Elvera had only a brother, who was now dead. Had the second girl had something to do with changing Elvera from a carefree, confident teen to an angry crone? Why else would she have photos of the two of them when she'd kept so little of her past?

Still staring at the photo, Michael tossed the drink he'd poured for himself down in one gulp. A second later he frowned at the empty glass. Water.

Chapter Twelve

Mackinaw City, Michigan-December, 1972

"Smuggling barbells into Seattle?" Cathy's husband teased as he set Margaret's suitcases in the trunk.

His mother-in-law didn't answer, since she was engaged in a tussle with Cathy about seating arrangements. "Sit up front with Gary," she urged. "I'll ride in the back."

"You're up front." Cathy folded the seat down and crawled clumsily behind it. Her growing belly got in the way of everything these days, but she managed it, adding, "There's no back seat in the pickup, so this will be a new experience for me."

Getting in, Margaret turned to shake a finger at her. "Well, don't be surprised if I steal your husband on the way to the airport." She squeezed Gary's arm. "You got yourself a real doll."

Catching Cathy's eye in the rearview mirror, Gary grinned good-humoredly.

"Don't forget to call when you get to Seattle, Mom," Cathy said as he steered the car onto the ice-crusted road. "The TV says the weather's bad all the way from here to there."

"Reverse the charges," Gary put in. "Don't want to wear out your welcome the first day."

"It's sure crappy here." Margaret peered up at the dark gray, flat-bottomed clouds. Icy rain hit the windshield, making tiny ticks. "Should have known better than to travel in December."

"Lucky for you, I have ten winters of driving experience behind me," Gary said.

"At least eight of them legal," Cathy added.

"A good driver and a sweetie besides." Margaret shed her mittens and tossed them onto the dashboard.

Cathy was pleased that Gary and her mom got along so well. He treated Margaret like a queen, listening to her long stories with apparent interest. His strong, reassuring presence in their lives had reduced her alcohol use. When Margaret agreed to visit her teetotaler sister in Seattle for Christmas, Cathy suspected it was because for the first time in ages, she felt able to spend a week without drinking.

Cathy studied her husband's profile, watchful as he navigated the slippery road. Though it sometimes bothered her that he took no interest in books, the news, philosophical discussion, or science, Gary was a good man. Orphaned himself, he'd insisted her mom come to live with them. "Family is supposed to be together, Cath."

Sometimes it was weird when Gary and Margaret laughed together at jokes so corny Cathy could hardly marshal a smile. But now she was pregnant. Having Mom with them (and sober) meant she wouldn't feel too guilty about going back to work when her six weeks of unpaid leave was done. Gary's income was a patchwork of seasonal labor and cash jobs, supplemented by unemployment checks in winter. Cathy's position at the county clerk's office provided them with much-needed health benefits. Margaret, who'd been forced to give up her bus-driving job due to vision problems, was more than willing to care for the baby.

"Use my car while I'm gone, Cath." Mom turned, her movement making the plastic seat squeak in protest. "No sense letting it sit idle."

"I will, thanks. I have a doctor's appointment on Tuesday, and Gary's working all week." A friend who did home renovations needed help, and the money he earned would bring a few luxuries. *If you consider a night at the bar watching your husband play pool a luxury.*

Her thoughts were interrupted by a soft curse from Gary. Margaret gasped. Peering between them, Cathy saw something massive in the road ahead. A forester's truck, loaded with logs, was out of the driver's control and coming directly at them. The scene unfolded in what seemed like slow motion, allowing Cathy time to conjure advice for escaping disaster in her head: *Turn right! No, left! Throw it into reverse! Speed up!*

"Hang on!" Pumping the brakes, Gary managed to slow the car and steer toward the ditch on the right, out of the truck's path. That was a relief, but a second later the truck's cab collided with a signpost on the opposite side of the road. Its abrupt stop sent the trailer swinging toward them, like a pendulum on its arc.

Hopeful thoughts raced through Cathy's brain. If the swing wasn't too wide, the trailer would miss them. If it didn't, the chain-binders might hold the logs in place. If the binders broke, the logs might spill into the ditch, not onto the car.

None of those things happened, but she didn't know that for a long time.

She awoke to the unfamiliar feeling she was both in a bed and above it. The smell of alcohol stung her nose. Hushed footsteps sounded on the tile floor. Her fingertips felt starched cotton sheets beneath them. People spoke to her and about her, but she didn't care—couldn't care—who they were or what they said. Over the next few days, words gradually penetrated her drug-fogged mind. She learned one tragedy at a time, as Doctor Willis judged her ready to absorb the information. Gary was dead. Her mother was dead. She had survived, Doc said with professional positivity, because she was in the back seat when the front of the car was crushed by a dozen thirty-inch logs. She should thank God she'd suffered only a concussion from impact with the side window and two broken femurs from the front seat slamming into her legs. And—he looked away when he said it—a miscarriage.

Father Yates came to visit, his face a mask of pious sorrow. He spoke of seeing through a glass darkly and being reunited in Christ some happy day. He left her with a *Revised Standard Version of the Bible* and a pamphlet on how Christians deal with grief. Paging through both, Cathy found no answers.

Why would we understand it later? Who was going to help her figure out how to spend the rest of her life without the man she loved, the woman who'd brought her into the world, and the child she would never hold in her arms? How was that fair?

For the first time, Cathy questioned the convenient phrases of religious conviction. Haltingly, she shared her doubts with the priest when he returned. His responses, platitudes about faith and God's unknowable plan, convinced her he knew no more than she did about life's biggest questions. Father's job was to comfort the grieving, and he'd been taught words chosen to do that. When those words didn't work, he had nothing more to offer. Patting her arm, he said that with time and prayer she'd start feeling like her old self again. Noting his recitative tone, Cathy realized that even after thirty years as God's emissary, Father had no genuine understanding of the confusion she was feeling. She couldn't be the only person he'd dealt with whose faith had faltered, but Father chose not to wrestle with life's whys. It was easier to be passive. It was God's will.

He prayed with her, though Cathy didn't feel like praying. Holding the hand closest to him, he asked the Lord for strength and healing for her. She felt the dry, cool touch of his fingers as his thumb rubbed gently across her knuckles. Despite his assurances that God knew exactly what she needed to return to her old self, Cathy did not feel better in a few days. In her heart she knew she'd never return to that old self again.

Her brothers, big men with walrus mustaches and work-reddened hands, took turns visiting each evening, saying little once they'd reported on the current weather. Although either could take an engine apart in the dark with a flathead screwdriver and reassemble it the same way, neither was comfortable with words. Speaking about feelings was nearly impossible. They mumbled, as if words had to be forced from unwilling lips, and a clumsy pat on her arm was both greeting and farewell.

What talk they managed was of practical things. Caleb's wife Barbie, a woman of almost irritating efficiency, arranged the funerals, composed the obituaries, and wrote and mailed thank you cards to everyone in town. In a rare moment of empathy, she also closed Cathy's room to visitors, shutting out well-wishers with nothing helpful to say and snoops only eager to report to the town how "poor Cathy" was doing.

No doubt there was plenty of talk about "poor Cathy" among co-workers, friends, and acquaintances. Cards came in the mail, phoned condolences arrived via Candy Stripers, and heart-felt messages from her church family were relayed by Father Yates, whose visits she couldn't summon the courage to turn away.

Curtis took care of the house, draining the pipes so they wouldn't burst and clearing the fridge and cupboards of food no one would return to eat. In his practical manner, he suggested she give up the lease, since it would be months before she could manage the seven steps from the ground to her front door. He took Gary's beagle home with him.

"She's doing fine with our two," his wife Ann, who came with him sometimes, reported, speaking softly in deference to the hospital setting. "I took your plants too. No sense letting them freeze."

"Thank you." The removal of such practical worries struck Cathy as the kindest thing, far better than perky assurances of brighter days ahead from those who had no idea what she was suffering.

One night when her physical healing was under way, Curtis shifted nervously in his chair, a sign he had something to say. "You'll be all right, Cath," he began, looking down at the sweat-stained cap in his hands. "I know this is bad, and I don't know how you handle it. But you're still young and pretty and everybody knows what a great girl you are. Guys will be lining up to date you." She must have made an involuntary sound, because his eyes met hers for a second. "I mean when you're ready. Caleb and me, we don't want you to lay there and worry. You'll find somebody, and things will work out okay."

Cathy struggled to come up with a response suitable to the comfort her brother was trying to offer. *A mate is like a pet? When one dies, you simply go out and choose another? God, no!*

Then she remembered God was no longer responding to her needs. "We'll see, Curt."

After three weeks in the hospital, Cathy was nearly insane. Grief, loss, pain, and anger mixed to fuel a constant roil in her gut that made it hard to use a civil tone when someone approached with meals, tests, or activities designed to speed her recovery. There was no recovery for the things that mattered most, and she wondered if there ever would be.

When the clip of high heels sounded on the tiled hallway, she hardly noticed, but as the sound drew nearer, she looked up. A figure swept into the room, ignoring the "No Visitors" sign. A mink coat, a fashionable crocheted hat, and lipstick so red it almost hurt her eyes.

"Elvera?"

E came forward, her gaze taking in the plaster that encased her friend's legs from thigh to ankle. "I came as soon as I heard." Taking both her hands, she set her forehead on Cathy's, eyes closed. For the first time since the accident, Cathy felt that someone understood what she'd lost.

That was it. A moment of silent communication. Elvera stepped back, blinking away tears she would never admit to.

But she was here, in person. Not a card of condolence, not flowers or money toward funeral costs. Elvera had come, even though aside from Christmas and birthday cards, they hadn't communicated in two years. Cathy's question was blunt, a sign of her stress level. "What possessed you to drive all the way up here?"

E ran a gloved finger down Cathy's cheek. "To get you out of here, Goofball. You need to be with me."

Chapter Thirteen

Cruise-Day 6, 8:00 a.m.

Khlong Toei Port on the Chao Phraya River allowed smaller cruise ships to moor relatively close to Bangkok's city center, and passengers on the *Happy Wanderer* were given two days to explore the great variety of offerings presented. Nearby was the food market, but there were also excursions by Sky Train into the heart of the city and guided tours to tourist sites on the west side. "Must see" choices were much discussed, including the Grand Palace with its Temple of the Emerald Buddha and Wat Phra Kaeo; the National Museum; the Museum of Royal Barges with its ornate collection of funeral barges for each member of the royal family; Dusit Palace; Wat Pho; Jim Thompson's House; Queen Saovabha Memorial Institute; and the Snake Farm. Those seeking a respite from populated areas could take a quiet walk through Lumpini Park.

When word got out that he was a Bangkok resident, Michael was asked for recommendations as to best use of time and finances. He cautioned the passengers to watch for unscrupulous tuk-tuk and taxi drivers who schemed to defraud tourists. He explained the snake shows put on by the Red Cross. He cited rules against see-through shirts or sandals at some of the holy shrines. It was a new feeling for him, being a sought-after expert, and he enjoyed the role, though he suspected that with time the repetitive, naive questions would become tiresome.

As he prepared Miss E's breakfast tray, Marilyn approached. "Inspector Lee is here." She said it out the side of her mouth, like a gangster in an old movie.

Guessing her curiosity had reached overflowing, Michael offered a plausible, though false, explanation. "The company suspects fraud in the ship's financial accounting. Lee approached me to help him investigate, since I'm newly hired and therefore can't be in on any schemes."

She opened her mouth to ask a question, but Michael put up a hand.

"The inspector would be angry that I told you that much, but of course I know your discretion can be trusted."

"I won't tell a soul, cross my heart and hope to choke." After a moment she added, "Invite him to stay for breakfast. You have work to do, but I'll see he gets a decent meal."

Michael suspected she hoped to provide Lee with more than that. "I'm sure he'll appreciate the offer."

Marilyn left, pleased to be in on the supposed secret, as Michael wondered what Lee wanted now. How could he protect Miss E from the pompous but determined cop?

Lee was on the observation deck, watching people come and go. "Good morning, Inspector."

Instead of returning the greeting Lee said, "I assume from your silence that Elvera Tharp has been behaving normally?"

Michael chuckled. "Miss E seldom behaves normally."

The response was an irritated gesture. "You know what I mean."

"The lady is as disagreeable as ever. No more, no less."

Lee smoothed his mustache, which Michael suspected was a tell, indicating he was about to lie, or at least not tell the whole truth. "I have decided to take you into my confidence, *Khun* Kanda." Lee used the Thai honorific roughly equivalent to *Mr.* or *Ms.* "You may play an important role in this matter, for I believe Miss E is part of, perhaps head of, a ring of people smugglers."

It was so unexpected that Michael blurted a laugh. "Human trafficking? Miss E?"

Lee shook his head abruptly. "People smuggling is different

from human trafficking in that those transported leave their homeland voluntarily."

Pieces fell into place in Michael's mind. Not drugs. Not contraband. People. An unseen visitor with long, black hair. "I see."

"What she does is a crime. There are laws governing the movement of people between nations. Elvera Tharp exploits Thailand's openness to tourism in order to break those laws."

"Why would she do that?"

A dismissive gesture indicated reasons didn't matter, but Lee said, "The business is quite lucrative."

"How does it work?"

Lee frowned at the docks below them. "The group calls itself Second Base, and they operate simply, keeping few permanent records. Members live normal lives, but from time to time they are asked to perform a single task. For example, a taxi driver might transport an illegal traveler to an extraction point."

"Like this ship."

"Yes." Lee glanced around as if an interloper might be creeping past at that very moment. "Other members secure false documents or provide temporary shelter." He flexed his hands. "Most group members know only one or two others by name or by sight, but I believe your Miss E knows them all."

"Then you intend to strike at the head of the snake, as they say."

"I do."

Noting the singular pronoun, Michael met his gaze directly. "Is this an official police investigation?"

Frustration showed briefly on Lee's face, and he touched his moustache lightly. "Those I work for are reluctant to believe that an elderly American tourist is an integral part of a criminal operation." His next revelation was part confession, part boast. "I have taken leave from my duties in order to see to the matter myself."

"Why are you so certain Miss E is your target?"

Lee's gaze went to the bright horizon. "A few years ago, I was patrolling the cruise ship docks at Laem Chabang when I saw an American woman leading an Asian man along the wharf. He was in obvious pain, and she supported him almost fully, though she herself had a noticeable limp."

"It was Elvera Tharp?"

"At the time I saw only a Western woman acting suspiciously." Lee paused, remembering. "Trailing them through a maze of crates waiting to be loaded, I lost sight of them for some minutes." His lips pressed together. "When I caught up, the woman stood on the wharf alone, looking toward the sea."

"She'd achieved what she came there to do."

Lee folded his hands. "I saw nothing, but the night was black. I followed her to a ship called the *Laughing Sailor*. There I learned her name, Elvera Tharp." After a pause he said, "Living entirely on cruise ships is convenient for the work she does, yes?"

Michael shook his head. "How would someone like Miss E get involved in such an enterprise?"

"She lived in Thailand many years ago, and rumors at the time claimed she participated in similar activities. Apparently, she has continued her criminal behavior for decades." He spread his hands. "The crimes have made her rich. How else could a woman without resources live aboard a luxury liner full time?"

"I find all this hard to believe, Inspector."

"Think!" Lee demanded. "A lone wolf persona keeps her separate. She demands only one steward, and with him she is bad-tempered, so the steward seeks to minimize his time with her."

"I thought it was pain that made her hard to deal with."

"Think what you like." Lee thumped a fist on the railing. "If I had been faster that first night, I'd have caught her with what they call a *package*." His tone grew agitated. "I'd have proof she's more than an eccentric American tourist."

Michael looked at Lee with fresh interest. "This quest seems personal to you."

"Each time she succeeds, our police appear more incompetent." Lee pulled himself to attention. "Other nations may ignore Elvera Tharp's schemes. Thailand will not."

"Other nations?"

He gave a single, curt nod. "When my superiors ignored my suspicions, I contacted Interpol and learned that Second Base operates world-wide."

"Why haven't they stopped them?"

Lee shook his head. "Today's Interpol has more serious problems to deal with, like terrorism, human trafficking, and cybercrime. The scale of this group is small, and its effects are painless in comparison." Lee's shoulders shifted under his shirt. "Still, when I present undeniable proof of Tharp's crimes, they will be forced to take up the case." He added as apparent incentive, "If Thai police apprehend Miss E, she won't be tortured or beheaded, as might happen in some less civilized nation."

"And a single clever policeman will become famous for unmasking an international criminal."

Lee shot him a resentful glance before offering another carrot. "In return for your help, I can perhaps do you some future service. It is seldom a bad thing to have a friend on the police force."

Understanding the implication Michael asked, "What should I do?"

"Each time Tharp leaves the ship, I believe she contacts someone in her organization. They arrange a time and method for a package to arrive at her cabin. Since she always returns to the ship alone and never has visitors, I believe the package arrives by boat and climbs to her balcony using some sort of ladder." As Michael struggled not to let his expression reveal that he'd already discovered that to be true, Lee finished, "Miss E insists on the same cabin each trip. That is, I think, because it's not visible from most places on deck."

"But a ladder would be easily spotted by someone standing on his own balcony."

"The ladder needs to be lowered for only a few minutes." Lee moved on to Michael's part of his plan. "I have no authority to search a foreign vessel, but if an employee reported to me that he observed an un-ticketed person in the lady's cabin, I could investigate that claim."

"I see."

"You will act as a good citizen should, Khun Kanda. You will search the room in the morning, find the interloper, and report it to me, yes?"

Though he maintained a calm demeanor, Michael was worried. Lee wasn't stupid, and he wasn't going to give up easily. "Of course, Inspector," he replied in a respectful tone. "I'm not the sort of person who'd stand by while the law is being violated."

Chapter Fourteen

Chicago-December, 1974

When Cathy set a large package on the post office counter, the clerk remarked, "Big one, eh?"

"Lots of nieces and nephews up north."

For a second year she wasn't going home to Mackinaw City for Christmas. She'd made excuses of busy-ness that her brothers accepted without argument. Dutifully she'd consulted wise store clerks for age-appropriate games for her nieces and nephews and wrapped them attractively before boxing up the lot and mailing it out. That would pretty much be all the Christmas giving, since E and Richard did little more than hang a wreath on the door. Cathy didn't mind. Christmas shopping reminded her of Mom, who'd loved buying presents for everyone. Christmas music annoyed her with its joyful songs and lyrics. Christmas Day would demonstrate that she was useful to no one. The Tharps' housekeeper, Mrs. Leon, would cook dinner, set the table, and clear away the mess afterward. No Christmas spirit required.

Cathy now knew that as an impressionable teen, she'd been wrong about the Tharps in many ways. They weren't nearly as wealthy as they worked at appearing to be. Though Franklin donated to charity, attended city events, and cultivated eminent people, he also fretted about which bills to pay in any given month. He made small economies that didn't show, like claiming he was too attached to his aging car to let it go.

Thinking back, Cathy realized the family's finances had been rocky for at least as long as she'd known them. "We own a place on Mackinac Island," had no doubt sounded impressive to their Chicago friends, but not one of them had been invited to visit

Braddock House. At fourteen Cathy had considered the place grand. At twenty-four she recognized the lies implicit in its neglected exterior and outdated appliances.

That wasn't all. E's marriage to the man she'd once called "Father's errand boy" was unhappy. Not only was the couple poorly matched, but the financial boost Franklin expected hadn't materialized. That was due to something called the Shakman Agreement, which Cathy learned about in an article she found in Franklin's study. The new law made sweeping changes to the patronage system that had long plagued Chicago's city government. Carlo Terzis had been indicted for racketeering only weeks after Richard and Elvera's wedding. Between expensive lawyers and rumored payoffs, buying his way out of prison had cost Terzis everything he had. Once the case against him was dropped, Terzis had scuttled off to Florida, leaving Franklin Tharp no better off for having pushed his daughter into marriage.

To his credit, Franklin didn't blame Richard for the mess, and to his credit, Richard kept Tharp Credit Services afloat without the expected influx of cash. Some of the policies he instituted apparently bothered Elvera, however, and once at dinner she'd hinted they might not be entirely legal. "Leave the boy alone," Franklin had ordered. "A good wife supports her husband, but you pick at yours like an angry harpy."

At that point Cathy had excused herself, saying she was feeling more tired than usual.

All that made E's rescue of Cathy from the hospital more impressive. Her friend had come for her despite financial and family woes, and Cathy intended to pay E back. As soon as she was able to stand and walk, she'd begun helping around the house. "If I do the evening dishes, Mrs. Leon can go home an hour earlier," she proposed. "I get to feel useful, she gets more free time, and you cut expenses a little."

Elvera seemed amused by this small economy, and the housekeeper was clearly horrified to have an intruder in her kitchen.

Cathy overheard E explaining that it was part of her friend's therapy.

At times it was like the old days. The two of them talked about things great and small. Cathy felt guilty about being the one left alive. She suffered from the knowledge that she'd never be able to get pregnant again. People back home had said it was Fate, a mystery, God's plan. She shouldn't dwell on it. She should look forward, not back.

E said none of those meaningless things. She let Cathy work through her pain, going over and over what might have made a difference that day. If they'd left a little earlier. If they'd taken a different route. If, if, if. It was masochistic, but Cathy needed to poke at the pain in her heart until scar tissue hardened the spot. E understood. They talked about sudden loss. They talked about guilt. They talked and talked, though words were hardly necessary between them.

Physical strength was slow to return, whether due to the injuries themselves, her mental state, or both, she couldn't say. Even after a year, when she could walk without a cane, Cathy tired easily, so she looked for quiet things to do. She read every book the Tharps owned, even previously unopened volumes of classic literature purchased solely to add atmosphere to Franklin's study. When she finished them all, she refused to go out to buy more. "I'll read these again," she told E. "I'm not sure how much I'm absorbing anyway." Rejecting that, Elvera went to a bookshop and bought the entire *New York Times* best seller list, both fiction and nonfiction, for her friend's reading pleasure.

Unwilling to live on the Tharps' charity, Cathy began acting as unpaid assistant to Franklin, who'd cut his office staff to one overworked secretary named Didi. Cathy kept track of Franklin's correspondence, scheduled his appointments, and made his travel arrangements. Didi, whom she never met but spoke with often on the phone, was grateful. "I'm so glad you help Mr. Tharp out," she told Cathy. "I'm swamped with the stuff Mr. Terzis wants done, and he's not a patient type."

"It's nothing," she replied. "I like feeling useful."

In the spring of 1975, when the snow started to recede, Cathy felt stirrings of life returning to her wintery soul as well. She conversed without being prodded. She listened to the radio and sometimes hummed along. She even agreed to go shopping when Elvera insisted they both needed something new to wear.

Father Yates hadn't been completely wrong, Cathy admitted. Letting go of grief was natural, even inevitable. But he hadn't been completely right either. She'd never be her old self again. The deepest part of her grief remained even as life whispered, *You're not dead. You must go on.*

Elvera wanted to start a clothing line, an idea her father called "ridiculous," and Richard termed "not financially feasible at this time." Cathy didn't care much about fashion, but in the face of their negativity, she gave E her attention, letting her talk about her ideas. At first it was all theoretical, but one day she confided, "Aunt Renee, who won't loan Dad a penny, is willing to bankroll me in return for a share of the profits after two years." With a grin she added, "She says a dog-grooming business would be better, but she came around to my way of thinking."

In a move that surprised everyone, Drake came to visit at Easter. He'd been scheduled for three months in Burma, but his mission wound up a few weeks early. When he returned home, he found that his wife, children, nanny, and in-laws had already left D.C. to spend the holidays in Florida. Rather than fly to St. Pete for six days with the Comptons, Drake caught a plane to Chicago.

E was busy developing contacts and support for her soon-to-be-launched business. Richard and Franklin went to the office early and returned late, which meant that Drake and Cathy were left together in the house. They renewed their old acquaintance, talking when they felt like it and ignoring each other when they didn't. Drake's conversation was fascinating, since he traveled all over the world.

"Putting out fires," was his term for the work he did, but he never elaborated on how those fires started or what he did to put them out.

Cathy felt comfortable with Drake, since he was the kind of person who never seemed to judge others. He let her talk about the loss of Gary and her mother, though she still couldn't speak of the child she would never have. Never once did he suggest she should "move on."

On Easter Sunday, Franklin, E, and Richard dressed in their finest and went to mass. Richard bought his wife a corsage for the occasion, orchids with a white ribbon. Cathy stayed home, as did Drake. After they'd gone, he asked, "Don't you go to church anymore?"

Cathy's answer was oblique. "Back home, a friend from high school came to see me in the hospital. She walked right past the *No Visitors* sign, took hold of my hand, and offered what she considered comfort. 'The Lord doesn't send us more than we can handle,' she said. 'You're tough, so you'll get through this.'"

Drake said nothing, though his eyes warmed with understanding of how that had made Cathy feel.

"I wanted to scream at her to get out." Cathy pushed her hair away from her face with an abrupt gesture. "I didn't feel tough. In fact, I felt like the next thing, the next whiff of pain, would crush me to the ground and leave me permanently shattered." She tried to smile. "I can't balance the loving God I learned about as a kid with a deity that sends tragedy as some sort of character test."

"A lot of people get that part of it wrong, but I doubt there's any sense arguing with them about it."

"No."

Drake leaned forward, his elbows on his knees. "Cathy, I can't imagine what you've gone through—what you're still going through, but I don't think it's a test of your strength or your faith. It's just the way the world is."

"What about you, Drake? Are you still a believer?"

He took a moment before answering. "At some point I gave up trying to understand life's mysteries. I stick with what I know is good and let others debate who's in control."

Hearing sorrow in his tone, she asked, "What do you really do at the State Department? What does 'putting out fires' mean?"

He struck a comical pose. "To quote Arthur Conan Doyle, 'I would love to tell you, but then I'd have to kill you.'"

The sound of her own laughter surprised her. "Really, Drake."

He leaned back in his chair, causing the Naugahyde to creak softly. "Mostly I go from place to place, trying to implement American foreign policy despite constant changes in said policy. They call me the Wild Goose, a play on my name and the fact that I wander all over."

"I'm sure you do a great job." He smiled, but his eyes revealed doubt. Whether he doubted himself or the policies, she couldn't say.

Drake seemed to sense that Cathy liked company, not necessarily to talk to, but as a reassuring presence. All her life she'd had family around her. Margaret, though not perfect, had always been nearby. For almost two years she'd had Gary beside her in bed, his chest against her back, his breath on her neck. And for months she'd had a new life inside her. She'd felt the quickening. She'd shared with Gary and Mom the tiny foot or hand that swept across her stomach, making its impatience to be born known to the outside world.

It was hard to be alone after all that.

Drake sat near her in the evenings, reading a book or newspaper. If she spoke, he immediately raised his eyes to hers and gave her his full attention. They discussed national issues, and though at times it seemed he might have said more than he did, they agreed on the basics. She liked that he saw her not as an invalid, not as Poor Cathy the Widow, but as a normal, functioning person with informed opinions on important things.

During Drake's visit, Elvera noted that he was good at drawing her friend out of her shell of grief. As a result, she took him aside the day before he left Chicago. "Cathy's been acting as Daddy's unpaid secretary, but she needs to get her life moving forward again. Encourage her to come to work for me."

Drake rubbed a hand across the back of his neck. "The fashion business doesn't sound like Cathy, E."

"Her old life is gone, Drake. She needs to get her mind off the past."

"Nothing can take a mind where it doesn't want to go. Shouldn't her new interests be her choice, not yours?"

"Ask her to think about it," E insisted. "She can't wander this house like a ghost the rest of her life."

Drake sighed. "I'll try."

Between Drake's gentle urging and E's pragmatic arguments, Cathy agreed to try working at Elvera's fledgling company. They discussed possible names like *Tharpbeau* or *Beautharp* but settled on *Mizz*, which Elvera said suggested elegance and energy. "Mizz like *Ms.* with a hint of *fizz* to conjure the idea of movement."

E fussed that everything had to be right for Cathy's initial visit, driving Jill, the young intern she'd hired, half crazy. When Cathy stepped off the elevator, Jill ushered her into E's office, where a shiny walnut desk was backed by a view of Chicago through floor-to-ceiling windows. "Welcome to Mizz Fashions," E said proudly.

"Nice."

E opened a door at one side of the room. "Your office." She pointed, and Cathy peeked into a space with a view of the city only slightly narrower than E's. On the windowsill sat a vase of daffodils, their bright yellow denoting optimism and new beginnings. "You can furnish it however you want."

"But what will I do?" she asked for the tenth time.

"Help me, Cath, like you did at my wedding, remember? I'll have a million things to do every day. I need someone I trust to see that the place runs the way I want it to."

"You need someone with experience and a business background." She gestured at the outer office. "Jill seems competent."

"She'd have to follow me around for months, asking questions you already know the answers to." E folded her arms. "To be honest, I need you as a buffer too. You're nicer than I am. You'll communicate with staff in a positive way, so they aren't always mad at me."

"People don't—"

"Oh, stop," E interrupted. "The other day I told a shipper, in what I thought was my most polite manner, that he was ripping me off on pricing. He hung up on me, and now he won't take my calls." She shrugged. "I'm assertive, which makes people angry—at least it does if you're female."

"I don't see you that way."

E chuckled. "For reasons I've never understood, Goofball, you like me even when no one else does."

Later, Elvera reflected that part of her speech had been truth and part sales pitch. Cathy needed a job. The settlement offered by the trucking firm had been laughable, but she'd refused to sue. She knew the owners and was aware that a judgment against them would bankrupt the business. As a result, her medical bills from the accident were still waiting to be paid. Gary had had no life insurance, so she was also making payments to the funeral home. Where else was Cathy, still shaky on her feet, going to find employment that would allow her to recover financially? If Elvera had to overstate her need for an intermediary, she was willing to do it. And in her heart, she admitted she was a bit of a bitch to work for—and to be married to, as Richard often commented.

Cathy's first day at Mizz was stressful. She'd been gone from the world of work—almost from the world entirely—for ages, so simply having a schedule was nerve-wracking. She was led to a stuffy, crowded room that smelled of jelly doughnuts and introduced to the staff, most of them her age or younger, as Cathy Charbonneau. "It's French," E said. "Automatic cachet in the fashion world. Besides, who can spell Przybylski?"

Cathy agreed, though she felt disloyal to Gary, who'd loved her enough to give her his name. More disloyal yet was the fact that it often took effort to remember exactly what he'd looked like. Had his eyes been more blue or green? And his hair. Had he parted it on the right or the left?

Added to her misgivings were details of a business she didn't know, fashion terminology she'd never bothered to learn, and the constant come-and-go of people who were confident, beautiful (at least on the outside) and...*expectant* was the word that came to mind. In business, people wanted things all the time. A person had to decide how much of their expectations would be—could be— fulfilled.

Of course, E made the decisions, all of them initially and later the most important ones. Yes, she could fit a short meeting with an up-and-coming designer between lunch and her one o'clock staff briefing. No, she wouldn't order more fabric from the company in India that had sent them insect-riddled goods. And no, she didn't have time to speak to her husband. Cath should tell Richard she'd meet him for dinner at such-and-such a place at six. As Cathy's confidence grew, E handed over decisions like where to make reservations for a client lunch or who should be acknowledged in staff memos in a particular month.

Like other things in life, the demands of business grew less fearful over time, mostly doable with the right amount of organization. Cathy became part of Mizz, earning a reputation for honesty and understanding. When E's mood turned snappish, employees went to Cathy, sometimes in tears. She explained that the boss carried great responsibility, which sometimes made her brusque, but she hadn't meant to be harsh. It became common practice to sound Cathy out on new ideas before approaching Elvera with them. Cathy could often tweak a proposal enough so that E didn't reject it halfway through the presentation. And if Ms. Charbonneau didn't think an idea would fly, most employees accepted that, saving themselves the pain of Elvera's blunt opinion.

Despite Elvera's sharp tongue and impatient manner, everyone at Mizz recognized her talent. Tough and competent, she entered the world of fashion with a work ethic that would have worn out three normal people, and a confident exterior that got her through the rough patches. She made mistakes but recovered quickly, using what she learned to build a stronger foundation for the business. She boldly misrepresented her prospects, workforce, and herself to industry leaders, first convincing them she could deliver and then running back to the office to make good on her promises.

Had it not been so stressful, it would have been funny to see the overworked Jill calling her former roommates at Northwestern to ask if they'd be willing to do some modeling…in four hours' time. No one had to know that the treats offered at client meetings, tasty bacon rumaki, nut-studded cheese balls, and such, came from home, prepared by Mrs. Leon and transported to the office in Elvera's car on Cathy's lap. E might be seen emerging from the back seat of a black sedan at some gala event and telling her driver, "Come back for me at one." The driver was Cathy, and the sedan was borrowed from a neighbor. "In fashion," E often told the Mizz staff, "appearance is everything."

To everyone's surprise except Elvera's, the business took off. Midwestern women liked the idea of a line created with them in mind. The frilly frocks and cotton coats popular in other places were impractical for Chicago winters, yet no fashion-conscious woman wanted to dress like Jeremiah Johnson. Mizz's first offering was a line of attractive but warm winter wear, and anyone who'd trod the Magnificent Mile in a too-thin coat took notice. Once they tried one Mizz fashion, women were eager to have a look at the rest.

Cathy often wondered if she was wise to stay on at Tharp House. E spoke to her husband in tones so cold as to chill whole rooms, and she frequently pointed out flaws in his wardrobe, his grooming, and his personal taste. She managed to insinuate with a phrase or a look that he'd never risen above his background, which was odd, since E never treated Cathy like a social inferior, never made fun of her "up north" accent or unrefined taste. It was hard to be in the same room with Richard and Elvera Terzis, because sooner or later E's claws came out.

For a time, Cathy felt sorry for Richard, who made no reply to his wife's taunts. But the more she came to know E's husband, the less Cathy found to like. Richard seemed like a pleasant person. He listened to Franklin Tharp's pompous ramblings as if every word he spoke was a gem. In social situations, he tended to ask question after question about others' opinions, though he seldom offered his own. Most people in the world of banking saw him as pragmatic, though once Cathy heard someone call him *ruthless*. It wasn't meant as an insult, she realized. Unless you were the one who suffered, ruthless was apparently good business practice.

What turned Cathy against Richard was the way he treated those below him in social status. Exchanges with clerks, servants, and other underlings were tinged with contempt, and his contempt turned nasty when something happened that he didn't like. Lost items, broken dishes, or small messes were never Richard's fault. Either someone else was responsible, or it should have been foreseen and prevented. More than once Cathy wondered why Elvera had married him after years of saying she never would, but her relationship with Richard was the one subject the two of them never discussed.

Cathy had been E's Matron of Honor at the wedding, but in the whirlwind pace of the weekend, she'd barely spoken to the groom. There'd been an uncomfortable moment when one of E's bridesmaids made a crack about his mother's horrible dress, unaware that Richard was nearby. He'd pretended not to hear, but during the father-daughter, mother-son dance, Mrs. Terzis had seemed near tears, while her son's stiff posture revealed a desire for the painful moment to be over.

Most of Cathy's memories of that weekend centered on Drake, who as Best Man had been her escort in the bridal party. Her face warmed when he greeted her with a hug, though she'd been at that time a happily married woman. Sensing how uncomfortable she felt among strangers she saw as more sophisticated than she, Drake introduced her as "our friend from Michigan," which lessened her feeling of being a hick from the sticks. When the response was, "Oh, Michigan. I've been to Detroit," he elbowed her lightly. To explain that Detroit didn't represent where she came from would be pointless, but it helped to know Drake found their ignorance amusing.

He'd watched over her the whole weekend, explaining how things would go and making sure she wasn't left standing in corners. She'd been cowed by the house, the church, the frenetic pace, and the level of attention to detail. E had arranged for her to have her hair and makeup "done" the morning of the wedding. "I'm told it's standard procedure," Drake said. "I think you look fine the way you are."

Since Cathy's approach to hair care was cutting a few inches off the ends every six months with sewing scissors, the salon visit was an experience. Thrilled by her long, thick mane, the stylist created a hairdo that suggested one of Cher's outlandish personas. Though Cathy didn't like it much, the other bridesmaids looked equally odd, with flowers stuck here and there in upswept, sprayed-to-stay "looks."

"Wrap it in toilet paper and sleep on a satin pillowcase," the stylist advised. "It will last a week that way." She'd laughed, picturing Gary's wide-eyed response if she returned home looking like Barbarella.

When she and E arrived at the church, Drake had seemed to be waiting for her. Complimenting them both, he sent E off to answer the photographer's questions while he stayed at Cathy's side. Things became awkward when Drake's wife Patricia arrived. A rail-thin woman with intense eyes and fingers that curled in like talons, she took one look at Cathy and judged her a threat. "So you're Elvera's little friend from Michigan," she said, her nose wrinkling. "Did you bring your chainsaw?" Her tone was louder than necessary, and two women standing nearby turned to look. "Maybe you can demonstrate tree-trimming after the ceremony." She laughed as if she'd said something witty, and a few of the others joined in.

Cathy was unsure how to respond, but Drake bumped her shoulder lightly, which she took as a warning, or perhaps a plea, to remain silent. Taking Drake's arm, Patricia pulled him away as if Cathy might latch onto him at any moment and drag him to her boudoir.

In the changing room, Cathy put on her dress and then helped Elvera decide on details such as lipstick color and where to stash a handkerchief. She felt useful as a reassuring presence for E, and she was able to avoid Drake and his wife until it was time to line up for the bridal procession. Thinking back on that day, Cathy's most telling memory of the ceremony was when Patricia turned to glare at her and Drake as they stood together in the sanctuary doorway. As they waited for their cue to enter, he spoke, softly and without turning to face her. "Patricia's insecure, and the fact that E can't stand her makes it worse."

"What's the problem between them?"

His smile was crooked. "Me, I suppose. Our parents always assumed Patricia and I would end up together, but E was never a fan of the idea."

"And being Elvera, she didn't bother to hide her feelings."

Peripherally, she saw Drake grin. "You know her pretty well." Straightening his shoulders, he said, "We're going to have a baby in December. I think motherhood will calm Patti down, and she'll stop thinking every attractive woman I speak to is trying to seduce me."

Cathy had left Chicago feeling both pleased and ashamed that the moments she cherished most from E's wedding were the two times Drake said, or at least hinted, that he found her attractive.

A few months after Elvera launched her new business, Franklin Tharp suffered a debilitating stroke. Following a two-week hospital stay, he was moved to a bedroom on the ground floor of his home and cared for by a full-time nursing staff. Though Cathy couldn't say she admired Mr. Tharp, she was moved by his pitiful state and did what she could to help, reading the newspaper to him and rearranging the room to suit his needs. At first his speech was too garbled to understand, but she soon became as good as the nurses at guessing what he wanted. Over time, he regained the ability to speak, but the right side of his body remained paralyzed.

Drake came home and stayed for a week, helping E deal with the crisis. He said little about his home situation, but from his frequent phone calls, Cathy guessed Patricia was unhappy with his absence. "I know I'm gone a lot," she heard him say as she passed the phone desk in the hallway. "I travel for work, Patti, and now with Father ill—" Once Franklin stabilized, Drake flew back to D. C. The next time they heard from him, he was in the Middle East.

Richard stepped into his father-in-law's shoes at Tharp Credit Services, and in time, a new normal came to be. Elvera visited her father each morning but never stayed long. It depressed her to see him so helpless, she said, and she trusted the staff to let her know if there was something to be concerned about. Cathy dealt with the different nurses, keeping a log of their observations and Franklin's progress. Each evening, Richard sat with his father-in-law for an hour, listening patiently to his slurred comments and playing games that could be managed with one hand, like Yahtzee and Parcheesi.

Richard had his own bedroom, supposedly so he and E could each have their own bath. Since Cathy's room was between the two, she realized in time that Richard never visited his wife's bed, nor did she visit his. In fact, Cathy often heard Richard leave the house after his evening visits with the old man. E never questioned his absences. In fact, she didn't seem to notice.

Worried that her presence might be a factor, Cathy moved from the bedroom next to E's to the maid's quarters at the back of the house. E was horrified. "Cath, the place smells like old floor wax, and the bathroom is the size of a telephone booth."

"But it has a fridge and everything." Grinning, she added, "It reminds me of the apartment on the island."

Though Cathy and E worked well together at the fashion house, for Cathy it was a job, not a calling. She learned the ways and lingo of the clothing business, but she didn't love it the way Elvera did. She knew E's plan was to keep her so busy she forgot the day she'd lost everything, and it worked, most of the time. Still, she couldn't help feeling she'd been spared for something more important than deciding whether to serve beef stroganoff or chicken Kiev at the company Christmas party.

Elvera first hinted, then suggested, then nagged at Cathy to begin dating. "It's been almost five years, Cath. Chicago is full of guys who'd like to meet a beautiful career woman. You don't have to marry again, but at least go out and have a good time once in a while."

Cathy always said she would, but she didn't. There were nice men, some deliberately steered her way, but she saw no point. She'd already been a wife. She'd never be a mother. Why play with a guy's affections?

She didn't miss sex, though it was the seventies and it was everywhere. Movies showed it in such graphic manner that she sometimes looked away, embarrassed for the actors. Nightclubs all but arranged sexual encounters, and who or how many would be involved was negotiable. Cathy wasn't sure what was right for others, but as far as she was concerned, celibacy was safe and comfortable.

One night when E had gone to New York for a conference, Richard became a problem. Though he usually treated Cathy with distant politeness, that night he knocked on her door, his smile betraying tipsiness, and held out a bottle like a sommelier. "A client gave me this wine today, and I thought I'd share it with you."

She struggled for a believable excuse. "That's nice of you, Richard, but I have a headache, and wine always makes it worse."

He dangled the bottle by its neck. "Don't you get lonely, Cathy?"

"What?"

"For a man." His gaze held a challenge. "I worry about you."

"Richard—"

He took a step forward. "It isn't normal for a woman who's young and attractive to be alone all the time. You had a husband, so you know what love between a man and a woman is. You must miss...it."

"Stop."

Seeing a threat in her eyes, he backed up a step. "I meant—I know men who'd treat you like you deserve to be treated." He set the bottle under his arm, as if putting it into storage for some other time. "I want to see you happy, that's all."

His words brought Billy Mason to mind. Billy had claimed he was looking out for Cathy's happiness, but E had saved her from his predatory ways. Now E's husband was the threat. No longer a naïve fifteen-year-old, Cathy said in a firm voice, "When I'm ready for a man, I'll go out and find one who suits me." Before Richard could say anything else, she closed the door in his face and turned the lock with a sharp clunk.

After much cajoling, Elvera convinced Cathy to celebrate the arrival of 1977. Dressed in Elvera's gown from last year, she attended a party with E and Richard at the home of a store owner E was cultivating. These days Cathy was less in awe of the city's wealthy, and E noted with satisfaction that she even managed to appear pleased, though not thrilled, to be there.

After a dinner that focused on a dozen different kinds of fondue, the small crowd moved to a large room where colored lights created a soft glow and a jazz trio played songs by Dave Brubeck and George Lewis. Searching out her friend in the crowd, E was surprised to see Cathy, wineglass in hand, deep in conversation with a man who might have stepped straight out of heroic mythology. Tall, with flawless skin, a chiseled face, and wide shoulders, he practically radiated strength and masculinity. "Who's that?" she asked a woman standing nearby.

"Jay Taksin," she replied. "He's from Thailand."

"A Thai named Jay?"

She shrugged. "His real name is unpronounceable, at least for most Americans. He was sent here by his government to explain the mess on their border and try to get help dealing with it."

"What mess?" Elvera seldom bothered with international news if it wasn't about fashion.

A flutter of her hand indicated the woman didn't pay much attention either. "I guess all the fighting in Southeast Asia drove a bunch of people out of their homes. The Thais don't want them in their country, but if they send them back to where they came from, they're likely to get killed." She gestured dramatically. "Jay says there are these huge camps filled to bursting with Cambodians,

Laos, and Vietnamese. Nobody can figure out what to do with them."

As Cathy listened intently to what the man was saying, Elvera congratulated herself for dragging her to the party. If anyone could reawaken a woman's interest in men, it would be an exotic, gorgeous type like Taksin. And though Cathy wouldn't pay attention to his social class, E guessed the man had a decent level of status in his home country. In fact, she thought she'd heard somewhere that the Thai government was mostly made up of men related to the king.

E's thoughts landed briefly on Cathy's husband. If Gary somehow returned from the dead, would Cathy see how small her world had been with him, or would she go back to Michigan and take up her old role as a small-town wife? The future Cathy once expected had been destroyed in an instant. How much did that kind of tragedy change a person? The outer Cathy seemed the same: calm and helpful, kind and caring. Still, E knew her friend saw things differently now. *When everything you expect from life is ripped away, are you ever the same person again?*

The next day Elvera learned she'd misinterpreted Cathy's interest in Jay Taksin. What impressed her wasn't the man himself, but the stories he told: children dying of neglect, women raped, fathers, sons, and husbands murdered as they fought to protect their families. Taksin's first-hand accounts lit a fire in her friend that E had never seen before. "Think of the horrors those people face every day, E. I'd like to help them."

"So what—you're going to join the Peace Corps or something?"

An uncharacteristically angry tone colored Cathy's response. "Should I go back to Mackinaw and sell trinkets to the tourists? Stay here and be the third wheel with you and Richard for the rest of my life?"

Elvera opened her mouth to say she needed Cathy to keep her home somewhat civil, but that was more honesty than she could manage. Things got worse by the day. E had started her marriage making excuses for Richard, telling herself he was driven to succeed because he was ashamed of his father's criminality. But nothing excused the satisfaction Richard took in besting others, or the way he pressed when he got someone under his thumb. Now that she knew her husband's black soul too well, E found it hard to be in the same room with him. She didn't even object to Richard's constant affairs. She saved her arguments for more important things, like keeping his business dealings within the law.

Richard ran Tharp Credit Services with the sharpness of a riverboat gambler, making deals that stretched the boundaries of ethics far too much for her liking. He always had a deal brewing that he claimed would be a killer, and sometimes it was. When it wasn't, Richard blamed outside forces. Someone had failed to do his part. The market had zigged when it was supposed to zag. Elvera herself was to blame at times, for not being supportive enough.

To be fair, the company had profited under his leadership. The nation was experiencing prosperity, with a decent growth rate, stable prices, and low unemployment. Credit cards were rising in popularity. As Richard's gambles succeeded, they were able to pay off her father's debts. There was light at the end of the tunnel.

That didn't mean E liked Richard's methods. They had a huge fight when she discovered Tharp Credit was mailing out "live" credit cards. The government had banned the practice in 1971, but Richard found ways around the ban and continued encouraging customers to wade farther into debt. "Why can't you abide by the law?" she asked when she found out. "I spend half my time watching what you're up to that might get us fined or even indicted."

"You're a baby," he responded. "Business is about winning, and you don't win if you don't take chances."

Though tempted to smack him, E had instead crossed her arms and issued an ultimatum. "If you can't operate within the law, I'll use the power of attorney Daddy gave me to fire you. Someone else will head Tharp Credit, and you'll be out on your ear."

They'd barely spoken since. At home, Cathy dealt with Richard. At work, Jill was their go-between. E's best times were when she could avoid speaking to her husband for days on end.

Though E foresaw a time when she and Richard would part ways, at present she wanted to focus on Mizz. In a year, maybe two, she'd have her business on solid footing. Then she'd take Richard on, financially, legally, and emotionally. Elvera Terzis would be no more.

With all that to consider, E was unwilling to lose Cathy to some hut in Thailand. Still, it was clear she was serious in her desire to change her life. "Listen, Cath, this is a really big decision. Promise me you'll give it some time. A month, maybe two. You know we've got tons to do before the spring line comes out."

Cathy agreed, though reluctantly, and E resolved to keep her so busy she'd forget the people suffering in faraway lands. People might need help in Thailand, but E wanted Cathy with her.

Chapter Fifteen

Cruise-Day 7, Midnight

On the second night of their stay in Bangkok, Michael didn't even try to go to sleep. Miss E had gone ashore at the first opportunity and returned some hours later, looking tired but resolute. Now he felt like a compressed spring, all kinetic energy. Dressed in black sweatpants and a long-sleeved pullover, he paced the tiny cabin where his roommate snored softly, counting the seconds that dragged by.

At twelve fifty-five he left, closing the door carefully behind him, and made his way to a cabin assigned to a party-girl type. She was screwing her way through the single men on the cruise, and he'd seen her and her conquest for the night enter the man's room after dinner. If past behavior was any prediction, Miss Sleazy wouldn't return to her assigned room until noon at the earliest.

Using his passkey, Michael entered the cabin and went straight to the balcony, where the moon shone above like a white balloon. As hoped, he had a decent view of Elvera Tharp's room, one level below and a few over. The curtains were drawn aside, and interior light spilled onto the tiny private space. On other balconies people sat or stood, talking, eating, or admiring the view. If she had something planned for tonight, it would be after things quieted. Sitting down on the balcony deck, Michael made himself comfortable with a pillow from the bed rolled at his back.

One by one, the balconies emptied, and the sliding glass doors closed. At two twenty-six a.m., only Miss E's remained open, though the lights inside her cabin went out. At two-thirty, a bright light from the interior blinked four times in rapid succession. Fifteen minutes later, the regular swish of oars pushing through water caught Michael's attention. A black rubber boat glided along the ship's hull, where watchers above were unlikely to see it. In the boat a man rowed, his back arching with effort. A woman sat hunched in the seat facing him. Michael remained still, though his legs cramped from staying in one position.

Miss E appeared in her balcony doorway and maneuvered her walker over the slider track. Reaching the railing, she opened the seat of the walker and took something out. Soft metallic sounds echoed over the water, but her body blocked Michael's view for a few seconds. When she stepped back, a rope ladder hung from the railing, its metal hooks cushioned at the top by a towel. Slowly, Miss E let the other end drop. The man in the boat caught and held it so it didn't knock against the hull.

As he watched the scene below, Michael recalled a crewman saying she'd called in the night to demand he unstick her slider. When it jammed with a package due, she must have been in a panic, but due to Miss E's reputation for eccentricity, the man had accepted her claim of wanting to see the sunrise.

Michael remained well back, watching through the balcony's enclosure panels as the woman climbed the ladder and climbed nimbly over the railing. Miss E bowed and said something in soft tones. The woman bowed back, though he read terror in her stiff posture.

Signaling the man below, Miss E pulled the rope ladder up, rolled it, and returned it to its hiding place. Almost silently, the boat retreated the way it had come. Miss E gestured for the woman to enter the cabin, but in a burst of emotion, the newcomer embraced her. Miss E put her arms around her for several seconds, and when they parted, the younger woman's posture was more relaxed. She bowed again, this time lower and longer. When she stood upright again, Miss E led her inside.

This was the woman who didn't like to be touched?

The door slid closed, and the blinds blocked his view. Michael was left with only the moon for company, and he was certain that when he delivered breakfast in a few hours, there would be no sign of a second person in Miss E's cabin.

That morning, as preparations were made to leave port, Michael reported by phone to Inspector Lee. "I can find no evidence that Miss E had accepted a…what did you call it? A package."

"I was sure there would be one last night." Lee's tone turned demanding. "You didn't fall asleep and miss the arrival, Khun Kanda?"

"I watched all night, and I searched the cabin this morning, as well as I could in the course of my duties."

Lee grunted impatiently. "Arrange an opportunity for a more thorough search before the ship reaches the next port."

Michael ended the call worried. Lee was determined, and Michael had no choice but to do as he ordered. He liked the idea of a new search of Miss E's quarters, but not so he could report his findings to a cop.

Within an hour, the horns sounded for a muster drill. Practice for emergencies was required at least once per voyage, to assure that passengers knew the procedures. They'd already had the obligatory one, but a fire in a storage area called for a second. Musters were unpopular with both passengers and crew, so there were rumbles of discontent as everyone made their way to their designated areas. There, in a real emergency, they'd be given information, accounted for, and evacuated if necessary. The fire turned out to be mostly smoke, but things were already underway by the time that was determined.

When Miss E left her cabin, Michael made his way upstream of the crowds of passengers. He'd catch hell for not reporting to his assigned post, but he'd claim she'd sent him back for some item. No one would doubt the likelihood of Miss E doing that.

Michael let himself into the darkened stateroom, noting that without its occupant, the place seemed smaller. Starting in the bathroom, he began his search. He found her on the floor of the clothes closet, and had he not been certain someone was there, he might have missed her completely. Only the toes of her cheap shoes gave her away. When Michael pushed aside the brightly colored kaftans, the girl, about sixteen and almost emaciated, looked up at him, her body tensed with fear.

She was pretty, though her hair was matted and the hand she pressed against her mouth had a raw scrape along the knuckles. In her eyes he read a hint of resignation. She'd probably been unable to believe she would escape whatever horrors she had experienced, and now her fears had proven true.

Michael put a finger to his lips. "Say nothing of this, not to her or to anyone," he ordered in Thai. "If you obey, you will be safe." When the girl nodded, he closed the closet door.

"I looked everywhere," he told Lee later. "There's nothing unusual in Miss E's stateroom."

"She must have a hiding place elsewhere on the ship," Lee said. "I am not wrong in this."

"I'm sorry I wasn't more help, Inspector. I'll continue to keep you informed."

"Do so," Lee ordered. "It is my aim to end this woman's crimes before your ship returns to Singapore."

Michael had hoped Lee would give up, but his comment indicated otherwise. Miss E was still in danger of being arrested.

Michael was determined that would not happen.

Chapter Sixteen

Chicago-November, 1977

Franklin Tharp suffered a second stroke in the fall of 1977, and this time the doctors couldn't save him. Cathy did her best to ease E's burdens, going with her to the church to speak with the priest, arranging a dinner for several hundred people after the service, and informing callers that Mrs. Terzis was resting but felt grateful for the outpouring of love and support for her father. She couldn't help but notice that the response from the community was *pro forma* and, like Franklin himself, lacking warmth and humanity.

When a car pulled up out front she went to the door, expecting another solemn visitor or respectful deliveryman. Instead it was Drake, and her face lit until she glimpsed Patricia scowling behind him. Farther back, the nanny helped their two children exit the car, picking up a blanket and some toys before following them up the steps.

"We got an earlier flight than planned," Drake said. "Courtesy of knowing whom to ask."

Cathy opened the door wide. "Please come in. Mrs. Leon has your rooms ready."

Drake stepped aside to let his wife and children, a sweet-faced boy and a lively younger girl, enter. Patricia sniffed as she passed, as if she'd caught a whiff of something objectionable. Drake shot Cathy a look of apology. "Where is Elvera?"

"In Mr. Tharp's study. She and Richard are going over some things."

Patricia turned to Drake. "He's not even cold yet, and she's in there figuring it all out."

"Patti," Drake began, but she started upstairs, her back stiff. Drake turned to the taxi driver who stood on the porch, loaded with suitcases. "Set them inside if you will. I'll take them up later."

Familiar with the house and Mrs. Leon's bottomless cookie jar, Drake's kids headed for the kitchen. After a shy greeting for Cathy, the nanny disappeared after them.

"How is she doing?" Drake asked.

"She hated seeing him struggle every day, so at least that's over."

"And how are you?" His expression conveyed understanding that time could dull but not remove the pain of the losses she'd suffered.

"I'm okay." She found herself wanting to tell Drake about Thailand, about Jay Taksin and his plea for assistance. After the dinner party, she'd gone to hear him speak to a local women's group. With fiery passion, Taksin described the confusing mess that had plagued Southeast Asia for two decades, draining Thailand's resources. As he showed slides that tugged at the heart he explained, "As many as two million Cambodians are currently homeless. My government tries to see that those at our border are fed, housed, and protected, but the job is too large for one nation to manage. We need help."

"Those poor Thais," a woman next to Cathy said softly. "How awful to have all that chaos right next door."

To Cathy it seemed one's sympathy might better be directed at the displaced thousands, but Taksin had gone on. "The chaos in Cambodia is not resolving; in fact, it seems to grow worse. Different factions vie to control the country, and periodically different groups—gangs, to be precise—sweep through, taking whatever food and valuables they can find and either enticing or forcing young men to join their ranks. Recently the nation came under the control of the Khmer Rouge, a group led by a vicious dictator named Pol Pot. They mistreat their own people terribly, which has caused even more Khmer people to flee."

"How many refugees are currently at your border?" someone asked.

"It is impossible to count accurately, since they shift from one camp to another as events unfold, but the United Nations recently estimated 60,000 at Nong Samet."

Someone else asked, "That's just one camp?"

"Just one." Taksin's smile was sad. "Supplying the camps is a nightmare." Another slide clicked into place, showing people crowding around an old army deuce-and-a-half. It was clear the truck couldn't possibly have enough food under its tarpaulin cover for them all.

"If they don't receive help, many of those you see in this photo will die." After pausing to let that sink in, Taksin continued, "We work with all the government agencies in the region, but a small group of concerned Thais formed our own organization in order to take more direct action." He smiled in a self-deprecating way. "I am here to ask you to pay for it."

Cathy left the meeting affected by the fire in Taksin's eyes. At the library she did some reading in the stacks, confirming his claims. Being diplomatic, he hadn't mentioned that American bombs had contributed greatly to the problem. In attempts to defeat the Vietcong, U.S. forces had destroyed homes, farms, and transportation systems in the countries bordering Vietnam. The American people and most of Congress had been unaware the raids were being carried out, but that didn't make the destruction any less real.

One op-ed she found was completely unsympathetic: *These people have been killing each other for centuries*, the writer claimed. *The U.S. cannot continue to serve as policeman for the world.*

Cathy disagreed, believing Americans couldn't absolve themselves of responsibility for the chaos they'd caused, even if other factors played into the situation. She admired Jay Taksin for focusing on how to fix things and not on who was to blame. And for forming his own relief group. "We're not as big as UNCOR or Catholic Relief Services," he'd explained with a smile that revealed white, even teeth. "But we are a sneaky lot, using alternate methods to outsmart the bandits and warlords and provide help to those who need it most."

It was hard to resist the pull of Taksin's personality and the desire she felt to be more than a cog in the business world. Her work at Mizz had allowed Cathy to catch up on her bills, so she owed no one anything, at least financially. The atmosphere at Tharp House was always tense, and Franklin's death was likely to ignite problems that had smoldered between E and Richard for some time. Cathy was ready to be somewhere else, ready to do something she believed was worthwhile. Two things held her back: loyalty to E and imagining herself in a foreign place, adapting to a strange culture, with no friends and no familiar faces. The idea was intriguing, but she didn't think she was capable of such courage. Even if it might help thousands of people.

As a State Department liaison, Drake no doubt knew about the situation in Thailand. He might even know Jay Taksin. If Cathy told him she wanted to join Taksin's group, would Drake approve, or would he pat her on the head and suggest she stay home and organize a funding drive for UNICEF?

Bonnie and Bobby emerged from the kitchen, each munching on a chocolate chip cookie. The moment passed, and Cathy didn't mention the dramatic life change she'd been considering.

Franklin Tharp's funeral day dawned bright and uncommonly warm for autumn. The service was dignified but long, with all the obsequies observed. The dinner afterward was noisy and cheerful, as funeral dinners tend to be. Once people have done what they can for the departed they strive for normalcy, relieved that they remain alive.

Cathy made sure the meal went smoothly, saw to the caterer's needs, and arranged for the parking attendants to get food and a soda. When it seemed everything was under control, she whispered in Elvera's ear that she was heading back to the house. E gave her a hug. "You've been wonderful, as usual. Thanks."

Outside, Patricia Compton-Tharp leaned against a railing, dragging on a cigarette as if she were taking her last breath. She wore a dress of black crepe in the empire style, which flattered her thin figure and showcased her large breasts. On the grass beside her was the veiled, wide-brimmed black hat she'd worn at the service.

"Well, well, Miss Cathy Whatever." Tossing the butt on the sidewalk, Patricia crushed it with a dainty foot. "What are you doing out here when you could be inside chasing my husband around the room?"

Cathy was so shocked that for a moment she couldn't speak. Finally, she managed in a carefully neutral voice, "I don't think that question deserves an answer."

Drake's wife leaned toward her, revealing a lot of cleavage and whiskey on her breath. "I've seen the way you look at him." Her upper lip curled. "And I've seen the way he looks at you."

"Mrs. Tharp, there is nothing between Drake and me. Nothing."

Patricia's voice rose to a scream. "You lying *whore*! You are screwing my husband anytime you get the chance, and I know it. Every time he comes to Chicago, I *know* Drake crawls into your bed."

A face appeared in the doorway, and the caterer asked, "Is anything wrong out here?"

"You're damned right something's wrong." Patricia pointed a red-tipped claw at Cathy. "*She* stole a man from his wife and children."

Unable to think of anything else to do, Cathy ran. Ignoring the shouts behind her, she fled to the street, where a taxi sat waiting for a fare. "Get me away from here!" she ordered as she threw herself into the back seat. As they drove away, she turned to look back. Patricia Tharp leaned over the metal railing, her face red and twisted, her eyes bulging. She was still screaming accusations. The sound stayed in Cathy's ears long after it was impossible to hear the words.

Back at the house, she could neither sit nor stand still. Pacing her room, she tried to decide what she should have done when Patricia started her rant. Walk away? Slap her, like they did to hysterical people in the movies? And what should she do now?

She was still pacing when a light knock came at her door. "Cathy?"

Drake. She considered pretending she wasn't there. She didn't want to face him, never wanted to have to face him again. Patricia sensed what Cathy thought she'd kept hidden. While it wasn't true she and Drake were lovers, she'd been in love with him since those first days on Mackinac Island.

"Cathy, please. We need to talk."

"Face your troubles," her mother used to say. "They're never as bad when you look them in the eye." She opened the door.

Drake seemed smaller somehow, as if what happened had diminished him. "I'm so sorry," he said gently. "I knew Patti was teetering on the edge of a breakdown, but I never thought—" Stepping back, he said, "We should go downstairs. God help us if we're found in your room."

She managed a shaky laugh. "I don't think God intercedes at times like this."

"No." He said nothing more until they were in Franklin Tharp's study with the door ajar. "I'm sorry, Cathy. So very, very sorry."

"No need to keep repeating yourself." It sounded bitchy, but she didn't care.

"Patti's parents took her to their place for tonight. Her father knows of a private hospital where her mother's gone more than once to 'rest.' They'll get her off the booze and pills." His grimace was meant to be a smile. "I've promised that if he can convince her to do that, I'll find work closer to home so I can keep an eye on her." He turned to look out the window at the dying garden. "I kept...I told myself it wasn't that bad."

Cathy knew exactly what he meant, since she'd spent much of her childhood telling herself the same things about her mother's problem. Patricia Tharp was a drunk who'd made the situation worse with what the Rolling Stones called "Mother's Little Helper."

Turning her focus to the present, Cathy asked, "What am I supposed to do now, Drake?"

"Anyone who knows Patti won't believe what she said."

Cathy slapped at the air disgustedly. "People want to believe things like this, and you know it. They'll say where there's smoke, there's fire."

His head drooped, but he tried again. "Elvera knows there's nothing going on between us. Maybe she can—" His voice wavered, and he added in a rush, "The worst part, Cathy, is that I wish it were true."

His words unlocked a part of her she'd kept tightly closed, and she wrapped her arms around herself to keep from reaching out to him. "Me too, Drake. It's wrong, but I do."

He stepped closer. "I fell in love with you that summer on Mackinac Island."

"Why didn't you say something?"

"Father and Todd Compton expected me to marry Patricia." Drake stretched a hand toward her and then pulled it back as if retaking control. "Until I met you, I had no idea that's not how it had to be."

She recalled how her mother had been sure Gary was Cathy's perfect mate. How much had that played into her feelings for him?

"We marry people with backgrounds similar to our own."

"Because we're expected to."

"I thought I was happy as Gary's wife. I told myself what I felt for you was some romantic dream I conjured up." After a moment she added, "When you said you were promised to someone else, I told myself the dream was over."

"I didn't know how to tell them I wanted to end the engagement. I'd disappointed my father in so many ways, but I knew." He looked away. "Before the wedding, Patti's father sat me down once and explained that she was what he termed flighty. 'If you're firm with her,' he said, 'she'll grow out of it.' I told myself I could do that, but in the end, I went all over the world to avoid dealing with a wife I don't love. And now she's had a breakdown in front of everyone, and it's my fault."

Cathy almost told Drake he wasn't to blame, but she knew that was useless. She had yet to convince herself that nothing she could have done would have prevented her father from leaving or her family from dying in a car accident.

"I should have been honest back then, with my father, with Patti, and with you." His eyes focused somewhere over her head. "But you were, what, sixteen?"

"Seventeen," she whispered.

"I left thinking that in a year, once you finished high school, I'd return to the island and make you fall in love with me. Then I'd tell Patti and our parents I couldn't go through with the wedding."

"The first part wouldn't have been difficult." Her smile was tinged with sadness. "I was crazy for you from the first chicken salad sandwich."

"You didn't show it. And the first thing you told Elvera the next summer was that you were engaged to be married. I figured you mustn't have felt the connection I did."

"I felt it, Drake," she objected. "I—" She stopped, unable to explain. Social distance. Fear of rejection. The old teaching that girls don't pursue boys. And most important, his mention of a fiancée. "I was stupid."

"I still think of you, Cathy. I can't stop."

Without conscious decision, she closed the distance between them and slid her hands around his neck. Drake pulled her close, bending his face to hers. The kiss was everything she'd imagined: sweet, hot, and tinged with joy and sorrow. When it was over, she clung to him, savoring the knowledge that if he could have done things differently, he would have.

"Oh, God!"

They stepped apart, every inch the guilty pair, as Elvera stormed into the room. "I spent the last hour explaining away what Patricia is telling everyone. Now I see that she was right."

"Elvera, no," Drake objected. "She's completely wrong."

"Should I forget what I just saw?" Elvera paused to calm herself. "Cathy, can I speak with my brother alone?"

Numbly, Cathy left the room, closing the door, but she couldn't make herself go upstairs yet. Since their voices rang with anger, it was easy to hear what was said.

"How could you, Drake?"

"How could I what, E? We've done nothing to be ashamed of."

"I saw you wrapped around each other like two pythons. Are you going to stand there and lie to me?"

"I've never lied to you, E."

"Geez, Drake. Old man Compton was about to back Richard's new deal with Bay Area Bank. Now he probably won't even take our calls, all because you can't keep your dick in your pants."

There was a long silence. "Your concern in all this is a missed business opportunity?"

"Well, no. That isn't all of it." E sounded ashamed of herself, and her tone softened. Cathy put her ear to the door, not caring who came along and caught her eavesdropping. "Drake, your wife is nuts. I get that occasionally you need to be with someone who isn't drunk or doped up. But did it have to be now, and did it have to be my best friend?"

Drake's voice went low, but Cathy heard every word. "I don't think we need to talk about this further, Elvera. In fact, right now I wouldn't care if I never speak to you again."

An hour later, when she'd calmed herself with time and a vodka and tonic, E went to Cathy's door and knocked. "Cath? We need to talk."

She got no answer, and when she turned the knob, the door opened to an empty room. Cathy was gone. She'd taken the old suitcase she'd brought from Michigan, her jeans, t-shirts, and tennis shoes. Everything else, anything Elvera's money had paid for, was left behind.

Chapter Seventeen

Cruise-Day 8, 8:24 a.m.

Michael had planned to follow Miss E on their next stop, Sarrahip, so he was irritated when Marilyn ordered him to help deep-clean a cabin where a passenger had become gravely ill. "We doubt it's anything contagious," she told the three crew members assigned to the duty, "but we don't want Legionnaires' or something like it. Here's what policy requires we do." She handed each of them a sheet with extensive instructions. "Thank your lucky stars she didn't use the pool, or we'd be in a world of hurt."

Michael tried to get out of the duty, saying he'd planned to visit friends in the area, but Marilyn put up a hand. "Low seniority gets the jobs no one else wants, Kanda. It's how the world works." Her last words were to the group. "Get it done while most passengers are ashore. That way we'll have fewer questions to answer."

When Miss E left the ship sometime that morning, Michael and the others were on the opposite side and two decks up, wearing rubber gloves and masks and scrubbing any surface the sick passenger might have touched since they'd set sail. The chore was completed by the time people began returning to the ship in twos and threes, carrying silk scarves or floral-scented, carved soaps they'd purchased at Buddha Mountain or Monkey Island. Miss E was absent at dinnertime, but she called when Michael was getting ready for bed.

"I've decided I want the shower chair," she said when he answered. "Can you get it for me yet tonight?" Glancing at the clock, he saw there were only three minutes left of what was technically night, but he said, "I'll bring it as soon as I can, Miss E."

"Good. I'll wait up for you."

Muttering to himself, Michael re-dressed and went in search of someone with keys to the storerooms. He didn't know the night staff well, but the mention of Miss E made the man on duty grin. "You're not the first to come in the middle of the night on an errand for that one."

First, they had to figure out where shower chairs were kept, but with the magic of computers, that wasn't too difficult. Next, they made their way to the correct storage area, down passages the clients would never see. In the hot, poorly lit storeroom, items were piled in no apparent order. It was hard to pick out individual things, but after some searching Michael said, "There." Against a bulkhead, under some deck chairs, they spotted a simple aluminum stool with a curved plastic seat.

Getting to it was the next problem. The two men moved larger pieces to reach the spot and then shifted the deck chairs, one by one. Finally, Michael reached the shower chair and carried it to the hallway while his companion restacked what they'd disturbed. Dusty and sweating from the effort, they exited the storeroom. Michael considered going to his cabin to freshen up but decided Miss E should see what he'd gone through to grant her untimely wish.

He knocked. "It's Michael, Miss E."

"Yes?" She sounded as if she had no idea why he'd be at her door at one-twenty a.m.

"I have your shower chair."

"Leave it outside the door. I'll come for it when I finish this row of beads."

He considered arguing, but what could he say? *I want to come in? I need to know what you're up to?* He held no sway over Elvera Tharp's mercurial moods. Setting the chair next to the door, Michael returned to his room and threw himself onto his bed, determined to forget Miss E and snatch the few hours of sleep available before he returned to duty at six.

When he delivered her breakfast later that morning, Miss E made no reference to the shower chair, which sat in a corner of the bathroom. She seemed unusually interested in her scrambled eggs, toast, and sausage, and she again dismissed Michael from cleaning duties. "I've hardly been here," she said, taking a slice of toast and then re-covering the plate. "The cleaning can wait a day."

Michael searched for an excuse to stay. If he listened carefully, would he hear someone moving around?

"I'll make up the bed," he said in a businesslike tone. "Then the place will look neat if you happen to have company." She didn't argue, though the set of her jaw said she wasn't happy about his cheerful insistence.

"There are tornados in the American Midwest this week," he said as he pulled the sheets up. "Isn't that where you're from originally?"

Her nostrils pinched. "Are you writing a book?"

"I might." He fluffed the pillows and set them aside. "I could call it *Meals and Insults with Elvera Tharp*."

"I'd sue the pants off you," she said grumpily. "My life is my life."

"Fine. I won't write a book." He pulled the bedcover into place, smoothed the surface with a hand, and turned to her, his expression earnest. "I would never gossip about you, no matter what I might learn."

"Discretion is commendable in a servant."

He ignored her condescending tone. "You do come from the Midwest, though. I hear it in your speech."

"Yes. Chicago."

"Do you ever go back home?"

"Home is not a place, Mike. It's a sense of belonging in a spot where one feels safe."

"You didn't find that in Chicago?"

"I did for a time." She sipped at her coffee. "But things have a way of changing. One day, home wasn't home anymore."

"Aren't there people there you'd like to see again?"

"I have no people, not anymore." Though she spoke calmly, there was a world of pain in the statement.

Sensing a softening of her protective shell, Michael said, "It sounds like you lost someone you cared a great deal for."

"Someone?" Her eyes, filled with pain, met his for a moment. "Too many someones, Mike. Too many. And once that happens, living becomes no more than a chore you have to face every day."

As he left the cabin, Michael found himself wondering what it would have been like to be raised by a woman like Miss E, one who might have encouraged his development, supported his curiosity, and allowed him to sharpen his wits on the stone of her experience.

Chapter Eighteen

Thailand-January, 1980

Thailand was beautiful. Cathy had never seen anything like it, though she smiled at the thought. What *had* she seen in twenty-seven years, outside a small portion of the Midwestern United States? Her home in Michigan was green in spring and summer, but here the green was intense, like a dial had been turned to its highest level. Her seatmate on the plane, a pedantic older man from California, said it was due to rain that fell daily for almost half the year. "Precipitation from May to September," he said in a tone that hinted she'd soon tire of it. "Nothing like you've experienced before."

Cathy stayed at Jay Taksin's house in Bangkok for a few weeks to acclimate to the time, culture, temperature, and newness of everything. She was somewhat nervous about staying at a bachelor's home, but the servants, three sober, silent maids and a gardener who never looked directly at anyone, seemed to regard it as normal. She was given a lovely room that faced the garden and a door that latched on the inside.

Made simply, in traditional style, the house sat on stilts. The high gable roof had a shape at its center that Jay said symbolized the halo of the sun but also allowed cooking smoke to escape. Long, overhanging eaves protected from sun or rain, and a latticed terrace invited outside lounging or dining in good weather. A high open space under the house provided storage for extra household items and bicycles.

Though Jay was a busy man, he took the time to show Cathy Bangkok's wonders. The markets, with rows and rows of jewelry shops and tailors who could custom-make clothing in an amazingly short time. She loved the flower market, where lotus flowers of many shapes and sizes scented the air, offered for sale as food, perfume, medicine, or memorials to be placed at shrines. Westerners called Bangkok the Venice of the East, Jay told her, and the eighty-three canals that cut through the city fascinated Cathy. The boats that crowded along them, serving as shops for sellers of fruits, vegetables, fish, and flowers, seemed both a colorful and efficient way of getting goods to customers. Smells seemed stronger there than anywhere else she'd been, but she couldn't identify individual odors. A blend of canals, plants, foods, and auto exhaust.

They visited the Golden Pagoda to see the Buddha whose gold had been hidden for centuries under a protective coating of stucco but was now on glorious display. Jay took her to a popular amusement place, Kimland, where talented kickboxers and graceful dancers performed. One afternoon he rented a motorbike. Cathy was nervous, since there were vehicles everywhere and few traffic signals. Drivers policed themselves—or did not. Ceding right-of-way was voluntary, and she witnessed the beginning of a disagreement between two taxi drivers. As Jay maneuvered around them, one got out of his car, a tire iron in hand. Cathy looked away, unwilling to see more.

Jay motored down some lesser streets to avoid traffic, and she saw the stark contrasts of Bangkok: lights and enticements for tourists, squalor and hopelessness for poorer residents. Everywhere noise, voices, engines, animals, and music flowing from the open doors of this bar or that. Bangkok was an assault on her senses, so much that was strange, so much that intrigued her.

Then they left the city. Jay wheeled with casual skill along narrow roads with rice paddies on either side, passing pedestrians and animal-drawn carts at a speed that was a little frightening. Here lotus flowers grew on the surface of the water while their roots reached down to the mud below. They carpeted the surface in shades of pink, and Jay stopped to let her stand at the water's edge for a few minutes, breathing in their scent and reveling in their numbers.

Those quiet moments in the country re-emphasized the craziness of Bangkok as they returned to the house. Cathy wondered which Thailand was real. Men in business suits or women in traditional *chut thai* (which Jay said meant "Thai outfit")? The white, quiet temples; the green, thick countryside; or the noisy, bustling city? In these tumultuous times, even the Thai people seemed unsure who they were.

New sights, new sounds, and new ideas assailed her daily, even hourly. It was strange to understand nothing of what was said around her, even when she guessed she was the topic of conversation. For a day or two Jay treated her formally, asking what she wanted to see and where she chose to dine. She left those decisions up to him, and he showed a sure sense of what would amuse or surprise her. Attractive, charming, intelligent, and concerned for humanity, Jay was unlike any man she'd met before. Cathy felt lucky to be his friend and ally.

Jay claimed the best restaurants were in hotels, so they dined at the Nana and the Asian, seated among Westerners, often reporters there to keep the American public informed on conditions in Southeast Asia. With his guidance, Cathy became more adventurous in her eating, trying fish paste and dishes flavored with various curries, lemongrass, basil, ginger, and coconut milk. Though Thai food was spicier than she was used to, she found she liked most of the unfamiliar tastes. Everywhere people were polite and friendly, augmenting or even replacing lingual communication with smiles and bows.

An incident about two weeks after she arrived in Bangkok deepened Cathy's understanding of Jay's work. She'd gone to her room for the night but realized she'd left the book she was reading on the terrace. As she went to retrieve it, she heard Jay and another man talking. The other began in Thai, but Jay ordered, "English, Ram. No sense letting the servants know our business."

"He pleads with us to get his son out soon." The man's English was heavily accented, and Cathy had to wait a beat before the words made sense. "The warlords search constantly for healthy men for their armies."

"It won't be easy to do," Jay warned.

The man's voice was raspy, but confidence vibrated in its timbre. "Have I ever failed you?"

Jay chuckled. "You have not, Ram. Do as you think best, and I'll see you when you return."

Before Cathy realized it, the conversation was over, and Jay was coming up the steps. She was trapped on the terrace, her white nightgown lit by moonlight.

"Cathy?"

"I'm sorry, Jay. I didn't mean to eavesdrop."

"I know you didn't. But what you heard must not be repeated."

Things she'd heard and noticed came together in her mind. "You smuggle people out of the camps."

He nodded. "When we can." Stepping toward her, he put a hand on her arm. It was a gesture of pleading, but his touch felt like fire. "You could be part of it, if you are willing."

"You want my help?"

"I need guides. You could lead those who might otherwise die in the camps to freedom."

Though the idea scared her, Cathy liked it. Delivering sacks of rice was one thing. Helping someone get a new chance at life was something else. "Do you think I can do that?"

Jay pulled her closer. "I knew it from the first moment I saw you."

"What if someone figures out what I'm doing?"

He chuckled. "Americans are seen here as oddly individualistic, and my people are a polite lot. Few will question what an eccentric Western woman does or where she goes."

After that, Cathy learned more about Jay's true mission. While he did provide supplies and call the world's attention to the situation at the Thai border, his most rewarding task was smuggling people out of the camps, where life was unbearably harsh. "Ram does the actual rescue work," Jay told her. "As often as we can, we remove those who are in danger from gangs, Khmer recruiters, or brutish warlords."

"Can't the government protect them—either yours or their own?"

A smile revealed how naïve her question was. "The governments of Laos, Vietnam, and Cambodia are in chaos and can't protect anybody. We Thais do what we can, but we are overwhelmed by sheer numbers."

"But with so many, how do you know who to help?"

"Resources are limited." He ran a hand through his dark hair and let it rest on the back of his neck. "We can help only those in dire need."

Cathy's job would be to take a post at an almost finished school some distance from the camps. In addition to duties there, she would secretly shelter the people Ram smuggled into Thailand. "At present, Ram himself leads them through the hills to safety," Jay told her, "but if you are willing to pick up the 'packages,' as we call them, and hide them for a day or two, I can send someone to guide them onward when it's safe. That will allow Ram to spend his time arranging more escapes, so we can help more people."

"Where do they go when they escape?"

"Mostly Australia, the U.S., or Canada. Finding new homes for them is one reason I travel so much." Catching his reflection in a mirror, Jay adjusted his collar. "Those who speak French might go to Quebec or Paris. Some stay in Thailand, hoping someday to return home. In those cases, we find a village willing to take them in. Rural communities often welcome a strong worker and an infusion of new blood."

"It's good work you do." Cathy helped him flatten the collar. "I'm glad to help, even if it is illegal."

Jay caught her hands in his. "You must never tell anyone what you do, not people you meet, not those you write to at home, no one."

"Of course."

They made up a backstory for Cathy to use at the school where Jay planned to place her. She'd claim to be a recent divorcée in search of a more meaningful life. Her hobby would be photography, which would provide an excuse to wander the countryside at different times of day. Jay bought her a camera and equipment, and she practiced until she understood f-stops and could take decent, if not particularly inspiring, photographs.

A problem they had to work out was Cathy's inability to speak any language but her own. After some discussion, she proposed a simple message system. "I learned a little beading as a girl," she told Jay. "What if we send information coded in bracelets? Four red beads could mean four days from now. Two blue beads could mean two a.m."

Jay nodded approvingly. "Simple for all to use." He put a hand on her arm. "You will begin important work soon. Are you ready?"

"I am," she replied. "I think I've been ready for a long time."

Chapter Nineteen

Cruise Ship-Day 9, 6:43 a.m.

"We'll anchor in Trat for two days," Michael said as he stacked Miss E's empty plates. "Do you have plans?"

"As a matter of fact, I'm going inland."

Michael stopped. "With whom?"

"With myself." Before he could speak, she added, "I've been on my own for decades, and I haven't died yet."

"I could go along and smooth the way." The look on her face signaled no, and he hurried on. "It's what I do—what I've done all my life. I can make the trip easier for you."

"For a big, fat fee."

He pressed his lips together. "You'd only have to pay my expenses."

The glare she focused on him was so sharp it almost hurt. "What's the attraction in traveling with me?"

"First, I've never seen this part of my country. Second, and here's more of that honesty you asked for, travel in remote areas of Thailand is hard for someone of your age and condition."

She regarded him slant-wise for several seconds before replying somewhat resentfully, "All right. Hire someone with a decent car. I'll pay our expenses and provide you a reasonable wage for seeing to the details." She sighed. "As long as we're being honest, I'll admit I've lost all desire to deal with snotty hotel clerks and greedy porters."

"What's the reason for the trip?"

Her manner turned icy. "If you want to come, keep your

questions to yourself."

"Fine." Michael suppressed a sigh of irritation. "Give me a time, and I'll be ready."

When the ship docked, they left together, Miss E leaning heavily on her cane and Michael slowed by an assortment of items she'd given him to carry, including a shopping bag loaded with gift-wrapped packages. He'd located a driver willing to do an overnight excursion, which he paid for from a neat roll of baht Miss E provided. The car was a beat-up Honda, but the motor ticked smoothly, and the seats were intact.

After Michael loaded their things, he joined his companion in the back. She spoke to the driver in Thai, though he claimed his English was "very excellent," and explained the route he should take. Under darkening skies, they maneuvered through the city and then traveled north on country roads, dodging squawking chickens, belligerent oxen, and unhappy pedestrians with equal carelessness. Unfazed by the near misses, Miss E wiped dust from her watch face and observed, "We should be there by six."

Cowed by her earlier outburst, Michael didn't ask where they were going. From her instructions he gathered their destination was a village near the Cambodian border. He spent half the time wondering what Miss E's purpose was, and the other half trying to figure out what Inspector Lee was up to. He'd gone quiet, which couldn't be good.

After a half hour of silence, Miss E made a single concession to Michael's curiosity. "I'm visiting old friends. With any luck, we'll be there and back before the rains start."

"This village is where you once lived?"

She looked out the window. "I'm not sure anyone I knew back then will still be around."

"You didn't stay in contact over the years?"

"When I left, I had no intention of returning." She smiled, and for once Miss E seemed human. "Now, I suppose, I'm feeling my age."

After a few hours she began pointing out landmarks. "That market's in the same place it was forty years ago." The car slowed slightly as it rolled through a village with a dozen businesses lined up along the road. The more established had awnings attached; the lesser ones were merely blankets laid on the ground with goods set in baskets atop them. A man weighed meat on a metal scale, a dozen children in shorts and t-shirts played between stalls, and a woman fried *roti* in a wok. Ignoring the cloud of dust the car raised, vendors squatting near the road shouted their wares. "Dragonfruit! Best of best!" A man held out a ripe mangosteen he'd cut in two with a machete. "Very good," he proclaimed, his smile showing more teeth missing than present. "Very good for lady."

Michael would have liked something to eat, but Miss E ignored the clamor. The driver navigated the crowd using the horn and a gesturing arm out the window, and then they were on the open road again. Looking at a battered map he found in the seat pocket, Michael realized they were heading toward the border, in the area where refugee camps had once been located. As a child he'd heard stories of the lawlessness in those places. His teachers had explained that the Khmer interlopers could not be allowed into their country, lest their corrupt blood and uncivilized ways destroy Thailand, the "land of the free."

That recalled what Inspector Lee had told him, and he asked, "Miss E, do you think a person should disobey a law he believes is wrong?"

She was staring out the window, and she didn't look at him as she answered. "In my experience, laws often support fears, not facts."

"For example?"

"Japanese internment camps. When World War II broke out,

fear said that Japanese Americans might spy for Japan or undermine U.S. efforts to win. No evidence supported that fear, and putting thousands of people into camps was a terrible idea. But in that moment, inhumane laws were drafted and put in place." With a sniff of disdain, she went on, "We don't like to admit it, but humans often operate by herd mentality, just like other species. Someone shouts 'Danger! Danger!' and we stop thinking for ourselves. We do terrible things, claiming it's necessary for self-preservation."

"Then we don't have a duty to obey established law?"

Now she turned to him. "I'm saying we have a duty to use the brains we're given. In 1942, the people in my country convinced themselves that thousands of innocent people deserved terrible treatment, simply because they were different from what we call *us*." She shifted her hips, grimacing as she sought a more comfortable position. "*Us* versus *them* is a huge waste of humanity, but it goes on and on. We never learn."

Michael lapsed into silence, wondering how far Miss E would go to follow the dictates of her conscience. Would she fight for some refugee's freedom? Kill to save his life? What drove her?

"There. I remember that temple ruin." She pointed to a pile of old stones with a structure at one end that might once have been a wall. She tapped on the window with a fingernail. "And right next to it, a cell phone tower. Can you believe it?"

When they finally reached their destination, a town called Bang Salung, there were cars, shops, and people everywhere. Old mixed with new, creating a colorful, noisy song of life. A bus hissed and roared ahead of them. A scrawny chicken pecked at something in the gutter while a woman in traditional clothing led a child wearing a Mickey Mouse t-shirt across the street. Overhead, electrical wires of several thicknesses stretched in all directions, crossing and re-crossing in a maze that no doubt made maintaining power a nightmare.

Miss E looked dismayed. "I don't recognize anything."

"We'll find what you came for," Michael promised.

She made a curt gesture. "You don't even know what that is."

He shrugged. "As soon as you tell me, I'll help you find it."

Glowering at the street, she muttered, "Nothing looks right."

"In my experience, hotel clerks know where things are," Michael said. "All we have to do is ask."

He was right. A clerk at the first hotel they came to was able to direct them to Miss E's former home. Since both he and the lobby looked clean, Michael booked rooms for the night before returning to the car. They located the house, which Miss E said had once stood alone on the hillside but was now surrounded by neighbors. She recognized its pagoda-style roof, which stood out from the flat ones around it.

When the car stopped out front, she again seemed uncertain. "I left this place to my housekeeper. Will she be here after all this time?"

"Things here don't change as much as they do in the U.S." Michael opened the car door. "Let me go ask if—Who is it you're looking for?"

"Nin." He nodded and backed away.

When Michael returned, he reported, "They say Nin died years ago."

Miss E bit her lip. "I was afraid of that."

Giving her a sly smile, he said, "Nin's husband is in good health, if that helps. His name is Ram, and he lives with his granddaughter."

"Ram?" she said sharply. "Ram and Nin...?" That seemed to be more than she could digest.

"I have his address. Do you want to go there?" When Miss E nodded, Michael gave the driver directions and climbed back into the car.

On a street called *Soi Lingopolo*, in a modestly elegant house with a good amount of space around it and terraces on three sides, an old man sat alone in the last rays of the setting sun.

"Wait here," Miss E ordered.

Michael almost objected. Curiosity had built all day, and he'd hoped to sit in on the reunion. Unwilling to destroy the fragile bond they'd established, however, he remained quiet.

A few seconds later she said, "I'm afraid you'll have to help me."

In fact, he had to lift Miss E from the car. Her grimace when he set her on her feet revealed the price she was paying for her nostalgic journey. Nevertheless, when Michael handed her the porcelain-topped cane, she straightened her back and started up the path, head high.

"Do you want the packages you brought along?" he called after her.

Turning, she shook her head. "For Nin, a gift would have been a sign of affection. For Ram, it would be an insult."

The man on the terrace had seen the car pull up. Now he watched as Miss E approached, his face blank. Though he was probably eighty, Ram looked...not violent, perhaps, but capable. Able to do whatever he felt required to.

When recognition lit the old man's eyes, he rose and came to meet his guest. At the edge of the terrace they both stopped. For a moment it seemed they might embrace, but in the end, they only shook hands. Leading Miss E to a chair, Ram invited her to sit. He called, and a woman came outside and was introduced. She bowed deferentially, speaking in an excited tone. Michael heard her voice rise in a question, and the man answered for both himself and Miss E. The woman went back inside, returning in a few minutes with a tray containing food and the makings for tea. Once they were served, she bowed again and retreated.

As they sipped their tea, the couple seemed to forget the world around them, and the visit went on for some time. Miss E's voice came on the breeze from time to time as she told some story, and Ram made low, guttural responses, sometimes laughter, sometimes murmurs of encouragement. He spoke too, and Miss E listened with interest. Michael watched them, fascinated, as their driver smoked one cigarette after another. What were they saying? Who was Ram, and what did he mean to her?

When she finally rose to leave, Miss E again put out a hand. Ram took it in both of his as he said something that seemed heartfelt. She made a small negative gesture, but he spoke again, insisting on his view. Finally, she bowed her head, acknowledging what seemed to be a tribute.

As they drove away, she said, more to herself than to Michael, "I never guessed Nin and Ram would marry."

Rain fell the next morning as Michael went out to explore Bang Salung. Passing a café near the hotel, he saw Miss E inside with a Thai woman of about her age. When she saw him in the doorway, Miss E gestured for him to come in. "Michael, this is Sunan. Many years ago, she taught me Thailand's language and culture."

Michael made a *wai*. "*Sawadee Khrap*, Khun Sunan."

The woman nodded politely. "Good morning, Khun Michael." Beside her was one of the packages he'd carried from the ship, a gift that had been unwrapped and set aside.

Miss E smiled fondly at her guest, and he marveled at how sweet she appeared. "Unlike Ram, Sunan has a telephone and a listing, so I called her last night and invited her to breakfast."

"I was most pleased," Sunan said. "It has been many years, and of course I thought—"

Miss E interrupted, which was rude but not unusual. "We won't ask you to hang around while we reminisce, Michael. Go off and see the town. We'll start back around ten."

He would have liked to stay, but it was clear that wasn't how Miss E wanted it. "All right. I'll pick up our bags, settle the hotel bill, and meet you at the car."

Michael decided to spend the two hours of time learning what he could about Miss E's life in Bang Salung. Walking back to the area where Ram and his wife had once lived, he visited several shops and made small purchases, asking apparently innocent questions as he did. Khun Ram, he learned, had been born in Bang Salung. No one knew, at least no one would say, what his vocation had been. Eventually he'd wed Nin, who'd once been the housekeeper for an American lady. "A lucky girl," said an old woman, obviously still jealous despite the passage of years. "Nin was only a servant, yet she got a fine house and a husband with money."

"Do you remember the American lady who gave Nin the house?"

"Oh, yes, yes. We would see her in her garden sometimes. She had a limp, and a scar here." She touched her cheek. "She had no babies, and I think for her that was very hard."

"Why do you say that?"

"Because she took children into her home. Every few months a different one."

"Where did they come from?"

She shrugged, but her eyes didn't meet his. "Who knows?"

"And where did they go, this parade of children?" As he asked, Michael slid a few baht across the table that served as her sales counter.

Staring at the money, the woman spoke, her voice low so that only he could hear. "Some said Ram sold them, but my mother did not believe the American lady would do that." She shook her head.

"She was good to them, though my father said they were worthless Khmer brats who should have been left on their own side of the border."

When they returned to Trat that afternoon, Miss E directed the driver to a Christian church near the center of town. "Wait in the car," she ordered.

For a time Michael obeyed, but curiosity got the best of him. "I'm going to stretch my legs," he told the driver. Absorbed in his phone and his smoking, the man nodded absently. Michael slipped silently around the side of the building, peering in windows. At the back he found a small office where a man in nondescript clothing sat behind a desk. Across from him was Miss E, and the two spoke seriously, each gesturing as if giving directions. Though Michael had only a slit of vision through the shutters, he saw the man hand her something that looked like a photo. She looked at it for a few seconds, nodded, and gave it back. From her purse she took an object he couldn't identify until she laid it on the desktop. It was a bracelet, like those she made in her stateroom.

Back aboard ship, Michael found another message to call Inspector Lee. He also learned he'd been scheduled to help with dinner that evening. Though he was tired from the long car ride, there wasn't even time for a catnap.

"I have important news," Lee told Michael, who put the phone on speaker and changed into his uniform as he listened. "I learned that Miss E will accept the final package of the voyage at your last port of call before the ship heads back to Singapore."

"One last chance to catch her. A lucky break for you, Inspector."

Lee's tone changed. "I understand you and she went somewhere together."

"She asked me to arrange a trip to the village where she once lived. She paid well, so I agreed."

"And what did you learn from this time with her?"

"Very little, I'm afraid. I've told you how secretive she is."

"When last I saw your supervisor, Marilyn, she invited me to dine with her any time I can manage it. I intend to tell her I can meet that night. You must find a place on board where I can hide after our, um, date."

"You plan to stay all night?"

"Yes. When Miss E's package arrives, you and I will catch her red-handed, as the Americans say."

"You are a very determined man, Inspector Lee."

"Do not fail me, Kuhn Kanda. The Americans have another saying, something about skeletons in one's closet. I have done some checking, and I believe I know about your skeletons."

Not all of them, Michael thought as he returned to the kitchen. *But even one is too many.*

Due to Lee's warning, fatigue from the trip north, and the press of his duties, Michael had an unusual moment of clumsiness. Hurrying to get a melon sliced for the dessert bar, he cut the webbing of his thumb quite badly. Ha'o applied gauze and tape, and Michael donned plastic gloves to finish his work, but the cut re-opened each time he flexed his hand. "Go see Doc R," Marilyn finally ordered. "He's as chatty as your old Aunt Mabel, but he can stitch that up for you quick as lightning."

Having never visited the infirmary, Michael had only seen Reuben Spangler when he came to the dining room for meals. Like Miss E, Reuben was an institution on Wild Goose Cruise Lines, a Brooklyn Jew who'd gone in search of warmer climates after medical school and never returned home. "Doc R" had served aboard ships for more than thirty years, always cheerful, always chatty. It was assumed he would hand out nausea pills and treat cases of sunburn until the day he died.

Though long gone from home, Doc R still had the Brooklyn accent and attitude. In a small but well-supplied sick bay that smelled of isopropyl alcohol, he took one look at the cut and ordered, "Sit. If you're not a crybaby, I'll fix you up fine in no time."

Michael's thumb had begun throbbing, and he winced as the doctor probed the wound. When he started a stream of conversation, Michael realized the physician was trying to distract him from the pain with conversation. For a while he paid little attention, but something the old guy said sunk in. "You were hired by the owner himself?"

"Drake Tharp realized when he bought his first ship that potential passengers would like the idea of a real doctor aboard." Examining his work, he nodded, adding, "He was a good man."

Michael was so interested he forgot to dread the next stitch. "He was related to Miss E?"

"Her brother."

He thought about the deference of the staff and the lack of charges for Miss E's treatment on Wild Goose Lines. "Is she part owner?"

"I don't think so." Doc R seemed pleased to be able to share what he knew of the line's background. "Drake traveled a lot as a young man, in the Foreign Service or something like that. When he left, he bought himself a cruise ship. The first one made money, so he bought another. I think it surprised him how profitable Wild Goose Cruises got to be."

"Wild Goose. Drake. I get it," Michael said. "How long has Miss E been sailing with us?"

"Four years, maybe five." The old man frowned. "The first few times, Drake came with her. That was shortly after his wife died." He paused, frowning. "Now she was something."

"What do you mean?"

"A witch with a capital *B*, that's what I mean." The old man apparently didn't believe the adage about not speaking ill of the dead. "Patricia was one of those people who attempted suicide whenever life didn't suit her. I dealt with it once. Screaming, swearing, bleeding—ecch. A mess."

"You saved her life?"

He waggled a hand. "That one never cut too deep or waited too long to call for help, if you get my meaning. The worst part was that I could tell the poor guy was used to it."

"Attempted suicide as a spousal management technique?"

He shrugged. "Some people have a deep need to control those they care about."

"You say she died. Was it…?"

"Suicide? Oh, no. Pancreatitis killed Patti Tharp, as it does many who abuse the booze." Squinting, he added one more stitch and then patted Michael's hand like a fond grandpa. "You did great."

"And when she was gone, Miss E started sailing with her brother."

"The lady has no use for doctors, so I seldom see her, but Drake seemed happier those last years." The doctor dumped the bloody gauze into a trash can and let the lid drop into place with a clang. "Keep it dry, and if you feel like hanging from the yardarm, use the other hand."

Michael rose to leave. "How did Drake Tharp die?"

"Massive stroke. I'm told his father went the same way."

As he left, Michael smiled to himself. One never knew when something that seemed like a setback was instead a step forward. Serendipity.

Chapter Twenty

Thailand-1980

It was almost inevitable that Cathy and Jay became lovers. He was an attractive man, and she'd been lost in her sea of grief for too long. Gently he seduced her, offering strength, encouragement, and passion to replace, however feebly, love.

Gary had been Cathy's only partner, and she found Jay's lovemaking surprising, sometimes embarrassing. He chuckled when she turned off the lights before disrobing or wrapped herself in a towel after a bath. "Why do you hide such a beautiful body from me?" he asked.

"It's my Catholic upbringing, I suppose. Fornication is a sin." *With you, I enjoy sin too much*, she thought.

"I do not consider what we do to be fornication," he responded. "Aren't we created with these feelings, that we might experience joy?"

His argument made Cathy see differences between what she'd been taught and what felt like truth. Prudishness had limited her experiences with Gary who, like her, thought of sex as something couples did but didn't talk about. A decade past virginity, Cathy had discovered there was more to physical pleasure than hurried couplings in the missionary position. Maybe Billy Joel was right about Catholic girls starting too late.

Jay was pleased that she'd accepted a role in his operation. "You must be ready when a call comes," he warned. "Ram often doesn't know when the chance for an escape will arise, so notice might be short."

Cathy had met Ram before he left Bangkok. A thin, hard man,

mostly monosyllabic, he called to mind the expressionless cowboys in Sergio Leone movies. He'd been barely polite to Cathy, and she guessed he had little respect for women in general, American women even less.

"How does he get people out of the camps?" she asked when he'd gone.

"It's best you only know your part." Jay touched her lips lightly. "Safer for all of us."

Cathy shivered. If she were caught, she'd be able to name only Jay and Ram. Secrecy protected her as well, making authorities less able to follow an escapee's trail to her door.

Though the prospect of danger frightened her, Cathy also felt a thrill of anticipation. This was what she needed: the chance to do something important. No more arranging events for pampered housewives. No more fake smiles when business contacts asked if there was "someone special" in her life. Cathy Charbonneau no longer struggled to look chic or be social. Now she would struggle to save lives.

On the day she reported to her post, Cathy almost chickened out. In a battered jeep that rattled her bones, she and Jay drove first to a small village near the Nong Samet camp for displaced persons. Jay showed Cathy the hut where she'd pick up her packages in the dark of night and lead them away from the horrors of the camp.

Leaving the border behind, they snaked uphill along a timid stream Jay said changed to a swollen torrent during the rainy season. Stealing glances over the edge, Cathy glimpsed between trees the sandy banks below, where a few dugouts floated along a pier. As their path rose, the sound of the river's passage went from a merry babble beside them to silence far below.

"The school is about two-thirds of the way up the mountain," Jay told her. "This road continues past it, through a pass, and down the other side." The jeep hit a hole and jolted sideways, sending a pain up Cathy's spine and giving a heart-stopping view of the drop below. Jay remained in control, his strong hands guiding the vehicle back from the edge.

The site he'd chosen for her, a school being built by a German missionary, had two advantages: its location, which was within a few hours' walking distance of Nong Samet, and a cave Ram had discovered in a rocky outcrop that rose behind the school. "The cave is perhaps twenty feet up and therefore removed from normal coming and going," Jay said. "Hide your guests there and provide them with food and water. Within a day or two, someone will come and take them on."

The plateau on which the Martin Luther School sat looked like a giant had sliced a chunk of mountain away with a knife. About half the size of a football field, the site was too rocky for farming but was central to several mountain villages. Four mud brick buildings had been constructed, two small huts for the live-in staff, and an even smaller hut for a privy. The largest building, the school itself, had at present half a roof and no interior walls. Cathy would help the women who'd founded the school get it finished and ready for use.

As they neared, she saw that the compound had a low, mud wall around it. It was meant to discourage wild animals, Jay said, adding that it wouldn't keep out earwigs, scorpions, spiders, and caterpillars that bit or stung with painful results.

"Your hosts will teach you what you need to know about living here," he said as she regarded her new home. "Ram will wait a week for you to settle in. Then he will expect you to begin your real work."

"It's...remote." Looking back the way they'd come, she asked, "Will you visit sometimes?"

"When I can." Jay met her gaze. "I realize this is not easy, Cathy, but think of the good you will do."

"What if I get lost trying to find Nong Samet in the dark?"

His voice took on a chiding tone. "The way is easy. You simply follow the road downhill and turn left at the end. The way back is the opposite: climb until you see the school."

She nodded, unwilling to admit to fear, and again Jay emphasized the need for discretion. "Don't question the guides or chat with the packages. Do only as Ram or I tell—" He rephrased. "—ask you to do."

"All right." Cathy lapsed into silence, wondering if she was capable of the deception required for the task. Never in her life had she lied to those around her. Never had she hidden her actions and motives from people who trusted her.

That brought a bitter thought. What had being trustworthy gained her? She'd been falsely accused before the whole world, and even her best friend believed she'd done wrong. Besides, deception was essential now, for the lives of the packages, and possibly her own life as well.

At the compound, Jay braked and put the gearshift in neutral. Two women emerged from the school building, the older one sheltering herself from the hot sun with a battered umbrella. Jay introduced Cathy to Gwen, a stiff-backed German who greeted her formally in stilted English, calling her "Miss," as if her name didn't matter. The other, a Thai of about Cathy's age, said in excellent English, "I am Sunan, Khun Cathy. Welcome to the Martin Luther Missionary School."

To Cathy's surprise, Jay remained in the jeep. As soon as she lifted her suitcase from the back, he pulled forward, turned the vehicle in a tight circle, and roared away. The sense of loss as she watched him go felt like a slap in the face. He didn't glance back once as the vehicle bounced and ground its way downhill.

It meant nothing, she told herself. Jay was a busy man, and the uneven road required his full attention.

"Come." Sunan's tone was kind. "I will show you your new home."

Cathy's time at the school was an education in a dozen ways. In her "real" work, she learned about demanding physical labor and doing without comforts she hadn't realized she'd miss, like Band-Aids and potato chips. In her secret job, she learned to continue despite fear—no, terror.

Sunan had once been an exchange student, sent to Duluth, Minnesota, for a year, where she'd learned English and observed Western ways. She quickly became a friend to Cathy, teaching her the language, explaining local customs, and answering questions about Nong Samet, which was almost exactly four miles from the school. Since her uncle worked there, Sunan was more familiar than most with its everyday operation.

A *de facto* city, sometimes called "007" because of the many intrigues within its confines, Nong Samet was a nightmare for those trapped inside. Though the camp had existed for years, there was little order inside its gates. No one could decide who was responsible for establishing rules, much less enforcing them. Because those in charge often failed to act, warlords swept in, leading ragtag "armies" of ill-equipped, poorly disciplined soldiers. Though a few tried to establish order, most were bullies who terrorized their own people.

"Why don't the Thais stop them?" Cathy asked.

"My people have little sympathy for those in the border camps," Sunan said sadly. "Most Thais don't understand what they left behind, and they don't see how the Khmer are forced to live in the camps. When they hear stories of lawlessness, Thais say, 'You see? Those people are savages.'" She shook her head. "Uncle says most at Nong Samet want only a chance for a peaceful life. His stories of their suffering make me cry for them."

She was tempted to hint she'd be doing something to help, but Cathy remembered Jay's warning, *Tell no one.*

Cathy established early on that she intended to come and go as she pleased. Gwen didn't like it, but free labor was hard to get, so she pursed her lips and said nothing. On her third day, Cathy announced she intended to be gone for the afternoon. Taking plenty of water and borrowing a coolie hat from Sunan, she headed for Nong Samet to explore it for herself. Though it was scary to strike out on her own and the sun sent heat rays like a giant, heavenly arc welder, she tried to think of it as a pleasant walk, like those she'd often taken on Mackinac Island.

That brought E to mind and led to a question that plagued her: Had she betrayed E by falling in love with her brother, or had E betrayed her by assuming she and Drake had acted on their feelings? The only possible answer was that it no longer mattered. They'd been friends. Now they were both on their own, for Cathy guessed E felt as isolated as she did, no matter how many people flocked around her.

Turning her mind to the present, Cathy looked out over the strange, beautiful land below: the river, the thick vegetation, the dry, dusty road. It was hot, but Sunan had warned that the rainy season would arrive soon. "Mostly it rains late in the day," she'd told the newcomer. "We do our work in the morning, though the skies will frown on us even then."

A rustling to Cathy's left made her stop and peer into the foliage, tensed and ready to run. She wasn't yet used to the idea that in Thailand, animals, insects, and even plants might kill an unsuspecting passer-by. Encyclopedia entries listed the large, dangerous animals roaming the land: tigers, elephants, wild oxen, leopards, and tapirs.

She told herself it was silly to be afraid, like tourists who came to Michigan terrified they'd be eaten by a bear. Wild animal encounters were rare and seldom happened on well-traveled paths. The trees she passed were just trees, not traps where snakes waited to drop on her head. The road was easy to follow, though its dust choked her. She reaffirmed her desire to see Nong Samet. *Think about what you will do to help. Don't think about bugs, tigers, bandits, or friends you'll never see again.*

The smell of Nong Samet, a mix of noxious human and automotive odors, hit her before she cleared a stand of trees and saw the place. First was a scattering of buildings that couldn't really be called a town. Cathy guessed the structures, tents, huts, and a few wood-frame residences, were related to the camp but not part of it: homes for aid workers and offices for the work international agencies performed to keep the camp supplied.

The camp itself was enclosed in seven strands of barbed wire topped with bamboo spikes. Uniformed guards armed with swords stood at the gate, glowering at all who approached. Standing atop a low wall with her camera, Cathy surveyed row after row of huts closely situated, several block buildings she guessed were offices and a hospital, and a few fenced enclosures that looked like holding pens. As she watched, a water truck drove through the gates, its engine knocking badly, and stopped. People hurried forward with buckets, jars, and pans to get their ration. She learned later that the daily amount varied due to conditions but was sometimes as little as fifteen liters per person per day. As the worker filled receptacles from a hose, children crawled under the truck to catch the cooling drops that spilled over. She stood transfixed by the scene for some time, taking pictures when she remembered to do so. Thousands and thousands of people who'd fled to escape violence, now caged like animals because no one knew what to do with them.

No, because people find it convenient to ignore the needs of those they don't consider theirs.

"Hello."

Looking down, Cathy saw an American in a faded tie-dyed t-shirt, khaki shorts, and Jesus sandals. His red hair was frizzy under a sweat-stained Panama, his nose sunburned and peeling, and she caught the scent of Noxema skin cream wafting from him.

"Hi." She stepped down from the wall and put out a hand. "Cathy Charbonneau. I'm teaching at the Martin Luther School up there." She pointed toward the west.

"Tim Adler. I work for UNBRO." When she looked at him blankly, he explained, "United Nations Border Relief Operation." He grinned, showing crooked teeth. "The dude with the food, dig?"

They moved to a shady spot between buildings, where Cathy learned about Adler's work in the camps. He'd seen them all, not just Nong Samet, and he wasn't shy about sharing what he knew. His colorful speaking style was entertaining, since the pale white guy from Muncie, Indiana, apparently saw himself as a cool black dude from the ghetto.

"The cats in Bangkok don't want to deal with no refugees, so they refuse to call them that. They're 'displaced persons,' who will all book it back home someday and just pick up their old lives, like magic." In a disgusted tone he added, "Course there's not much left after all the bombing we did, and if there is something, somebody else has probably claimed it, but it'll all be happy and shit." He jabbed a thumb over his shoulder. "Thai government refuses to relocate these people, even to countries willing to take them." His lips twisted. "Jive jackasses."

"Why wouldn't they want them to relocate?"

Adler huffed disdainfully. "The Thais want the Khmer people to go back home and form a buffer between Thailand and Vietnam." When Cathy frowned, he explained, "Khmers and Thais both hate the Vietnamese, partly from religious differences and partly what they consider the Viets' aggressive nature." He swept a few sweaty curls off his forehead and then replaced the hat. "There's a whole lot of support in Thailand for Pol Pot, the guy in control in Cambodia right now."

"But isn't he killing off anyone who's smart enough to oppose him?"

"Pretty much. The West sees him as a monster, but old Pol is trying to do exactly what the Thais want—keep Vietnam inside its own borders." He gestured over his shoulder at the gate to Nong Samet. "These people are up Shit Creek. They can't go home, but they're never going to be allowed to go anywhere else."

When Cathy parted from Adler, who became "Tim" over the course of their conversation, she promised to visit again soon. What he'd told her reaffirmed her determination to help Jay make his Thai version of the Underground Railroad a success.

Cathy worked hard at the Martin Luther School. Though Gwen's squint said she disapproved when Cathy didn't spend the first and last hours of her day on her knees in prayer, she came to respect her volunteer's strong back and willing hands. Together the three women and a few day laborers finished the school building, using mud, reeds, lumber, and tin scavenged from various places. They divided the space in half, one side for Gwen to teach older students and the other for Sunan, Cathy, and the little ones.

Once the building met her exacting standards, Gwen made an overnight trip to fetch a pastor who'd promised to come and bless the school, driving non-Christian spirits out so they couldn't interfere with her work. Left idle for two days, Cathy decided to trek to the refugee camp at night to make sure she could manage in the dark. It wasn't hard, but the unease she'd felt in the daytime was multiplied at night, and she couldn't stop herself from shivering every few steps. The rain had begun, though Sunan said it would become much worse. Clouds blocked the moon and stars, so she felt as if she might lose her way and go tumbling down the mountainside. That wasn't likely, since the path had been deepened by the passing of many feet and had easily discerned edges. Pulling her raincoat with the hood up, she stepped carefully to avoid protruding rocks or slippery spots. Within a short time, her tennis shoes were soaked and made squishy sounds as she walked.

When she reached level ground, Cathy was pleased with herself. She'd only shied once when a strange bird called from a spot overhead. She'd recovered quickly, telling it softly, "Hush, bird. Go to bed!"

Nong Samet was almost invisible at one a.m., with only an occasional light here and there. According to Tim, there was no electrical system, only a few gas-powered generators, and no telephones. As she watched, furtive figures slunk through lighter spaces. Since most inhabitants spent their days scrounging for necessities and standing in line for the limited services available to them, anyone still moving around was probably up to no good. Night was a time of intrigue and danger, for women the possibility of abduction and rape, for men "recruitment" into one army or another in the array of warring Cambodian factions. Families hid pretty daughters and strong sons, hoping to protect them from forces they had few ways to resist.

Ram went into the camps as an aid worker. While there, he spoke with potential escapees and plotted how best to get a package out. Jay spoke of Ram's courage, explaining that if an extraction was easy, his confederate was almost offended. "When a plan of intricate detail and certain danger is required," Jay said, "Ram really comes to life."

Looking down at the dark camp, she wondered if Ram was even now in there somewhere, whispering to some desperate person, "It is time."

When she'd been at the compound for ten days, Ram putted up the road on a motorbike, strode into the courtyard like a visiting potentate, and approached Cathy, who was hammering an ill-fitting board into place on the door frame. After a glance to assure the other women were busy with their tasks he asked, "Are you ready to begin your work?"

"I am."

Though Ram's eyes revealed doubt, he apparently accepted Jay's judgment of her abilities. "It will be soon."

Cathy suppressed her fears. "I won't fail you." Movement caught her eye, and she glanced at the schoolhouse doorway, where

Gwen frowned at them. "What did you tell Gwen you came to see me about?"

He frowned. "I told her nothing."

"That won't work." She bit her lip. "Hug me."

"Hug? What is hug?"

"Like this." Sliding her arms around his neck, she embraced Ram, who reacted with almost comedic revulsion. "Hug me back," she ordered. "They need to think we're, um, attracted to each other."

After a moment, Ram's arms closed around her. It was like being embraced by an oak tree. "Okay," she said, and he immediately let go. "Do that each time we meet and when you leave as well."

His mouth was a line of disapproval. "If you say it must be so."

She led the way to her quarters, where she went inside and got the bracelets she'd made. Explaining the simple coding system, she gave him a bag of loose beads to be added to the original band to provide specific information about her assignments. Pocketing the items, Ram gave Cathy a second wooden hug, got on his motorbike, and rode away.

Whether they'd been convincing or not Cathy couldn't say, but no one asked her about Ram's visits. Gwen was absorbed in her Bible and the school. If Sunan was aware that Cathy had secrets, Thai politeness demanded that she appear not to notice.

After the in-person visit, Cathy began receiving messages from Ram in the form of bracelets. "Reading" the beads, she saw how many packages to expect and when and where she should meet them. Cathy added a marker of her own, a bangle that was uniquely hers, to send on with a package so the guides recognized their legitimacy. The simple system worked well, allowing communication even when participants didn't know each other or speak the same language.

On the date indicated for a pickup, Cathy would leave after midnight, travel to Nong Samet, and visit what she thought of as the Designated Hut to take charge of a package, usually one person but occasionally two. Returning to the compound, she led him or her to the small cave on the cliff above. The climb was steep but not impossible, and the cave was back from the edge far enough that those below couldn't see it. When the chance of pursuit had lessened, usually after a day or two, her guests simply disappeared. Once there was some sort of glitch, and Cathy received a note from Ram in stilted English. *You must see the view from the top of the mountain. Sunrise is best.*

Getting the idea, she led her current package to the mountain peak the next morning. They were met by a stern-looking Thai farmer who wordlessly pulled back his sleeve to reveal one of her bracelets on his upper arm. When she showed her own in return, he spoke gruffly to the young man in a gravelly voice. The youth nodded obediently, bowed his thanks to Cathy, and followed the older man down the path.

Cathy never learned what happened to the people with whom she shared those nerve-wracking days, and she often wondered how the packages, often children, fared in places where they had no family or friends. While the abrupt shift in lifestyle was undoubtedly difficult, whatever happened once they left the cave had to be better than life at Nong Samet.

Using a book borrowed from Tim Adler, Cathy memorized basic phrases in Cambodian: "You are safe." "I can help you." "Be very quiet." Later she learned the same phrases in Laotian and Vietnamese. The plight of the children tore at her heart. Most were terrified, having known no life but armed guards, land mines, and poisonous bamboo stakes. She taught herself one more helpful phrase. "You will find peace soon."

The physical part of her work got easier. She could travel the trail in almost total darkness, wait in a cramped position for hours on end, and climb up to the cave without getting short of breath. The mental part never did. Terror gripped the back of her neck like a steel-gloved hand each time she left the compound, and it stayed with her until she was once again safe in her bed. Cathy hid her fear, for it would do her charges no good to see their guide start at every sound. Each package sent on his or her way pleased her, though she was always aware that rescuing one person was a small thing. So many were left behind.

One day Sunan reported that Nong Samet had a new administrator, a Cambodian lawyer named Arum Seng who, rumor said, was determined to maintain distance from all the factions of Khmer politics. Seng worked to make the camp safe for residents. "Uncle says Seng joins with laborers on projects rather than simply ordering things done," she told Cathy as they swept the dirt floor of the school. "He plans roads and clean-up projects and works to see them carried out." After a moment's hesitation, she told a darker story. "But he is not a man to tolerate evil. Two bandits who bragged openly about their exploits were found at the edge of the camp with their throats slit."

If Seng had ordered the bandits' deaths it was harsh, but Cathy guessed he felt it necessary to show the lawless at Nong Samet that order would be achieved, one way or another.

Though Cathy considered her a friend, Sunan treated both Western women as if they were above her in status, allowing them first choice in food, chairs, everything. Gwen received the best treatment, since Thai culture demands respect for age. Sunan acted almost as Gwen's servant, making her bed and laundering her clothes, kneeling over a tub of water and scrubbing industriously at the stains. Cathy thought Gwen took advantage of the younger woman, but nothing she said to Sunan changed her behavior.

When Sunan approached one day with a deference even greater than usual, Cathy realized she had a message that was difficult to express. "Khun Cathy, please pardon my rudeness, but I fear you are putting yourself in danger."

She didn't admit to anything. "Life is often dangerous in this place."

Sunan seemed disappointed in the vague response. "Please consider carefully what you do. There are things at work here you cannot know."

She was probably afraid the school's reputation would be tainted if Cathy's activities were discovered, and she was completely correct to feel that way. Aware she had no right to put the school in jeopardy, Cathy still couldn't make herself give up her important work. "Thank you for your concern," she replied formally. "I promise to consider seriously what you have said."

Chapter Twenty-One

Cruise-Day 10, 5:00 p.m.

Despite six stitches in his left hand, Michael managed to get Miss E's dinner tray to her on time. Any camaraderie he thought they'd built during their two days on the road together had disappeared completely. He clucked in commiseration when she said her chicken breast was dry. He murmured apologetically when she complained the potatoes were lumpy. And he offered a packet of sugar when she claimed the salad dressing was too vinegary. When he'd adjusted the slider's blinds twice and she still wasn't satisfied he asked, "Is something wrong, Miss E?"

"What have I been saying?" she demanded. "Half-mashed potatoes. Blinding sun. Chicken cooked hard as pemmican—"

"That's not what I'm asking." When she stopped, surprised at the interruption, Michael took a deep breath and went on. "Why are you being so nasty?"

"I'm not—" She couldn't finish the lie. "Did you think I didn't see you lurking outside the window at the church? Did you think my friends at Bang Salung wouldn't tell me you were digging into my past?"

After a deep sigh, Michael said, "I did it because I worry about you." He leaned toward her, lowering his voice. "You have secrets, Miss E. I think they might put you in danger."

Her lips went flat. "I've told you I can take care of myself."

"By pushing people away. That isn't smart."

"I see. You're a fount of wisdom and I'm some dumb old hag."

He refused to let himself be distracted by her taunts. "When you get a new steward, the first thing you do is find his weakness and go

at it, so he's set back on his heels and unsure how to deal with you."
He counted on his fingers. "Ha'o wants to be liked, so you
convinced her you'll never like her, no matter how hard she tries.
Darrin is proud of his body art, so you belittled him for having it.
Your first comment to me was about how my looks are fading. It
was…deflating, until I realized that's exactly the reaction you
wanted." He took a breath. "You don't have to worry that I'll betray
you, Miss E. Anything I see you do or learn about you won't be
passed on to anyone. Ever."

Grudgingly, she nodded. "Good to know."

"Now, will you tell me what you're so afraid of?"

She shook her head impatiently. "I'm not *afraid* of anything. I
admit I find it…convenient to keep people from becoming
chummy." She rolled her eyes. "Not that it worked with you, Mister
Persister."

He bowed theatrically. "I'll agree you're good at being bitchy
if you'll admit I've worn you down a little."

Her lips twitched, but she didn't smile. "I won't let people force
me to behave as they think I should."

"But there are better ways to communicate that than tossing TV
remotes at earnest young women."

"To be honest, Mike, one gets to a point where playing nice
when you don't feel like it is simply too much effort."

His reply was more fervent than he intended. "One certainly
does."

She didn't seem to notice. "I'm not the only one. Emily
Dickinson stayed home. Montaigne moved to the country and wrote
letters to the world. Mark Twain turned bitter and sarcastic." She
made a comical moue. "I cruise the seas and say whatever comes
into my head."

"No filters."

She put a finger to her lips. "It's actually quite freeing."

Michael folded his hands at his waist, lest she chide him for taking the "fig leaf pose." "I want to help you."

Her nose twitched like a dog with the scent of game. "With what?"

"With whatever you need."

She sniffed once. "I'll keep your offer in mind."

"I care about what happens to you, Miss E."

"Are you trying to say you see me as a person and not a fussy old bat with issues?"

"You are definitely a person to me." He smiled, adding, "A pain in the ass, but still."

She chuckled. "Don't the oft-quoted 'they' claim that pain makes you stronger?"

Sobering he said, "I never saw pain as a lesson in patience or an opportunity for growth."

"No, it isn't a lesson, and I'll pass on further growth opportunities, if you don't mind." After a moment she observed, "I get the sense you've had your own painful experiences."

He thought about how to reply. "There have been times when I desperately needed help, but I had no one who was willing to provide it."

"And now you want to help me. I suppose that's commendable."

Michael's eagerness colored his tone. "Then you'll let me know if there's anything I can do?"

She smiled, though a hint of sadness remained in her eyes. "I wish we'd met earlier in life, Mike. Perhaps we could have helped each other through the bad times."

Chapter Twenty-Two

Martin Luther School, Thailand-January, 1983

"Time flies," people often say, and Cathy found it to be true. She was so busy at the school that it surprised her one day when Gwen said, "New Year's Day. Ours, not theirs."

January 1st, 1983. A decade ago, she'd been a wife. A few years ago, she'd been top executive assistant at a fledgling fashion company. Now she was a teacher by day and a people smuggler at night.

Teaching was not something Cathy had ever believed she'd be good at, but the children who came to the Martin Luther School convinced her otherwise. They were grateful for the opportunity to learn, and she experienced none of the discipline problems she'd heard U.S. teachers complain about. Gwen leaned heavily on religion, telling her students that God sent the hot sun and heavy rains so they would remember to worship Him. Cathy didn't preach and was therefore better liked. The students' favorite was Sunan, who served as an example, a Thai who read books and had traveled in an airplane. She understood children as Gwen never would, and when the older woman went away for some reason, Sunan often suggested a nature walk or outdoor games instead of sit-down lessons. At those times, there was sure to be singing.

When it came to fashion, Elvera Tharp had a golden touch. She sensed which trends would succeed in the Midwest and which should be avoided. She had an eye for what the well-dressed Chicagoan wanted and needed, particularly in winter clothing. While she wasn't exactly beloved in the business, fondness had nothing to do with success. Mizz bloomed. Profits rose. The media praised Elvera's taste and "feminist example."

Richard made himself useful after Franklin's death, guiding E through the legal maze that in the end left her in control of everything. Drake had retreated to D.C. to try to save his marriage, and when Richard offered to buy out his interest in Tharp Credit, he readily agreed. Richard became chief executive officer but, aware of her husband's tendency to skirt the law, E stipulated in his contract that she could fire him at any time, without explanation or redress. "You get what you've always wanted," she told him, "but to keep it, you have to behave yourself."

Cathy's departure had been a shock, both to Mizz Fashions and to E personally. Though she tried to be angry with her, what Elvera felt was loss. She had no one to talk to anymore. Things she'd saved up from her day's experiences, little irritations, humorous anecdotes, questions to be batted back and forth in search of solutions, abruptly all those things had no audience, no receptive ear. Though she knew lots of people and socialized regularly, E felt she had to be constantly on guard, even in a casual conversation. "Poor Elvera," she imagined any one of her friends saying in her absence. "She's just so…"

How that sentence ended didn't matter. It felt like everything she said and did was filed away for later dissection. The reason was jealousy, of course. She had succeeded by herself, not through her husband's efforts or her father's backing. That didn't make the fake smiles over chicken cacciatore at Sabatino's any more palatable.

The Mizz staff was supportive, but she maintained distance from them to avoid appearing to have favorites. Friends from school drifted away into lives taken up by children and tennis lessons. No one stepped in to serve as Elvera's friend. No one seemed to care about Elvera the person. No one got her jokes, shared her world view, or identified with her struggles. The girl from Mackinaw City, Michigan, so different from her, had done all those things, practically from Day One.

The two people closest to Elvera had caused her public shame, and Richard, who had never liked Drake, found it delightful. E held her head high, refused to talk about it, and pretended it didn't matter. Discreetly, so as not to add to her husband's enjoyment, she hired a private detective to find out where Cathy had gone. When he didn't find her in Michigan or in Illinois, E realized her friend was truly done with her. She had to move on. Naming Jill as her new second banana, she did.

Things were going so well that what happened was more cliché than tragedy. Elvera dropped mustard on her blouse at lunch. Having a meeting at two with some Tokyo buyers, she needed to change, but Jill was out of the office on some errand. On the way to the meeting, E stopped at home to get a clean shirt.

She entered the house quietly not by design, but because she was practicing the pitch for the afternoon meeting in her head. It was raining, so she slipped off her damp shoes at the door. Padding up the stairs, she paused when she heard noises coming from Richard's room. He'd gone to work as usual, and Mrs. Leon had the day off, so she'd expected nothing but silence in the house. Turning the knob, E quietly opened the door. Jill and Richard lay on the bed, naked and writhing, oblivious to anything but each other.

Closing the door softly, she tiptoed away. Richard's unfaithfulness was no surprise; she'd known that for years. It wasn't even terribly upsetting that he used their home for his trysts. But she'd gotten used to having Jill around. No real friends, no loving husband. And now, E thought ruefully, she'd lost a damned good executive assistant.

She managed to make it through the day, but her mind was divided: half on work, the other half on Cathy. E wanted to cry on her shoulder, but that was impossible. She had no idea where Cathy was.

Though she seldom believed in luck, E admitted that it sometimes strikes when least expected. Paging through a newspaper to make sure the ad she'd paid for was prominent and perfect, she noticed a small announcement. Jay Taksin was back in Chicago, speaking to various groups on the refugee crisis in Southeast Asia.

Suddenly she realized why no one had been able to locate Cathy. She was in Thailand.

That night when Taksin finished his talk, Elvera watched him deal with the small crowd of adoring women who purred approval of his message and offered more with their eyes. A couple of the braver ones touched his arm or squeezed his shoulder, as if they couldn't resist.

E couldn't blame them; the man was even more attractive than she remembered. When the others finally left, she waited until he looked up and saw her standing in a dimly lit corner. "Mr. Taksin, I'm Elvera Tharp-Terzis. I believe you can put me in touch with Cathy Charbonneau."

As Taksin looked her over, she admitted to herself that he was good. The admiration in his eyes wasn't boorish or creepy, but he didn't try to hide it either. Stepping lightly, he descended the dais and approached her. "Shall we find somewhere to have a drink while we talk?"

E smiled. "I'd like that." A woman would have to be careful with a man like Jay Taksin, she thought, but the rewards might be worth the risk.

Their affair was heady and satisfying, at least in the early days. Jay was passionate where Richard was cool, verbal where Richard was silent. It felt like she was paying Richard back for all the women he'd bedded, and it didn't matter to E that he didn't know. Jay was a perfect choice as a lover, since his time in Chicago was limited. As pleasant as their assignations were, she had no interest in a long-term relationship.

Then she began to see a negative side. Jay was volatile, even frightening at times. The first instance was when he caught a hotel maid looking at a necklace he'd bought for Elvera. Flying into a rage, he accused the woman—She was little more than a girl—of intending to steal it. "I saw Saks Fifth Avenue on the box," the terrified woman sobbed. "I only wanted to see what was inside."

Fearing Jay might strike her, E put a hand on his arm. "She was curious, Jay. Don't make a fuss."

"I *will* make a fuss." He shook her hand off, but he let go of the maid's arm, and E saw the marks his fingers had left. "She will be fired."

The girl left in tears, and Jay called the hotel manager demanding her employment be terminated. It was good, E thought as he ranted, that Jay Taksin would soon move his fundraising efforts to the West Coast. There was a side to him she didn't like very well.

It came as a shock when Jay told her he'd adjusted his schedule so he could stay longer in Chicago. Things got worse when he confessed that he was in love with her. "Jay, you don't love me," E almost shouted. She stopped herself before the rest came out: *any more than I love you.*

"I want you to be my wife, Elvera."

"Have you forgotten that I'm already married?"

Taking a strand of her hair, he touched it to his face. "Richard is not the man for you. I am."

Seeing almost manic conviction in his eyes, Elvera suppressed a shiver. "Finish your speaking tour," she said, keeping her voice calm. "When that's done, we'll talk."

Though he didn't like the idea, Jay eventually agreed. Once she'd put him on a flight out of O'Hare, Elvera went to a nearby church for the first time in months and offered a fervent prayer that he'd meet a woman in Denver or Sacramento or Seattle and forget her. She confessed her sin and felt pleased when the priest's demand matched her own desires: "Give up this man," he enjoined sternly. "Return to your husband."

"I will, Father," E murmured obediently. She had no intention of ever seeing Jay Taksin again.

But three months later, a horrifying truth dawned. Elvera had stopped taking birth control pills due to warnings about its safety. They were unnecessary, since sex with Richard was nonexistent. At the beginning of their relationship, Jay had confided with some chagrin that he was sterile. "The doctors can find no cause," he said, "but I have been with many, many women and never once made a child."

When she missed her first period, E hardly noticed. Her cycles had been irregular since she quit taking the pill, and things were busy at Mizz. When she threw up her breakfast twice and felt so sleepy at times that she could hardly navigate, she blamed it on a germ she'd picked up somewhere. Rinsing the bile from her mouth with water, she told herself that illness could mess up a woman's cycle. The Monthly Monster would show up soon, no doubt in the middle of a workday, when it was least convenient.

Midway through the third month, Elvera stared at her lily-white underwear and realized she couldn't ignore the truth forever. She was carrying Jay Taksin's child.

When he returned to Chicago, Jay's ardor had not cooled. Elvera told Beth, her new personal assistant (whose greatest virtue was that she was too old to be of interest to Richard), to say she was too busy to see Mr. Taksin. Three days later Beth reported, "He's become quite insistent, Mrs. Terzis. I'm not sure what to say to him anymore."

She'd already begun buying looser skirts and pants, and her breasts required a bigger cup size as well. "Keep repeating the message," she told Beth. "He'll get the hint eventually."

But he didn't. As Elvera was getting dressed to go to work one morning, Mrs. Leon tapped on her bedroom door. "There is a man downstairs—" Before she could finish, Jay brushed past her and into the room. "Elvera, what are you trying to do to me?"

"Jay." It was some relief that Richard had already left the house. The housekeeper stood in the doorway as if on guard. "It's all right, Mrs. Leon. He won't be staying long."

Mouth tight, the older woman retreated, leaving the bedroom door ajar in a tacit sign of disapproval.

"Why are you avoiding me?" Jay demanded.

Checking to be sure Mrs. Leon was out of hearing she said, "Jay, our relationship is over. I don't want to see you again."

He was looking at her oddly, his anger for the moment replaced by something else. Elvera wore only underwear and a slip, and she leaned forward, trying to hide the bulge at her belly.

"You look different."

"You're mistaken."

"I don't think so." Coming to her, he cupped her chin. "Your face is rounder. Your shape has changed. You are pregnant."

"No."

Stepping forward, Jay gripped her arms. "Lie to your husband if you like. You can't lie to me."

"I told you, no." Pulling herself away, E retreated. "It's not true."

It was as if she hadn't spoken. "I *knew* you were meant to be mine."

"Jay—"

Again, he paid no mind. "We must move quickly. There is a city in this country where a divorce is granted in a short time, yes? We will go there today. You'll rid yourself of Richard, and then we'll be married."

"Listen—"

"My family will arrange a second, more proper wedding when

we arrive in Thailand." He nodded with satisfaction. "My child will be born in my homeland."

"That isn't possible. Richard—"

Jay's face reddened, and he jabbed a finger at her. "Everything I have said will happen." When she opened her mouth again, he said, "Divorce him or do not, as you wish, Elvera. I have disposed of better men than Richard Terzis before eating my breakfast in the morning."

E froze as the meaning of his words sunk in, and she felt her hands clench. She'd made a horrible mistake.

Jay began pacing, his manner frenetic. "I felt it from the first. You are the woman I was born to marry. This is now proven by the fact that you carry my child, a thing no other woman has been able to do." Stopping before her, he grasped her arms again, squeezing so hard she winced in pain. "Do you see? Nothing—no one—can stand in the way of our future."

This was not the cosmopolitan gentleman who'd told her how lovely she was over a bottle of expensive wine. This was a madman who'd casually threatened to murder her husband. Jay wanted E, but even more, she suspected, he wanted her child. She hadn't considered the baby until that moment, but suddenly it was hers. Hers to care for. Hers to protect.

What could she say or do to make its father go away?

"I didn't realize you loved me so much, Jay." She stroked his face softly, though at that moment she'd rather have petted a grizzly bear. "I see now that you and I must be together."

His manner softened, and he embraced her tightly. E forced her body to remain relaxed as she spoke. "You're going to have to give me a little time. It will take a while to arrange a divorce, and if I'm moving to Thailand, I'll have to sell my company."

He leaned back to look into her eyes. "How long?"

Inside her head, she was figuring frantically. "Three months."

Jay released her abruptly. "The child will be born by then."

"No," she lied. "I'm not due until late December." Touching his face again she said, "Go back to Thailand. Prepare your family for this wedding." His brows lowered, but she added in her most convincing tone, "How will they react when you present them with the prospect of a pregnant, Christian, American divorcee joining the family?"

Though he didn't want to, Jay saw the logic of her argument. "I suppose some preparation is necessary."

Raising her face to his, Elvera kissed him as ardently as she could manage. "Come back in three months, darling, and I'll be yours forever."

He pulled her close, and she forced herself to seem soft and inviting. "It seems an eternity."

"Yes," she replied. "But then we'll be together, and so happy."

Chapter Twenty-Three

Cruise-Day 11, 5 a.m.

Glynis found Michael in the dining room, where he was replenishing the pudding selections. "Ha'o says you worked for the Chailangka family on Wireless Road in Bangkok until recently. Is that right?"

Pausing, Michael turned to her. "I was the grandfather's caregiver until he died last fall."

Her pretty face lit with pleasure. "I can't believe it! We probably saw each other in the elevator sometimes. I watched the Yoosamran brats back in 2017. They live just a few floors below."

"Interesting."

"Little monsters, they were. Couldn't wait to get away." She tilted her head coquettishly. "I can't believe I never saw you in the building. I think I'd have noticed."

"I spent my time with the old gentleman. He was quite demanding."

"Too bad." Reaching, she pinched his shoulder playfully. "We mighta got to be good friends, you know?"

Michael smiled. "Yes. I'm sure we'd have become close if we hadn't both been so busy."

"You spent time in the States, too, I hear." When he didn't respond Glynis said, "I'd love to visit New York City. Did you ever go there?"

"No."

"Not one for talkin' about yourself, are ya? Your ma slap you silent when you was a kid?"

"No," Michael replied. "My 'ma' never raised a hand to me in her life. Now if you'll excuse me, I need to get the rest of the desserts out."

Chapter Twenty-Four

Thailand-October, 1983

It had been a particularly brutal day. Rain fell—no, it went beyond that. Rain assaulted them, coming straight down at times and then, when the winds kicked up, turning almost parallel to the ground. The house was loud with it, and they had to shout at each other to be heard. When it was necessary to go outside, water beat them like a thousand clubs, soaking their clothes and stinging any exposed skin. No children came for school, so Cathy, Gwen, and Sunan sat in their hut, reading, writing, or dozing.

They didn't hear the truck's approach, and they jumped when someone pounded on the door. Gwen got up to answer, and there stood Elvera, looking like a figure in a *Carol Burnett Show* skit. Her outfit was completely unsuited to monsoon season. The extra fabric in the legs of her fashionable pants was so saturated that she had to hold the waistband with one hand to keep them up. Her shirt clung to her body, and her dark hair laid against her forehead like wallpaper. Though she had never looked worse, Cathy's response was a bolt of pure joy. Elvera was here.

Setting her suitcase down, E held out her arms, her bat-wing sleeves dripping streams of water onto the dirt floor. "Do I get a hug for tracking you down in the middle of nowhere?"

Cathy embraced her friend, ignoring her squishiness. "How did you get here?"

"It wasn't easy." Turning, Elvera waved and a truck geared up, turned around, and headed back downhill. "I had no idea something that awful could be called a road."

Closing the door, Cathy shut out some of the noise before hugging her again. "I've missed you," she said in her ear, and the tightening of E's arms said more than words could.

"Have you got an extra bunk?"

"An extra—But what...?" E's expression stopped Cathy's question. She was exhausted, and in her eyes was something like desperation. Why she'd come, what she wanted, those questions could wait. "Sure. We'll make room, right, girls?"

Gwen's nod was almost imperceptible, and even Sunan seemed doubtful of the stranger in their midst. Leading E to her corner of the hut, Cathy said, "Let's get you some dry clothes."

Since Elvera seemed on the verge of collapse, Cathy gently helped her remove her wet garments. Noticing that E's panties were a bloody mess, she dug out her precious box of menstrual pads and handed her one. The other women politely looked away as E took care of the problem.

"I'm sorry to just show up," she said in a voice smaller than Cathy remembered. "I didn't know what to do, and it seemed like if I could be where you are, we'd figure it out together."

"You need to rest," Cathy said. "Tomorrow you can tell me your adventures." Again unlike herself, E nodded meekly, turned her face to the mud-brick wall, and promptly fell asleep. Cathy was left to assure her housemates that whatever had brought her friend all the way from Chicago was important...and temporary.

The next morning the rain lessened somewhat, and Gwen and Sunan went to the school in hopes a few children would brave the weather. Elvera had slept in Cathy's bed, though there wasn't much difference between it and the dirt-packed floor where Cathy stretched out beside her. She watched as Cathy brewed tea on a small brazier and filled two tin cups. "I told Richard I had to see you," she said as Cathy handed her one. "He acts like he doesn't care what I do, but he tends to find out everything somehow. He's—" Flipping her hair back with both hands, she let the sentence remain unfinished.

"Richard knows you're here. That doesn't explain why you

came."

"First things first." E squared her shoulders. "I want to apologize for the thing with Drake. I knew better."

Cathy made a gesture that swept away any blame. "You'd had a horrible day. Anyone might have been…"

"Judgmental? Bitchy? Mean?"

"Since you put it that way, yes." A smile took the sting from it. "You know I would never…"

"Yes, I do. No matter how much you wanted to, Cath, you'd never sleep with another woman's husband." Frowning, she added, "Unlike most females in the Western world."

"What?"

"Nothing."

"All right." Cathy handed E her cup, and she sipped tentatively. "You've apologized. Now what?"

A smile from Elvera, the first genuine one since she arrived, showed understanding that she was with the person who knew her best. E hadn't come to this wild place only to apologize, and now Cathy was ready to hear the rest.

"I've known where you were for a while, but I figured you didn't want to hear from me. Unfortunately, something came up that overcame my respect for your privacy." She stopped, unsure how to go on.

Cathy reached out and squeezed her knee. "Whatever it is, E, I'll help if I can."

"I've been having an affair." Shock must have shown on Cathy's face, because Elvera hurried on. "I know, it's stupid and wrong. But he was different from Richard or anyone I've ever known."

"Different?"

"Strong, passionate." She looked at her irregular, dirty fingernails, so unlike the head of Mizz Fashions. "It was wonderful."

"Was?"

Elvera ran a hand through her matted hair. "I considered it a fling, Cath. I was furious with Richard—it doesn't matter why—but I met this man and there was this…attraction between us." She swallowed before going on. "I thought we'd have a little fun and then go back to our lives when it was over, but…he says we're meant to be together."

"How did you respond to that?"

"I reminded him I'm married. I used the church as an excuse." Her expression indicated she knew how lame that was. "He didn't buy it."

"With no kids, you could probably get your marriage to Richard annulled, if that's what you want."

E shook her head. "Tharp Credit would turn into a complete mess if Richard and I split up."

For a moment Cathy wanted to swat her. "E, the business can't dictate your future. If this man makes you happy—"

"He's no Knight in Shining Armor," E interrupted. "In fact, I found out he isn't shiny at all on the inside."

Cathy set her cup aside and leaned her chin on her hand. "If you didn't come here for romantic advice, then why the long trip?"

Elvera wrapped her arms tightly around her middle. "I got pregnant."

"By your—by the man?"

Her shoulders moved, signaling assent and aversion at once. "Yes. The baby was his, not Richard's."

Cathy's face turned dark. "Was?"

That brought a weak chuckle. "I could never have an abortion, Cath. Too many years with the nuns."

"What did you do?"

"First, I told Richard I was going to visit you for a while."

Cathy gestured at the one-room house with its meager furnishings. "E, this isn't exactly a vacation spot."

"I didn't come here to stay. In fact, I left Chicago weeks ago."

"I don't understand."

"I went to Bangkok, had the baby, and left him at an orphanage. They'll keep him until I return."

"How does that help?"

She rotated her shoulders as if getting ready to face the future. "I need to convince Jay to leave me alone, so I'm going to tell him I had a miscarriage. Once he's out of the picture, I'll tell Richard there's a Thai orphan I want to adopt. No one will know he's mine except you and me."

Cathy's brain had stuck on the name. "Jay?"

"Jay Taksin." E tapped the tin cup a few times with a fingernail. "He seemed so...exciting. One day he's tramping through the jungle, rescuing people. The next day, he's dining with kings." She grinned. "Gorgeous isn't bad either."

"I know what you mean," Cathy said. She thought of Jay's visit a few weeks earlier, when they'd gone for a walk that ended in lovemaking along the river. "So beautiful," he'd said as they lay recovering from their passion. Brushing her hair back from her face, he'd said it again. "So beautiful." Though she didn't love Jay, it was embarrassing to learn how little she meant to him, and how easily she'd fallen under his spell.

Unaware that Cathy's thoughts had wandered, Elvera went on. "I'll stay here a few days. We'll take some photos together. When I see Jay again, I'll say the miscarriage convinced me that God wants me to work on my marriage. Once he's convinced there's no baby, he'll accept it."

Cathy felt dizzy trying to take it all in. "Richard didn't notice you were pregnant?"

"He made a crack once about me letting myself go, but it was more to hurt my feelings than anything else."

"You are a little rounder than before," Cathy acknowledged.

"I'll get back to my old self in time," Elvera said confidently. With a flash of her usual wit she rubbed her backside, adding, "The ride up here in that truck probably shook off a pound or two."

That afternoon Cathy told her companions that her friend would like to stay a few days. "We don't invite people for tea, Miss," Gwen said irritably. "This is important work we do here."

Since there was nowhere else for her to be, Elvera heard the comment. "I can work," she said. "I'll do whatever you need me to do."

Gwen seemed doubtful, but Sunan said, "Perhaps she could go with me to take supplies to the villages." To Elvera she explained, "We sometimes get shipments of food and medicine from churches, and we share what we can with people in the outlying areas."

"I could help with that," E said.

That came as a relief to Cathy, who had one package hidden in the cave and another to pick up at Nong Samet that night. Still she warned, "The trip isn't easy, E. It's mostly uphill, and you'll have to carry a lot of weight."

"I can do it." Even Gwen had to smile when E raised her arms, flexed her biceps, and said in a deep voice, "Me strong like bull—or in this case, musk ox."

Elvera had never been so tired in her life. When they loaded their packs to capacity and then hefted them onto their backs, she'd been optimistic, even enthusiastic. That was before they started uphill. Within an hour her thighs screamed with pain, the straps of the pack felt like sword blades cutting into her shoulders, and her recently traumatized female organs felt like they might fall out onto the ground and drag behind. She tried to hide from Sunan how irregular her breathing was, but the other woman sensed her fatigue and made frequent stops.

Along with exhaustion, E struggled to calm acrophobia like she'd never experienced before. The trail was at first laid with planks and bordered with a handrail, but those amenities soon disappeared, and she felt as if she were balanced on the edge of the world. It was beautiful, to be sure: the deep-green base, neatly terraced crops, roofs that slanted over hillsides, and the river so far below that it looked like a velvet-brown ribbon tossed carelessly across the valley. She couldn't help imagining how easy it would be to slip on a loose rock or a patch of wet grass, how her own weight would send her rolling down the incline—How far? A half mile? More than that? Whatever the distance, no unplanned descent would end well.

Still, E was proud to be part of the mission. Her family had often sponsored charitable events, and she and Richard donated to worthy causes, but this felt personal, and she kind of liked it.

At the first village, an untidy assemblage of straw huts with a smoky fire pit in the center, the reception was different than she expected. Their gifts were rejected by a cantankerous headman with a horrible case of warts, who apparently saw outsiders as devils, no matter what they offered. He spoke roughly to Sunan, waving at her as if she were a bothersome insect. Despite that, Elvera saw children peeping through holes in the hut walls, eyeing the visitors' bags of goods. Sunan remained deferential, but the old man banged his fist on a rickety table and pointed toward the trail. E almost laughed, because the man reminded her of Father's friends, shaking their jowls and insisting credit would never replace cash in America.

Looking around the circle of adults, she noted interest on several faces. A few smiled shyly when their glances met, but the old man glared them into submission. Again, E was reminded of times back home when church leaders, school officials, and sorority presidents discouraged interaction with "outsiders" as a way of controlling their people.

As they left the village and continued up the mountain, the two women met a group of boys shepherded by a man in bright orange (Sunan called it *saffron*). They pulled their mule to one side to let them pass, and the monk made a dignified *wai* in response. When they were gone, Sunan said, "He will find the headman more receptive than we did, and he will leave the village with a boy or two more in his little group."

"He's going to make them all into monks?"

Sunan shook her head. "Monastic life is often temporary. A boy taken in by the monks escapes poverty, learns moral principles, and earns respect for his parents. If he finds a spiritual calling, he may stay in the order. Otherwise he returns to normal life with no stigma attached."

"Then you and the monks compete for the same children?"

"We offer them a view of the outside world, and the monks offer a view inside their souls." After a moment Sunan added, "I cannot say which is better."

She pointed to their next goal, a few houses perched almost at the mountaintop. "From there we will visit three villages on the other side that might someday send children to our school."

"Will it discourage you if we're sent on our way again?"

Sunan's smile was mischievous. "Often children come to school whether the headman approves or not."

"He doesn't notice them going and coming?"

"He will pretend not to. These petty kings strut and rant, but they cannot stop people from wanting to educate their children.

Parents don't openly contradict them, but in the end they do as they choose."

The path was full of switchbacks due to the steep incline, and several times Elvera looked down on the school building. She imagined Cathy inside, arranging things and humming as she worked. She seemed more content here than she'd ever been in Chicago. Cathy needed to be needed, and in Thailand her courage and self-confidence had grown. Tragedies and disappointments she'd experienced, the loss of her family, the gap she felt between herself and her brothers, her government, even her church, might have crushed her, but in Thailand, Cathy had found new reasons for optimism.

Since the mess with Jay began, Elvera had changed too. She admitted to herself that her reputation for bitchiness was earned, at least in part. She'd treated Richard badly, allowing him no shred of pride. She'd bullied Cathy into working at Mizz, though Drake had warned that the job wasn't right for her. Now Cathy was doing what she chose, and while E didn't see it as rewarding enough to outweigh flush toilets and clean sheets, she knew her friend had found something to believe in.

Using her limited Khmer vocabulary, Cathy tried to reassure her companion. "Safe now."

It was clear the girl didn't believe that. She kept looking over her shoulder as if expecting to be caught and dragged back to the camp. It felt odd, traveling with a package in daylight, but after Sunan and E left, Gwen had decided to attend services at a small Christian church a few miles north. She'd gone off on her bicycle, leaving Cathy with enough time to reach the camp, get her "guest" from the hut where Ram had hidden her, and bring her safely to the cave before Gwen returned, as long as there were no delays. She'd borrowed some of Sunan's clothes, so anyone who saw them would not suspect the girl at her side was an escapee.

"Safe," Cathy repeated, hurrying the pace a little, though the girl was so weary her path arced left and right rather than making a straight line. Clouds had hung low overhead all morning, and the level of humidity rose by the minute. It would rain soon, and the climb to the ledge would grow slippery. Better to push the girl now and save her a treacherous climb later.

At the school she communicated *Wait here* with gestures. The girl leaned against a post, eyes half-closed with fatigue. In the storage shed, Cathy filled her knapsack with food unlikely to be missed. Going back outside, she led the way to the steep rock face that backed the compound. Adjusting her knapsack, Cathy started up, demonstrating to the girl where the hand and footholds were. When they reached a ledge, she pointed to a faint path leading to the cave, about ten feet farther up, its entrance concealed by jutting rocks. "Come. Hide here."

Obediently the girl climbed up the gentler slope through the rocks. When they neared the cave entrance, Cathy clicked her flashlight on and off twice. A face appeared from the darkness, a girl about the same age as the newcomer. When she spoke in a welcoming tone, the weary girl smiled for the first time. Crouching, she entered the cave, which held the bare necessities: a jug of water, some blankets, and a slops bucket. Sliding the knapsack off, Cathy set its contents between them.

"Make it last," she said, holding up fingers. "One day, maybe two."

They nodded, and the new girl used one of her two English phrases. "Thank you."

Leaving the other girl to explain what would happen next, Cathy made her way back down to the compound. When she reached the ground, she turned to find Elvera standing at the corner of the building.

She gasped in surprise. "What are you doing here?"

"Sunan made a deal with some village chief, medicine for his wife's eczema in exchange for letting the kids come to school. I volunteered to come back for it."

When Cathy didn't speak, she asked, "Who was that girl?"

She couldn't lie to Elvera. "I'm helping her escape from a refugee camp on the Thai-Cambodian border, a few miles from here."

"You smuggle people into Thailand?"

"Jay's men do the actual work. All I do is hide them until someone comes to guide them on."

"That's all? You risk your life for people you don't even know?"

Cathy thought for a moment. "Do you remember when you came to the hospital, E? I was a wreck, in a place where I was miserable, and you came and took me away. That's what we do here: rescue people with no hope and give them a chance for a different future."

"But you can't help them all."

Cathy pushed a strand of sweat-damp hair away from her face. "We do what we can."

"But it isn't your job to help. The government hires people to see to their needs."

"Sit back and let someone else do it; is that what you're saying? If I know these people need saving and I don't do something, what kind of person does that make me?"

E rubbed at her forehead. "I don't know, sane, maybe?"

Cathy paused, frustrated by her inability to make Elvera see. "Do you remember your housekeeper on Mackinac Island, Laura?"

"Sure. Really long hair, quiet and efficient."

"Her husband used to beat her. Did you know that?"

"She told you?"

"I saw the bruises, the way she flinched when he came up behind her." Cathy bit her lip. "I didn't say anything, didn't do anything about it."

A casual wave banished any possible culpability. "Women like that don't know anything else. They—"

"Stop!" Cathy ordered. "Don't you dare say she chose to be abused."

That brought a pout. "I didn't mean that. I meant—"

"You meant she was too dumb or too lazy or too…something to get herself out of a bad situation." Cathy gestured toward the unseen camp to the east. "The bigots among the Thai people claim the Khmers at their border should have stayed and fought for their homeland. Since they weren't 'tough enough' to do that, they deserve to live like animals."

"What has that got to do with—?"

"You implied that abused women choose to be punching bags for their husbands. It's the same thing." Cathy looked away, her mouth twisted. "We convince ourselves that others aren't like us. We're sure we'd do differently—do better—if we faced what they face. That arrogant thinking lets us forget they are people in pain. We absolve ourselves of responsibility and refuse to help them, because, hey, it's all their own fault."

E wasn't ready to give in. "You're breaking the law, Cath."

"You can't turn wrong into right by taking a vote, especially when the people voting don't understand the situation."

Taking a different tack, she asked, "Do the others know?"

Cathy snorted a laugh. "Does Gwen seem to you like the type who'd bend the rules?"

E chuckled. "Not really."

"Sunan suspects, I think, but she isn't part of it."

"Then you're putting them in a tight spot."

Cathy didn't argue, since that question often plagued her. It was, she had decided, a matter of weighing pluses and minuses. "E, you need to forget what you saw."

"You said Jay arranged all this?"

"Listen, I know you and he are in a mess, but Jay's work is good. He could stay in his nice house in Bangkok and ignore what's going on here. Instead, he tries to help."

E's eyes narrowed. "You're sleeping with him."

Cathy shrugged. "Like you said, he's different."

"I'm not sure he's all that noble, Cath."

"We're none of us angels. If Jay takes people out of that hellhole and gets them to a place where they might have a chance, I'll help him. Even if it's wrong by some people's standards."

Suddenly E's irritation vanished, and she wrapped her arms around her friend. "I don't know enough to say who's right, Cath. But I know you are one amazing woman."

Cathy hoped Elvera would leave before another package arrived, but that didn't happen. A local boy came by the next morning to offer her a bracelet. He left pleased with the money she paid him and unaware he'd served as messenger between her and Ram.

E wasn't fooled, and she approached Cathy as the boy disappeared down the trail. "If you're going to that camp, I'm coming with you."

"It's dangerous enough for me alone. I can't drag you along."

"You don't have to drag me. I can walk."

"But I chose to do this. You didn't."

Arguing got her nowhere, and Cathy didn't know why she tried. It was Elvera, after all, and she usually got her way in things that mattered to her. They started for Nong Samet together in the rain that afternoon, wearing ponchos and rubber boots and leaving a disapproving Gwen glaring after them. Sunan had not yet returned, and E insisted the chief's wife could wait another few days for her cortisone cream.

"I've portrayed myself as a bit of a slut," Cathy confided as they made their way down the slippery hillside. "Saying I have a date gives me an excuse to be gone overnight."

"Gwen allows that?"

"She has no say. I'm a volunteer, and I do the work of three sluts."

E put her hands to her face in mock embarrassment. "Is it common here—the slut thing?"

Cathy chuckled. "Mission work, the Peace Corps, whatever, is noble stuff, but it doesn't change human nature. Send a bunch of young, healthy individuals to a land far away from home, and you and God will have to look the other way when they slip into each other's sleeping bags from time to time."

"I bet more than one sweet young thing goes home P.G." Elvera hesitated. "Not that I should talk."

"What's it like?"

"Having a baby? It hurts like hell." E's face softened. "But I had no idea what it would be like to get handed a piece of myself that somehow lives and breathes apart from me." After a moment she added, "I fell in love the first moment I saw him."

Tears came to Cathy's eyes, but she blinked them away. A moment like that was impossible for her, but she didn't begrudge her friend the love she'd discovered. "It had to be horrible to have to leave him."

"I can't tell you." A few steps on she said, "But it won't be that long. I've got my story worked out, and Richard won't care enough to argue."

"I'm glad, E."

"Don't worry, Aunty Cath. I'll let you spoil him rotten."

"Deal." After a moment she said, "My guests in the cave moved on some time last night."

"How do you know they're all right?"

"The guide leaves a sign." Showing E the bracelet she wore, she explained the beaded messages.

"Clever."

"Another tribute to Laura. She did beautiful beadwork, and she showed me the basics."

E shook her head. "The woman lived in my house, and you know six times what I ever knew about her."

"We all see different sides of people. Part of it is what they choose to show us, but the other part is what we look for in them."

E went silent, apparently pondering that.

The day grew warm, and their packs, loaded with flashlights, food, and water, grew heavy. For the last part of their trek, the rain felt like standing under a waterfall, but it slowed as they entered the village. They were able to push back their hoods and raise their faces to a lighter sky.

Cathy led E to her observation spot to give her a bird's eye view of Nong Samet. "It's so big," E said.

"At times, the population is larger than Cambodia's capital, Phnom Penh."

They retreated to a tea shop to wait until dark, when the camp closed for the day. An exodus of Westerners in cars, on bicycles, and on foot exited the gates in the last hour. Cathy explained that guests were strictly supervised inside the camp and almost never allowed to spend the night. Once activity slowed, Cathy led the way to a hut outside the wall that was minus most of its roof. Its door hung crookedly on one hinge, and the windows were mere holes in the wall. Inside, she turned on her flashlight and moved a broken table aside, revealing a trapdoor. After knocking in a pattern that was clearly a signal, she pulled it open.

In the beam of her flash was a boy of about ten, rail thin and clearly terrified. "Come. I will take you to safety," Cathy told him in Khmer.

He said something in a low voice, but Cathy put up a hand to stop him. "No Khmer." The fear on his face was replaced with frustration. "I will take you to safety," she repeated.

The boy began to cry, repeating the same words over and over. Cooing softly, Cathy pulled him to his feet. It was clear he was torn between escape and whatever held him back, but she gestured for him to follow. "Quiet," she warned in Khmer before opening the cockeyed door. Covering his dingy-white tunic with a dark blanket she'd brought along, she led the way outside. The boy choked back his tears, emitting instead an occasional soft hiccup. Elvera hurried him along with a nudge to his back, and Cathy smiled to herself. E was learning that what had sounded like an adventure at the compound was chilling here in the dark streets.

When they turned onto the road up the mountain, Cathy stopped to give the boy dried fish and crackers, which he fell on like a starved puppy. "He keeps saying something about his sister," she told E. "At least I think that's right. *Bangosrei*."

The boy's eyes turned to them at the word, and he repeated it. Reaching into his clothing, he pulled out a photograph and handed it to Cathy. Shielding the light with her hand, she directed the flash at a curled, cracked picture of the boy and a girl several years older than he. She stood with a protective arm around him, her face solemn. She was beautiful, with balanced features, luminous eyes, and a haunted look that hinted at secrets that would never be shared.

"It's not a bad shot," E said, "though they could have set it up better."

Cathy almost laughed aloud. "Not much scenery in the middle of a concentration camp, E." She gave the photo back to the boy and hefted her pack again. "She's probably been his stability his whole life."

"Now he'll never see her again," E said. "That's got to be hard."

"The other thing he says is *ban tinh* which I think means "buy." He repeats those words: *sister* and *buy*."

E was horrified. "Someone bought this kid's sister? What do we do about that?"

Cathy sighed. "It's the way things go around here. My friend Tim says you can buy a woman in the camps for two dollars. For a virgin you might pay as much as four."

"Somebody needs to do something." E's voice rang with outrage. "No one should have to live that way."

Cathy might have reminded Elvera of their earlier discussion, but she said nothing, touching the boy's shoulder before leading him up the path to safety.

Elvera was silent as they traveled, troubled by the situation and with keeping up on the steep incline. After a while she said in a breathy wheeze, "We need to know if you understood him right."

A few steps on Cathy said, "Sunan speaks pretty good Khmer."

"But you'd have to tell her what you're up to."

In the slice of moonlight that peeped through the clouds, E saw Cathy's shoulders rise and fall. "I think she already knows."

The next morning, while E got Gwen out of the way by feigning interest in the school curriculum, Cathy approached Sunan. She agreed to help, and taking the camera as a prop, the two climbed to the cave where the boy, Sakda, waited.

"Sakda's mother is dead," Cathy told E later. "His father is dying of some lung ailment, probably TB. The man sold his daughter, whose name is Daw, to get enough money to smuggle his son out of Nong Samet."

"But I thought you said you guys don't charge for your help."

"Bribery is a way of life here. Sakda's father probably had to pay several people off just for a chance to meet Ram and ask for his help."

"Sell the girl to save the boy." E blew out a puff of air. "Given the circumstances, a lot of Western fathers would make the same choice."

"It's sad, what happens to girls in this world."

E stood abruptly. "We need to go get her. If the brother gets to escape, she should too."

"Elvera."

She touched her chest. "There's money taped inside my bra. I'll buy her back."

"Or we could rent a jet pack, fly in, and pluck the girl out of danger." Cathy turned from sarcasm to logic. "We're not allowed inside Nong Samet. If we were to get in, we have no idea how to find the girl. And if by some miracle we found her, we'd have a snowball's chance in hell of getting her out." She rubbed her neck. "Jay might be able to arrange it, but Daw could be…damaged by the time we find him and enlist his help."

And I certainly don't want to run into him. Once she realized that Cathy saw Jay as a heroic figure, E had shut up about her experiences with him. Jay Taksin might be a great example of concern for humanity, but Elvera wasn't sure the man was completely sane.

Biting at her lip she asked, "Didn't you tell me the current camp administrator is a decent guy?"

"That's what Sunan says, but how would we get to him, and why would he listen to us?"

E turned to look at the suitcase she'd brought, packed with completely unsuitable clothing. "What if a rich American stopped by? Could she charm her way in, do you think?"

Cathy grinned. "Elvera Maude, you are utterly crazy."

It was like a hastily composed surprise party. E dug out two outfits, one for herself and one for Cathy, talked Sunan into accompanying them as interpreter, and led the way down the mountainside, leaving Gwen standing with her arms akimbo, mumbling insults in German.

"Where might we get a car?" she asked as they walked.

Sunan replied, "My cousin has one he uses as a taxi."

Raising her shirt, E took some cash from her bra. "Will he let us borrow it for the day?"

Sunan swallowed. "For that you might buy the whole car, Miss."

E put some of the money back. "Arrange for us to use it and have him fill it with gasoline." She turned to Cathy and held out more bills. "We need bodyguards." At her blank look, E explained, "Who'd believe that two American women of importance would wander around Thailand without protection? Find two healthy-looking men, get them something decent to wear, and tell them they're going to be actors in a little play."

The only way Cathy knew to find what E wanted was to go to her friend Tim. When she told him the story, he blinked as if she'd sprouted a second head. "Are you trippin', Cathy? You're going to sashay in there and ask the top dude to let some Cambodian girl leave because her daddy sold her to a warlord?"

She'd expected that reaction. "If you knew my friend Elvera, you'd be more optimistic."

"Chick must be something else." Tim stared at the ground for a moment. "Tell you what. I'll find your bodyguards, and I'll come along. Seng knows me, so he won't boot you and your kitty at the get-go."

"I wouldn't want to get you into trouble, Tim."

He swept her objection aside with a freckled hand. "I'll tell the dude your girl is for real a rich American. You two have to do the rest."

"I bet he'll laugh and send us on our way, but E is determined to try."

It was almost noon when a dilapidated Mercedes pulled up at the Nong Samet Camp gate, where a flag hung limp and puddles from the recent rain lined the road. Tim was at the wheel, since it turned out that neither of the two men he'd hired could drive. Squashed between Tim and one of the "bodyguards" was Sunan. The other rode on the trunk, muttering in Thai because he hadn't been chosen to ride up front. In the back seat were Cathy and Elvera, dressed in outfits ill-suited to the temperature and the terrain. E had coached everyone to appear bored, as if they were used to such experiences.

A wide, smooth road cut through the camp's center for perhaps a quarter mile but then turned to a muddy track. On both sides, row upon row of six-person huts stood so close there was hardly room to walk between them. Beyond them were tents of various materials for those even less fortunate than the hut-dwellers. There were no gardens, play areas, or organized activities. "They can't start a business or grow stuff," Tim explained. "Kids don't go to school."

"Why?" Elvera demanded. "That's inhuman."

"The Thais don't want them to think of the camp as home," Tim said, adding, "But yeah, it's a shitty way to live." His words were reinforced by blank stares of hopelessness on the faces of those they passed.

Tim had told the guard at the gate they were there to see Seng, passing on a little of the cash Elvera had provided to convince him that was a good idea. He repeated the bribe several more times, and each instance got them closer to their goal. It took several hours of waiting here and then waiting again over there, but finally they were ushered into the presence of Arum Seng, commander of Nong Samet. Cathy's first glance at the man brought the word *decorum* to mind. His appearance was neat. His desk was neat. His bamboo-and-thatch office was neat. It was clear that Seng liked things in order. How would he react to an odd proposal from a possibly crazy American businesswoman?

Conveying the reason for their visit was a cumbersome process. Seng seemed impatient, his handsome face tense, but E spoke directly to him, letting Sunan translate while she spoke in a pleasant but firm voice.

"He wants to know why this woman is important," Sunan said when the reason for their visit had been established.

Unable to admit they'd already smuggled the girl's brother into Thailand, they'd come up with a plausible lie. "Tell him I saw a photo taken by a reporter," E said. "Daw is exactly what I want to model my new fashion line, which will showcase traditional Asian clothing."

As Sunan translated, Seng's flared nostrils revealed disapproval. He barked a few words, and Sunan relayed the message with some embarrassment. "He says this is, um, nonsense."

"This woman will turn the eyes of the world to this place," E said. "With her I will highlight the dignity of the Khmer people and the urgency of their plight."

In reply Seng barked a question that needed no translation.

"Daw's face will appear in every magazine in the U.S. and Europe." E made an elegant gesture. "She will in time speak for her people in a way no other Khmer can manage."

"Khun Seng says he can offer a dozen beautiful women who will serve your purpose."

"I want this one."

Seng's face didn't soften. "He says you are a...stubborn woman."

E grinned. "Tell him he doesn't know the half of it."

When Sunan translated, Cathy saw the slightest glint of humor light Seng's eyes. Though his posture remained stiff, he gave an order, and two of his men left the room.

"We must wait while his people try to locate the girl."

With a gesture, Seng indicated they should sit, and they made a circle on a straw mat in the center of the room. Tea was brought in, but if they'd expected the camp commander to have more than the residents, they saw no sign of it. Everything, from the cups to the quality of the tea, was acceptable but not exceptional.

They held an awkward conversation, with Seng asking questions that E answered with glib lies. Why had she come to Thailand? Looking for clothing designs and unique fabrics. Where was she staying? She named an expensive hotel in Bangkok. Feeling her face warm and knowing her cheeks were bright red, Cathy feared Seng would notice, call them liars, and order them to leave.

But no. He'd fallen under the spell Elvera could cast when she chose to. Though Seng's face remained impassive, the way his eyes rested on E as Sunan spoke revealed admiration for his confident American visitor.

It was a relief when noise outside the room indicated Seng's men were back, but as they entered, Cathy's heart sank. Daw was half-carried in, and she stood upright only with support. Her right eye was swollen closed. Her lip was badly split. They'd come too late to save her from the trauma her father's decision had caused.

Growling low in his throat, Seng asked several rapid-fire questions. Sunan stopped translating, perhaps in fear of his angry countenance. The men's answers displeased him, and he gave a series of orders. Daw's supporters helped her to a seat beside Cathy, where she slumped forward, hiding her face in her hands and swallowing sobs of pain and humiliation. Turning to Elvera, Seng gave a longer speech than he had thus far.

"Khun Seng is sorry this has happened," Sunan reported. "The matter will be dealt with." As Cathy pictured more corpses at the camp fence tomorrow morning, Sunan said, "He wants to know if she is still...suitable for your purposes."

E nodded. "If she agrees, I'd like to send her to the U.S. as soon as it can be arranged."

All eyes turned to Tim, who seemed confused but willing to help. "There are visas for compassionate transport. I'll see what I can do."

The camp commander spoke again, and Sunan looked relieved. "Khun Seng suggests I take Daw to the infirmary now, so that her, um, injuries can be treated."

"I should have thought of that right away. I get excited." E flashed Seng a smile that was downright flirtatious, and he flushed slightly. As Sunan helped the girl to her feet, Cathy sent her a look. Sunan nodded, indicating that when they were alone, she'd tell Daw they intended to reunite her with her brother.

Even though they hadn't saved Daw from harm, Cathy felt good to know she would soon be safe. Working as a team, Cathy Charbonneau and Elvera Tharp had made a small but satisfying difference in the world.

When they'd thanked Seng and left his office, Cathy went to find Sunan and Daw. Elvera turned to Tim Adler, who seemed dazzled. "That was killer-diller, lady."

"Thanks, but I need a telephone so I can begin making arrangements for Daw's arrival."

"Two problems with that, Dudette." He looked at his watch.

"We don't have phones here, and it's two a.m. in Chicago."

"Can you get me to a phone?"

He shook his head. "Best I can do is a ham radio operator I use when I need to confab with home. He hooks me up with another and another, and eventually we get to a phone line."

"Let's do that."

"But like I said—"

She raised a hand. "I doubt the person I'm going to call will mind waking up for this."

Several hours and much bother later, a woman answered her telephone in Chicago, Illinois. She had apparently been sleeping deeply, and her voice was husky. "Hello?"

"Jill? It's Elvera. I have a proposal for you."

"Proposal?"

"Wake up and pay attention. Would you like your job at Mizz back?"

Jill's voice became stronger. "Is this a joke?"

"No, it's not. I need you to be my surrogate for a while. You'll run everything and answer only to me. Does that sound okay?"

Jill's hesitation was brief. "It sounds wonderful. I—Thank you, Ms. Terzis—I—"

"This is an overseas call, so I can't chat. I'll write up my instructions and get them to you, and I'll send a letter to my lawyers giving you the power you'll need to manage the company in my absence. I expect you to have my new campaign organized by the time I get back."

Ending the call with Jill's thanks still ringing in her ears, E spent several minutes writing out instructions for what she'd already begun thinking of as her Khmer Line. Adler busied himself with paperwork, allowing her time to work. When she was satisfied, E addressed two envelopes and gave them to him. "Can you get these to Chicago for me?"

"Sure thing."

"And you'll send Daw there as soon as possible?"

He nodded. "I think with your money, my skills, and Seng's influence, we can have her on a plane to O'Hare within a week."

"Great." She leaned back in her chair. "Now can we talk about something else?"

"Sure." Rising, he took two lukewarm sodas from a shelf behind his desk and handed one to her. "How can I further serve the delightful head of Mizz Fashions?"

"I need information." E leaned her chin against her knuckles. "About Jay Taksin."

Adler's face told her most of what she wanted to know, but she listened closely as he talked. "Cathy digs him. I kinda thought I should say something to her, but here's a news flash: Chicks don't take one guy's word that another guy is a jerk."

"But you know for certain that Jay—Mr. Taksin—is a jerk?"

His mouth quirked. "He's one slick dude."

Elvera leaned back, folding her arms across her chest in a gesture that was almost defensive. "Tell me what you know."

Some of Tim's odd language fell away as he turned serious. "Jatukamramthem Taksin is the seventh son of a minor member of the Thai royal family. He's been a con man his whole life, real good at the whole fakin' people out thing."

"He gets money from rich Americans by telling heart-tugging stories of the poor Khmer people."

Adler scratched at his beard. "I've heard he keeps most of it."

"Have you heard anything about Taksin and people in the camps?"

Adler smiled knowingly. "You mean that he smuggles them out? He does, if they can scrape together the money to pay his price."

E leaned forward. "He charges for his help?"

Rubbing his fingers together Tim said, "Life is all about the bread for Mr. Taksin."

"But those people have nothing."

He shrugged. "Look at what you saw today. Daw's dad sold his daughter to save his son, right?" When she nodded, he pointed a finger at her. "Taksin probably hatched that deal."

"In exchange for Sakda's freedom."

"Dude's got a real talent for evil." He added a warning. "I've heard that people who piss him off get dead, so I don't advise taking him on."

Remembering Jay's threat to kill Richard if she didn't divorce him, Elvera felt sick. She'd been deceived by his smooth manner, at least for a time. And Cathy believed he was a saint. How would she react if faced with the truth of Jay's perfidy?

Adler watched Elvera, apparently trying to assess how she was taking the news. "Can't you let our government know what Taksin is doing?" she asked. "It's not right."

A grin revealed how naïve that was, and Tim raised both hands, mimicking a scale. "They know. The dude does little favors for Uncle Sam, and they ignore his less-than-nice activities. Get it?"

E put a finger to her forehead in a parody of heavy thought. "Pro-Western propaganda in Uncle Ambassador's ear?"

"Don't hurt to have connections to the royal family, no matter how distant. Besides, our people back home like the picture Jay paints." Adler spread his hands. "We got our asses kicked in Vietnam, and then America's citizens found out how much we contributed to the messes in Laos and Cambodia. They like to think of Thailand as the white-hat good guy of Southeast Asia, fixing what's broke with nobility and grace."

"It's all about how things look."

Tim's smile turned rueful. "Isn't that how things usually is with the gov'mint?"

Sunan stayed in the village, since the next day was her uncle's birthday. On the walk back to the compound, E felt the humidity like a blanket on her skin. More rain was coming, though it seemed the earth was soaked beyond what it could absorb. It was hard to imagine the rainy season until one lived through it.

Sakda still waited in the cave above the school, and Cathy fretted about his future. "Someone is going to come to take him on soon. How will we reunite him with Daw if we don't know where he is?"

"I'm going to take him to Tim Adler's house," E responded. "You'll tell Jay's men that he ran away."

Elvera didn't let on how hard it had been to convince Adler to take the boy. His arguments were strong: How did the two of them rise above all the others at Nong Samet? Why should Tim risk his position and his agency's reputation for them? Where was he was supposed to get a second compassionate entry passport? It had come down to money, and to his credit, Adler succumbed to a bribe not for himself, but for his work. Elvera promised twenty percent of Daw's earnings as a model, sent directly to Adler to use as he saw fit.

"Having seen you in action," he'd said in parting, "I'm betting that within a year I'll have the bread to do some real good in this place."

Elvera explained her plan. "Tomorrow morning, announce that I've gone home. I'll leave Sakda at Tim's house and head back to Bangkok."

"You'll never find your way in the dark."

"You said it yourself, Cath. I just keep going downhill."

"We need to talk about this some more."

E took her friend by the arms. "Cath, he'll be fine. I'll be fine."

"Are you sure?"

"I'm sure."

They'd come within sight of the compound, which was dark and silent. Removing the remaining food and water from her pack, Cathy gave it to E, who stuffed the pockets of her expensive jacket until it hung like a clown suit.

"Take the flashlight," Cathy whispered. "I'll pack your things and set the suitcase out front."

"Okay. I'll pick it up after I get the boy."

"Wait until it's quiet before you bring him down—" Cathy winced as if struck. "Oh, E, I won't see you again for who knows how long."

"I know. I hate it too, but it has to be this way." She hugged Cathy fiercely. "I'm so glad I came. I'm glad we're...all right."

Cathy returned the embrace. "We're all right, E. We always will be."

The rain began sometime after two a.m., pounding on the roof like a hundred tinkers mending pots. Around four, a boy came to the teachers' hut, pleading for help. The roof of his house had collapsed, and a cross beam broke both his father's legs. Gwen, who was known as a healer, agreed to go and see what she could do for him.

With Gwen on a mission of mercy and Sunan still with her family, Cathy was left to organize a shipment dropped off the day before, outdated but usable textbooks donated by a school in Nebraska. When day dawned, gray as it was, she began unpacking boxes and shelving the books out of the damp as best she could.

When a vehicle sounded in the distance it registered, but she paid little attention. Trucks often passed the school on their way over the mountain, a shorter though rougher route than the main road. Sometimes drivers stopped to have tea with them; other times they went by with a downshift and a wave.

This vehicle stopped, and Cathy looked out the window to see an old army Jeep. The driver's face was shielded by a wide-brimmed hat that dripped with moisture, but she shivered nonetheless. She knew the set of those shoulders and the tone of his skin. Jay.

On the way to the door, she practiced the lies she'd have to tell. Casually she called out, "Hey, Stranger."

"Cathy." Jay stepped inside and hugged her, his touch both familiar and frightening. When he released her, he asked, "Where is Elvera?"

"Elvera?"

The smile stayed in place, but his eyes were cold. "I know she came here, Cathy, and I'm sure she told you about us. I need to talk to her." After a pause he added, "About the baby."

"She isn't—"

He put up a hand to stop the lie. "I spoke with the driver who brought her here."

Nothing but truth would do. "She doesn't want to see you, Jay."

"She has my child." His voice cracked on the last word, and he took hold of her arms. "Is it a boy, Cathy? Do I have a son?" She said nothing, but he read the answer in her eyes.

"It is a boy. Cathy, do you know how I've longed for a son?" His tone was pleading. "I love Elvera, and we will be a family. I would give my life to protect them."

"It isn't going to work—"

He raised a hand, and Cathy thought he was going to slap her. Then she saw a shift in his eyes, and his manner turned pleading. "Did she give me a chance? Did she let me show how our life could be together? No. She did not even tell me there would be a child. But when I saw it, I said to myself, 'This changes everything.'" His eyes met Cathy's. "I am the man Elvera needs, one she can love and respect."

Cathy's mind wavered for a moment. If Jay had a chance to talk to E, could they work things out? She certainly didn't love Richard, and Jay seemed to truly care for her.

As Cathy argued with herself, Jay added a new wrinkle. "Please don't let jealousy dictate your actions." He touched her face, a loving gesture that felt false. "You and I have…a past, but what we had was not love. I beg you to step aside, for the sake of Elvera's happiness."

Cathy shook her head, stunned. Did Jay think she'd keep E's location a secret due to envy? As if a blindfold had dropped from her eyes, she realized Jay didn't know her at all. Because that emotion would motivate him if the situation were reversed, he assumed she was the same.

Examining his face with new clarity, she saw the manipulator behind the attractive mask. Impatience and agitation made him less smooth and more transparent. His eyes, which had once seemed so warm, looked as cold as flat stones to her now. The mouth that had pressed on hers was tense. His body seemed coiled like a spring, its energy barely under control. Everything she'd once believed about Jay Taksin was wrong.

"E is afraid of you."

His smile faltered. "I was…upset when I learned she was pregnant. I will make things right when I see her."

Cathy felt her lips tighten. E had gone to great lengths to be rid of Jay. Now E needed her help. "She went home, Jay."

"And my son?"

"She didn't tell me anything about a baby."

His smile turned ugly. "You were never a good liar, Cathy."

"I—"

The force of Jay's blow sent her staggering backward against a bookshelf. It toppled over, spilling its contents, while she barely kept her feet. Jay stepped toward her with fists clenched. "Where is the child?"

"Jay—" A second blow sent her to the floor, and she tasted blood on her lip. "I don't know."

"You know, and you will tell." Jay stood over her like an evil Titan. "No woman will come between me and my son."

Elvera had been leaving Tim Adler's house when she saw Jay Taksin pass by in a Jeep, his tires splashing water on passersby. She recognized him at once, despite the slanted view and heavy rain. His posture revealed determination; his speed indicated he had a goal in mind. If he'd been to Nong Samet, he knew that she and Cathy had been there the day before.

"Tim!" she called. He hurried out to see what had upset her. "I need to get to Cathy as soon as possible."

Adler didn't know the whole story, but he heard the fear in E's voice. "My driver took Daw to Bangkok. He won't be back until tomorrow." He pointed to several trucks lined up to be loaded with goods. "You could hitch a ride with one of them." He checked his watch. "If you can wait half an hour, I'll come with you."

"I can't wait, but once I find her, we might need a place to hide for a while." Adler frowned, and she feared he might try to stop her from leaving. "Everything will be okay if I go get Cathy and bring her here."

"Okay," he said doubtfully. "I guess those guys are your best bet."

The first truck in line was ready, stacked with an assortment of bags and crates. "Are you going over the mountain?" E asked the driver.

He stared uncomprehendingly, but one of the others translated, and the first man nodded. "Yes, yes."

With the second man's help, E bargained for a ride to the school. "We must go quickly," she insisted, waving a wad of bills in his face. Eyes on the money, the man gestured for her to climb into the cab, which had no windows and a stretched canvas for a roof. To sit, she had to move a crate of chickens to the floor and splay her feet around it. The chickens weren't pleased. Rain fell inside the cab almost as hard as outside, but the driver climbed in, rammed the truck into gear with a sure hand, and they roared away.

After a ride even more uncomfortable than her initial one up the mountain, Elvera exited the truck at the compound. Dread twisted her gut when she saw Jay's Jeep parked in front of the mud hut. The place was silent except for the truck engine, and after a moment she waved the driver on. Slogging her way to the door, she opened it cautiously and peered into the hut. No Cathy. No Jay. No one.

Going back outside, she splashed through puddled water to reach the school, where her worst fears were realized. The place was a battlefield, strewn with broken glass, torn books, and, she noted with even deeper dread, spatters of blood. Hurrying back outside, she checked the other buildings. Empty. Where was Cathy?

The cave! If Cathy had been able to climb up there, she could pelt Jay with rocks and keep him from coming after her. E raced around the building, praying. *Please, God, let that be what happened.*

It was not. Looking up through the downpour, she saw Jay standing on the ledge above. One hand gripped Cathy's hair, holding her upright as she slumped, half-conscious. The part of her that was awake registered Elvera's appearance, and she cried, "Run, E! Take the Jeep and go."

"No, Elvera!" Jay shouted over the pounding rain. "If you want your friend to live, climb up and join us."

Her mind swirled with possibilities. If she ran, Jay would almost certainly kill Cathy in reprisal. If she promised to marry him after what she'd done, he'd call her a liar. She had to bargain with him, offering the baby's location for Cathy's life. Jay no longer trusted her, so he'd keep them both alive until he was sure she'd told the truth. It was certain that once he had the child, he'd kill both her and Cathy. In Jay's diseased mind, they were his enemies now.

E had to appear compliant, hoping to placate Jay until they got a chance to escape him. She prayed that Cathy would guess what she was thinking and react accordingly. A memory gave Elvera hope: the night on Mackinac Island when Cathy had appeared like an avenging angel to save E from rape. By joining forces, they'd been able to triumph. If they were going to get out of this, they had to do something like that again.

"I'm coming up."

Her ascent was slowed by rain, slippery rocks, and naked fear. She had to force herself to keep going, to climb when every instinct told her to run. As she neared the lip, E couldn't banish the notion that Jay might send her to her death with a single kick.

No, she told herself. *You have something he wants*. Once she reached the ledge, she and Cathy would defeat him, somehow. Together.

When she reached the top, Jay's expression was smug. "I'm glad you decided to cooperate, Elvera."

E glanced at Cathy, trying to gauge how much help she'd be in a fight. She remained on her feet, but it was an effort. Her face was a mess, and E promised herself Jay would pay for hurting her. "Let Cathy go. She doesn't know anything."

As she hoped, Jay turned to look at his battered victim. "She'll go free once you—"

E lunged at him with as much force as she could muster. Hands out, she aimed for his broad chest, hoping to knock him backward with the unexpected attack.

Though the move surprised him, Jay turned his shoulders and shifted one foot, like a bullfighter. E's right hand missed him entirely; the left hit him a glancing blow as she stumbled past. As E struggled to regain her balance, Cathy came to life, pushing Jay toward the drop-off with a guttural, "Bastard!"

Jay stumbled from the force of this second attack, but he didn't fall. Instead he turned, grabbed Cathy's shirt, and tossed her over the ledge with an almost casual gesture. Her eyes met E's for an instant, pleading either for help or for forgiveness at leaving E to deal with this madman alone. Then she was gone. The cry she emitted was cut off by a fleshy thud that broke E's heart.

"Cathy?" Pulse pounding, E rushed to the edge and looked down. Her friend lay on the ground, arms and legs splayed. A trickle of blood ran from one side of her mouth and disappeared into her hair.

Jay spared no time on her. "Where is the child? He is mine, and I will have him."

Still stricken, E didn't answer.

"Elvera." His fingers pinched her arms painfully as he turned her away from Cathy's motionless body. He began shaking her, so violently that her head grew fuzzy and her legs couldn't hold her up. "My son. Where is he?"

"Cathy!" Her teeth clacked together. "Murderer!"

The shaking continued until E had trouble remembering where she was. "Elvera!" Jay shouted in her ear. "Tell me, and you will live." His tone turned even harsher. "He is *mine*."

She was losing consciousness, and he must have seen it, for he stopped shaking her and pulled her close, staring into her eyes until he saw that she was again able to think. His voice turned coaxing. "Tell me what I want to know, and I will leave you in peace."

What peace could she have now? Cathy was dead. She was

faced with the prospect of losing her son to this monster. Anger filled her, so deep she couldn't hold it inside. "Go ahead. Kill me. I'll never tell you."

The blow knocked her to the rocky ground. Pain shot through her back, her head, her shoulder. "I will not bargain with you, Elvera. Tell me." A kick to the gut left her curled into a ball and gagging.

When she could speak again, the words came out in chunks. "I—hate—you."

That brought another kick, and she cried out. Jay leaned over, speaking into her ear. "I have not yet begun to hurt you, E, but understand this: I know how it is done." He glanced around. "In a place where no one can hear you scream, you will tell me what I want to know." Grasping her shirt, he punched her in the face. Black curtains closed on her vision, and for a while she knew nothing.

When she woke, it was to the hum of an engine under her and the continued roar of rain above. Opening an eye—Only one would open, and it offered blurred images—she realized she was slumped in the passenger seat of the Jeep. Jay drove, his hand on the shifter and his eyes on the road ahead. In the back of the vehicle was Cathy—Cathy's body, she amended. Her face was turned away, as if even in death she couldn't bear to watch what would happen next.

Every bump sent pain through Elvera's torso, like fire-tipped spears. Bones were broken, but there would be worse when Jay got to the destination he'd chosen. Once he beat the baby's location out of her, she too would die, and he'd bury her and Cathy in the same, shallow grave. No one would ever know what became of them.

Her son. She had to protect him.

Desperately she tried to think of a way to escape. The road was even more treacherous than usual, and Jay held tightly to the wheel as the Jeep slewed and slid in the mud. That was good, because he hadn't noticed that she'd regained consciousness. That wasn't exactly the right word. She was at best semi-conscious. Fuzzy vision, an inability to concentrate, and a blinding pain in her skull signaled a likely concussion. Covertly E tried moving her free arm. It obeyed, but the resulting pain suggested it was broken. She didn't dare move again lest she drew his attention.

Blinking to clear her vision, Elvera fought waves of nausea as her traumatized brain's reacted to the rough ride. She was sorely tempted to shut her working eye and rest, but part of her knew that if she wanted to live, she had to act. Outside the Jeep, she saw for the first few seconds only smears of green and brown, but gradually the eye began sending better images. Trees dripping with moisture. Green hillsides dotted from time to time with grayish rock outcrops. A footpath lined with handrails.

Jay was heading upward, over the mountain. She recalled the steep drop-off and the river far below. "I wouldn't try this road at night," she'd said to Sunan the day they followed its path.

"It's very bad during rainy season," she had replied. "A small mistake can lead to tragedy."

Beside her, Jay downshifted as the ascent steepened. Elvera saw a wide expanse of sky over his shoulder. Did she have the strength to do what she was thinking? She licked the corner of her mouth, where blood made the skin taste like iron. Jay used desperate people to make himself rich. He ruined lives without compunction. He'd murdered Cathy. A man like that could not be allowed to raise her child.

Reaching out, E grabbed the steering wheel and wrenched it to the left with every ounce of her remaining strength. Caught by surprise, Jay turned to look at her for the tiniest moment.

That instant of inattention was enough to negate any chance he might have had to correct his path. The front tire was already over the side when he jerked the wheel back to the right. As the rest of the vehicle followed the direction E had set it on, Jay roared with helpless fury. Turning onto its side, the Jeep traveled downhill, rolling over and over as it went, striking trees and rocks, until it splashed into the river. There the engine continued to spin the tires for a few seconds before it gurgled and died.

Bangkok, two weeks later

She woke to a faraway grating noise that went on long enough to become irritating. It took a while for annoyance to make her open her eyes and look for the source. Though she couldn't tell where the sound came from, she realized she was in a hospital room. A glance revealed tubes coming from her arm, a white sheet pulled up to her chest and folded back on itself, and a heavy metal frame beyond her feet. She made a noise that was much smaller than she'd intended. Her throat was dry, and her tongue felt like someone had pumped it full of glue. The horrors of Jay's attack returned, and she whimpered once.

Something rustled to her right and Richard appeared, his face pinched with concern. "You're awake. Thank God."

She looked at him blankly and tried again to speak, but he put a hand on her shoulder. "Your jaw is broken. They had to wire it shut, but they tell me you'll be fine in a few weeks." In the falsely cheerful way people use when putting a good face on a bad situation he added, "Food has to come through a straw, but you get as many milkshakes as you want."

The next sound she made was a question, and he nodded as if she'd made herself completely understandable. "A village woman found you on the hillside, barely alive."

The door opened and a tiny, dark-haired nurse came in. "She has awake. This is good." Taking up the hand not attached to tubes, she went silent as she counted the pulses. "You are very lucky," she said in careful English when she finished. "Your husband brought you here to see that you have the very best doctors."

When she turned to Richard, brows quirked in surprise, he explained, "When you went missing, Elvera, I realized I don't want to live without you." He took hold of the hand the nurse had released. "If you let me, I'll spend the rest of my life making you happy." He seemed not to notice her frown but went on, "They found Jay Taksin's body in the river and…Cathy too." As tears filled her eyes he said, "I had to do the identification. She was—" Thinking better of that he said instead, "I'm so sorry, sweetheart."

In time she learned she had multiple injuries, including a shattered hip, but nothing that threatened her life. Once it was clear she was on the mend, Richard confessed that he knew about the baby. "When you get out of this place, I'll bring him to you. Would you like that?" She nodded. "We can stay in Thailand if you like." He glanced out the fly-specked window. "I'll have to return to Chicago periodically, but this is a beautiful country. We'll raise the boy here, together." Richard's gaze met hers. "He's lucky you survived, Elvera. What chance would the poor little guy have if both his mother and his father had died in that accident?"

Though Richard offered paper and pen, she couldn't summon the energy to try to explain her thoughts. Jay was dead. Richard was willing to raise the child. That was enough for now. Everything else could be straightened out when she was stronger.

A memorial service was held for Cathy, and friends she'd made in Thailand came to pay their respects. Her brothers were notified of her death, but being practical men, they neither had the body shipped home nor traveled halfway around the world to honor a sister who was beyond earthly help. Richard went to the service alone, while she wept on and off all day. Images of two girls, two young wives, two women starting a business, and two combatants facing a monster on a mountaintop played through her mind. Only the hope she'd soon have a child to care for made life bearable.

Chapter Twenty-Five

Bangkok-1984

The Garden of Children Orphanage was not the best of its kind, but it wasn't the worst either. Children housed there were fed simply but regularly. They were not mistreated, though they experienced little of love or even affection. The manager, Khun Maarit, was almost never seen to smile, except in a professional grimace she had developed for when prospective parents visited. With the woman who now stood before her, she didn't bother to even attempt that. The visitor was obviously poor. Bruises on her face and arms indicated a recent beating, and she could barely speak for fear and trembling.

"What is it you want?"

It took the woman a few seconds to form the words. "I want a child. A son. Please."

Maarit looked her up and down, but her second impression was no better than the first. "You seem hardly able to care for yourself. How will you raise a child?"

The story came out in a rush. "My husband is a hard worker and not a bad man, but I am not able to bear a child for him. It weighs on his heart, making him almost mad at times." Her eyelids hid her eyes as she added, "It is my fault, and I deserve his anger."

"So he beats you."

"If he had a son, Kiet would be happy." Her expression revealed hope for a better future.

Maarit doubted her visitor had enough brains to figure out that a man who beats his wife for one thing will beat her for another. A child wouldn't change things, at least not for long.

That was not her concern. "There are fees for this. Can you pay?"

The woman opened her hand to reveal a pitiful roll of baht. "I have this much."

The sum she offered was laughable, but Maarit had other considerations. An American woman had come recently, asking to leave the child she was about to bear at the orphanage for a month or two. She'd given Maarit money for his care, but she had not come back for the boy. The child seemed always to be hungry, and Maarit sometimes stopped at his crib, wondering what she should do with him. Experience told her a mixed-race child would be hard to place, despite his strong limbs and symmetrical features.

Now Maarit studied Kamon Banyen, who blushed and fidgeted before her. She was the opposite of the boy's birth mother, dull-witted and disadvantaged. Maarit had smiled when she took the American woman's money, but she'd secretly despised her brash, rude ways. She didn't want to look at her bastard, half-breed son for even one more day.

The peasant woman's face broke into a smile when Maarit said, "You are in luck, Khun Kamon. I have a fine boy you may take home with you today."

Richard bought a house for them in Bangkok. "The owner died violently," he reported. "Some believe that means his ghost will hang around the place, but we won't worry about such foolishness, will we." More solicitous than she'd ever seen him, Richard hired a housekeeper to get the place ready. When she was able to leave the hospital, he pushed her wheelchair over the cool tile floors, showing her the house and letting her choose the room she wanted for hers. One with a wall of windows overlooking the garden pleased her, and he smiled. "I could have guessed that would be your choice."

For himself Richard chose a room on the opposite side of the house, smaller than hers and facing the street. No doubt he planned to bring women in that way, but that was Richard. Numb with grief, recovering from multiple injuries, and depressed, the last thing she wanted was a man, any man, in her bed.

The Tharp businesses were halfway around the world, but Richard created an office in a small side-room, installed a telephone, and stayed up late talking to clients and employees during their business hours. Four weeks after her release from the hospital, he declared it was time he returned to the U.S. "Some things can't be done long-distance," he said at breakfast, "but Nin will take good care of you."

Released from the device that had allowed her jaw time to heal, she was able to say, "I understand."

Meeting her gaze Richard said, "I believed I've located the boy." As a pulse of infrequent joy rushed through her veins, he went on, "Unfortunately, the orphanage says their records are private. I explained that the child's mother is presently unable to travel, but the woman in charge is about as warm as Lake Michigan. I'm working to convince her to release the boy to me."

"How will you accomplish that?"

"When I'm in Chicago, I'll pick up documents that prove I'm married to the woman they know as Mrs. Smith. I'll bring back a photo of the two of us as visual proof." His lip curled, and the old sardonic Richard showed. "No doubt I'll have to include financial incentives as well, but we should have him with us soon."

If anyone could do it, Richard could. He was an expert at conniving, and though it wasn't an attractive trait, it was useful in situations like this.

"I don't care how much it costs," she said. "I want him with us."

"I know, darling," he replied, "and I know what my role is in this."

Richard was gone for two months. During that time, driven by the prospect of having an active little boy who would need a functioning parent, she worked to regain her strength. With it, some of her enthusiasm for life returned as well. The horrors of Jay's attack remained, but in time the scenes she relived became muted, like movie scenes watched so many times they lose their chilling effect. Though she understood that the brain blurs tragedies over time, it made her angry. Her dearest friend was dead. How could her heart rejoice at the flowers that appeared in her garden?

Her Catholic upbringing offered what felt like the possibility for future peace: penance. Giving up something allowed sinners to atone for mistakes, to remind themselves that actions have consequences. Her means of atonement had to be something difficult to live without, something meaningful.

Music, she decided. All of it, all the songs Elvera and Cathy had loved and the singers they'd discussed on lazy summer afternoons, would be banished from her life. Denying herself that joy would be penance for living through the day her best friend died. She would no longer sing, listen, or even hum. Silence would remind her of past failures.

When Richard returned, she was in the kitchen chopping vegetables. She looked up, saw his expression, and knew the news was bad. "The child, he—." He choked out the rest. "The boy died."

Suddenly he was holding her up as her knees swung weakly beneath her. The knife she'd been holding clattered to the floor and spun there, gradually slowing to a stop. "Darling, I'm sorry. I didn't want to tell you on the phone, but I shouldn't have blurted it out like that."

Leading her to a chair, he got a glass, filled it with water, and ordered her to drink. When she had recovered a little, he told the story. With documents and photos, he'd convinced the orphanage manager to open the records. "The boy simply died." At the question in her eyes he added, "I had the translator read the death certificate to me. *Cot death*, he called it: the unexplained loss of a child under a year old. There are theories about why it happens, but honestly, no one knows."

"His mother wasn't there to take care of him," she mumbled.

"Nothing suggests such deaths are related to who looks after a child."

She didn't argue, and Richard fell silent, no doubt aware he'd never convince her. Refilling her water glass, he set it before her. Then he took up the knife she'd been using and set it out of sight. She didn't move or speak, and after a few moments he left the room. In a short time, the young housemaid came in and finished paring the vegetables. Obeying her master's orders, Nin pretended to stay busy in the kitchen after the task was done, to make sure the mistress didn't retrieve the knife and use it to slice her own wrists.

Chapter Twenty-Six

Cruise-Day 12, 11:30 a.m.

The kitchen hummed with activity. Marilyn paced the aisles, urging both speed and attention to detail. "The Captain's Dinner is the passengers' big night out," she told her staff. "Tomorrow they'll go ashore for the last time, and then it's full steam for home. We want to give our guests great memories, so let's be ship-shape."

There was lunch to be served as well, so Marilyn split her crew. Michael, Glynis, and two others were charged with setting out a simple soup-and-salad menu for mid-day, while more experienced hands applied themselves to the elaborate dinner preparations.

"I still can't believe I never saw you in Bangkok," Glynis said as they carried steaming pots of soup into the dining room. Sliding the vessel into its spot over the warmer with a metallic clunk she added, "I even visited the Chailangkas' place a few times when I was chasing the Yoosamran brats. Never saw you there."

"Yes, it's funny how that happens."

"Ow!" Glynis blinked rapidly. "I think I've got an eyelash stuck to my contact lens." Leaning toward Michael she asked, "Will you look?"

Obediently he studied her eye for a few seconds. "Nothing there."

Glynis touched his chest lightly. "See anything you like?"

Michael shook his head at her persistence. "I'll get the last pot of soup. You fill the cracker baskets."

In the cubby at the back of the kitchen was a pouch marked *G.S.* In it was a lipstick, a lighter, and a contact lens case. "Be right back," Michael told the cook as he palmed the case. "Have to use the rest room."

Chapter Twenty-Seven

Bangkok-May, 1984

"Madame, you must eat something, or you will become sick."

When Madame didn't answer, Nin set the soup and bread on the table and tiptoed out.

The aroma of the broth brought Mackinac Island to mind. The housekeeper there, what was her name? Laura. She recalled the long braid that hung down the woman's back, swinging slightly as she moved around the kitchen. One day when the weather turned cold and the wind came in raw off the straits, she'd made cabbage soup. After ladling out two bowls from the stainless-steel pot, Cathy had broken crackers into hers, making it thick and lumpy. Watching, Elvera said it looked gross, but when she tried it, she'd admitted it wasn't bad.

Elvera. Cathy. So different. So alike.

She spent several days in a dark room, unable to calm her roiling brain. *Think of something else,* she would order, but a stressed mind doesn't follow orders. Her thoughts ran in a circle. The boy would have made up for everything. Now she faced a useless life with no path to meaning.

She thought often of death, of those who die unwillingly and those left behind with no reason to go on. She even tried willing herself to slip into the abyss. Lying in bed, she tried to let go by listing the reasons for doing so. Each time, she merely fell asleep and woke the next morning to her unwelcome life again.

"We could adopt a child here in Thailand," Richard suggested, but she squinted at him as if he'd spoken in a foreign language. Clearing his throat nervously he said, "We'll talk about it later."

But they didn't, and after a few tries he left her to her brooding. Within a month he found it necessary to return to Chicago again, and a month after that he called to say he had to stay for a while. Business was problematic. Prices were going crazy, and the dollar was weak. It was best if he remained close to things.

She hardly noticed his absence. Inhabiting her home like a restless ghost, she brushed her teeth when she thought of it and washed her hair when Nin said it was time. Though she was able to walk, she often forgot to rise from the chair and do it. She was like a four-year-old, capable of self-care but needing to be reminded what that was.

Then one day a woman showed up who changed everything. "My name is Terri Schultz, Mrs. Terzis," she said when Nin left them alone together. "I've come to ask for your help."

Ms. Schultz—Her manner suggested she would prefer the neutral title—was walnut-colored and burned dry from hours in the sun. Her athletic body was built for action and was seldom still. She had dressed for the heat in khaki shorts and a shirt washed so many times it was hard to tell what color it had originally been. From her homely face shone two eyes so blue and bright that they looked like aquamarines set in wet sand.

"My help?" With those two words, she managed to convey the ridiculousness of the idea that a crippled recluse could assist anyone.

Schultz' gaze took in the cane and the dent in her hostess' jaw that pulled her mouth slightly to one side. "I was about to contact Cathy Charbonneau when she—when she died. I'm sure you know that the situation on the Cambodian border is only getting worse."

She shook her head, indicating she hadn't been paying attention.

"Cambodia is under the control of the Khmer Rouge."

"I know that much. They've terrorized their own people for years now."

"Well, the Vietnamese invaded, intending to kick the Khmer Rouge out. Now the camps on the Thai border are battlegrounds for the opposing armies. Nong Samet was destroyed by shelling at one point, but it's been rebuilt and renamed Site 2."

"And the Thais still won't let the Khmers relocate?"

"The policy's the same. They're expected to go home when things settle."

A flash of her old fire returned. "How many years will that take?"

Schultz grimaced to indicate she had no answer. "More people come to the border every day."

"I'd hoped it would get better."

"We all did." Shaking her head Schultz said, "Each time we gain a little on the problems, things fall apart again. International agencies do a great job of bringing in aid, but as Cathy probably told you, food and supplies often fail to reach those who need it, those it was meant for."

Was this woman another Jay Taksin, come to wring money from the rich American with stories of tragedy and danger? *When you trust too easily, innocent people die.*

"Why are you telling me this, Ms. Schultz?"

"I didn't know Cathy," she replied, "but Tim Adler was a good friend. He's gone back to the States, his father died, but he always said how great she was." With a flash of white teeth, she added, "I think he had a crush on her. Anyway, he admired you as well and thought you might be approachable."

"For what?"

Schultz clasped her hands in her lap, as if willing them to be still as she got to the point of her visit. "I came to Thailand with AID two years ago. When my hitch was done, I stayed, working with local Thais who do what they can for the refugees. We have no legal status, so my job is begging people like you for funds to buy food for the camps."

"Established international agencies bring in aid every day."

Schultz' eyes flashed with irritation. "And everybody from warlords to camp guards helps himself. They either keep the stuff or sell it to the people it was meant for in the first place." She paused, obviously trying to regain her pleasant manner. "Our group gives goods directly to those in need, and we take nothing in return." She frowned, adding, "The problem is that we seldom have much to give."

Part of her wanted to say, "Of course I'll help." Another part ordered, *Don't be a dope. Good people are fooled every day by con artists. 'Save this!' 'Rescue that!' 'Give us money, and we'll do great things.'*

"Ms. Schultz, you want me to help you circumvent the laws of Thailand, the rules that all the governments involved have agreed on, and the guidelines of international relief agencies. Am I supposed to believe that you know more than all those entities do?"

Schultz sat back, as if tempted to give up, but she tried once more. "We're on the ground, Mrs. Terzis, and we see things at that level. Our actions aren't tied to political concerns or diplomatic complexities." Her chin rose a little. "We don't give a damn what's said at the U.N., in the U.S. Senate, inside the throne room in Bangkok, or any other place where lunkheads stand up and give speeches about what can't be done." She blew a strand of curly hair off her forehead with an angry puff. "We see people in desperate need, and we feed them." She leaned forward earnestly. "You were close to Cathy Charbonneau. We thought—"

In a bolt as clear as sunlight, she recognized that Terri Schultz was nothing like Jay Taksin. Her arguments, though unpracticed, were heartfelt. Her unkempt appearance revealed time outdoors in tough conditions. She was genuinely concerned for the people in the camps. It was impossible not to think how things she'd learned at

Mizz might be used to set up a better system for soliciting donations, something more effective than showing up at a stranger's home looking like a vagabond and suggesting vague, unspecified projects.

"I'll give you money," she said, and Schultz' eyes widened with surprise. "But I want to go along."

Schultz blinked several times as she considered that. "You're—um, not healthy, Mrs. Terzis, and we're a long way from the camps."

"I'll get better," she replied. "I'll find a house in the Cardamoms, and we'll use it as a base of operations." When Schultz opened her mouth to say something, she hurried on. "Cathy told me the Thai people consider Americans odd. If I pay well, and I will, who'll question what the crazy Western lady does?"

Though Schultz looked doubtful, she seemed to understand there'd be no negotiation. "If that's what it takes, Mrs. Terzis, we accept. But I have a condition: you must follow orders. You're a fashion designer who's been in this country less than a year. We can't have an enthusiastic amateur putting us all in danger."

"I'll do exactly as you say."

When she called Richard and told him what she planned to do, he was vehemently opposed. "Darling, you cannot save those people. They've been killing each other for decades, hell, centuries. Buying food for them is like tossing money into a bottomless pit."

She hadn't mentioned she'd be participating. Withholding that knowledge from Richard made the whole idea somehow sweeter. "I control the finances," she said firmly. "It's what I want to do."

Reluctantly he established an account at a Thai bank for her to draw from. "Keep good records," he ordered. "I'll call it charitable giving and figure a way to get some sort of tax break out of it."

Once again, she had a purpose for living. Once again, she felt useful to the world. Hiring a man with a car to drive her to the border, she searched for a suitable place to live. She wanted to avoid the area where the Martin Luther School was located, so that left either north or south of the camps. A few miles south of Site 2, near a village called Bang Salung, she found a house on a hillside, removed from neighbors and solidly built. The owner had moved away because of the chaos at the border, and he was happy to rent the place to her. His delight was the first step in establishing among the locals that the American woman now living in their midst was a little soft in the head. She moved in, bringing Nin with her. A lifelong city dweller, the housekeeper was terrified by life in the country for the first week. After she stopped worrying about bandits and tigers, Nin began to enjoy the slower pace of village life.

Though her damaged hip didn't allow her to do as much as she'd have liked, Bang Salung's newest resident again had reasons to work toward recovery. She was able to walk, though she limped noticeably. Watching from outside the camp as the goods she paid for were delivered, she chafed at her limits. She couldn't drive a truck or a Jeep, since all the vehicles they used had standard transmissions, which meant operating a clutch. Still, she was part of things, and she celebrated with her colleagues after each successful mission.

One night the men returned with a boy of about ten. "He was trying to hang himself from the perimeter fence," they said. "His parents are dead, and another family took over their hut. He had nowhere to go."

When she expressed shock that a child would try to end his own life, Terri said, "Suicide is pretty common. They have nothing to look forward to, so it's the only solution they can see for their pain."

"What will you do with him?"

Terri sighed. "Good question. I have nowhere to keep him, and if we set him loose, he'll either be recaptured or make another attempt."

She tapped her lips with a knuckle. "I'll take him home with me."

"What?" Terri shushed herself and went on in a lower tone. "Elvera, if you're caught with a Khmer refugee in your house, at the very least they'll throw you out of Thailand."

"Do you recall how surprised my housekeeper was when you came to my door? That's because no one visits, ever. Only she will know he's there. When he's stable, I'll see about relocating him."

Terri snorted a laugh. "How? Have you got a pocket full of blank exit visas?"

She'd come to trust Terri and believe in her abilities, so she replied, "Before the accident, I worked with a group that smuggled people out of the camps. If I can revive the pipeline, we might be able to help others get out of that hellhole."

Terri's expression turned scornful. "All sixty thousand of them?"

"Of course not. But we'll do what we can."

"Are you going to foot the bill for both the food and the escapes?"

"I have the money," Cathy Charbonneau replied. "I wasn't sure why I lived through an experience that should have killed me. Now I believe it was so I can spend the Tharp fortune doing what's right."

"Cathy," Richard had said that first day after the nurse left the room. "Elvera is gone. Her will leaves everything in trust to Drake's children." He spoke slowly, watching her, and she guessed he'd spent days formulating his argument. "I want to take care of you and the baby. When I saw you lying there..." He looked down at the hand with which he held hers. "You and E were both so battered that no one could say who was who. I thought, 'Elvera can live on. Great things can be accomplished in her name.'" He squeezed Cathy's hand, but she pulled it away.

Though his nose pinched briefly, Richard's tone remained patient. "Whatever you think of me, I've dedicated my life to Tharp

274

Industries." He bit his lip as if bracing for disappointment. "If you tell the authorities the truth, I'll lose everything I've worked for. But if you do as I suggest, you'll control E's wealth and spend it as you see fit. When Drake's children are of legal age, you can turn everything over to them. With the things I've put into place, their inheritance will only increase between now and then." He raised a palm as if swearing an oath. "I'll do whatever you say, but please, think this through carefully."

Her eventual agreement had been due to several factors, not the least of which was an inability to care about the future. Though the doctors did their best, she was in considerable pain. She couldn't talk to anyone about the decision; there was no one with whom she could discuss such a shocking deception. Richard's arguments were persuasive. Elvera's child needed to be located and cared for, but neither of them had any right to him. If she went on pretending to be E, the Tharp family businesses would provide for him.

There was one more thing. Cathy felt she owed Elvera a life. If she'd been more discerning, E would never have met Jay Taksin. She'd still be alive. Cathy had hoped to make up for her failures by providing for E's son, but now he too was dead. The only thing she could do to redeem herself was to save other lives, for herself and for Elvera.

The boy Terri had rescued from Nong Samet was almost too weak to walk, but Cathy shared her cane with him, his small brown hand atop hers, and they entered her house together. She told Nin she'd hired him to do the outside chores. Though doubt showed on her face, Nin took the boy to the back yard, where she doused him under the hand pump to remove the worst of his dirt. Back inside, she fed him leftover sticky rice and fish. When he'd eaten, she laid a blanket for him in a corner of the kitchen and stayed nearby until he fell asleep. "Sleep is good," she told Cathy after she tiptoed away. "It is the best thing for great sadness."

The next time Cathy saw him, the boy looked like a different child, with a haircut, a light behind his eyes, and a shy smile for "Khun E." Language was a barrier, and her few phrases of Khmer were soon exhausted. She learned his name, Binh, but not much else. "Safe," she told him in his own language. "Here. Safe."

She showed Binh the raised garden, where she grew vegetables and flowers in crates stacked to waist level so she could reach them without kneeling, bending, or stooping. When she pulled a stray weed, the boy immediately mimicked her action, pulling a pea plant and holding it out to show that he wanted to help. "This one is good," she told him, pressing the seedling back into the soil. Pulling a weed, she said, "This is bad."

Eyeing the patch with a serious expression, the boy located a weed of the same type and pulled it. "Very good." She clapped her approval. The joy on his face was heart-warming, but she wondered what Terri's people had told him. *Please this woman or you'll be sent back to Nong Samet?* Wishing she could assure him that he need never go back, she patted his shoulder. He was so bony he almost didn't feel human.

Watching Binh change from a frightened, feral creature to a child who could smile, Cathy felt a reawakening of purpose. It was good to fight injustice, even on a small scale and with no guarantee of success. Leaving Binh in Nin's care, she went to look for Ram.

Soon after they moved to Bang Salung, Nin had begun reporting stories of a local strongman who held sway in the village, though he operated no recognized business. Rumor said he was a smuggler, providing goods to those at Nong Samet who had money to pay. Ram was wealthy, which impressed some, and he behaved like a prince, which cowed others. Thus far she had avoided coming face to face with him, though she guessed he knew all about the strange American woman. Well, not *all* about her.

By the time she'd made her way downhill to the village, her hip ached and sweat ran down her spine. She found the man who'd been Jay's second-in-command outside a noodle shop that smelled of peanuts and soy. Smoking a cigarette, he watched the villagers go about their daily tasks through slitted eyes.

"Khun Ram," Cathy said, making a *wai*. "We have met before."

"Perhaps." His tone implied that recalling a woman's face was beneath his dignity.

"My name is Elvera." That made his brows quirk in denial, but she went on quickly. "I came to offer work that could bring you good profits." Remembering his love of risk, she added, "There is danger as well."

Ram seemed to understand instinctively that he was to keep her real identity to himself. "I will hear your proposal, Khun Elvera," he said as if granting a favor. Noting her crooked stance, he kicked a chair a few inches in her direction. "Please sit."

An hour later they had a deal to revive Jay's network of people smugglers. Terri Schultz and her group would identify candidates at Site 2 in imminent need of rescue, and Ram would arrange their escape. Elvera Tharp's money would fund the operation. "These people are not to be abused in any way," she said firmly. "Man, woman, or child, each must be treated with respect."

Ram made an abrupt snort. "If there is money to be made, they are safe with us."

Moving permanently to the house outside Bang Salung, Cathy arranged to buy it from the absent owner. Already unhappy about how much money her "humanitarian nonsense" was costing them, Richard demanded to know what she saw in the place. "It's beautiful," she replied.

Richard countered by pointing out the lack of sanitary facilities, its proximity to the border camps, and its isolation from "civilization." "Don't expect me to visit. Bangkok is foreign enough for me."

The threat was a relief. "If we need to meet, I'll come to

Bangkok."

He wasn't finished. "If you have a problem out in nowhere land, how will you get help?"

Knowing his worry stemmed not from concern but from fear of losing his position as Elvera Tharp's business manager, she replied, "I have friends in Bang Salung. Do your thing, Richard, and I'll do mine."

Cathy was pleased when she found a Unitarian pastor who arranged for Binh to settle in Manitowoc, Wisconsin, where there was, for reasons she couldn't fathom, a large contingent of Hmong people. Though he had no living family, the boy would be raised among those who spoke his language and shared his customs.

Being part of the planning was different from being a cog in Jay Taksin's organization. Rescue missions called for many things, from lack of adequate sleep to the possibility of crossing paths with some power-mad warlord who'd beat them bloody for interfering with his plans. Cathy constantly fought the fear their activities would be discovered by the authorities. If that happened, she and Terri would no doubt be deported, but their Thai friends would face harsher punishment. Being responsible for so much possible danger was hard on her nerves.

Ram made light of the perils. "A man must test the limits of his courage, or he is no better than a woman." Cathy didn't point out that Terri Schultz took as many chances as Ram did. Since he was so useful to them, his chauvinistic opinions were best ignored.

Though adept at arranging escapes, Ram had no idea how Jay had smuggled the refugees from Thailand into other nations. Cathy guessed he'd used a combination of family influence and tricks that played the system. Ram agreed enthusiastically with the second part. "Khun Jay liked fooling people very much."

Since she lacked Jay's government contacts, Cathy broke the problem of people smuggling into two parts: transport out of Thailand and resettlement in a new country. For the first, the always-resourceful Terri came up with the idea of bribing a clerk in the Passport Division to make copies of documents submitted by legitimate travelers. Using the duplicate papers, Terri bought a ticket for the escapee to travel on the same day as the real person, but on an earlier flight. When the duplication was noticed, which wasn't all that often, the second person's identity was checked and verified. Workers usually concluded that someone had entered the ticket information in two different places by mistake. Cathy and Terri spread the "mistakes" as widely as possible, so the pattern wasn't noticed and investigated.

Resettlement was Cathy's job. She contacted churches, social justice groups, and concerned individuals to find those willing to help her charges establish themselves in a new place. Countries like Canada, France, and Australia had fairly open policies for allowing immigrants in, and often newcomers could simply ask for and get legal status once they arrived. When that wasn't the case, friendly individuals and organizations took the refugees in, taught them English, obtained identity papers, and helped them become, or at least appear to be, legitimate residents. Former refugees who did achieve citizenship were encouraged to share what they knew of conditions in Cambodia and the border camps in whatever ways they could. Some were more able than others, but word began to spread. Even the war-weary United States could no longer ignore the chaos it had contributed to in Southeast Asia.

One afternoon Cathy was reading in her garden, a beautiful spot that overlooked the village below and the river beyond. Depending on where she chose to sit, she could smell jasmine, magnolia, or lemongrass, and she found each one soothing in its own way. A sound made her turn, and there, framed by a bamboo trellis, was Drake. Her first reaction was a rush of joy, but it was quickly followed by burning shame. Drake had come to see his sister, and that was no longer possible.

"Cathy?" His voice was a croak.

"Drake, it isn't what you think—"

He was already hurrying forward, and he took her in his arms. His strength, his support, even his familiar masculine scent, opened Cathy's heart, and she admitted to herself how much she loved this man.

"Cathy," he repeated, his voice a whisper in her ear. "When they told me you were dead, I almost lost my mind."

"It was E who died, Drake. I'm so sorry." He moaned once, and she groped for words, but he pulled her closer, stroking her hair. As always, he understood her without explanation, without words.

Nin brought cool drinks. She must have noticed their embrace was not that of brother and sister, but she behaved as if everything was perfectly normal.

Once they were seated near a sweet-scented hibiscus, Cathy told Drake most of it, doing her best to make Elvera seem blameless. Judging from the sadness in his eyes, Drake read between the lines. "E never should have let Dad pressure her into marrying Richard." After a beat he added, "Not that I was any great shakes at avoiding parental expectations."

"Things are still difficult for you?"

"Patti can't seem to get her demons under control." He paused. "Cathy, E was overwrought that day, with Dad's death and Patti going off like that. She never believed you and I would..."

"I know. It was a bad time for all of us."

Turning away, he spoke to the flowers around them. "When you disappeared, I wanted to scour the earth, find you, and stay beside you for the rest of my life. But I had the kids to consider. I told myself when they were old enough to understand..." His lips pressed together briefly. "Then word came that you were dead. E was badly hurt, and Richard had gone to Thailand to be with her." His body tensed, recalling previous agitation. "I couldn't get hold of him for some time. When he finally called, he said Elvera couldn't speak due to a broken jaw."

She looked down at her hands. "Richard excels at turning an ounce of truth into a pound of persuasion."

"I wanted to come then, but he said Elvera had a lot to work through. He claimed she hated the idea of me seeing her with a limp and a scar. He sent weekly reports on her health, even photos." Drake shook his head ruefully. "Always from a distance, and a little blurry."

Resisting the urge to touch her disfigured face she said, "It's true. E wouldn't have wanted anyone to see her weak and broken, even you."

Drake ran a hand through his hair, and she noticed his temples had gone silver. "I shouldn't have trusted Richard. When I had to come to Southeast Asia this month on business, I decided it was time to see for myself, no matter what Elvera or Richard or...anyone said."

She guessed the pause had omitted his wife's name. "And it's worse than you could have imagined."

"No." He met her gaze. "I knew—I sensed—that E was beyond my reach. If any part of her was left, she'd have contacted me. I imagined her brain-damaged, unable to feed herself or construct a coherent sentence." His smile was sad, yet it was still a smile. "What I never guessed was that I'd find you in her place."

It was time to explain her reason for deception. "Did E tell you why she came to Thailand?"

He frowned. "To see you. Since I'd been here, she called for suggestions on where to stay and such."

"Then you and she talked after...I mean..."

Drake smiled. "We put that sad mess behind us not long after you left, but Patricia is so...emotionally fragile...that E suggested we let her believe we'd cut ties completely."

How difficult it must be to have a wife so insecure and petty. She didn't say that aloud. "I bet E got a kick out of fooling everyone."

"She did." He chuckled grimly. "Not only did Patti think she'd won some imaginary battle, but there was also a sharp drop in the number of Compton nieces and nephews dropping by my office to hint they could be the next big thing at Mizz Fashions."

"Your office? What are you doing for a living these days?"

"I started a travel enterprise that's worked out well. All that running around the world for State counted for something after all."

Cathy realized she had to tell Drake about Elvera's son, because she needed him to understand why she'd made the bargain with Richard. Keeping her gaze averted, she explained how E had come to her with news of a baby and how she'd died before she could retrieve him from the orphanage. "I thought if I found the child and gave him a good home, I'd be doing her a service," she said, "but he died before we could get him out of that place."

"And now you're trapped in Richard's schemes." He made an angry huff. "The man always manages to get what he wants."

Her voice filled with self-recrimination. "For a while I believed he meant to help."

"I hope—I hope he treats you well, Cathy."

"We aren't...a couple, if that's what you mean. He sees to the businesses and sends me money to live on."

"Be careful." The tilt of his head reminded her of E, a stab of memory so sharp she almost cried out. "Richard puts profit over prudence. That's what E told me once." After a pause he asked, "Is this life enough, Cathy? I can help you return home, if that's what you want. We'll claim you had amnesia or something."

She considered becoming Cathy Charbonneau again, going back to Chicago or maybe living quietly in Michigan, the life of a normal person with a job that paid the bills. No stress, no danger, no threat of discovery. But that would end their work at the camps. Reaching out, she touched the petals of a nearby flower. "I'm content here, Drake, though I know it's wrong of me to spend money that should be your children's."

"They'll be fine," he said, chuckling. "My cruise line is growing, so they're financially secure. If you're happy here, that's all that matters."

Happy wasn't the right word. The work was stressful, and her physical limitations made life in a backwater village difficult. And Richard? Only a month before, he'd visited Bangkok and insisted she come "home" with him. The week had turned uncomfortable when he tried to charm his way into her bed, apparently determined to bind her to him in every way possible. Angry at her rebuff, he'd complained about the money she "wasted" on refugees. "Elvera certainly had you pegged," he snarled at one point. "She said you're like a little kid, trusting anyone who smiles at you."

"She never said that."

Richard gave her an arch look. "You don't suppose that things you did contributed to E's death, do you? I mean, it was you who took up with that Jay guy in the first place."

How did he know so well how to undermine her confidence? Looking back, Cathy realized that when she'd been half-dead and Richard had seemed so kind and caring, he'd probed until he knew everything: how she felt, what she'd seen, and what had happened in Elvera's last few days of life.

Regarding him coldly she'd said, "I've started sleeping with a pistol under my pillow, Richard. I'm telling you about it so there isn't some horrible accident in the night."

Had Elvera considered her hopelessly naive? Even if she had, she'd never have said it to Richard. Cathy blamed herself for Elvera's death, for being blind to Jay Taksin's dark side. Once she'd expected people to be honest and good. Now she knew, and was determined to make herself remember, that too many are neither honest nor good, at least when they see a chance to benefit themselves.

That reminder made Cathy check her wristwatch and say, "It's been good to see you, Drake, but I think it's time you went back to your wife."

Chapter Twenty-Eight

Cruise-Day 12, 6:55 p.m.

The Captain's Dinner was a great success. Passengers came dressed in their best, and the crew outdid themselves to make the meal pleasing to all the senses. A trio played mellow jazz, lighting was dimmed, and each table had an attractive arrangement of soft-scented tropical flowers.

The only hitch came when Glynis turned up in the kitchen with something wrong with her eyes. Irritated, red, and caked with a yellow rheum, they watered constantly, and she squinted like a newborn puppy under the bright lights.

"Out of this kitchen!" Marilyn ordered after a single glance. "You can't be anywhere near the food or our guests."

"I was fine this morning," Glynis griped. "I don't know what happened."

"Get down to Doc R and get some medicine," Marilyn ordered. "And stay in your cabin until we get back to Singapore. I don't want whatever you've got to spread, and I certainly can't have the guests seeing you looking like one of the undead."

Chapter Twenty-Nine

Thailand-December, 1984

As "the lady on the hill," Cathy took in Khmer, Vietnamese, and Lao nationals desperate to escape the chaos in their homelands and the deprivations of the camps. Aware they could help only a fraction of those in need, she and Terri looked for people who might later tell the world about conditions in Southeast Asia. Daw, now a model of growing renown, was doing that, exactly as Elvera had hoped she would. The Khmer woman's beauty captured the eye, and her popularity allowed her to speak for her people, citing their proud heritage and pointing out the horrors of their current situation. "Cambodia was for over five centuries a great civilization, with the largest city in the pre-industrial world," she was quoted in a magazine article. "If the nation that built Angkor, a city for one million people, can fall into ruin, any civilization can. When such things happen, nations and people must help and support each other."

Daw's success was encouraging, despite a few self-righteous pundits who claimed a fashion model should "shut up and smile," apparently believing she had no right to an opinion despite first-hand knowledge of the topic. Others, however, urged world leaders to educate themselves on the situation, which was what Cathy and her friends wanted to hear.

Eventually Cathy shared her secret with Nin, since it wasn't fair to include her in illegal activities without her knowledge. Nin merely smiled. "I have seen this, madam, and I think you are a very good person." Her eyes sparkled as she added, "If they find one of your people here, I will make a stupid look and say, 'But sirs, I do only as my crazy employer demands.'"

Cathy's life was solitary but not lonely. She worked in her

garden, growing vegetables that would have amazed her family back in Michigan. She read books, mostly historical romances where everything worked out happily in the end. She attended village festivals, fingering the lovely silks or choosing cleverly woven baskets. It was at times embarrassing, since the locals treated her as if she were royalty. She wrote long letters to Drake, which she burned in the brazier as soon as she finished them. Still, she imagined his face as she wrote, his smiles at her little jokes, his concern when she mentioned soldiers who came to the village on the trail of an escapee. *They never suspect me*, she assured him in the text. *I pretend the camps terrify me and fret breathlessly about how the people there might crawl under the fence and murder me in my bed. I am always assured that any escapees are caught within hours and sent back where they belong. The villagers say nothing, though they must suspect I am not what I seem to be.*

Though they'd expected their partnership would last months, maybe a year, Cathy, Ram, and Terri operated together for almost a decade. Terri often stayed at Cathy's home in Bang Salung, where they allowed people to believe they were cousins. When Ram took to stopping at the house to visit, Cathy suspected he was attracted to Terri.

Though they were in general satisfied with the operation, the work was neither pleasant nor easy. At times their charges were difficult, though not intentionally. Some feared being captured and returned to the camps. Others begged Ram and Terri to go back for family, friends, or lovers, which was usually impossible. A few were too young or too stressed to understand what was happening, so it became difficult to keep them out of sight and quiet. One summer Cathy discovered they'd taken in a spy. She told Ram and was concerned when her guest disappeared in the night. He refused to speak of it, and as they laid freshly washed clothing to dry on sun-warmed rocks, she asked Terri, "Do you think Ram killed her?"

Her response was pragmatic. "Only if he had to."

It was hard to hear what the packages had been through, though she always listened patiently and sympathetically. Women whose husbands had been taken by warlords were reluctant to leave but terrified at the prospect of spending another day in the camps. Children cried themselves to sleep, knowing they'd never see their parents again. She met young men who'd mutilated themselves, smashing a foot or cutting off a hand to escape serving Pol Pot. Where did such desperation come from?

Success helped Cathy keep going even when the packages were difficult, tragic, or ungrateful. She promised them life would be better someday, though she couldn't say how far off that "better" would be.

On rainy days, she often sat at the window, conjuring visions. Elvera the last time she'd seen her, drenched, anxious, and angry. Jay Taksin, the lover who'd struck what he meant to be her death blow without the slightest hesitation. The child she'd carried as a young wife. The child she would have cared for and raised for Elvera's sake.

It didn't matter now. They were all dead, and she was left to lead Elvera's life. Though she couldn't force an ounce of interest in the business E had loved, Cathy hoped her actions at Bang Salung would have won Elvera's approval. E had almost single-handedly saved Daw. Now Cathy saved others like her.

Sometimes as she watched the rain come down, E seemed to be standing beside her, and once she whispered in her ear: *It's good, Cath. You're doing good things with the life you were given.*

At other times it was Drake's voice she heard, but the message was the same. It didn't matter, since neither of them was available to her.

Chapter Thirty

A Village North of Bangkok, 1990

Maceo stayed outside, though rain fell from the sky like spilled pudding. His father was in the house, drunk, his temper as bad as usual. The boy heard the blows his mother took, heard the cries she tried to stifle. When his targets begged for mercy, Kiet grew meaner. The best thing, Maceo had learned, was to let him hit you until his arms grew tired. Then he'd stumble to bed, tossing comments over his shoulder about how it was your fault for making him angry.

The boy kept his head lowered, watching water run over his bare feet. Around him the insular world of his village in the Thai midlands was blurred by rain that rinsed the color from everything. The hillside had turned from blinding, emerald green to a dark, fecund olive. The huts of his neighbors looked almost black, their thatched roofs flattened and turned deep brown by the damp. And the sky above, had he dared to raise his face to it, was a mix of lowering grays. No bright spot anywhere.

Squatting under a spindly tree in the muddy yard, Maceo waited. When the sound of fists hitting flesh ceased, he waited some more. Water ran down his head, over his nose, and off his chin. So familiar was he with his father's beatings that he knew exactly what his mother had endured. Kiet always began with a slap to the face that made one's ears ring. Then he attacked the body, raining blows on the stomach and gut. When his victim could no longer stand, Kiet resorted to kicking the legs, arms, and back. Blows to the back were the worst, because there was no way to protect from them. Twice Maceo had peed blood after a beating and had a hard time standing upright for a day or two.

Though he sometimes felt sorry for his mother, the misery was her fault. She'd brought him into this world. She chose to stay with

Kiet despite the brutal maltreatment they received from him. She might have left when Maceo was a baby, so he'd never have known his father was a monster. If she'd found a way to have no babies, Maceo would have been born to some other couple, or never been born at all. Better.

After the house had been quiet for some time, the boy crept inside. His father's snores shook the place, and he made his way to his bed in total darkness. As he fell asleep, he heard his mother moaning softly.

In the morning he woke early and slipped outside. When his father staggered to the door, already irritated by stabs of sunlight signaling a new day, Maceo was busily hoeing the vegetable patch his mother had planted. Rubbing his hair, Kiet turned and went inside to get ready to begin his day of fishing on the river. Soon he stumbled down the path, his feet shuffling clumsily on the rain-soaked ground.

Maceo went inside. His mother lay on her bed, and one look at the black smudges under her eyes told him she was badly hurt this time.

It seemed she'd been waiting for him. "Maceo, my gift from God."

"What's wrong?"

She laid a hand on her stomach. "The hurt—" She left that unfinished. "I have something to tell you."

"I'll get the healer." What he wanted was for her to let go of his arm so he could get away from her pain-wracked face. Her hand traveled down his arm and closed on his hand. How long had it been since she touched him in love? Fear and misery had closed them each in separate cocoons, and now the feel of her rough fingers unnerved him. What did she want, this woman who'd brought him into hell?

"You are not my son."

For a few seconds he didn't comprehend the words. Had she read his thoughts and disowned him because of them? No. In her eyes he saw she was telling him a thing he needed to know.

"Whose son am I?"

She patted his arm, and her hand felt cold on his skin. "I took you from an orphanage in Bangkok." Her voice was weak, revealing both emotional and physical pain. "I could not bear children, but I hoped Kiet would be pleased to have a son." Her forehead creased. "For a while he was, but soon he returned to his old, angry ways."

"What was the name of the orphanage?" Her eyes had gone blank, and he shook her. "The name?"

"The Garden of Children. It sounds beautiful, does it not?"

She drifted into unconsciousness, and her grip on him loosened. Maceo stood up, his eyes already searching. Somewhere in this house was information on the Garden of Children Orphanage. He had to find it and put it somewhere safe before his father—no, the man who *pretended* to be his father—came home.

Chapter Thirty-One

In mid-1993, the Thai government closed the camps on the Cambodian border, announcing that conditions were stable enough for those who'd been displaced to go back to their homes. "Go back to what?" many asked, but the Thai hosts said only, "Go." Implied but unspoken was, *We never wanted you here in the first place.*

Cathy fretted briefly about what Ram would do for a living, but when she told him, he came as close to laughing as Ram ever did. "For a man of my talents, there are always ways to make money."

Reassured, Cathy shook his hand formally and wished him well. Nodding gravely Ram said, "My wish for you is that you will find new ways to be happy, Khun Elvera."

He was perceptive, because she'd been wondering what she would do now that she was no longer needed in Bang Salung."

"I'm sure I'll think of something."

Ram nodded. "I think yes. Not everyone discovers what makes happiness in a lifetime, but you now know what it is for you." With that he bowed, backed away, and then turned on his heel and left.

Terri had become a good friend, and parting from her was difficult. "What will you do now?" Cathy asked.

Running a hand through hair that was half silver these days Terri said, "I'm going with them."

"With the Khmers returning home?"

She made a disgusted noise. "What does home mean to them? Their coalition government is a mess. There's no plan for resettlement." She looked toward the camp. "Most of them know nothing but this. Even for those who remember home, decades of war have erased what they had. Are local authorities going to kick current residents out so the original owners can have the land they once farmed and live in the houses they built?" Her voice shook with angry sorrow. "They'll need someone who isn't afraid to rattle cages."

Cathy almost said, "I'll go with you," but her damaged hip would make her more liability than help in a crowd of needy travelers. "You know you can call on me if you need something."

"I do, and no doubt I will," Terri replied. "You're the best, Elvera."

She remained at Bang Salung for two months, helping Terri when she could and then, with great reluctance, closed the house. She'd been happy there, or at least content. Though she tried to tell herself it would be entertaining to return to the city, she'd become a lover of solitude. Even Nin's bright chatter irritated her some days. What, she would ask herself, was wrong with silence? Still, there was nothing to do in Bang Salung now, no one to shepherd to freedom.

Her return to Bangkok made Cathy's promise to Terri a lie. She entered the empty house after a long day of travel, weary and uncertain what should come next. Nin sniffed at the odor of a place too long unaired and immediately went to work opening windows. Cathy wandered behind her, looking aimlessly at things that belonged to her but seemed to suggest someone else. When had she last sat on the comfortable chairs and thought of nothing? Who had she been when she bathed in the enameled tub and used the fluffy, white towels stacked on a shelf nearby?

As she tried to re-orient herself, Nin brought her a stack of letters. "The neighbor has been saving these until someone came to get them."

Pleased to have something concrete to do, Cathy sat down at

her worktable to read her mail. As she opened heavy, cream-colored envelopes festooned with stamps of many denominations, disaster after disaster poured out. Tharp Credit Services had folded overnight, leaving both investors and employees unpaid and angry. Mizz Fashions had filed for bankruptcy. A handwritten letter from Jill, mailed six weeks earlier, warned of a pending fraud investigation. Since then, attorneys for and against that prospect had sent official-looking notices, all clamoring for Elvera Tharp Terzis' immediate attention. And finally, a document with a blue cover informed her that she was now divorced from the Party of the First Part, Richard D. Terzis. It had probably taken some doing to accomplish that without her knowledge, but talented lawyers had long been part of Richard's circle.

The money was gone. So was Richard.

In the next hour she learned that she was several months behind in payments on the Bangkok house. Elvera Tharp-no-longer-Terzis, once Cathy Charbonneau, owned nothing but a house in a remote border village. She had nothing but unpaid bills. Though she guessed Richard had diverted a good deal of money for himself before disaster hit, any accusation she aimed at him would ricochet back at her. She'd stolen Elvera's identity and for a decade used E's money for her own purposes. No matter what excuses she gave, the blame would settle on Cathy.

For days she sat by the window, looking at the garden that had once helped her regain a sense of tranquility. Someone else would see its next blooms, would perhaps sit in this very spot to admire them. She'd come to consider Thailand home, but that was an illusion. Home itself was an illusion, as was security. She chuckled aloud, though it was a bitter sound. Since she was herself unreal, how could anything else be true?

At one point she got mad at Elvera for leaving her, the less talented one, to cope with everything. Had Cathy died and Elvera lived, she'd have protected Tharp Industries, kept better track of Richard, made Mizz a huge success, and maybe even saved her son.

E had been the one with guts and drive and assertiveness. Why did Cathy Charbonneau have to stumble along alone, uncertain what to do next?

Eventually she stopped wallowing in self-pity, got out a pad of paper, and listed her resources. Her bank accounts were frozen, but she kept cash on hand, since she never knew when Terri would show up with a pressing need. The furniture could be sold, as could her jewelry, but it would have to be done quickly, before creditors swooped in and took everything. If she let the gardener and Nin go, she could afford to remain in Bangkok for a few months. After that, she had no idea where she might end up. Bang Salung, maybe, where the people knew her. The question was what she would do there to earn her living.

Rising, she roamed the house, looking out one window and then a different one. Nin brought food, begging her to eat it, and she tried, if only to ease the woman's worry. Nin's anxious face brought up another question. How would she earn a living now that Elvera Tharp had no way to pay her wages? At her age, with no dowry, Nin was unlikely to find a husband. More unhappiness for which Cathy was responsible.

Cathy Charbonneau had family, and she recalled the poet's line about home being where they have to take you in. Could she show up on her brothers' doorstep and say, "I wasn't really dead and now I need you to take care of me?" She couldn't imagine doing that.

Still, it was not a good time to be Elvera Tharp. News reports were full of the collapse of Tharp Services and the imminent demise of Mizz Fashions. They called Elvera "reclusive," which was true, and "demanding," which she resented for E's sake. Employees from decades back told stories of being terrified of her. She was "driven." She was "waspish." Cathy wondered how much Richard had contributed to stories of his wife's domineering personality. Character assassination hidden behind a lowered head and a rueful smile.

As Cathy or as Elvera, she had no way forward.

The only workable plan was to give up the house in Bangkok and find a job in Bang Salung, perhaps as a teacher. She and Nin took her jewelry and some other small items of value to a shop, where Nin haggled to get the best price. Cathy left feeling a little better. They could survive for a month, maybe two.

"More mail," Nin said when they returned to the house. Wrapped in plain brown paper, the small package had no return address. Torn between dread and curiosity, Cathy tore it open, unwilling to stop to look for her letter opener. Inside was an envelope containing two airplane tickets: one from Bangkok to Chicago and the other from O'Hare to Pellston, the closest airport to Mackinac Island. With it were two bits of cardboard taped together, and between them was an iron key. The card said: *Bought the house on Mackinac Island. If you need a place to go, it's there for you. D.*

Chapter Thirty-Two

Though Maceo could barely tolerate the man who called himself his father, he never revealed his hatred in even the smallest way. Kiet was morose after his wife's death, crying into his beer and telling the boy it was only the two of them now. The urge to beat his son deserted him temporarily, probably because Kiet suspected he'd killed his wife. He told the neighbors Kamon had fallen sick and died suddenly, and they pretended to believe him. A few gave Maceo pitying looks, but a boy was, of course, his father's to command.

While Kiet drank himself into oblivion every night, Maceo agreed with his drunken ramblings. There was nothing they could have done. His mother had been a saint. In the daytime he ran the household, using his father's meager earnings to see to their needs. With careful dishonesty he put aside small amounts of money, and as his nest egg grew, Maceo made plans. The people at the orphanage were unlikely to share their records with a boy of twelve, so he had to wait until he was older, until he looked like a man. The time until then would be used to hone his skills. As much as Maceo hated Kiet, dealing with him taught valuable lessons. He learned how to manipulate others by showing concern, uttering sympathetic words, and most of all, concealing his thoughts behind a pleasant mask.

Having two faces became Maceo's entertainment. On the outside he was amenable, even ingratiating. He cooked Kiet's favorite meals. He washed his sweaty, fishy clothes. While Kiet ranted about the weather and the vagaries of fortune, Maceo dreamed of the Garden of Children, where he would learn his real name, find his real family, and demand to know why they had abandoned him to Kiet's inhumanity.

One day Kiet brought home a new woman. Pleased to have a companion in his bed again, he was almost pleasant for a few weeks. He didn't seem to notice that she wasn't pretty or clever or even loyal. When Kiet wasn't around she looked at Maceo and raised her dark brows suggestively. He pretended not to notice.

The boy knew already that women were weak. Local girls and even a few women with husbands wanted to have sex with him. He was handsome, they said, and different from other men in the village. He found it almost laughably easy to say the right words, touch their hands at the proper moment, and get what he wanted from them. Though he liked the physical release sex provided, he didn't like the women much. Their soft eyes and smooth skin reminded him of his mother—the woman he'd thought was his mother. Weak. Worthless.

Maceo was generally disliked among the village men, which he attributed to jealousy. At times he had to defend himself with his fists, but he was generally able to win, being big for his age and completely ruthless in a fight. When possible, he chose stealthy reprisal over combat. A man who threatened him for stealing melons found his rooster dead at his doorstep, its head twisted almost off. A boy who called Maceo names tripped and fell, knocking out a tooth. He swore something stretched across the pathway had tripped him, but no one could find it.

Though it couldn't be proved that Maceo was to blame for such incidents, people understood in time that insulting or harassing the "banana boy" resulted in fierce, secret revenge. The wisest of Maceo's enemies learned to leave him alone.

The one person he couldn't summon the courage to oppose was his father. Years of pain had left Maceo powerless before Kiet, and while he hated himself for it, he accepted abuse from him like a dumb beast. Still, things went better with the woman there, so he spoke to her with grave politeness and avoided her longing glances.

Then they woke one morning to find her gone. Turning to his son Kiet demanded, "What did you do to make her angry?"

Maceo swore he'd done nothing, and they both knew who was to blame. In a moment of anger Kiet had slapped her, knocking her to the ground and splitting her lip. Though he'd controlled himself enough to walk away afterward, the woman had seen where things were going.

"What did you say to her?" Kiet's voice grew louder. "You said something, you—" The crude name came with a blow to the face, and Maceo was on the ground before he knew it. Instinctively he pulled his legs up to protect his guts. Kiet kicked him sharply between the shoulder blades, and pain shot through him like an electrical current. He gritted his teeth to keep from moaning.

Flashbacks to earlier beatings made him tense, expecting more, but Kiet was out of practice. Muttering about stupid women and ungrateful children, he turned and headed for the box where he kept his beer.

By noon Kiet was in a stupor, seated with his back in a corner so he stayed upright. Maceo had crawled to his bed, where he lay nursing his stinging cheekbone and aching back. As strength returned, he uncoiled a little, testing the damage. Bruising for certain on his back and arms, but he could breathe and move normally. His right eye was swollen shut, and there was a cut along the cheekbone. At the water bucket he wet a cloth and cleaned himself up. The cut would heal. The bruises would fade. His hatred for Kiet would remain.

Eventually Maceo heard Kiet stumble into the bedroom, and soon there were loud, snuffling snores. Getting up, he moved slowly to the man's bed and stood watching him. Hating him.

Ten minutes later, he left the house forever.

Maceo guessed any search for him wouldn't last long. Who would care if Kiet Banyen's strange son, the loner who looked so different from the rest of them, had run away? No one he could think of.

Chapter Thirty-Three

Mackinac Island, Michigan, October, 1994

A strong breeze crossed the straits, making it feel colder than forty-eight degrees. The chill didn't deter the woman who stood at the bow of the ferry, watching the island grow bigger as they neared. At the dock, a dozen blanketed horses stood in a column of twos, waiting to be loaded onto the boat and taken to winter quarters. Mackinac Island was closing down for the year, and those who remained would be few. Soon the straits would fill with ice, and boats would no longer bring supplies from the mainland. The island would become a world unto itself.

That was exactly what she needed. Cathy was in search of the past, of the days when she'd known what happiness was.

"Can I get a carriage for you, ma'am?"

When did I become ma'am? she asked herself, but the answer came quickly. Her halting gait, the gray in her hair, and an air of defeat made her look older than forty-four.

"I want to walk, but will you have one of the drivers take this bag to Braddock House and leave it on the porch?" The young man glanced doubtfully at her cane, but she gave him money, and he took the suitcase to a nearby wagon and told the driver what was needed. The cart man caught her eye and waved, indicating he'd do as she wished.

Leaving the dock, Cathy made her way to the street, then to the road that led uphill, and finally, slowly, to Braddock House. Her hip pained her almost from the first, and she chided herself for being a sentimental idiot. Still, she enjoyed every step and every memory.

The house seemed embarrassed by its run-down appearance.

The path to the door was choked with dead leaves, but she waded through, climbed the steps, retrieved the suitcase left there, and slid the key into the lock. She looked up, almost sure she'd heard laughter from the turret above. The house was silent. Of two silly girls who'd known nothing of life, one aging woman who knew too much of it remained. She'd been young, and now she was old—at least she felt old. She'd been poor, then wealthy, and now she was poor again. She'd once believed life was kind to people with good intentions. Now she doubted she'd ever feel like laughing again.

It was colder inside than out. The house was dark, the furniture the same as she remembered, though now it was covered with dust and dead insects. Was it possible no one had been here since 1968?

Of course not. When it hadn't sold, Franklin Tharp had rented the place out as a vacation home. E had argued for renovation but never got her father to agree. Looking at the shabby curtains and peeling wallpaper, Cathy guessed that over time, fewer and fewer visitors cared to vacation in a musty mausoleum.

She half expected Elvera to come clomping down the stairs or Laura to peek out from the kitchen, her long braid swinging. Even E's parents came to mind: Franklin Tharp with his pedantic lectures on Ojibwa culture and Doris with her small-minded but well-meaning advice. What would she say if she learned Cathy's naiveté had led both girls into danger, and that E's "improper behavior" had resulted in tragedy?

A shiver brought Cathy back to the present. Her first need was heat. The living room had a fireplace and pocket doors she could close to keep warmth inside. Wadding up newspaper from 1972, she tossed it onto the grate and made a crisscrossed stack of kindling from a small box on the hearth. Atop that she placed a couple of wrist-sized logs. After a brief search, she found a box of safety matches and lit the paper. The acrid smell of burning hit her nose, and she backed away, watching as the tinder built enough heat to ignite the slender bits of wood. They in turn would burn hot enough to start the logs and make a real fire.

Belatedly she realized she should have checked the chimney before making a fire. The flue might be choked with soot, leaves, or even dead birds. Leaning in, she tried to see up the brick column, but smoke and heat drove her back. After a few minutes she concluded with some relief that there was no blockage. Adjusting the damper, she sat back on her heels and watched. The room would take a while to warm up, but she felt a glow of that single accomplishment.

Once the fire was established, Cathy left the room, closing the doors behind her. Upstairs she dug out four blankets, shook them vigorously to dispel the dust, and tossed them down the stairs. The couch would be her bed, one of the blankets a pillow. She checked the fire, added another log, and then took two candy bars from her coat pocket and ate them as she watched the flames. When the candy was gone, she went in search of something to quench her thirst.

Roaming the downstairs, she found a bottle of distilled water in the laundry room, still sealed. It recalled the days when Laura had wet the Tharps' clothing by sprinkling water on each item, using a pop bottle with a special attachment. She'd rolled the garments and let them sit in a basket until they were uniformly damp. Then she ironed, expertly fitting the point of the appliance into tucks and along seams. As a kid, Cathy had envied E's crisp sleeves and perfect pleats. Now what came to her mind was Laura's assiduous attention to someone else's comfort.

Taking a cup from the kitchen, Cathy poured some water and carried her beverage to the slightly warmer living room to check the fire. It burned merrily, the wood making little pops as it turned into heat. Next, she peeked at the house's single bathroom and confirmed her fear. The toilet was inoperable. Since she'd lived for years without modern plumbing, that problem was easily solved. Trekking into the back yard, she looked for the outhouse she remembered, but it had apparently been torn down. Not bothered by that, she peed behind the well house.

When she went back inside, her little nest had warmed nicely. Taking off her coat, Cathy hung it over a chair, stuffing her hat and gloves into the sleeves. Putting a couple of large logs on the fire, she pulled back the top two blankets of her makeshift bed and climbed in. They felt damp and exuded a musty odor, but it didn't really matter. Her body heat would warm them, and the smell wasn't bad compared to some she'd endured. For the first time in weeks, Cathy fell into a deep, dreamless sleep.

The next day she walked to town, determined not to let her hip dictate what she would and would not do. Most of the tourist stores were shuttered, but as she'd hoped, the library was open. Inside she approached the desk where a middle-aged woman with half glasses was stamping the day's mail with a date stamp. Cathy applied for a library card, explaining that she'd be at Braddock House indefinitely.

The librarian squinted at her. "Are you the daughter? Elena?"

"Elvera," she corrected.

"I thought it was you. I mean, I don't exactly remember you, but people talk. You used to be all over this place as a kid, and then you went off and started your own business...was it in New York?"

"Chicago."

Nodding as if she'd known that all along the woman said, "I bet you need some time away from the rat race."

Did she not know her visitor was at the center of a huge financial scandal? It was possible. Chicago was miles away geographically and eons away metaphorically.

"The rat race. Yes." Turning her temporary library card in her hand she asked, "The local woman who used to take care of the house, Laura Wolf. Do you know how I can contact her?"

The woman's face revealed pleasure at having a juicy bit of gossip to share. "She's in prison in Ypsilanti."

"Prison?"

"Killed her old man with a beer bottle." Shock rendered Cathy speechless, but the woman was eager to tell her story. "She claimed he beat her so they reduced the charge, but you can't get away with murder in this state." She tapped the counter for emphasis. "She got six years."

"When was this?"

She did some mental figuring. "My husband retired in 1990 from sailing." Pride made her elaborate. "His boat was the *Stewart J. Cort,* the first thousand-footer on the Great Lakes. Anyway, that was the year it happened." After a moment she added, "I guess Laura might be free by now, if she behaved herself."

"Good. I need her help."

Though Cathy was never sure how the message reached Laura, she showed up at the back door a few weeks later. She looked older, which wasn't surprising after so many years. Her black hair had turned gray, and the braid was gone. Wrinkles radiated from her dark eyes. She seemed in no way diminished. Still strong, still prone to silence. "It's good to see you, Laura."

Her brow furrowed. "You're not—"

"No, I'm not. Come in out of the cold. I'll make tea, and then I'll tell you a story."

Later, when the tea was cold and Cathy's secrets had been shared, Laura said, "A person thinks she's got it tough, but there's always some who have it worse."

"Do you want to tell me about Darby?"

She sniffed. "You can probably guess most of it."

"I knew he didn't treat you well."

"Everybody knew it, but when it came down to saying it out loud, they all backed away." She licked her lips. "Darby was drunk, like always. He started smacking me around, like always. But that night I—I don't know. I couldn't take it anymore." Laura went silent, and Cathy waited for her to decide how to tell it. "Both my kids left home as soon as they could. Carrie used to call me up and say, 'Mom, come to Vegas and live with me and Josh,' but I didn't. I don't know why I didn't."

"Men like that get inside your head."

She nodded. "That night he broke a glass. That was it—a broken glass, but he cut himself on it, and somehow it became my fault. He slapped me hard and called me a lazy slut. I was working on a quilt for our new grandson. Darby grabbed it off my lap and used it to wipe the blood off his hand." She looked down at the table. "I'd been sad all day, thinking I might never see that baby." Another pause. "Darby always said if the kids wouldn't come home to see us then to hell with them."

Her breath hitched, but she pulled her lips tight. "He tossed the quilt on the floor, kicked it into a corner, and started to walk away. There was an empty beer bottle on the table next to me, and I—I pegged it at him. I'd never done anything like that before, but—" She cleared her throat. "It hit him in the back of his head, and he went down. His forehead hit the kitchen table. He was dead when the EMTs got there."

"They called that murder?"

"Manslaughter." Laura rubbed at her nose with a knuckle. "They made a big deal out of the fact that I'd drunk that beer. There were plenty more empties in the trash, and since nobody bothered to test my blood alcohol level until the next day, they said I was hammered." She licked her lips. "The prosecutor was running for judge, pushing a tough-on-crime stand. He used every drunken Indian image you can imagine."

"That's ridiculous. You aren't like that."

Laura smiled. "Says the kid who knew me a hundred years ago."

"If you weren't drunk, your lawyer should have presented evidence."

She shrugged. "My lawyer wasn't much interested in my case, since I didn't have any money. And that drunken Indian stuff goes a long way with some people around here."

"So you went to prison."

She nodded. "Met lots of women there that had it worse than I did."

Faces appeared in Cathy's mind. Daw and others who'd suffered at the hands of men who saw them as property. And Elvera, who'd paid for a man's anger with her life.

"How are things now that you're out, Laura?"

Another shrug. "Carrie still wants me to come out West, but I don't think her husband's all that thrilled at the idea of an ex-con mother-in-law in the house. My other girl doesn't communicate much." After a pause she added, "She knows what Darby was, but in her mind, it was me who should have been different."

Cathy waited a few seconds to let Laura recover from the sting of her own child's rebuke. "Where are you living now?"

"There's a shelter in Petoskey that lets parolees stay for ninety days."

"Here's the thing. This hip of mine makes it hard for me to keep up a house. If you don't mind working at your old job for no pay, I can offer room and board."

"How are you going to live if you've got no money?"

"I have a little saved up, so I'll be okay for a while. After that, there's tons of stuff in this house that's really old."

She glanced around. "You got that right. Mostly junk."

"These days they call that junk *vintage*, and people pay a lot for it." Cathy grinned at her new housemate. "Drake tells me the internet is becoming a great place for selling things, even for private citizens. There's something new called eBay, and he's going to help me learn how to use it." With a grin she added, "I wish old Mr. Tharp could know that using credit cards has become so popular. He'd be thrilled to hear that he was right all along."

Drake had written early on to suggest that she set up an email account, a method of communication Cathy had heard about but never tried. Now she went every few days to the island library, where patrons were allowed access to dial-up internet. Though cumbersome, email put Cathy in touch with Drake in a way that was both faster than mail and more private. Despite that, they kept their messages platonic, as suited brother and sister.

Sell anything you want to from the house, he'd said. *The Internet will give you a wide enough audience to make it worthwhile.*

When she fussed that his children might want the house's furnishings someday, he replied, *My kids are modernist pagans who think anything made before 1984 should be burned in the city square.*

But the money from the sale should be theirs, she'd countered.

The money is mine. Until I'm dead, I can do with it as I like.

Since climbing the stairs was difficult and heat was expensive, Cathy had made the living room into her bedroom. When Laura returned with her pitifully small store of belongings, she took a room off the kitchen that had been the larder. "Doris Tharp would roll over in her grave," she said, "but we don't have anything to keep in there anyway."

That winter they lived mostly on canned soup and sandwiches, bologna, peanut butter, and for a treat, grilled cheese. Cathy's experience as a photographer served them well as she took pictures of items they wanted to sell. Her computer skills grew slowly, and there were times when she muttered words under her breath that her mother would have frowned at. Gradually, with determined effort, she learned how to make attractive postings with detailed information and enticing prices.

When they made a good sale, Laura prepared what she called

"a real supper." Those meals, though still simple, included baked chicken or a ground beef casserole, and they dined in style, using Doris Tharp's china and setting out her silver-plated candlesticks. Afterward, they washed the delicate plates and cups and replaced them carefully in the cupboard lest they chip them. "We might as well enjoy them," Cathy would joke, "because someday they'll be gone." And in time they were.

Though Laura had no interest in learning to use a computer, she entered enthusiastically into the process of getting items from the house packaged for shipment. Furnishings from the unused upstairs went first. They got a nice price for the master bedroom furniture, and it took four men to carry the sleigh bed out and load it on a wagon. Small pieces like lamps, bedside tables, and even ashtrays created minor bidding frenzies. The good silverware left the kitchen carefully wrapped in old towels. Heavy draperies, somewhat sun-bleached but sold as "authentically aged," required sturdy boxes and cost the buyer extra postage. Paintings went one by one, and they discovered quite by accident that a rather stark landscape by a semi-famous artist was worth a thousand dollars. That bought groceries and a refurbished computer for Cathy, so trips to the library were no longer required.

Laura learned to call Cathy "Elvera," though her mouth quirked every time she said it. She was never idle, growing vegetables in the short summer season and scouring wooded areas for firewood in the fall. Her talent in almost any handicraft delighted Cathy. "You should sell your stuff," she said one day when Laura showed her a finished afghan in vibrant blues and greens.

"Who'd buy it? Everybody I know has family that can knit and sew and bead and whatever."

"Around here that's true, but out in the big, wide world, they've lost those talents."

"And how do I reach people in the big, wide world? We live on an island, in case you forgot."

Cathy smiled. "I can sell your things online, like we do with the furniture. We'll use eBay, but I bet someday there'll be a site just for artistic people like you to show what they can create."

Chapter Thirty-Four

Bangkok, 1994

It took Maceo a full day to reach Bangkok, begging rides from passing trucks and motorists who took pity on his battered face. It was another day before he gathered the courage to wade into the swirl of traffic, noise, and unfamiliar smells. Hunger drove him, both a need for food and the yearning to know who he was. He bought rice from a street vendor and sat down next to the stand after she handed him a palm leaf piled with food. Shoveling it into his mouth with his fingers, the boy tried to puzzle out what to do next.

The single sheet of paper carried in his pocket had no street address, only a few handwritten sentences that said Kamon Banyen was given permanent custody of Baby Boy 320. He asked passersby for directions to the Garden of Children but got helpless shrugs in reply. Bangkok was not like his village, where there was one of everything and everyone knew where it was. The city had perhaps a dozen orphanages, and the teeming mass of people coming and going had no time to help a stranger find a particular one.

A woman selling sandals from a pushcart had an idea where it might be, but her instructions were too vague to be useful to a person new to the city. Several times Maceo drew beeps from car horns and curses from cart drivers as he wandered bewildered along streets that all looked alike to his untrained eyes.

Finally, he approached a bicycle taxi driver who nodded when he heard the name. "It's near the Oriental Hotel. I can get you there in twenty minutes." He became less friendly when Maceo confessed he didn't intend to pay for a ride. The store of money he'd managed to save was dwindling so quickly it was frightening, since everything cost more than he'd imagined. He smiled earnestly, hoping the man would pity him, but nothing came for free in

Bangkok. Turning away, the driver resumed his general cry: "Anywhere in the city. Relax while I do all the work."

With a well-known landmark to narrow his search, Maceo found others willing to direct him. "Follow the river," a woman said, pointing. "When you reach the hotel, ask the porters out front how to find the place you're looking for. They know the city better than most."

When she turned to point toward the water, Maceo helped himself to a sample of the vendor's wares. Nibbling at the still-warm fried bread, he began walking, his progress slowed by the wonders he saw along the way. Bangkok was a long-established city locked in a struggle with the modern world. On one hand were structures ranging from old to ancient: apartment buildings, temples, shrines, and shops. On the other was new construction. Sometimes Maceo had to turn away from the river to skirt ongoing projects: street-paving, sewer installation, and skeletal frames for buildings that would stretch, it seemed, to the sky.

Traffic was a nightmare, but he was a fast learner and soon darted effortlessly across roads choked with cars, carts, and even an occasional elephant. Copying other pedestrians, he shook his fist, demanding passage, or joined clumps of street-crossers, finding safety in numbers.

The sun had long passed its zenith when he reached his destination. The building where he'd begun life was squeezed among others much like it on a street that had nothing of beauty and plenty of need. Three stories high, the Garden of Children had wide balconies in front. Taking a narrow alley, Maceo peered through a latticed fence to gain a slitted view of the back. Large windows overlooked the enclosed space, their shutters open to allow any breeze that might happen along to pass through. The yard was full of life. On one side grew neat rows of vegetables. On the other a group of perhaps twenty children of various ages kicked a ball back and forth, their cries high-pitched and joyful. A young woman who seemed bored and listless watched over them.

Spotting a sign for lodging nearby, Maceo decided to spend the last of his precious coins on a room for the night. Arriving at the orphanage ragged and dirty wouldn't inspire those in charge to answer his questions, but if he appeared serious and presentable, the lazy optimism with which most people judge strangers would work to his advantage.

He bargained the room's price, using a combination of flattery and a story of parents who'd died in a house fire. His father had awoken him, Maceo told the host, told him to flee, and then gone back for his wife. They had died in each other's arms, and now Maceo was on his way to tell his mother's sister, who didn't yet know of the tragedy. The woman was almost in tears when she lowered the price of his stay to a minimum.

Leaving his knapsack on the bed, Maceo roamed the streets until he spotted a clothesline hung with items suited to his size and purpose. After assuring that no one was around, he vaulted the fence and stole a shirt of finer quality than he'd ever worn and pants that turned out to fit him quite well. The communal bathroom at the inn was a pleasant surprise, with water springing from the tub tap at a turn and a toilet that took a bit of figuring. After watching a fellow guest use it, Maceo tried it himself, flushing more times than was necessary to hear the rush of water through the pipes and watch clean water replace what had been in the bowl.

When he left the room the next morning, Maceo was clean, well-dressed, and rested. Examining his image in the fly-specked mirror, he noted that his face had healed nicely. He decided he looked much older than his age. Old enough to be taken seriously.

A small brass plaque near the door of the orphanage identified it, though the letters were obscured by years of weather and dirt. The woman who answered his knock was the one he'd seen with the children the day before. She frowned when he asked to see the person in charge, for a time refusing to even relay his request. When Michael insisted, she sniffed loudly, raised a finger to signify he should wait, and closed the door in his face. After several minutes she reappeared and ordered him to follow, her tone indicating if it had been up to her, he'd have been sent packing.

Inside, the temperature dropped a few degrees, and the harsh glare of sunlight turned to soft dimness. As they crossed the foyer, Maceo glanced out the open rear door. In the yard the children played with their ball, and happy laughter reached his ears. *How much better life would have been here,* he thought. *No Kiet. No beatings. No shame.*

Her slippered feet rustling on the steps, his guide led him up a wide staircase to the second floor and knocked at a heavy wooden door. A low voice called out permission, and the woman opened the door and gestured for him to go in. Maceo entered an office where a woman in her fifties sat behind a large, black desk. She seemed almost a part of it, since she too was mostly black: black hair and eyes, black blouse. Though he couldn't see the rest of her, he guessed she wore black shoes and pants—no, he decided, probably a black skirt.

"I am Maarit. What do you want, boy?"

He took on the manner of a man back home who had always seemed afraid he'd be beaten for speaking. "I am called Maceo, Khun Maarit. I hope you can tell me more than that, for I don't know my real name."

That brought a frown. "Why have you come to me?"

Showing her the adoption document, he told his prepared story, which was mostly true. "The woman who raised me, Kamon Banyen, died some years ago. The man I called father, Kiet, died recently." He arranged his features in a sad expression. "At the last, my mother told me I was adopted from this place."

The director's expression turned even stonier as she perused the single sheet. "I cannot say if this is true."

"It's true," Maceo said. "There is the document."

She made an impatient gesture. "Documents may be falsified."

"I don't think so." He leaned forward. "Please, Khun Director, tell me who my real parents were and what happened to them."

He expected Maarit to turn and consult the files behind her, but either she remembered every adoption she'd arranged or his had been special. "Kamon came here wanting a child, and I gave you to her."

"Did you know her husband was a monster?" His tone was calm, though his heartbeat rose in his chest.

She eyed him dispassionately. "She said he would welcome a son."

"A lie I have suffered for all my life."

Khun Maarit rearranged items on her desk, setting a file aside and aligning a pen. "I have no way of knowing how such things will turn out."

"I need to know where I came from. Who I am."

Her lips tightened. "Our records are secret."

He could no longer pretend to be calm, though he kept his voice low. "You gave me to a woman no better than an idiot, whose husband beat her—and me—whenever it pleased him. You owe me the truth."

"I owe you nothing." With a sweep of her hand, Maarit erased his years of pain like dust from her desktop. "What you make of yourself now is all that matters."

How easily she absolved herself of guilt. Was it she who'd cowered in fear, who could not relax for a single moment? How was he to make something of himself after years of horror?

Maceo enunciated his words carefully. "I demand to know the names of my mother and my father."

"I cannot help you, boy."

A knock sounded, and the woman who'd brought him upstairs opened the door enough to speak to Maarit. "They're here. Shall I bring the children inside?"

"Yes." Rising from the desk, Maarit went to confer with her employee. As she passed, Maceo saw he'd been correct. Black, sensible shoes and a black skirt that fell to her ankles.

Surveying the room, Maceo noticed four filing cabinets along the wall. In one of them was the information he wanted—no, *needed*.

When the younger woman left, Maarit returned her attention to him. "You must leave now. I have people downstairs who are interested in adopting a child."

Forcing his voice to remain neutral he said, "Might I at least see the room where I slept as a baby?"

As she considered, he easily read her thought. If she acceded to his request, this troublesome boy might leave without making a fuss that would upset her potential clients. "Very well, if you don't stay too long."

Leading him down the corridor, she ascended the stairs to the third floor and opened the door to a barracks-like room. At one end, an open casement window looked down on the courtyard where he'd seen the children playing. Footsteps clattered below, and he imagined them queuing up to be inspected by a couple who'd choose one for their own. Two rows of beds, ten on each side. Between them were shelving units, each with four drawers, each drawer marked with a child's name written in Thai script. One drawer each. At one side of the room was a nursery of sorts, four cribs with the accoutrements of baby care piled on a chest of drawers in the center. He'd no doubt slept in one of those cribs.

Who had left him here, not caring he'd be alone and unloved? Someone heartless. Had his mother died in childbirth, so his father abandoned him? Had they both been killed in some tragic accident, and no family member stepped up to take responsibility? Whatever the explanation, his fate had at some juncture come from heartlessness. Someone could have saved him from the life he'd led.

The woman who stood impatiently behind him was heartless as well. She'd failed to protect a child entrusted to her care and now absolved herself of all responsibility. *I have no way of knowing how such things will turn out.* Exactly how much interest had she taken in his welfare?

Coming down the center aisle, Maarit stopped beside him. "You are lucky I was able to find parents for you, boy. Most mixed-race children never find a home."

Could she ever understand what she'd done to him? Looking into her eyes, he saw that she could not. In fact, she would not even try.

On the street a few minutes later, Maceo retrieved his knapsack from the bushes where he'd hidden it. He stuffed the file he'd stolen from Maarit's office into the bag, put his head down, and strode away as if on some errand. He was gone long before his crime was discovered.

Some distance from the orphanage, he located a spot behind a restaurant out of sight from the street. Behind a pile of discarded crates, he made himself a simple campsite. For some time he lived there, emerging each day to forage for food and learn his way around the city. Evenings he studied the file he'd taken from Maarit's cabinet, using a flashlight stolen from a bin in the market.

Along with charts that tracked his weight and feeding habits, he found handwritten entries that were probably Maarit's. The paper was of different sizes and in different shades of ink, in a hand so small it was often hard to decipher. The story that emerged fascinated Maceo.

Sept. 10, 1983:

Peg Herring

Received a telegram from an American woman who proposes to come here during the last days of her pregnancy. I am to arrange a midwife, after which she will leave her child with me for a span of time. I was (illegible word) to agree to her proposal, but she assured me the financial support the child receives will be (illegible) and continue for as long as we care for it. I agreed and will see to her childbearing myself, since I am as able as most doctors. The money she offered will help with repairs, since the house has become quite (illegible).

While she did not explain her reasons, I suspect the woman's husband is unaware of the child's imminent birth.

On another sheet dated Oct. 18, 1983:

Our guest has come and gone. Her pregnancy was well advanced when she arrived, but she'd been wearing a (unknown word) to hold herself in. Only three days into her stay, during which "Mrs. Smith" wandered the place like a caged tigress, she went into labor. After an uncomplicated delivery, she slept for ten hours then was on her way, leaving her son behind. I received two payments: one for the orphanage and another for myself, with instruction that I treat the child as my own. In three months, she will either return for her son or send more money for his care.

The child is healthy, and my workers report he is no trouble.

January 16, 1984:

I have heard nothing from the Smith woman, and the three months we agreed on are gone. The child thrives, but each time I visit the nursery I chide myself for believing the American's lies. I have been (illegible), and it humiliates me. I have no true name for Mrs. Smith and no way to contact her. It infuriates me to feed her child with my limited funds when she is fully capable of paying for his care.

February 20, 1984:

A woman from a village in the north came yesterday, wanting a son. While she could not pay much, I gave her the Smith woman's boy. The child who reminds me of my mistake will no longer raise his eyes to mine and smile his mother's smile.

November 27, 1984:

A man with curiously small ears has visited twice, asking about the American woman's boy. When he first came I pretended to know nothing, but he visited again today, bringing proof he is her husband. He showed me a marriage license and a wedding photograph of himself with Mrs. Smith, younger than when I saw her but certainly the same woman. I had a moment of (illegible), but I soon learned the man had not come to take the child. Instead, he wanted my assurance the boy would not reappear at some time in the future and embarrass his parents. When I told him the child had been placed with a Thai family, he seemed pleased. Leaving me with a generous donation, he suggested the matter should be forgotten.

This time I was not so trusting. While I spoke with the American in my office, I sent my assistant to search his car. She found there a document that identified him as Richard Terzis of Chicago, a city near the center of the United States.

United States. Richard Terzis. Chicago.

After reading Maarit's words over and over for several days, Maceo dug a hole in the dirt and buried the file. Everything he needed to know was now indelibly etched in his memory.

Peg Herring

United States. Richard Terzis. Chicago.

In a newspaper discarded on a bench, Maceo found an account of Maarit's death. She'd been found on the tiled walkway at the back of the orphanage, and the reporter cited a visit from a "mysterious" young man only minutes before. The police officer in charge of the investigation saw nothing sinister. "The visitor was only a boy," he was quoted as saying. "After he left, the lady went upstairs. Standing at the window, perhaps to wave goodbye, she obviously grew faint and fell to her death."

Maceo chuckled at the idea of Maarit having the vapors. The reporter, undaunted by disagreement from his official source, hinted at suicide, suggesting the visitor might have brought bad news. "The sadness of a moment should not lead to self-harm," he lectured his readers. "No matter what sort of blows life deals, one will find better days if she only perseveres."

"Some don't deserve better days." Tossing the paper aside, Maceo turned his mind to how he might find Richard Terzis. It would not be easy. The trail was old. Money, or rather the lack of it, was a daunting problem. He could beg, but he was too old to be pitiful and too physically developed to appear unable to provide for himself. He might find work on construction projects in the city, but that would limit his ability to do as he liked. In the end, petty theft seemed the easiest survival method, at least until something better came along.

He knew a fair amount of English, learned from the couple who'd built the school in his village. The man had often said Maceo had an ear for languages, and for once he'd bested his schoolmates in something. That was a beginning, but if he intended to find Richard Terzis, he had to expand his language skills.

Loitering in cafes and on hotel porches where tourists gathered, Maceo took in the rapid cadence of American speech, the slurred endings, and skipped explanatory words. At night, in his alley camp, he would practice, separating the disparate parts into intelligible, interchangeable words and phrases. "What sounded like "Jeet?"

320

turned out to be, "Did you eat?" and the reply, "About to," apparently meant, "I have not but intend to do it soon." In time he understood the gist of most conversations, though there were words and phrases he couldn't decode, such as, "The Tigers' chances look good." From the pleased way it was said, Maceo didn't think the speaker meant the sort of tigers with which he was acquainted.

One day he was approached by a middle-aged British tourist. "I'm told you sometimes serve as a guide for those new to the city," he said, and Maceo without the slightest twinge of guilt, claimed he was a Bangkok native who could show a visitor all its sights. The man, whose name was Edgar Thornton, seemed pleased.

As it turned out, Thornton was mostly interested in finding young, beautiful prostitutes. Though he knew little of such things, Maceo promised the best of the best. He struck a deal with a tuk-tuk driver, who made a great show of taking the man to a "special" brothel, driving up and down the streets for some time only to end up four blocks from their starting point. Pleased with his first experience, Thornton accepted Maceo's offer to be his guide on an exclusive basis. Maceo couldn't believe his luck when Thornton mentioned his business in Thailand would take at least a year to complete.

The man was arrogant and condescending, but Maceo approached the job as a course in Western culture. By agreement he arrived at the hotel most mornings—not too early—and waited until Thornton showed himself. Maceo then escorted his employer around the city, riding on the back of the tuk-tuk or in front with the driver when they took a taxicab. Sometimes Thornton had an agenda related to business; other times he simply demanded, "Show me something good." Since he was completely new to Southeast Asia, it was easy to find him fresh experiences. And after a day of sightseeing, there were always willing women.

With what he earned, Maceo was able to get a room and eat regularly, though of course he never dined with his employer. While

Thornton chatted and flirted in some tourist bar or dim-lit brothel, Maceo squatted outside, ready to return him safely to his hotel, no matter what shape he was in when the evening ended.

After a few months, it was hard not to speculate on his future. Since he'd proven so valuable, might Thornton recommend him to other travelers? Suggest he be given a job at the hotel? In his wilder dreams, the man invited Maceo to come with him when he returned to England.

That was before he heard Thornton tell his friends about "my native." Maceo arrived at the hotel early and chose a waiting spot near the table where Thornton usually breakfasted with friends. A screen of climbing plants hid him from sight, but he heard the man's plummy voice clearly.

"Only half a cup, little darling," Thornton told the waitress. "My native, Maceo, will be here for me soon." He went on in a lower tone, apparently speaking to other men at his table. "He's vulgar as all get-out, but quite punctual for an Asian."

Maceo froze, listening with every cell in his body.

"You've kept him around all this time," one of the other men said. "Surely you found him competent."

"He's strong as an ox," Thornton said. "Keeps the pickpockets away when I can't stay on my pins after an evening of celebration. But honestly, that's about all that recommends Maceo, and I won't miss him when I return home next week." He must have taken a forkful of food, because the next words were muffled by chewing. "The boy is the very picture of a peasant—knows nothing of civilized society. He lies constantly, but of course they all do that. His English is mangled, and if you ever watched him eat, you'd think he was born in a cave somewhere." Maceo heard the clink of a spoon against china as Thornton stirred. "If he didn't work dirt cheap, I'd have dumped him long ago."

"Then you don't recommend him as a guide?"

"I suppose he's all right," Thornton said with what Maceo

imagined was a casual shrug. "If you don't mind traveling with a street urchin who smells of sweat."

Maceo slunk away, torn between pain and hatred. After all the effort he'd put into pleasing that simpering, self-important prig! The months he'd spent trying to find experiences that excited Thornton's jaded tastes. The smiles he'd conjured when he was ordered around like a pet monkey. "Wait outside, Maceo." "Return in one hour, Maceo." "Get me another beer, Maceo." He'd been efficient and amiable at all times, but now he realized Thornton was the type who'd never admit he'd been well-served.

What should he do? Thornton owed him two weeks' pay, and Maceo had hoped for a large tip as well, though Brits weren't as generous with gratuities as Americans. Could he swallow his pride and finish the job as Thornton's guide?

The answer was simple. He had to.

While waiting for his flight to England, Edgar Thornton fell from the balcony that circled the Bangkok airport's main floor. Initial speculation was that he'd leaned too far over the railing, probably attempting to see the departure board. The amount of alcohol in his system had no doubt impaired his balance.

Before he died however, Thornton said a name: "Maceo." The policeman in charge of the case learned from the man's friends who that was, but they didn't know where the youth lived or anything else that might help to locate him. Officers were told to be on the lookout for a tall, mixed-race youth, but the city was large, and the population dense.

In his old campsite behind the restaurant, Maceo wondered if it had been a mistake to run. If he'd let the police find him and ask their questions, what could they have proven? Still, his name on a dying man's lips made him afraid to return to his room, which meant he lost access to his money, his clothes, everything he owned.

The next few months were miserable. He stayed out of sight

during the day and emerged at night to forage for food. Hunger pains cramped his stomach most of the time. His sleeping place was damp, odiferous, and open to the weather, yet he sometimes had to defend it from interlopers who saw it as preferable to what they had. After living comfortably for months, Maceo hated every second of his return to degradation, and he swore that if he got a second chance at stability, he would never suffer poverty again.

His reason for coming to Bangkok often returned to mind, but the quest for his parents hardly mattered anymore. Richard Terzis had no doubt returned to America long ago. Slouched against a wall one cold night, drinking in the last of the light before he crawled behind his pile of trash, Maceo forced himself to be realistic. The police were looking for him. His stomach held only the insufficient remains of someone else's meal. If he starved to death in that alley, it would hardly be noted, much less mourned. Edgar Thornton's word came to mind: he was indeed "vulgar," too young, too rural, too inexperienced…the list went on. Any chance he might get to America and find the one person who knew his parents in that huge, unknown country was extremely small.

What, then, should he do?

He could return to his village. Kiet's brother had no sons, and if Maceo begged humbly enough, he might take him in. That was a bitter pill to swallow, since Uncle Lek had often said aloud what most others thought: that Kiet's boy "didn't look right." In a village where everyone knew his ancestors for generations, Maceo would always be an outsider. If he returned, he'd have to hide how much he hated Lek, but at least Aunt Pensri would feed him.

"Boy? Are you hurt?"

How had someone found his hiding place? Had he made a sound that betrayed the despair he was feeling?

"Boy?" The voice was female, and she spoke in English. "Do you need help?"

Peering out, Maceo beheld an extremely homely woman

standing a few feet away, her body bent toward him. Her face looked smashed in, like an apple that had rotted from the inside. She was at least half again his weight, and her body seemed too large for her spindly legs and arms.

Searching his mind, he came up with the correct English word. "Hungry." Recalling proper sentence structure, he said the whole thing. "I am hungry."

Her bulging eyes seemed to extend toward him. "I'll buy food if you'll talk with me about your future."

Standing quickly, he bowed. "Yes. Yes, please."

Her name was Adeline, an incredibly kind and even more naïve American. Against all advice, she roamed the streets of Bangkok, inviting the dregs of the city to accompany her to the nearest noodle shop for a meal. Since she'd never bothered to learn Thai, her offers were usually refused. When she found someone who understood and accepted, Adeline was so happy it was almost pitiful. After only a few minutes in her presence, Maceo guessed that for most of her life, no one had appreciated this ugly, inept woman.

While he slurped down his first meal in days, Adeline told Maceo about Jesus and how He loved him so much that He'd died for him. Acting as if he'd never heard the story before, he pretended great excitement at hearing that Jesus could change his life. He also asked if he might have a second bowl of noodles, which Adeline readily agreed to. Maceo then asked, in his most ingratiating manner, if he might shake her hand, which resulted in the first of many hugs he would get from her, a warm, somewhat damp embrace that lasted longer than he was comfortable with.

Adeline, he learned in time, was the daughter of a successful, now-deceased evangelist. She used the money "Papa" had left her to further his work. Being unable to attract crowds of listeners, as her father had, she'd chosen to become a missionary. Having once seen a documentary on the country, she'd chosen Thailand as her target and invested everything she had to set up a home where she could save young men from the streets of Bangkok.

Maceo soon realized he could stay with Adeline indefinitely if he accepted her narrow brand of Christianity. Had she been more discerning, she might have wondered at the new boy's immediate enthusiasm for her unsanctioned rescue and eccentric demands. In truth, he was more than willing to pretend Jesus had crept into his heart if it got him into a warm, dry place and resulted in three meals a day.

Pleased with her newest convert, Adeline led him to her house, a large structure in a decent neighborhood. The entire second floor was a dormitory for the young men she rescued from the streets. When Maceo realized he would not be expected to provide sex, it was some relief, though he'd have done whatever the woman wanted. Her intent really was saving the boys from the streets, and along with Bible lessons, Adeline fine-tuned their English skills and taught them mathematics, geography, and history. Since she had no interest in Thailand's past, the boys learned a great deal about the Women's Suffrage Movement and the Battle of Little Big Horn. Maceo had never realized the people of India had such a large population living in the United States.

The mission was informally run. Five other boys currently in residence ranged in age from eight to seventeen. They eyed Maceo warily, and he wondered how many of them were as uninterested as he in becoming shining examples of Christianity. Within a few weeks, he knew them well enough to answer that question. Two were actual converts. The others liked sleeping in beds and being fed regularly, so they played their benefactor's game.

Recognizing the need for employment, Adeline helped her charges prepare for jobs at hotels and restaurants that catered to the growing number of Western visitors: tourists, ex-soldiers, news people, and government agents, both open and covert.

Like a hungry tiger, Maceo ate up everything she had to teach him. His spoken English improved, and he learned to read and write it as well. After six months, he was able to get a job at a restaurant. He hated the place, but no one there could have discerned that. He was always pleasant and apparently willing to do as he was told. All the time he was learning about civilized behavior, about Westerners, and about how easily most people are satisfied with a servant's smile and an amiable manner.

It was Adeline who changed Maceo's name to Michael. "Both names mean that you came from God," she told him, "but the people you serve will be more comfortable with a name they can relate to." Oddly, she'd already renamed two of the other boys Michael. It had been her father's name, and she was fond of it.

Maceo was content at Adeline's, though it was sometimes hard to keep up the facade of being a devoted Christian. He disliked the droning prayers, the uncomfortable kneeling, and the dry bread Adeline insisted on dropping into their open mouths, as if they were baby birds.

Still, life with her was comfortable, he was well fed, and he was learning things that made him less rural, less vulgar. He might have settled for the life Adeline envisioned for him, but an opportunity arose that reawakened his old desires. One day in December, their hostess informed her boys that through the generosity of her father's home church in Texas, she could offer one of them the chance to go to America. "You must all work hard," she told them, her hands waving like flags. "Only one of you will be chosen, but if he does well, it could pave the way for another boy to follow in a year or two."

In a year or two? Michael was determined to be chosen for the first spot. His English was good. At sixteen, he was a prime example of Thai manhood, attractive, personable, and healthy. He was perhaps not as assiduous in his studies as some of the others, but he redoubled his efforts, hoping Adeline would pick him.

When the time came, she did not.

The chosen one was another of the boys she'd re-christened with her father's name, Michael Chusuk. Though he'd been with her for about two years, roughly the same time as Maceo, Michael C was Adeline's favorite. "He loves learning and he loves the Lord," she would croon, her homely face wreathed with smiles. "Michael C would rather talk about the Bible than eat."

Adeline explained, with great breathiness and wide gestures, that Michael C would soon leave for Texas. "There he will study very hard, become a doctor, and one day return to Thailand to help his people." She beamed at Michael C before turning back to the others. "I encourage you to follow his example, asking for the help of Our Lord Jesus Christ and dedicating yourself anew to Him and to your studies."

Maceo found Michael Chusuk pompous and smug, but from that day on, he cultivated the young man's friendship. Chusuk was flattered, since the others avoided his company. In the evenings, the two began exploring the city together. They marveled at bulldozers and steam-shovels. They stared at posters outside movie houses where women in skimpy dresses looked longingly at men with hair as light as sand or red as clay. It fell in waves over their foreheads, like waterfalls frozen in time.

Once Maceo convinced Michael C to sneak into a movie house with him. They didn't stay long, since Chusuk was smitten with guilt as soon as they were inside. In the short segment of the film he saw, Michael glimpsed a world he could hardly imagine. Adeline seldom spoke of the modern U.S. making instead rambling speeches about the "old days," when everyone in the nation had been taught good morals and worthwhile values. Watching the movie, Maceo understood Adeline's objections. Women like her had no place in the America of *Charlie's Angels*.

When the day arrived that their star pupil was to leave for Texas, Maceo asked if he might go with him to the airport. Adeline, who had contracted a vicious case of diarrhea, agreed that someone should see Michael C off. The result was that Maceo was the one who got on the airplane heading to America that morning. Michael Chusuk was never seen again.

Chapter Thirty-Five

Cruise-Day 12, 9:30 p.m.

One would have thought Marilyn was a teenager from the way she blushed and giggled through the late dinner she shared with Inspector Lee. Michael lingered near their table, enjoying Lee's painfully evident discomfort. The inspector made a valiant attempt to seem interested in his companion, but his expression revealed confusion as she tossed more idioms into her conversation than usual, declaring herself "pleased as punch" to see him and suggesting he looked "right-down scrumptious."

"It must be difficult to manage such a varied group of individuals," Michael heard Lee say, gesturing at the workers of different nationalities who were clearing the tables and cleaning the room.

"You don't know the half of it." In a poor attempt at a Gilda Radner impression Marilyn said, "It's always something, you know?"

"I understand that Miss E is particularly troublesome."

Michael's work at the dessert table slowed to a snail's pace so he could hear what was said. "Miss E is family. I don't know who's been tattling, but what Susie says of Sally says more of Susie than of Sally."

That confused him even further, but Lee said, "I met her some years ago, when she lived in Thailand."

"I didn't know she lived here," Marilyn gushed. "No wonder this is one of her favorite cruises." She went on in a confidential manner. "Miss E's niece, who is our CEO, would like the old lady to give up cruising and settle in somewhere near her."

"What does Miss E think of that idea?"

Marilyn giggled again. "As far as I know, nobody's had the nerve to bring up the subject." She set her wineglass down, took up the bottle, and refilled both their glasses, though Lee had barely sipped at his. "It's only a matter of time. Her age, her hip, the arthritis—she won't be able to be on her own much longer."

"No," Lee agreed. "She cannot continue doing as she has been."

Chapter Thirty-Six

Bypassing a man with a sign that said *Welcome, M Chusuk,* Michael melted into the airport crowd. He had no idea where to go or how to get there, but he had no desire to further his education and even less to study medicine. Looking around, he congratulated himself. Against all odds, he'd made it to the United States.

After using the bathroom for its usual purpose, he lingered until it was empty and then freshened up a little, using a paper towel to wash his armpits and teeth. An interesting heating device fastened to the wall intrigued him, and he used the flow of warm air to smooth some of the wrinkles from his clothes.

As he wandered the building, observing behaviors and listening to conversations, Michael felt anxious yet energized. He didn't understand a lot of what was said, but he was confident he could adjust. While he didn't understand Americans well, he told himself that every culture has naïve types who can be manipulated if one knows how to go about it.

A map hung on the airport wall brought a moment of crushing doubt. Corpus Christi, Texas, was a great distance from Chicago, Illinois. How would he make the trip with little money, no understanding of travel methods, and stolen papers?

It would not happen today or even tomorrow, he realized. He would have to acclimate himself to this new country and learn how things worked. The envelope of cash Adeline had given the other Michael would not go far, judging from the prices he'd seen posted in airport shops. Perhaps things would be cheaper in the city.

As he left the terminal, a static-laden loudspeaker announced, "The free shuttle to Howard Johnson's will leave soon. Please board if you are going into the city." A man with a bullhorn stood next to a van, and Michael watched him for a few seconds, noting that he didn't seem to care who got on the bus. From a second map of the local area, he realized the airport was some distance outside the city. The van was there to provide transport to Mr. Johnson's home, and apparently, he had quite a few guests arriving. Michael figured he could ride into the city in the van, and when he got there claim he'd made a mistake. Heart pounding, he climbed aboard and took a seat at the back. Nothing happened. A few people even smiled at him. During the ride he watched and listened. A large, pale man spoke most of the way. He had three grandchildren, one of whom was apparently destined for athletic stardom, though only ten. The woman next to him had been airsick on the plane, "Not tossing my cookies sick, but really nauseous, you know?"

When the bus stopped to let them off, Michael realized that Howard Johnson wasn't a person but the name of a hotel. As his companions trooped into the lobby to register, he followed and, once inside, slipped down a hallway and began to explore. One wing of the building was under renovation, with the doors to the rooms removed and the furniture and carpeting missing. Workmen moved in and out with tools and materials, but Michael decided if he came back later, when they'd stopped work for the day, he could sleep in one of the gutted rooms as long as he left before they started work again in the morning. Returning to the lobby, he checked the time on the wall clock above the clerk's head. Three p.m. He'd explore the neighborhood a bit and slip back in once the carpenters' tools fell silent.

Within view of Howard Johnson's were five restaurants, including one attached to the hotel itself. Michael chose the one that was farthest away and put on an ingratiating smile for a waitress dressed in a blue-and-white outfit that made her look like a schoolgirl. He ate what she brought him, chicken cooked crisp and something called *fries* that he didn't care for. He ate all of it, not sure when he'd be able to eat again. When the food was gone, the woman asked if he'd like "pah." He said yes, though he wasn't certain what that meant. She rattled off a list of choices, from boysenberry to peach. He chose the last thing she said, since he had no intention of eating it. He simply needed her to believe he intended to stay longer. When she left to get his pah, Michael went to where a sign said *Restrooms*, bypassed both *Men* and *Women,* and located the back exit. The alley there felt almost like home, and he was settled in behind some barrels, invisible, when the angry waitress came out, the check she'd prepared for him clutched in a fist she set on her ample hip as she glared at nothing.

After waiting to be sure the woman wasn't still looking for him, Michael left his hiding place and went looking for clothing. Wandering through several different shops, he watched as people picked up items and disappeared into small rooms to try them on. If a garment pleased them, they took it to a clerk behind a counter and paid for it. If it didn't, they put it back on a rack or table. When Michael felt ready, he went to a display of denim pants that looked old but were in fact new. Holding different ones up until he found his size, he took a soft cotton shirt marked "Large" from a table and carried the items into one of the fitting rooms. There he put them on, carefully removing the tags and applying them to his old clothes. He folded the shirt he'd been wearing to look like the one on display and hung his pants by the clips attached to the metal hanger. Once that was done, he peeped out, watching until both clerks were busy. Exiting the fitting room, he left his old garments behind and walked out wearing the new ones. Later, in his borrowed hotel room, he examined himself in the mirror and decided he looked like a real American.

On his first full day in Corpus Christi, Michael walked the streets, becoming familiar with the place. At One Shoreline Plaza, a large building that loomed above the downtown area, he stood watching crowds of people pass. He wasn't certain what he wanted—*who* he wanted—but he thought he'd recognize opportunity when he saw it.

Resting on foam carpet padding in the hotel room the night before, he'd come to grips with some truths he could no longer avoid. He'd been lucky to get this far, but he could go no farther without help. He couldn't fly to Chicago, and he had no idea how to get there any other way. According to the television set that blared continuously in the hotel lobby, it was winter in the north, with bitter cold and snow that would last for months. Even if he managed to get to Chicago, Michael feared he'd freeze to death within a week.

Common sense demanded he stay in Texas until winter was over. He'd learn how to act like an American. He'd perfect his American English. When summer came to Chicago, Michael would find a way to get there, and he would search the city until he found Richard Terzis.

As Michael waited for something that looked like opportunity, a woman got out of a car. Head lowered, she stepped quickly across the sidewalk, her high heels clicking rapidly, and headed toward the South Tower. The man who'd opened the car door for her wore a uniform jacket, which indicated he was a hired driver, not a husband or friend. What drew Michael's attention to the woman was a large birthmark that spread over the lower right quadrant of her otherwise pale face. Not only was the mark dark purple, but the skin was also rough and bumpy looking. It drew the eye, evoking pity or disgust, depending on the viewer. Aside from the glaring imperfection, the woman was hardly noticeable, a plain face and a shapeless body, a pitiful bust line and not much rear either. Though her clothing was well-made and probably expensive, her posture was apologetic, almost furtive. She looked like a peasant masquerading as a princess.

As she hurried inside, Michael drew several conclusions. The woman was financially comfortable but socially insecure, no doubt due to her facial deformity. She wore no wedding ring, though she was at least thirty. Someone like that, desperate to experience love, would be susceptible to an attractive man who ignored her imperfection. All that was in his favor.

But Michael was half her age. Though his goal was a sexual liaison, he'd have to start with an innocent relationship and build from there.

Ignoring the suspicious glare of the security guard, he followed his prey into the building and noted the floor where the elevator stopped. When the car returned, Michael boarded it and rode to the same floor. The doors opened with a discreet chime, revealing a hushed office furnished comfortably and expensively, with indirect lighting and lots of wood paneling. A receptionist with caramel-colored, straight hair that fell over the shoulders of her boxy jacket looked up expectantly. "Can I help you?" Her tone suggested she'd already decided he wasn't important.

"A woman came here that I think was once my teacher. Miss Swift?" He'd chosen the name from the side of a passing delivery truck.

"There's no one named Swift here."

"I am almost certain it is she because of the…" He touched his cheek as if unsure of the word. "She was a very good teacher, Miss. I learned English from her back in Laos."

"You're mistaken. The woman you saw has never been a teacher."

Michael feigned eagerness. "Is my English not very good?"

She seemed partly amused, partly impatient. "You speak very well, but I doubt that Miss Logan could even find Laos on a map." She straightened her desk blotter. "I can't help you."

"Thank you. You have been very kind." Michael pressed the elevator button. He might have added, *and informative,* since the receptionist had unwittingly revealed the client's name and status, Miss, not Mrs.

Perfect.

When Miss Logan came out of the building an hour later, Michael was ready. As her driver pulled away from the curb, he stepped from behind a post, thumped the side of the car with his fist, and fell to the ground. Someone screamed, and the car stopped with a scrape of tires.

Michael lay on the pavement, clutching his hip. Getting out, the driver launched into a diatribe about careless pedestrians. Michael groaned. Soon the back door opened, and he heard the click of heels on pavement. "Are you all right?"

"I—will—be...okay." He spoke through clenched teeth, keeping his features drawn tight.

"I'll go inside and call for an ambulance."

"No, please." He extended a hand beseechingly. "I need to—" He glanced around. "I need to go."

Kind, gray eyes met his. "You're illegal."

He looked away as if ashamed. "Please, go on your way."

She hesitated, and Michael held his breath. She might do as he said, not as he wanted. After a few seconds she asked, "What if I take you to a doctor who won't care what your resident status is?"

"No, I—"

"I can't leave you in the street. When my doctor says you're all right, you can go on *your* way." She smiled as she said it, a joke between them.

He feigned reluctance. "Miss, I don't know you."

"I don't know you either," she replied, "but people help people. That's how things should be."

Susan Logan was a good person, too kind to leave a man in apparent pain and too naïve to realize how easily she'd been manipulated. After Michael's injury was proclaimed to be minor (He'd slammed his thigh into a fire hydrant to raise a convincing bruise), she offered to take him to lunch. "It's the least I can do after my car knocked you down." Her driver eyed Michael with distrust, but Michael had determined that the man worked for the car service, not Susan, so he ignored him.

"You did nothing wrong, Miss," he told her. "You are as kind as you are lovely."

Seeing the blush creep up her neck, Michael knew he was in. Lunch was pleasant, and he allowed her to drag out of him that he'd come to the U.S. on a student visa, now lapsed. "University was not for me," he told her, letting his eyelids droop with fake sadness, "but I love your country. It is peaceful here, while there is great killing in my homeland. I want to stay, but without school or a job, I cannot get a green card."

She sipped at what she called a Coke, though it was clear. "What if you worked for me?"

He frowned. "How could that be?"

"My grounds man is getting old. You could help him clean the pool, trim the hedges, and mow the grass. If you're willing, I'll help you apply for legal status."

"I could not ask you to do that."

"You didn't ask, Michael. I offered."

"I am most grateful." Gravely he put out a hand to shake hers, sealing their agreement. "You will not be sorry."

It took Michael two months to seduce Susan, though she believed it was the other way around. When she cried afterward, sobbing out that she was a terrible person, that he was too young and she was too hideous, he kissed four points on her face: forehead, chin, cheek, and birthmark. "I have loved you since the day we met. That cannot be wrong."

In the years that followed, Michael learned the advantages of being rich, or at least living with someone who was. Susan's natural reluctance to mix socially meant she maintained a small circle, and most of them tolerated Michael because of their fondness for her.

By watching her friends and family, he learned how to dress and act, what to eat and drink, and how to pronounce it correctly. Michael became adept at conversing amicably without providing a single shred of significant information.

His biggest problem was Susan's father, who made harrumphing noises whenever Michael was in the room. "Daddy doesn't like anyone," she'd say, waving away his concerns. "You could be Asian royalty and he'd still mutter and fuss." To minimize friction, Michael began staying home when Susan visited her parents. He suspected the old man poured caution in her ear at every opportunity, but Susan seemed immune to it.

Michael's passion to find Richard Terzis faded as his new lifestyle pushed old resentments into the corners of his mind. He succumbed to the comforts of life with Susan, and each year when spring came, he told himself there was no hurry about going to Chicago. The secret of his birth would be there when he was ready to look for it. For the present, he was enjoying the life he'd always felt he deserved.

Though Susan wasn't a socialite, she did attend a few charity events. She insisted that Michael go along, and she introduced him to others as her protégé. While he guessed few believed their relationship was platonic, plenty of current celebrities were involved in winter/spring affairs. He'd claimed to be twenty when they met, and a dozen years between lovers wasn't unique.

In 2003, when he returned from a trip to Houston, Michael was met by a police officer who told him Susan was dead. Inside the house, a detective named Weller, who smelled of stale cigarette smoke, waited to interview him. When he cleared his throat like a water buffalo and said, "Mr. Chusuk, I have a few questions," Michael concluded he was the principal suspect in Susan's death.

"Whatever I can do to help." He pressed his mouth with a knuckle. "This is unbelievable."

"I understand you flew to Houston Wednesday morning. Why?"

He swallowed hard. "Susan and I had a disagreement. We needed a cooling-off period."

The muscles around the detective's eyes relaxed a little. He'd known about the fight and expected Michael to try to hide it. "What did you quarrel about?"

Taking out a silk handkerchief and wiping at his nose, Michael replied, "She wanted us to marry."

"And you didn't want to do that?"

Laying a hand on his chest, Michael met the detective's gaze. "Look at me. I'm a poorly educated resident alien. If we married, people would say Susan had been tricked by a—Who is it? —a Romeo." That was precisely what he surmised Susan's father had already told the police. "I didn't want people to gossip that she was a fool. She was not."

"You don't deny that you and she were lovers?"

He sighed as if disturbed by the man's assumptions. "I cared for Susan more than I imagined I could care for anyone, Detective, but I didn't want to come between her and her family. Her father barely tolerates me now. Can you imagine what he'd say if we announced we were getting married?"

He'd struck the right note. Weller had read old man Logan as vindictive and bigoted. Logan had no doubt thrown his weight around, assuming the investigation would go in whatever direction he demanded.

"How did she die?" Michael begged. "No one will tell me."

"It appears Ms. Logan got up sometime Wednesday night, tripped, possibly on the belt of her housecoat, and fell down the stairs." Weller's tone had edged away from treating Michael as a suspect. "Can you give me a detailed account of where you've been since Wednesday and the names of people who can corroborate it?"

Opening his wallet, Michael took out a ticket stub. "This shows the flights I took going and returning. I'll write down contact information for the friends I stayed with in Houston."

Weller nodded. "That should do. And Mr. Chusuk, I'm sorry for your loss."

Michael's friends in Houston had no idea he'd left their place at midnight via the fire escape, driven through the night in their car, and slipped back into their guest room just before daybreak. "Thank you, Detective. If there's anything I can do to help you learn what happened, please let me know."

A real sense of loss hit when Michael discovered that everything Susan had, her home, her car, everything, belonged to her father. The day after her death, Logan and two of his employees, both intimidating types, arrived to order him to leave. Aside from his clothes and some personalized gifts Susan had bought for him, Michael could take nothing. No tangible rewards for three years as her lover, confidante, and confidence-builder.

Still, he told himself, he'd learned a lot from Susan. He knew quite a few rich Americans, and he knew how to deal with them. And Michael was barely twenty years old.

Chapter Thirty-Seven

Mackinac Island, January, 2004

In the first few years of the new millennium, Cathy and Laura became financially solvent, though hardly well off. As 2004 wound down, as the leaves changed color and the nights turned cold, they shut off the nearly empty upstairs by closing grates and laying foam panels over the stairway openings. Cathy canned the vegetables grown in a sunny spot out back and picked and dried the last of the flowers she'd coaxed from the rocky soil. Laura wrapped the water pipes with heat tape so they wouldn't burst when real cold arrived. They bought a small propane heater for the living area, and when the temperatures dropped dramatically at night, they assured each other that cold was better for sleeping anyway.

The pace of the island slowed, as always. Boats still arrived from St. Ignace and Mackinaw City, but fewer tourists stepped off the metal gangways. Horses still pulled carriages and carts along the streets, but their numbers lessened as handlers came to move a few at a time to winter quarters. Employees who'd spent the last five months staffing fudge shops, hotels, and bicycle rentals began to melt away, the American kids heading to college and the foreigners returning to places like Denmark, Honduras, or Sri Lanka. Though Braddock House wasn't part of the Mackinac Island hubbub, even there on the hill, the quiet grew quieter.

Cathy was surprised one afternoon when Laura came in the back door, leading a girl of about fifteen who wore clothing too light for the weather and too suggestive for her age, which was about fourteen.

"I heard a bump in the well-house, looked in, and found her hiding there." Laura slid an arm around the girl's shoulders, and she met Cathy's gaze as she added, "I promised her we won't call the police."

The girl's wide eyes and tear-streaked face suggested panic was imminent. "If you tell on me, I'll run!"

Her tone, expression, and posture recalled children Cathy had dealt with in Thailand, kids whose trauma had convinced them no one could be trusted. Stepping forward, she bent so that her eyes met the girl's straight on, aware that eye contact sometimes steadies jangled nerves. "What's your name?"

"Star."

"Are you running away from someone?" When she nodded Cathy asked, "Your parents?" Star shook her head, and new tears spilled down her cheeks. Cathy felt her jaw tighten. "Has someone hurt you?"

The girl sank against Laura, almost upsetting her. As they exchanged a look over her head, Cathy backed away, letting Laura hold Star while she cried. When her sobs turned to soft moans, Laura led her to the couch and sat her down on the colorful afghan that covered a worn spot.

"You need to tell us everything," Cathy said while Laura got a glass of water. "If we can help, I promise we will."

The story Star told between gulps of water was not all that unusual, but tragic, nonetheless. She'd run away from home one night after her stepfather knocked her to the floor, his reason that time being that she hadn't refilled his coffee cup quickly enough. Desperate to escape his abuse, she'd fallen into something worse. "A guy gave me a ride from Marquette to some little town where they have a casino. When he stopped to gamble, he said I had to get out. I stood outside the place all night, not sure what to do, but then this guy Doug came along. He said I looked cold, and he offered to buy me breakfast." She swiped at her nose with the back of her hand. "He seemed really nice."

Naïve, Cathy thought, *as we all are at that age.*

"When was this?"

Her eyes rolled upward as she remembered. "Monday."

Three days. "This man bought you food. Then what?"

"He said he'd take me all the way to Detroit if I wanted, and maybe even get me a job down there. He was really polite, you know? We stopped in Escanaba and he bought me stuff. Makeup. These clothes." Tears started again. "Then he got a motel room and he said I—I owed him for all that. He said I had to—He—"

"We know what he did," Laura interrupted. "What happened after that?"

"He brought me to Mackinaw City, where he had this, like, sailboat."

"Did you tell him you didn't want to go with him?"

She nodded. "He said if I made a fuss, he'd turn me over to the police and they'd take me back home. He said my stepdad would really teach me a lesson for running away." She wiped her nose again, this time with the hem of her shirt. Laura rose, got a box of tissues, and set it beside her on the couch. "He kept saying 'I never hurt you, did I?' and I said like, 'Well, no,' and he said girls gotta, like, pay for their meals and clothes and all that somehow."

"So you went with him."

"Yeah. Except there was two more guys on the boat. They—" Her voice broke.

"We know, sweetheart." Laura stroked her hair. "We know."

"You've been on Doug's boat since Tuesday?"

"The first two nights they locked me in this cupboard thing. Last night they got all drunk, and when…when they were done, they went to sleep without locking me in. Once they got to snoring, I sneaked out and went over the side." A tiny scrap of pride showed as she added, "The water's cold, but I can swim really good."

"And how did you get up here?"

"I was scared to stay in town, so I started uphill, thinking I'd hide in the woods till they left. When it got daylight, it felt like everybody in the world was looking for me, you know, so I looked for a place to hide until it got dark again." Her tone turned defensive. "Your shed wasn't locked."

Laura hugged the girl again. "Star, you're safe now. We'll help you."

More attuned to consequences than her friend, Cathy asked, "Do you think they'll come looking for you?"

The girl's darting gaze hinted that she wanted to lie, but she didn't. "They planned to take me out to North Dakota, to some oil field where there aren't many girls. Doug said guys there pay a lot for, um, sex."

"The Bakken Fields." The area was known as a human trafficking nightmare, and their mention of it indicated the men who'd abducted Star weren't amateurs. Not wanting to scare the girl more than she already was, Cathy said, "We'll get you to somewhere safe. When you're ready, people there will help you decide what you want to do."

While Laura got out her spare nightgown and made a blanket bed for Star in a corner, Cathy emailed her old friend Terri Schultz. *I have a package in Michigan that needs to be moved. Any idea how things work these days?*

It was a relief to get a quick reply. *Still in business, world-wide. Buy a track phone and call this number.*

Terri didn't know what she was asking, but the next day Laura took the ferry to St. Ignace and found a dust-coated specimen in an electronics store. Once Cathy figured out how to make it work, she made the call. "This is Terri."

"It's Elvera. I can't believe you're still…helping people."

"Still plenty who need help," Terri replied brusquely. "We call ourselves Second Base. What you got?"

Before she explained the situation with Star, Cathy felt compelled to account for her sudden disappearance from Thailand. "I know I said I'd help your cause, but—"

"We heard what happened," Terri cut in. "I'm guessing when the government and the lawyers got done with you there was about enough money left to buy a jar of peanut butter and a box of crackers."

"I'm surviving." As she said it, Cathy realized how little she missed the wealth she'd had. What she did miss was the feeling of contributing something positive to the world. Aside from taking Laura in, what had she done since leaving Thailand that was the least bit worthwhile?

Unaware of her thoughts Terri asked, "What's the situation with your package?"

She told her about finding Star in their shed and learning of sex traffickers operating in the area. When she finished Terri said, "The U.S. isn't my area of expertise, but we'll get her somewhere safe."

"I wish I had a way to repay you."

There was a pause. "You're near the Canadian border, right? Would you be willing to do what you did before, give packages a safe place to stay until something permanent can be arranged for them?"

"I have to discuss it with my, um, housemate, but if she's okay with it, I'd love to."

Star left by boat the next night, and while her tearful thanks still rang in their ears, Cathy presented Terri's idea to Laura. "We'd be a halfway house for people on the run from war and other bad things. It's illegal, and you're a convicted felon. If you're caught—"

Laura chuckled. "Then we'll need to make sure we don't get caught."

Within a month they were expecting their first boarder, a boy from Myanmar named Noor. Though Cathy had been unaware of turmoil there, Terri explained that in the nation that had been Burma back when they learned geography, the Rohingya, a Muslim group, were persecuted by the Buddhist majority. Though the situation was confusing, Cathy trusted Terri's judgment. If the boy needed to leave Myanmar, she would do what she could to help.

In the dark of night, Laura went to meet the boat that brought Noor across the strait. When she returned, Cathy saw a child who reminded her of many she'd seen in Thailand. Noor's eyes seemed too big for his face. He had bitten his lips raw, and he stared blankly into the distance, unwilling to speak and unable to meet either woman's gaze.

As the boy slept wrapped in three blankets, Cathy told Laura what she knew of his background. "Noor's birth was never registered in Myanmar, since Muslims aren't supposed to have more than two children. Travel is restricted, and they're often harassed, their businesses destroyed, crops burned, and families attacked because of their religion."

"People are bastards sometimes," Laura commented.

"This boy lost his entire family in one night. His mother saved his life by hiding him in a cupboard, but he heard the whole thing."

For several days, Noor inhabited Braddock House like a ghost, saying little, eating little, and sleeping only for short periods. They communicated with him using gestures, but aside from a weak nod or shake of his head, he made no attempt to reply. Winter meant few choices in terms of fresh fruit, but Laura managed to find things he was familiar with, grapes, melon, and once a pathetic mango. Rice was easy, and Cathy consulted the internet for ways to prepare fish dishes Noor would find familiar. As the days passed, he became more responsive, reminding Cathy of her own recovery from grief. What seems unbearable becomes bearable in time, because something in the human spirit won't allow us to give up and die.

By April, when the signs of annual renewal began on the island, Noor conversed hesitantly in English and sometimes smiled. His dark eyes were still haunted by tragedy, but he liked a video game Cathy found at the library that allowed players to race around an oval track while rival drivers zoomed in and out ahead of them. Once when he won, Noor laughed aloud.

Word finally came that he was to go to Canada, to a Muslim community outside Toronto. "Will they speak his language?" Cathy asked the man who contacted her. "He's been through so much."

"His host family speaks Burmese," the man answered. "Several others in the neighborhood came to Canada because of the troubles in Myanmar. He'll be okay."

Easy for him to say. Cathy and Laura had become fond of Noor, and it was hard to let him go. In the lonely days after he left, Cathy told Laura stories of her activities in Thailand. "It was rewarding," she said, "but I only knew those people for a few days. It's harder this time, after having Noor with us all winter."

As tourist season neared again, the pace picked up with Terri's organization as well. She and Cathy spoke regularly on the phone, and one day Terri said, "Elvera, I told a few of our people about your house on the island. For some time, we've talked about the need to establish a base of operations. We need someone reliable who will take calls, deal with emergencies, and keep track of who can do what."

Laura was a hundred percent behind the idea. "You're good on that computer," she told Cathy as she tested the spring catch on an intricately beaded bracelet in gold and black. "Your friend knows you can be trusted to keep things organized."

"I suppose I am perfect for the job," Cathy agreed. "It's not like I ever travel very far from home." She felt her spirits lift as she made her decision. "If they can use a lame, fifty-plus people-smuggler dispatcher, I'm happy to be the one."

Chapter Thirty-Eight

Texas-December, 2004

Susan Logan's father used his influence to harass his daughter's former lover whenever possible. Homes that had been open to Michael in Corpus Christi were now closed. No one offered a hand in friendship, and he suspected warnings had gone out that anyone who associated with Michael would earn endless enmity from the old man. It was time, Michael decided, to leave the city and his Michael Chusuk persona behind. Selling the things Susan had bought him netted enough cash to purchase a new identity from a hairy, smelly, computer nerd who barely looked up when he handed over a set of documents at a wobbly table in a third-rate coffee shop. None of that mattered. He was now Michael Silver, a naturalized U.S. citizen.

Though he toyed with the idea of picking up the quest he'd put on hold, Michael's enthusiasm for locating his parents had dimmed. One or both might be dead by now, and from what he'd heard, Chicago was a dangerous place, with murders in the streets every day. Besides, it was winter again, and he hated the cold. The easiest path forward was to find another Susan and take up the soft life again.

Crashing a New Year's party at a fine hotel, Michael meandered through the crowd, smiling like he belonged there and sipping cheap champagne. Near the end of the evening he met Dottie Rawlins, a widow whose husband had been a moderately famous rodeo rider. When he first noticed her, she was telling a group of partygoers her troubles. "Life ain't the same these days," she said in a nasal whine. "I sure wish Clint hadn't jolted his poor old body till it gave up and died."

Though well off, Dottie was naïve, having been sheltered by her male kin as a girl and married at seventeen to a man who took over where her daddy had left off. At fifty, Dottie was without a man's steadying hand for the first time in her life, and she had no weapons with which to resist Michael's charm and good looks. Within a week of their meeting, she told friends she planned to take "that pretty boy" home to her ranch outside Nacogdoches. The Rawlins family was shocked when she did, and investigation into Michael Silver's background began. As far as they could learn, Silver had emigrated to the U.S. in the early nineties with his parents, who were now dead. He'd worked in hotel management for the last few years. He had no police record, not even a traffic ticket.

The problem, Michael learned later, was that Clint Rawlins had known his wife well. While Dot had plenty of spending money, the ranch belonged to Clint Junior, "lock, stock, and whiskey-soaked barrel." Still, it wasn't a total mistake. Dottie provided the lifestyle Michael desired, and aside from a healthy appetite for sex, made few demands on him.

The Rawlins family despised Michael, and he heard Junior refer to him once as the "slope gigolo." That was okay. He didn't care what they thought or said or called him, as long as he was handed an appropriately frosty drink when he wanted one and someone else cleaned up the messes he left behind.

During his time with Dottie, Michael learned, by pure happenstance, something that rekindled his interest in his parents. Dottie's ten-year-old grandson, Russell, had a stammer. Most of the boy's family either embarrassed the kid when he stuttered or ordered him to stop, as if mere willpower could produce the desired result. Though he'd never spent time around children, Michael earned the boy's regard simply by waiting in patient silence until he got out what he wanted to say. They became, if not friends, at least allies. The boy sought Michael's company, and since he had little else to occupy his time, he allowed the kid to hang around.

Russ loved computers, where his stutter was no handicap, and he showed Michael his sticker-covered laptop, opening a whole new world to him. When he realized technology could help him complete the search he'd abandoned years ago, Michael cultivated Russ' friendship with purpose, soaking up everything the kid could teach him.

It took a while, because he had to do his research when Russell wasn't around, but eventually Michael found an article about the demise of a Chicago business once headed by Richard D. Terzis. According to the writer, Terzis' wife had been the real power figure, managing things from Thailand. When the business failed, no one had been able to reach her for an interview. She and Terzis divorced. There was a photo of the couple in their younger days, and, looking closely at Terzis, Michael recalled a line from Maarit's journal: *A man with curiously small ears visited, interested in the child.* This had to be the right Richard Terzis, but the article said he'd left Chicago after the failure of Tharp Credit Services. There was no indication where he'd gone.

It took an additional month of research to locate the name online again, but when he did, Michael chortled aloud. A fundraiser for an aspiring presidential candidate was being held in Dallas, and the organizer was Rick Terzis. Michael signed up for the event, using the name Russell Rawlins and paying the hefty fee with one of Dottie's credit cards.

At the gala, he watched Terzis from a distance, trying to get a sense of the man's character. Terzis was a people pleaser, smiling, laughing, or touching others on the arm to show appreciation for their wit and wisdom. Despite his apparent geniality, Michael sensed an invisible wall between Terzis and others. His responses came a beat late, as if he ran them through a filter and gave back what he believed the listener wanted to hear. *Been there, done that.*

When he got a chance to shake hands with Terzis, Michael asked, "Are you Rick as in Frederick or as in Richard?"

Looking slightly uncomfortable, he said, "Richard, but I detest that name." His eyes narrowed. "Forgive my asking, but are you

Thai?"

"Good guess. I'm Michael Silver. I Americanized the surname when I got my citizenship papers. Far too many letters in the original for people here to deal with."

"Are you enjoying the evening, Mr. Silver?"

"Very much. The crudités are excellent, and the company is stimulating."

Michael didn't extend the conversation but instead moved on to others in the senator's party. The donation he (Dottie) had made brought VIP treatment. It was flattering to be courted by men who walked the halls of Congress, to hear them speak casually of "Dubya" and others he'd seen only on the news. Though he'd met wealthy people before, wealth melded with political influence was doubly attractive. These people enjoyed their cars and their yachts, but they also steered the country in the direction they wanted it to go. Money was a tool to them, and the nation was their chessboard. That made Michael ask himself a question. Since Richard Terzis had supposedly lost everything in the fall of Tharp Credit Services, how did he fit in with this crowd?

With discreet questions, Michael learned that Terzis had made himself useful as a facilitator, using his years in business to make things work for the senator. "He's a pretty interesting guy," one man said. "He lived overseas for some time, in Hong Kong or somewhere like that. Then his wife bankrupted the company and divorced the poor schmuck, leaving him with nothing." A raised eyebrow hinted at his belief that one could expect nothing else when a woman ran a business. "Terzis knew Senator Dawkins from years back, and since he'd done so much work overseas, the senator offered him a job." He shrugged lightly. "Having some international experience on staff makes Dawkins look less like a hick."

Michael circulated through the crowd, bringing conversations around to Terzis without being obvious about it. One man called him "savvy," which Michael interpreted as *He knows how to bend the rules.* Another termed him the senator's "go-to guy," which he translated to *He does the dirty work.* While the official story was that the senator valued Terzis for his foreign experience, Michael concluded his actual job was hatchet man, working to control the way the ambitious politician was seen by the outside world.

Late in the evening, when the party was breaking up, Michael drew Terzis aside. "You need to find me a place on the senator's staff."

Terzis gave him an assessing look. "Doing what?"

Michael met his gaze. "Whatever you tell me to. Officially I serve as your driver, or something like that. I stay in the background, but I handle tasks that need to be done…discreetly."

Terzis' expression revealed interest, but he was also cautious. "If I wanted someone like that, why would I hire a complete stranger?"

"I'm in the U. S. illegally." At Terzis' surprised look, Michael smiled. "Now you know something that could get me deported. I can't betray you without screwing myself." When Terzis frowned, he went on, "I'm not on anyone's radar. I move quietly, and I take care of business, as they say."

"That's not—" Terzis stopped, and for a moment Michael feared he'd moved too fast. Then he asked, "How far are you willing to go?"

Michael quirked a brow. "Unless you want to start a nuclear war, I've probably already done it."

"I see." He paused to consider. "We move around a lot. Would you be able to come with us?"

Michael thought about Dottie, who'd begun asking bothersome questions about where her money was being spent. "Give me a week to tie up some loose ends, and I'll be there."

Richard, now Rick, Terzis had managed to reinvent himself, shedding past failures and a near escape from prosecution for fraud. "I spent years trying to save a company that was doomed from the start," he often told listeners. "My wife and her father..." He would let the words trail off as if he didn't want to damage anyone's reputation. "Really, it was nobody's fault."

"My ex was once a fiercely competitive businesswoman," Rick told Michael when he asked about Elvera Tharp one night after dinner. The remains of their meal lay between them, and his fingers felt sticky from shrimp sauce, despite his having wiped them on the fine linen napkin.

Scotch flowed freely in and out of Rick's glass, which Michael had discovered made him more willing to speak of the past. "Then there was an accident. Two people were killed, and they found Elvera half-dead. The trauma she experienced and the pain she dealt with afterward changed her. She refused to leave Thailand. She insisted on running both businesses long distance. She wouldn't listen to my advice. The situation became impossible, and there was nothing I could do but get out."

Every scrap of information Terzis let slip in conversation sent his new personal assistant to the internet for more information. Reading on Rick's laptop late at night, Michael drew his own conclusions. Terzis himself had killed Tharp Credit Services by making increasingly risky deals. Then he'd bled his wife's fashion design company dry to save himself. When even that wasn't enough, he'd absconded, leaving his wife to face the mess he'd created.

Looking at grainy black-and-white photos of Elvera Tharp, Michael searched for clues that she was indeed his mother. Weren't their noses similar in shape? Wasn't that forthright gaze identical to the one he saw in the mirror? Michael found the old question stirring his mind and his emotions. Why had she left him at the Garden of Children?

"Fiercely competitive," Terzis called her. Had she been unwilling to take the time to raise a child? Embarrassed that her son was illegitimate? Or that he was half Thai? Was Elvera Tharp a bigot who'd screw a handsome foreigner and then refuse to acknowledge his son? One of the most upsetting things Michael learned was that Elvera Tharp's Bangkok house was less than a mile from the Garden of Children Orphanage.

There were other questions too. Why had Terzis come looking for him all those years ago? Not out of concern for his welfare, Michael was certain of that. Had Terzis confronted Elvera with knowledge of her affair and demanded she abandon the boy?

But she'd been the one with the money and power. She could have—should have—insisted on keeping her son. She was busy, yes, but wealthy women's children are often raised by nannies. At the very least, Elvera might have placed him with a loving family and provided funds for his care.

No explanation proved Elvera Tharp to be anything other than a faithless woman, a spoiled rich girl who tired of things and dropped them like discarded toys. She'd tired of Richard Terzis, so she had an affair. She'd tired of being a mother before she'd spent even one week in the role. Apparently Elvera had even tired of her precious fashion house in the end, leaving a subordinate to manage it.

Michael read everything he could find about the rise and fall of Mizz Fashions. At first the business was wildly successful, and Elvera was hailed as a genius. Its fall was sudden, but insiders must have known there were problems. If Elvera had cared about Mizz, why hadn't she returned to the U.S. and tried to save it when the financial reversals began?

In an article called "Disastrous Business Failures of the Nineties," he learned that Mizz's creative director, Jill Elliot, had worked to the bitter end to try to save the company. In Elvera's absence, Elliot had launched an impressive campaign of Asian inspired fashion with a Khmer woman named Daw as the focal point. It had been a big success, but years later, things had gone downhill. At the last, Mizz left its suppliers, employees, models, and other creditors unpaid and angry. Jill Elliot didn't have the resources to keep Mizz afloat, and Elvera Tharp hadn't seemed to care that it was sinking.

Had the accident Terzis spoke of caused brain damage? That might explain her loss of interest.

Michael searched until he found a frustratingly brief account. *Police in Sa Kaeo Province report the deaths of two people in a motoring accident. Killed were American missionary Cathy Charbonneau and Jatukamramthem Taksin, a cousin of Thailand's Prime Minister. Their vehicle slid off the mountainside due to heavy rain. A third person, U.S. businesswoman Elvera Tharp, was gravely injured but is recovering in a Bangkok hospital.*

Typing *Cathy Charbonneau* in the search bar brought no results. Entering *Jatukamramthem Taksin* got only one new item, a programming note for a 1980s women's group that wasn't much help. *Mr. Jatukamramthem Taksin spoke to the Women's Overseas Relief Committee about the conditions at Nong Samet, a camp for displaced Cambodians on the Thai border.* Being neither Cambodian nor the child of refugees, Michael saw no connection to himself.

He went back to the article on the failure of Mizz Designs. Jill Elliot claimed profits from Mizz had been regularly transferred to Tharp Credit Services. The year of the collapse, Elliot had tried contacting Elvera Tharp in Thailand to discuss the matter but received no response. Eventually, fearful for her own reputation, Elliot called the authorities to report financial irregularities between the two businesses.

She was too late. The money was gone. No doubt aware of the looming crisis, Richard Terzis submitted his resignation and left Chicago. Legally, he was a hired hand, with no personal stake in the mess Elliot insisted he had created. Though evidence seemed to confirm his mismanagement, Elvera Tharp was the responsible party, the owner of both businesses. A few members of the media expressed shock at her failure to press her ex-husband's culpability; others claimed she should have been more watchful. Ms. Tharp remained silent on the subject.

Banks and lawyers were left to sort out the mess of who owed whom and how much. Workers were devastated to learn that not only had they lost their jobs, but they also had no pensions to look forward to. There was no recourse, because neither Tharp Industries nor Elvera herself could meet present obligations, much less future ones.

Tharp's wealth was seized and used to pay her creditors pennies on the dollar. The house in Chicago and everything else she owned was sold, the money tossed into a fund that would never stretch far enough to satisfy everyone.

Elvera made no response to any of it. A reporter sent to her home in Thailand for an interview was told she was at her summer place in the country, which only heaped fuel on the public's anger. Most people had one home. Elvera Tharp had three, and newspapers printed pictures of two of them, the sprawling bungalow in Bangkok and the dignified mansion in Chicago. "Palatial" the captions termed them, reminding readers that Tharp had cheated hundreds out of what was due them.

Elvera was the subject of dozens of editorials, both professional and amateur, on the lack of humanity among those born with silver spoons in their mouths. Former employees told of her "driven" personality. Some writers expressed sympathy for Terzis, who'd worked his whole adult life for the company and been, according to one employee, "hand-picked by old man Tharp for his daughter to marry." Unnamed sources said Richard had been given the impossible task of minding the finances of two large businesses while his wife lived like a queen in Siam. One writer opined it was a shame that Terzis, whom he'd interviewed personally, now had to scramble for a living, betrayed by Elvera Tharp just like everyone else.

Like a cat coming out of free fall, Terzis had landed on his feet. Now, as he prepared his old school chum for a 2008 run for the Presidency, his operating maxim was that honesty and politics never go together. "The best way to win," he told Michael, "is to convince voters that your opponent is more dishonest than your guy." Rick Terzis had what he called a "sixth sense for secrets," and he dug up dirt on others like a hound going after a rabbit. "I can always tell when someone shades the truth," he'd once bragged. That made Michael cough uncomfortably, but Rick had slapped him lightly on the arm. "You've lied to me more than once, Mike, but you've proven your value with your extra assignments, so it doesn't matter."

Michael's first "extra assignment" had been dealing with a young woman who objected when the senator, drunk as he often was, groped her in the cloakroom at a party. Michael seduced her, arranging a hidden camera in his hotel room that captured her face on film but not his. The woman received a copy, along with a letter that explained her choices: say nothing against the senator or see the recording pop up everywhere.

That had shut her up, and similar incidents had, as Terzis said, proven Michael's value. Rick recognized in Michael a kindred spirit, someone who would do whatever it took to get what he wanted. The senator they both worked for didn't seem to care how they accomplished his goals. In fact, he didn't want to know.

That evening, freed to wander by generous amounts of Scotch, Rick's mind focused on the past. "I don't always know what a person's secret is," he said, "but I know when there is one." Taking another drink, he added, "My wife used to think she had me fooled, but she never did. Not once."

Michael's interest quickened. "Mrs. Tharp had secrets?"

"Never fooled me once." Richard's words had gotten slushy. "I knew about her Thai lover long before he drove them both off a cliff." Though Michael did his best to get him to elaborate, Rick went silent, pouring himself another Dewars and staring into its amber depths.

Two more of Michael's questions were answered. His father was Jatukamramthem Taksin, and he was dead.

Because they saw life similarly, Michael and Rick's partnership was successful for some time. If Rick was the senator's hatchet man, Michael became the blade. If an opponent's wife got a speeding ticket, Michael found someone who'd swear she'd been drinking at a bar a few hours earlier. If a candidate's daughter went out for the evening, photos in which she looked dazed and out of control showed up on social media the next morning. And if the candidate himself had a meal with a woman other than his wife, Michael found a waiter who, for a small fee, would suggest to reporters that the two had seemed a little too cozy together. All Rick had to do was express a desire for some mud, and Michael arranged it. He was always able, with amazing speed, to turn the media's attention to somewhere more interesting than the Senator's latest gaffe.

It all went well until it didn't. A reporter who had more integrity than most investigated the all-too-convenient scandal fodder Rick provided to the press. Through dogged determination and nights without sleep, the young journalist learned that Michael's services to Senator Dawkins included crimes such as extortion and fabricating evidence. Naïvely, the woman took her findings to the senator, believing she should give him a chance to correct any untruths before submitting her work for publication. Dawkins immediately turned on his employees, launching a "probe" to "cleanse the negative aspects" from his campaign and "return to the issues."

The attempt to save himself didn't work. Dawkins was out of the race before most Americans even recognized him as a contender. Because of his disavowal, Rick and Michael were investigated and eventually indicted for multiple crimes. Rick blamed Michael, as anyone who had been paying attention should have expected. Claiming his employee had gone "off the rails," he provided "recently discovered" evidence of assaults Michael had committed, including one where he'd beaten a man almost to death. Michael was tried and found guilty. He didn't even attempt to blame Rick Terzis for the crimes. Since the case came down to a white, natural-born citizen's word against a foreign-born half-caste, there was little doubt who'd be believed.

Perhaps in response to his loyalty, Terzis never mentioned Michael's illegal status. The bogus citizenship documents the smelly computer nerd had provided held up, and Michael was not deported. Instead he went to prison for a term of no less than seven, no more than ten, years.

Chapter Thirty-Nine

Cruise-Day 13, 10:22 p.m.

When he arrived at Michael's quarters, Inspector Lee seemed stressed. "Your supervisor is quite fixated on sex," he said distastefully. "Luckily, she became very tired after the meal."

Lee didn't need to know that Michael had slipped three sleeping pills into Marilyn's coffee at dinner. "We need privacy," the policeman said to Michael's roommate in a peremptory tone. The shy Malaysian excused himself, giving the two men a look that made Lee chuckle. "I fear I've ruined your reputation, Khun Kanda."

"I'll survive."

Lee pulled two sheets of paper from his jacket pocket. "I brought this, in case you're having second thoughts about our arrangement."

As he scanned the sheets, Michael struggled to keep his face blank. "How did you get this information?"

Lee seemed pleased to hear the strain in his voice. "Once I suspected you were not a Bangkok native named Kanda, I went in search of your real identity. These days, everything is digitalized, and I found that your fingerprints match U.S. records for a convicted criminal named Michael Silver." Folding the papers, Lee returned them to his pocket. "You have served your time in Texas, but here in Thailand, you could face charges for stealing a man's identity." After a pause he added, "If you help me catch Miss E tonight, I will forget what I know about you."

Michael spoke slowly, as if reluctance weighed his tongue. "All right, Inspector. That's fair enough."

Nodding stiffly, Lee got down to business. "Have you found a location where we can observe Miss E's balcony?"

"There are passengers in all the cabins, but it's visible from a spot a few decks above."

Lee shrugged. "As long as the post is inconspicuous."

"What happens if she does take on a…package?"

Lee took a small video camera from his pocket. "I will record the incident. When the ship reaches Ho Chi Minh City, I will call the authorities there and have them arrest her."

"Have you told anyone else about this?"

"No." Lee put the camera away. "I want visual evidence, so they are forced to act."

"You realize this will probably get me fired."

Lee was unmoved. "You will also be fired if your employers learn you're here under a false name."

Michael sighed. "I'll do as you want, but please, keep my part in this as quiet as possible."

Lee touched his mustache lightly. "I will be happy to, Khun Kanda."

When Michael led him to the place he'd chosen, a storage shed for lifesaving equipment, Inspector Lee seemed pleased. Two decks above Elvera Tharp's cabin and some distance sternward, Lee could remain out of sight, both from below and on the deck itself, yet have a clear view of his quarry's balcony. "We'll be comfortable here, I think, Khun Kanda."

Michael took on an aggrieved air. "One of the crew is sick, so I'm on duty until late. I'll come back as soon as I can, but if anything happens on that balcony, you'll see it."

"Something is going to happen. I'm sure of it." Lee's voice was uncharacteristically gleeful, and he grasped Michael's arm briefly. "Join me as soon as you are free. Once I film the crime, we will go directly to Cabin Three. You will open the door with your passkey, and we will catch Tharp with the package. At that point, she will be unable to deny her involvement."

"No," Michael agreed. "She won't." He paused at the door. "I should be back just after midnight."

Lee settled in among lifejackets and floats. "That should be perfect."

Michael left, unhappy with the fact that Lee knew as much about him as he did. Michael's careful planning might all be for nothing…unless Lee's night took an unexpected turn.

Chapter Forty

Prison was bad, but not catastrophic. Michael learned quickly how to get along, and before the first year was out, he enjoyed many things the public believes incarcerated felons don't have. He had a cell phone with internet capabilities, and his free hours were spent surfing the net for every scrap of information on Elvera Tharp, Richard Terzis, Cathy Charbonneau, and Jatukamramthem Taksin.

Over time, Michael put together a theory that made sense to him. Elvera and Richard's unhappy marriage had led to her having an affair with the Thai known as Jay. She'd run away with him to Thailand, but he'd died in the accident that also killed her childhood friend Cathy, who'd been working as a teacher. Elvera's injuries explained why she hadn't returned to the orphanage on time, but they didn't account for Michael being left there permanently. Had Elvera lost her memory, forgetting she had a son? When her lover died, had she lost interest in their child?

One way to answer that question. Find her and ask.

Released in 2015 (He'd been a model prisoner), Michael found himself once again with no money, no prospects, and a rekindled desire to find his mother. The first task he set for himself was hunting down Richard Terzis, which took time and ingenuity. Changing one letter of his last name, Richard had established himself as Rich Tersis in Tampa, Florida. He made his living as a rental agent for high-end properties.

From an unattended till at a diner where he'd had lunch, Michael stole enough money for a bus ticket to Tampa. There he went back to his old ways, sleeping in empty houses and stealing food. For three days he watched Richard come and go. When he was ready, he broke into the man's condo, sat in a chair facing the door, and waited for the key in the lock that signaled his old boss's return.

"Hello, Dick."

His response was almost comical, but Richard recovered quickly. "Michael. It's good to see you, kid."

"Funny you should use that term. I figured out whose kid I am."

He tried to appear lost, but his shifty gaze betrayed him. "What?"

"On November 27, 1984, you went to an orphanage in Bangkok, looking for a child left there by an American woman. That woman was your ex-wife, Elvera."

Terzis licked his lips. "You're E's son."

Michael moved impatiently in the chair. "Aside from giving birth, what did she ever do to make me hers? My father was killed in the accident that crippled her, yes?"

The muscles around his eyes flexed as Richard tried to decide what to say. When he spoke, his voice held an odd note. Fear? Falsehood? Eagerness? "You're Thai royalty, Michael. I can help you prove it."

"Third cousin to some government functionary? What would that do for me?" When Terzis didn't reply, he asked the question he'd come to have answered. "Where is Elvera now?"

With a helpless gesture he replied, "Last I knew, E was in Bangkok."

"The house she lived in was repossessed years ago."

"Then I can't help you," Terzis said. "I know she'd be pleased to know you're alive."

"I intend to tell her," Michael replied. "In fact, I'm very eager to meet my mother."

"That's good." Terzis sounded honest, but Michael knew better.

"Her brother Drake probably knew where she is, but he died a while back."

"I found you. I'll find her too." Michael took out a pistol he'd bought in a Miami alley. "Where do you keep your cash these days, *Dick*?"

"Cash? I'm afraid I haven't got any." He spread his hands as if demonstrating penury. "It wasn't just you who suffered when Dawkins dumped on us. I've had a hell of a time keeping body and soul together."

"You have no soul," Michael countered, "but I'm willing to bet you have a little money." He glanced around the room. "It's bound to be close by, where you can get at it." He pointed the muzzle at Richard's right knee. "Think the old fogies in this building will be able to figure out where a single gunshot came from?"

Terzis must have known he meant it. "Wait. In the credenza." The door was cleverly concealed, but when he pressed a certain spot, a hinged panel opened with a slight click, revealing a safe.

"Open it."

Knowing full well what his former employee was capable of, Terzis didn't argue. *Familiarity breeds concession,* Michael thought, pleased with both the sentiment and the phrasing.

Terzis took a fat envelope from the safe and tried to hand it to Michael. "Set it on the kitchen counter." He obeyed, frowning when he saw an unopened bottle of Dewars on the countertop. "Have a drink," Michael invited. "In fact, have eight or ten."

Chapter Forty-One

Mackinac Island- July, 2015

A carriage pulling up outside the house was unusual enough, but when Laura helped an obviously traumatized girl out, Cathy moaned slightly. Laura had again found someone in need of rescue. Though she waved the driver away with a cheerful smile, her expression turned serious when he was gone. Putting an arm around the waist of her companion, who crouched like a slapped puppy, Laura helped her climb the porch steps.

Cathy opened the door for them, noting that Laura's companion was a Native American girl of about sixteen. Bruises on both her arms looked like finger marks, and above her left eyebrow was a dried cut that had not been treated. "This is Anne." Laura's glance warned Cathy not to ask questions, so she merely stepped aside and followed them to the kitchen. Helping the girl to a chair Laura ordered, "Rest for a minute while I get something to put on that cut."

When Laura had cleaned the wound with astringent, she suggested that Anne lie down for a while. "Could—could I take a shower first?" she asked in a thin voice. "I feel—I'd like to shower."

Cathy almost spoke then, but another look from Laura stopped her. A rape victim, which she guessed Anne was, shouldn't wash away the evidence. Laura's glance telegraphed there would be no accusations made and no charges filed.

Clean and dressed in a spare nightgown, Anne went to Laura's room to rest. Once she was gone, Laura told Cathy the story she'd coaxed from the girl on the ferry from St. Ignace. "Anne's father has molested her since she was twelve. Her mother either can't deal with it or doesn't care. A week ago, on her birthday, he said he was taking her out for a Sweet Sixteen celebration." Laura's eyes hardened as she said, "The party turned out to be a help-yourself-to-my-daughter event for several of his friends. When she tried to refuse, her father beat her into submission."

Cathy covered her mouth with a hand. "Where do people like that come from?"

"Straight from hell, if you ask me." Laura made an angry gesture. "Anyway, I was getting groceries, and I saw her, walking between two men. They never let go of her arms, which looked odd. When she raised her face, I saw the cut." Laura blinked a few times. "I got mad."

"How did you get her away from them?"

"I pretended to trip and grabbed her as if to steady myself. I whispered in her ear, 'Tell them you have to pee.'" She smiled. "The girl's no dummy. She didn't let on I'd said anything. I went into the ladies' room and waited, and pretty soon, in she came. When I asked if she needed to get away, she started to cry. After I got the short version of her story, I told her to crawl out the window and wait for me at the ferry dock, behind the ticket booth. Then I went out to where the men were standing. I told them a girl in there had asked how to get to the state police post."

"Which is nowhere close to the ferry dock. Good one."

"Once they were gone, I found Anne and brought her here." Her eyes sought Cathy's. "I had to."

Cathy agreed, though they both recognized the danger. Anne was local, which meant her father and his perverted friends would easily find out where she'd gone, who Laura was, and where she lived.

"I'll call and get her moved right away."

Within an hour, Cathy had arranged for a boat to pick Anne up at one a.m. on the uninhabited side of the island. A guide would take her to a Shelter, Incorporated safe house, where she'd be protected, counseled, and given options for her future.

Since the girl had nothing, they each contributed to her needs: a hairbrush, some underwear, and other necessities. When the little stack of items was gathered, Laura went upstairs to search the closets for a suitcase of some kind. After some door slamming, Cathy heard her start back downstairs. A second later there was a crash followed by several smaller thuds. Cathy and Anne hurried to the staircase and found Laura sprawled halfway down, her face distorted with pain. The bag she'd been carrying had bumped its way to the landing and settled at their feet.

"Are you all right?"

"My knee," she gasped. "It twisted when I fell."

Though Laura insisted she'd be fine by the time they had to leave, the immediate swelling of the joint and the pain that showed on her face said otherwise. "I'll take Anne to the boat," Cathy said. "Put the leg up and ice it. In the morning we'll decide if you need to see a doctor."

"You're going to walk all the way to Brown's Brook and back? Your hip gets worse every day, no matter how hard you pretend it doesn't."

Cathy waved the objection away. "It will take me longer than it would you, but I can do it." In the end Laura gave in, though she didn't like it. Taking her sturdiest cane, Cathy escorted Anne down the path.

It had been a while since Cathy was actively involved in an escape. She hardly thought about the danger, since she needed all her energy to hide her pain as they made their way to the shore. Though her hip objected at each step, it held her upright, and she told herself that was all that mattered. Once Anne was safely away, she could take her time getting back home and rest there as long as she needed to.

When the driver of the boat turned out to be a man, Anne panicked, clinging to Cathy and sobbing. "He won't hurt you,"

Cathy said gently. To the man she said, "Show her your bracelet." He pulled back his jacket sleeve to reveal a silver chain with a core of beads at its center. "That's how we prove we're the good guys," Cathy told Anne. She showed her own bracelet, as their procedures required, to assure the driver he hadn't ventured into a trap. "It's old school," she said, "but it's worked for a long time."

Standing on the shore, she watched as the craft puttered quietly away, its engine on low. When the operator finally opened the throttle, the sound quickly faded. The boat was headed to Ludington, on the Lake Michigan coast. After that, Cathy had no idea where Anne would end up, but at least she'd never have to see her father and his disgusting friends again. Turning, she began the long walk home.

As she reached the edge of town, a siren sounded. In seconds, people stepped outside their homes, peering into the darkness to find the source of the trouble.

A woman Cathy knew slightly had turned to look up toward the island's center. "What's happened?"

"Oh, honey." The woman put a hand on Cathy's arm and pointed to where a red glow in the trees signaled disaster. "My son got called out. He says your house is on fire."

The next morning, Cathy sat with the police and fire captains as they tried to make sense of the night's events. "I went for a walk," she said for the fourth time. "I often can't sleep at night, so I walk until I can relax."

Seeing the men glance at each other, she discerned what they were thinking. A disabled woman from a house on the hill taking midnight strolls along the lakeshore? Who was she kidding?

"Mrs. Wolf was asleep?"

"I assume so." They'd found her in the kitchen, where the fire started. Initial reports said Laura's injuries were inconsistent with death by fire. The puzzled look on the fire chief's face and the way the police chief stroked his chin before asking his questions revealed they had suspicions about what had gone on at Braddock House.

Cathy knew. The men Laura had robbed of their prize came for Anne and, finding her gone, took their anger out on Cathy's oldest living friend. *Must everyone I get close to die violently?*

The police chief had heard things. "Ms. Tharp, were you aware Mrs. Wolf had a run-in with a man named Ben Simmons recently?"

She paused to choose the right words. "She knew he'd mistreated his daughter. Laura is—was upset when women were treated badly."

"Where is the girl now?"

The carriage driver knew Anne had come to the house. "Laura brought her here to calm her down. Then she bought her a ticket for the ferry and gave her enough cash to get to a relative—an aunt, I think."

He shook his head. "She hasn't contacted anyone in her family."

Cathy feigned confusion. "Then I don't know where she could be."

A stir outside the office caught everyone's attention, and they turned to look out the open door. "I've come to see my sister," Drake Tharp said.

Drake's appearance made all the horrible things that had happened a tiny bit less so. They embraced briefly, and the feel of his arms around her sent strength coursing through her veins. After a few seconds Cathy forced herself to let go of him, and she kept her gaze at his shoulder, not daring to meet his eyes. In minutes, the police chief was apologizing for keeping Ms. Tharp from resting, though Drake had made no accusation. He added his assurance that no one believed the two women at Braddock House were guilty of any wrongdoing.

"They tried to help an abused child. We're looking for the girl's father, and if he's at fault for this, he'll pay." Though Drake had no way of knowing what had gone on, he thanked the chief for his concern and said he'd like to take his sister somewhere she could rest.

He'd reserved a suite at an island inn, but before they went there, he suggested Cathy stop at a store and buy what she needed for the next few days. She owned nothing but the clothes she wore, which stunk of smoke. Each time she moved, the odor stirred memories of standing on the lawn, watching her headquarters, her home, and the magical place of her childhood turn to blackened timber and smoldering ash.

Once she had clothes and sundries, they traveled to the hotel in a carriage, the horse clip-clopping through a light rain, its hooves sending up water droplets that spattered the windows. The feeling of safety that came from being there with Drake made Cathy want to cry and smile at the same time. How many times had she dreamed of traveling anywhere, in any fashion, with him by her side? In fruition, the dream was bittersweet, and she entered it on a mental balance sheet: for every sweet moment in life, one that's bitter. For every good thing, a loss.

At the inn, she showered and changed while Drake took her old things outside and tossed them in the trash. A change of clothing couldn't erase the terrors of the night, but it helped a little. Drake ordered room service, and while she told herself she shouldn't be hungry, Cathy ate most of the food while he sampled bits of this and that. "Thank you," she said when they'd finished. "That was good."

"You should probably rest."

She wasn't ready for that yet. "It was awful, Drake. The place went up so fast."

"I'm sorry, Cathy. About the house, and about your friend."

She told him everything then, starting with Anne but going on to Noor and Star and all the way back to Daw and Sakda. She described how brave Elvera had been during the rescue, and how she'd discovered that she only felt alive when aiding people no one else would or could help. "I think Elvera would approve of what I've done, but now…I suppose it's over."

He was silent for some time, and she feared he thought she was insane. To be fair, when she stood back to look at thirty years of risking everything to obtain unclear, often unknown, results, she probably was.

Drake finally spoke. "I told you once that my job at the State Department was putting out fires in Southeast Asia. My actual job, at least part of it, was investigating the movers and shakers in the area, so we didn't get blind-sided when scoundrels like Jay Taksin did things that put the U.S. in a bad light."

"You knew about Jay?"

He nodded. "I knew of him. I warned my superiors that he was no good, but some in our government found such men useful." Another pause. "If I'd known you had met him, or that Elvera had fallen under his spell, I'd have said something."

Remembering the moment when she'd almost asked his advice about going to Thailand, Cathy said, "It was my fault. I was so stupid—"

Putting his hands on her arms, Drake looked directly into her eyes. "None of this is your fault, Cathy. You joined Taksin's group because you wanted to work for good in the world." He turned away, his expression grim. "We knew he misrepresented himself, but his uncle held a high position in the Thai government. And since Taksin pushed for more U.S. influence, we excused his crimes."

"Governments often do what's convenient, not what's right." Cathy's tone turned regretful. "I'm going to hate giving up my small contributions to justice. They made me feel useful to the world, despite my age and condition."

"I know what you mean," he said. "Since I turned the cruise line over to Bonnie, I often feel like what the young people call an oxygen thief."

She touched his arm. "Drake, you've been a good husband to your wife and father to your children. Wild Goose Cruises provides enjoyment to lots of people. I know you give generously to charity, both your time and your money. Why in the world would you say you aren't useful?"

Drake put a hand on hers. "I could have done so much more. I saw the same things in Southeast Asia that you did. I knew those camps were horrible. I told myself it wasn't my job to worry about them." Pulling his hand back, he sighed. "But you, Cathy Charbonneau? You waded in and helped where you could, as much as you could." Meeting her gaze, he added, "If I'm not mistaken, you're still doing it."

She made a small huff of derision. "My 'wading in' as you call it, has at times resulted in tragedy. We've had packages get lost. One that I know of drowned trying to cross a river during a monsoon. Some were caught and returned to Nong Samet." She bit her lip before continuing. "My actions caused the deaths of people I knew well, even loved. Jay. Elvera. And now Laura."

"And how many benefited from your actions?"

"I don't know, but can you weigh a life and say, 'This one is worth the loss of another'?"

"You must believe what you do is worthwhile," he said gently. "You've kept at it all these years."

It took a while for her to answer, but in the end, she said, "I do. Despite everything."

Drake paused, apparently thinking something through. "Would you like to continue, Cath? Maybe not right now, but when you're ready?"

"I don't see how I can. I'm old. I'm lame. And now I haven't even got a house, much less—" She stopped, realizing how self-pitying that sounded. "Drake, I'm going to be okay. I'll get an apartment. Elvera Tharp qualifies for Social Security, so I have an income."

"What if I could offer a place to live and the possibility of continuing your work?" He grinned, and the boy she'd met in 1967 shone through the old man's face. "No government assistance required."

Chapter Forty-Two

Cruise-Day 13, 11:01 p.m.

When a knock sounded on the door of Cabin Three, Cathy knew who it was. She put down the book she'd been reading. "Come in, Michael."

He obeyed, but his manner was different from what she'd seen before. Leaning his back against the cabin door as if guarding against her escape, he said, "We have to talk, Miss E."

"I suppose we do."

His expression was grim as he said, "I didn't become your steward by accident."

"I know." That stopped him cold, but she went on, "You're a perfect blend of your mother and your father." Speaking almost formally she added, "In case you don't know your name, it's Franklin Daniel Tharp."

He let out a breath, as if a valve that had been building pressure suddenly released. "Yes, Miss E. I am indeed the child you abandoned."

"If you've come for money, I'm afraid there isn't any." She turned her gaze to the ocean. "If you came for your mother, she isn't here either. Like you, Michael, I operate under an alias." Taking a photo from the table, she handed it to him. "My real name is Catherine Charbonneau Przybylski. I'm the one on the right."

He stared at the picture, though he'd seen it before. "You're not Elvera." It was an admission, not a question.

"My hair tends to curl. Hers was smooth as silk." She smiled. "I envied her that. In the sixties, curly hair was a curse."

"I should have seen it. A rich girl would have had that crooked canine tooth straightened." Laying the photo aside, he asked, "Why do you pretend to be Elvera?"

"My reasons changed over time, but in my defense, the deception always served a higher purpose."

"Did you know about the child she had in Thailand?"

Her gaze faltered momentarily, but she met his eyes again. "I did."

"Yet you left me there."

"Elvera's husband convinced me you were dead."

"Richard Terzis? The man was a born liar."

"Was?"

"I'm pleased to inform you that Richard is now deceased."

After taking a moment to process that, she said, "When I finally told Drake the whole story, he said exactly what you did. 'Richard is a born liar.'" She smiled as she said Drake's name. "He spent a great deal of money trying to find you."

"Why?" Michael sounded both angry and disbelieving.

"You were his nephew. He would have included you in the family for Elvera's sake."

"Now who's the liar?"

She remained calm. "Drake hired an investigator in Bangkok. He located the orphanage where E left you for what she intended to be a short time. Your file was missing, but a woman who had worked there for a long time recalled the name of the village your adoptive mother came from. When the detective went there, he learned that your parents were dead and you had disappeared."

Michael seemed confused. "Drake Tharp must have known you weren't his sister."

Again her gaze dropped, and she said to the floor, "Drake and I were in love. He stayed silent to protect me from charges of fraud and theft."

"Lovers." Michael smiled. "Now I understand."

"No, you don't *understand*." She'd meant to be gentle with him, but his assumption of guilt made her angry. "Drake was not the sort of man to break his marriage vows." Her voice softened. "When things fell apart in Thailand, he helped me return to the States. To separate myself from those who knew me or Elvera, I lived for years on an island in Michigan."

"Until Mrs. Tharp died and you two could be together." Though she thought Michael meant to sound sympathetic, it didn't come off that way.

"As I've told you before, my personal life is personal."

"Fine. Let's ignore your sex life. Drake Tharp arranged for you to live on his ships."

"Yes. He stipulated in his will that I can sail on any Wild Goose ship at no charge for as long as I live."

"The flowers on your meal trays are a tribute from him."

She raised her hands, palms up. "I once commented that the only thing I missed from living ashore was my garden. To fix that, Drake decreed I should get flowers every day."

"Thus, Miss E became a legend on the line." Michael's brow rose as he added, "But you have a sideline, don't you? Smuggling human cargo."

She bowed as if the comment was an accolade. "That sideline, as you call it, came into being long ago, when your father and I helped displaced Khmers escape the refugee camps on the Thai border. When he died, I continued the work. The last few years, Drake helped by allowing us to operate aboard his ships."

"My father worked with displaced Khmers?" The emotion in Michael's eyes made her heart go out to him. She knew how it felt to wonder what sort of person one's father had been.

"He did." Cathy saw no purpose in telling Michael the full truth. "If they'd lived, your parents would have come for you and taken good care of you."

There was an extended silence. At the end of it, Michael's tense shoulders relaxed. In a soft voice he said, "I've been angry at them for so long." He smiled, and Cathy noted he tilted his chin the way Elvera had when she was pleased with herself. "Now that I know, I can put my anger behind me."

"I'm glad to hear it."

He gestured at the balcony. "Is it possible that I could join your group and help people escape from dangerous places?"

She shook her head. "We're shutting it down. Apparently, some Thai policeman is determined to call me to account. I might even face arrest."

"Surely your friends will rescue you."

"They'll try." She shrugged. "Either way, this is my last mission. Second Base will go on. Computers and cell phones will replace bracelets and fake jewelry ads. A new generation will take over the fight."

Michael nodded to where the slider stood open. "You'll have one last package tonight, I think."

She shook a finger at him, her expression rueful. "I thought from the first you were cleverer than most."

"I want to see how it's done." His expression was earnest. "I won't tell a soul. I swear it."

Cathy examined Michael's face, so like Elvera, so like Jay. "Be here at four a.m., and I'll show you the system in action."

He glanced at his watch. "Four? That's when we leave the harbor."

She let him see a flash of her old irritability. "Do you imagine I don't know the schedule? Don't be late."

Returning to where the inspector waited, Michael whistled softly before opening the shed door. Lee peered out suspiciously but relaxed when he saw who it was. "Done with your work, Kanda?"

"Not quite." With a quick motion, Michael stabbed Lee in the heart with the knife he'd concealed in his hand. Lee slumped sideways, making a soft thud as his shoulder hit the shed wall. "Wait for me," Michael told the corpse as he closed the door. "Once we're far enough out, I'll give you a proper burial at sea."

Chapter Forty-Three

Laughing Sailor Cruise Ship-January, 2016

When Drake proposed using his cruise ships to transport victims of chaos to new homes, Cathy had argued against it, citing the risk to his business. Drake insisted it was perfect. "Wild Goose ships stop at ports all over the world. If your people bring packages to our docking points, we can move them to a new place, even a new country, within days." She admitted it would be simpler: no false papers needed and no chance of detection by airport security screenings, which were much enhanced since 9-11.

She argued anyway. "What if we're caught?"

He merely smiled. "Authorities in most countries will be reluctant to risk their relationship with Wild Goose Cruises, since we regularly unload hundreds of wealthy passengers who boost local economies like you wouldn't believe."

Their first cruise together was a combination of romance and reconnaissance. Cathy found that she loved the sea, the smell of it, the vast emptiness of the horizon, and the peace it brought to her soul. Experiencing it with Drake was even better, and she was delighted to learn that he'd chosen the ship's colors, silver and red, for her. "You once told me you preferred silver to gold," he said, "and red is for your birthstone, the ruby."

The reconnaissance part was learning the ship's procedures and layouts. They peered into corners and looked over railings. He procured the schematics of his other ships so they could determine where the differences lay. They discussed the possibility of having packages brought on board in trunks or disguised as porters. In the end they decided the simplest thing to do was drop a ladder over the side in the dead of night, have the stowaway climb to Cathy's balcony, and hide him or her in the cabin until it was time to reverse the procedure in a friendlier port.

For months, Cathy struggled to deal with her guilt over Laura's death. The conviction that she was a pariah who endangered everyone she cared about hung in the back of her mind, like an old sweater she didn't want but couldn't make herself throw away. She'd pushed her mother to go to Seattle; the result was death. She'd brought Jay into Elvera's life, and they'd both died. When she made Laura part of her schemes, she too had paid the ultimate price.

Though she tried to hide her sadness, Drake sensed her mood. "Laura's death was not your fault," he said one night at dinner.

"People always say that when they know something was a little bit your fault," she replied without looking at him.

Drake set his wineglass down and looked out at the calm, flat water outside the window, apparently searching for the right words. "Do you think Laura felt good about what the two of you did for people in trouble?"

"Well, yes, but—"

"Without you, what would she have done in the last half of her life?"

Realizing where he was going, she grimaced. "Probably worked in a bar in St. Ignace."

"Then if the bad thing that happened to Laura is a little bit your fault, so is the good, right? That's all we can hope for in life, that the good we do balances out any unintentional evil."

Cathy didn't respond, and Drake looked at her over the glasses he'd recently begun wearing. "From what you've told me, Laura wasn't the type who'd want to hang around in some nursing home until she hit ninety."

"No, but those men beat her to death."

He nodded. "That's hard to think about. But because of what they did, they'll be in prison for the rest of their lives."

"What about Laura? Her life is over."

He leaned forward, and the light reflected on his hair, now as silver as the candlestick between them. "Your friend died doing what she thought was right. Don't negate her sacrifice by taking the blame onto yourself."

"You're right," Cathy said after a long pause. "Laura was one of the strongest women I ever knew. I need to allow her the choices she made."

After their initial voyage, Cathy notified Terri she was again ready to accept packages. She created a website that supposedly offered jewelry for sale but in fact allowed communication about when and where packages would be sent and received. In Central America they picked up their first package, a boy from Guatemala whose police officer father had been killed by the gangs he'd opposed. A cousin had brought the boy to Santo Tomas where a sympathetic priest contacted Terri, who arranged for him to be brought to the ship.

The mission of mercy had a rocky start. When the horns blew and the ship began to move, the boy became hysterical. Though Cathy and Drake tried to reassure him, he didn't understand English and couldn't be calmed. He cried aloud, overturned a table, broke a lamp, and closed himself for hours in Drake's bathroom, kicking the door periodically and shouting demands and pleas in some Amerindian language. Drake finally phoned the priest, who was able to calm the boy's fears, but it was clear they needed a story to cover the noise and the damages.

"We could say I have nightmares," Cathy suggested.

"Bad dreams don't cause people to kick holes in doors."

She thought for a moment. "When her business collapsed, the media trashed Elvera's reputation."

Drake grimaced. "For weeks they reported every ridiculous thing anyone ever said about her."

"That can help us now. Tell the crew your sister is volatile. She broods. She's irritable. She goes on the occasional bender. When crazy things happen in her cabin, she's not to be disturbed. You want her to be allowed to live on her own terms, no matter how odd they seem."

"I can't do that," he objected.

"You can," she replied. "You have to."

He let out a long puff of air. "All right, but I think we'll have to get lawyers involved. Elvera must be completely free to do as she pleases, whether I'm around or not."

Cathy laughed. "Wouldn't she love that!"

On their fourth mission together, things almost fell apart. In Pattani, Cathy went to pick up a package, a village mayor who'd tried to bring a group of separatists to the bargaining table with local officials. Someone who didn't want the negotiations to succeed tossed a firebomb into his home, causing extensive burns to the mayor's legs. Together Cathy and Drake managed to get him onto the ship, but the next day a Thai policeman knocked at her door.

"Khun Tharp, I have questions concerning a man named Wirat."

"I'm sorry," Cathy said. "I don't know anyone by that name."

"You were seen with him last night, on the dock."

"Last night? I was here in my cabin."

"Our information does not match with this." Though he was polite, the man's eyes challenged her honesty.

"Officer—"

"Lee," he supplied.

"Officer Lee, I have no idea what you've heard."

"Seen, madam. I saw you on the docks with an injured man."

She licked her lips. "I'm afraid you're mistaken."

A knock at the door was followed by Drake's voice. "Are you decent, E?"

She let him in, feeling her spine relax a little. "Drake, this is Officer Lee of the Royal Thai Police. He seems to think I was out strolling the docks last night with some nefarious purpose."

"Really." Drake's eyes met hers for a moment before he turned to Lee. "My sister has difficulty walking, sir, so she seldom ventures off the ship alone. And she and I were together last evening, watching a movie." He looked at her questioningly. "What was it called, Elvera?"

"*The Prisoner of Zenda.*"

"That's the one. She went to bed around midnight, I think. I looked in on her an hour or so later, since she sometimes needs a pain pill in the night. She was sound asleep."

Lee's lips went tight. "I suppose one does not dispute the word of the owner of the shipping line."

Drake apparently took no umbrage at the implication. "Not without making many of your fellow Thais unhappy."

Spring, 2018

"Welcome aboard, Ms. Tharp," said a young man in a blinding-white uniform as she limped up the gangplank. "I'm Assistant Chief Steward Banizek." After a pause he said, "We were all sad to hear of your brother's death, ma'am. It was quite a shock."

Instead of meeting his gaze, Cathy turned to survey the ocean. How empty the world seemed without Drake. "Thank you."

Picking up her bag, Banizek led the way to her cabin and pushed the door open, allowing her to precede him inside. "I don't think you've sailed on *Billows South* before, so let me explain the amenities."

As he rattled on, Cathy's mind wandered down its own path. She and Drake had sailed together many times. Together they'd planned—plotted, Drake said—how to most efficiently use the cruise line to move packages. Cathy had given the role of dispatcher to Terri, who at seventy-eight declared herself too old to serve as a guide any longer. Though both felt their age, neither was willing to give up the work entirely. "It's the only thing I do that makes me feel useful," she told Terri.

"Yeah," her old friend had replied. "You and me are old biddies, but we ain't dead yet."

Drake enjoyed the intrigue. "I sometimes used deception in my days with the State Department. Of course, in those days it was hard to tell if I was helping good guys or bad guys."

"Sometimes we still can't," she replied. "We've had some duds go through Second Base, but usually our people do well in their new lives."

"That's all we can ask." She was pleased at his use of *we*. They were together in all senses of the word: sailing together, working together, being together. It was wonderful, though the hard burn of passion had turned to a soft glow of intimacy. Drake occupied the connecting cabin, and in private they were free to touch, kiss, laugh, or simply sit companionably side by side. Perhaps karma was a thing, she thought. Perhaps she'd made up for her mistakes by helping others. Being apart from the man she loved was in the past.

In 2017, Drake had gone to his daughter's for Thanksgiving. Though she was always invited, Cathy had refused to go along, afraid she'd give away somehow that she was not Elvera. There might be photos. Family stories would be told, and she might get the details wrong. Though she sometimes spoke on the phone to Bonnie, who now headed Wild Goose Cruises, she didn't trust herself to spend too long with those who'd known Elvera Tharp well.

Somewhere in the Mediterranean, she was called to the captain's quarters and told the news. They let her speak to Bonnie, who said through her tears, "It was peaceful, Aunt E. He was watching football, and the Bears were even winning. He just— died." Her voice caught, but after a moment she went on. "I'm glad you and he were so close these past few years. He was happier lately than I'd ever known him to be." After a beat she said, "You should come to Virginia. We'll help you find a place to live, somewhere they'll take good care of you."

"That's kind of you, Bonnie. I'll think about it and let you know." She ended the call, feeling as if her chest was being squashed in a press.

Drake was gone. The last person on earth who knew who she really was. The last person she'd loved. Nothing remained that made her feel worthwhile. Nothing except the work.

"I can sign you up for bridge if you're a card player," her steward—Banizek—was saying. "And we have musical evenings, lots of different types—"

"I'm not interested in those things."

"Well, let's see. They show movies most nights at eight, and there are trivia contests on Thursdays. Or—"

"I don't enjoy social interaction much."

He frowned momentarily, but his beaming smile returned to full wattage a second later. "You're a tough one, Ms. Tharp, but I promise you this: I will find something that pleases you. It's my job to see that you're entertained."

Damn, she thought. *I'm going to have to figure out a way to keep these helpful little elves out of my business.*

Chapter Forty-Four

Cruise Ship-Day 14, 4:00 a.m.

Tapping on Miss E's door at 3:58, Michael used his card to let himself in. She was dressed in dark jeans, black sneakers, and a navy-blue sweatshirt that said *Bimini Bay*. Her expression suggested she'd put one over on someone, and he guessed the victim was him.

"The package?"

"I made other arrangements."

He opened the slider and stepped onto the balcony. "At least show me how it's done."

As she stepped outside, the engines droned far below. The horn hooted, and the ship began to move. Grasping the railing, she said, "The last leg begins."

Miss E moved more easily tonight, and he guessed she'd taken an extra pain pill or two. "They come along the water line, there." She pointed. "On every ship in the line, Drake and I found the cabin that's least visible from above. On *The Happy Wanderer*, it's Cabin Three."

He watched her mouth move, like a cobra watching a mongoose. When she stopped talking, he said, "They call you 'ornery.' Did you model your Miss E persona on my mother?"

"To be honest, I did channel E a little. She was never able to tolerate fools or foolish behavior, and I suppose that's what people mean when they say a person is ornery." She smiled thinly. "But sooner or later, life gives each of us plenty to be ornery about."

The lights of the city grew smaller and fainter behind them. Their course split the Gulf of Thailand, 774 nautical miles back to Singapore.

She turned toward him. "Michael, I know you came here to kill me."

He spoke in a mocking tone. "Miss E, you're very perceptive."

"You've killed before."

That surprised him. "How do you know that?"

"The investigator I mentioned earlier reported that Kiet Banyen was smothered."

"I wonder who cared enough to notice how that bastard died."

"A woman at the orphanage in Bangkok fell from a window."

"Maarit sold me to an idiot and then refused to give me the truth of my birth." He took a step toward her. "Those who stand in my way don't stand for long."

"Then there have been others?"

Michael's laugh was louder than intended, and he paused to see if anyone came outside to investigate. No one did.

Though he went on in a quieter voice, Michael's words bubbled with anger. "Of *course* there were others. *I* had to make my way in the world. *I* had to deal with pampered women with no idea how hard life can be." He stopped, and his breath shuddered in his lungs. "And when I finally reached the truth, I found that the person responsible for my unhappiness is already dead. I am denied the justice I spent my entire life looking for."

"There is no justice for what happened to you, Michael. Still, most people who experience a horrible childhood don't turn to murder."

Grasping her arms, he pulled her close and shook her. "You should have tried harder to find me."

Miss E's gaze remained on his. "There are many times when I should have done things differently. Would you believe that I once insisted my mother ride in the front seat of the car, and she died because of it?" Her voice suddenly turned weak and wispy. "I wish I could change what happened to you, Michael."

He let go of her arms abruptly, and she staggered to remain upright. "Wishes don't erase your shortcomings, Miss E."

"True." Turning her back on the ocean, Cathy took hold of the balcony rail. Anyone who saw them there would have assumed they were enjoying the warm, clear night. The stars overhead seemed almost touchable, like a stage set. Reflected moonlight waffled on the water below, its effect both beautiful and eerie. "Then I'm to be your next victim."

"I mentioned in the kitchen today that your pain has been increasing, and you've told me more than once that you'd be better off dead. In the morning I'll find your balcony door open." He shrugged eloquently. "I'll wring my hands and say I should have done more to stop you."

"You're good with a story, like your father was."

He shrugged. "Consider it a kindness, Miss E. From what I can discern, your life has been over for some time."

"You're right about that," she said sadly, "but in everything else you're completely, terribly wrong."

He took hold of her arms again, and anger shook his voice. "You could have found me after Elvera died." The grip tightened. "You could have saved me from that monster, from the pain and deprivation I grew up with."

"I failed then," she admitted. Grasping his belt with both hands, she added, "But tonight, I'll save the world from another kind of monster."

With a sudden, powerful movement, she threw herself backward, over the railing. Her impetus carried him with her, before he realized what was happening, before he could reach for a handhold to save himself.

Miss E went silently, but Michael let out a cry of rage as he followed her down, into the dark water below.

391

Author's Note:

Events in Thailand described in the book are based on fact. The camps were as described, as were the attitudes of the governments involved. The character of the camp commander, Arum Seng, came from my reading about a lawyer named Thou Thon, who in the early 1980s did his best to ameliorate the worst of the conditions at Nong Samet. Due to the extremely complicated politics and rivalries of the time, I have simplified some of the events.

In order to help Cathy survive on Mackinac Island, I moved the creation of eBay ahead one year. Its actual start was August of 1995.

About the Author

Peg Herring reads, writes, and loves mysteries. As an educator she once set the school stage on fire (just a little one). As a driver she's been so lost that she passed through the same town in Pennsylvania three times in one day. Family and friends have lost count of how many times she's locked herself out of her house. As the award-winning author of several best-selling mystery series and standalones, it's much safer if she sits in her office and writes, either as herself or as her younger, hipper alter ego, Maggie Pill.

Visit http://pegherring.com for Strong Women, Great Stories

Books by Peg Herring

All books are available at major booksellers in print and e-book formats. Many are also available as audio books.

(Series are listed in order)

The Kidnap Capers (Suspense with cozy tendencies)
KIDNAP.org
Pharma Con
The Trouble with Dad
***

The Simon & Elizabeth Mysteries (Tudor Era Historical)
Her Highness' First Murder
Poison, Your Grace
The Lady Flirts with Death
Her Majesty's Mischief
***

The Loser Mysteries (Contemporary Mystery/Suspense)
Killing Silence
Killing Memories
Killing Despair
***

Clan Macbeth (Historical Romance, Medieval Scotland)
Macbeth's Niece
Double Toil & Trouble
***

Mercedes Maxwell Suspense Series (with Historical Implications)
Shakespeare's Blood
Charlie Dickens' Documents
***

Standalone Mysteries
Somebody Doesn't Like Sarah Leigh (contemporary cozy mystery)
Her Ex-GI P.I. ('60s-era mystery)
Not Dead Yet... ('60s-era paranormal mystery)

***

Maggie Pill's Cozy Mysteries
The Sleuth Sisters Mystery Series
 The Sleuth Sisters
3 Sleuths, 2 Dogs, 1 Murder
Murder in the Boonies
Sleuthing at Sweet Springs
Eat, Drink, and Be Wary
Peril, Plots, and Puppies
Captured, Escape, Repeat
***

Trailer Park Tales
Once Upon a Trailer Park
Twice the Crime This Time

Visit Maggie at http://maggiepill.maggiepillmysteries.com